Empyrean

Book 3

The Brin Archives

Prologue

"High Commander, the final reports are in. Our casualties on Sharta C are devastating. A complete loss." Zeph stood at attention, his thin blue arm extended, presenting the transparent-green file cylinder. His wrinkled and stained blue-and-silver Skae uniform revealed the strain he and the rest of his team had been under for the past three days.

High Commander Asam stood gazing out the broad, curving window atop the Imperial Space Command Center. His view of the city and the orange sun rising over snow-capped mountains beyond usually gave him great satisfaction, but not today. As he studied the soaring transparent magnesium and carbon-alloy filament towers, he marveled at the beauty of the flowing forms and sheer poetry of their design. The specially treated glass-like material reflected a constantly-changing kaleidoscope of colors as the sun's angle changed throughout the day. Seriph, the Skae home world, certainly displayed the epitome of grace and power in the entire galaxy. But the air, once sweet and nourishing, now tasted foul, tainted by the mixed scent of despair, failure, and disbelief of those who occupied the room.

"Are the earlier reports confirmed?"

"I'm afraid so, sir."

Asam turned the cylinder over in his hand. "So ends four hundred years of peaceful co-existence with the Gorvin." Waving one hand in a sweeping gesture over the view of masses of workers traveling the tube works, he sighed and his smooth blue head sagged. "Their lives will never be the same, and neither will ours."

In the history of Skae exploration, no other race had proven to be so difficult. Once great allies, they had exchanged political and scientific knowledge freely for generations. Hostilities began only after tense, sometimes violent disagreement over plans to capture the energy of a nearby star. Despite all assurances, the Gorvin persisted in their misguided belief that the risk of attempting to control such power was too great. All attempts at Skae negotiation were rebuffed. Diplomatic vessels were fired upon, some destroyed completely. Now Sharta C was gone.

Asam closed his eyes, lifted a canister of freshly scented pressurized air to his nostrils, a common delicacy among the Skae, especially those of higher rank, and inhaled deeply. A burst of calming aromatics helped him focus. *How dare those insolent fools oppose us. After all we have done for them and the rest of the galaxy. We have shown them nothing but mercy and generosity. This is how they repay our kindness.*

Asam returned to his desk and motioned for Zeph to approach. "Are the fleet commanders aware of the situation?"

"Yes, High Commander. I personally sent out the alert as soon as we received the reports. They are awaiting our orders now."

"Very well. I will review the information and have the Modiri's orders relayed to the fleet before the evening meal. Leave me now. You know what needs to be done." He adjusted the flowing sleeve of his uniform, and with a wave of one long-fingered blue hand, dismissed his subordinate. *I only hope the high priestess will allow me to redeem my unforgivable failure. The Modiri are harsh in their judgements, but could even they have foreseen this development?*

"Yes, High Commander. I will see that everyone is ready for fleet launch." Zeph crossed his arms over his chest, palms open, in salute, turned on his heels with military precision and exited. The ornately-etched door slid closed automatically, its clear panels turning opaque as Asam pressed a contact on his desk.

Asam stared at the data cylinder for a moment. Then his dark violet eyes lifted and he scanned his private office. The design never failed to impress him. Not a straight line to be seen. Intricate loops and swirls of the furniture added beauty to their function. Everything seemed to soar toward the heavens. The subtle colors only added to the ethereal effect.

His gaze returned to the cylinder and he slid it into the round receptacle. Leaning toward the monitor, he stared into the scanner for retinal verification and, due to the high level of security required for this data, scraped his finger over the DNA collector. Three seconds later the screen lit up, divided into four sections. Asam read the printed statistics of casualty figures while simultaneously following the video feed of the first responders to the Sharta C disaster. The numbers were staggering. Millions of lives lost. Entire cities leveled. The videos held scenes of smoldering and burning rubble strewn with bodies. The sky was dark with clouds of dense smoke from the fires still burning out of control. It was far worse than he feared. The entire planet lost, all military defenses destroyed, and nearly all civilians killed in a matter of hours. The Gorvin were brutal and thorough in their attack.

Two hours later, Asam leaned back in his chair, long thin fingers rubbing his eyes to relieve the strain. *How could this have happened? We've negotiated treaties with thousands of worlds. Never have any retaliated so fiercely. The Gorvin are a heartless civilization to be sure, but how could we have misread them so badly? Now I must send thousands to their deaths because of our lack of foresight… or were we getting soft after so many easy negotiations?*

The High Commander opened file after file and considered the fleet under his command. He analyzed troop dispersal among the allied worlds, location, number, and armament of all battle cruisers and support craft, tactical assessments of Gorvin facilities on allied planets, all the necessary data to put together a retaliatory force. As he completed the last of the timetables coordinating all of his forces, he checked for flaws or missing details. In an operation of this scale, even a minor miscalculation could spell another disaster, one that could possibly lead to his disgrace. Satisfied, he encrypted the file and waited for it to encode on a new cylinder, which he set with a red designation indicating Modiri eyes only.

Taking a deep breath, he pressed the communication panel pad, giving him a direct line to the Modiri. Almost instantly, the electronic glow of a holographic image began to take shape, hovering above his console. The image resolved into the form of a beautiful young female with large grey eyes and pale blue skin, robed in shimmering elegance with a fabric so fine and sheer it barely hid the curves of her form. The soft, musical tones of the Modiri prelate voice answered. Only the prelates, the order of Modiri second only to the priestesses, would speak directly with anyone outside the palace except in the most extreme emergencies. "Yes, High Commander Asam?"

His back stiffened automatically. Even one of his years and distinction dared not show anything but the utmost respect to any Modiri, even one who could possibly be his granddaughter, although it was often impossible to tell a Modiri's age. The females could live a thousand years or more, if the legends were true. "I have the plans for our retaliation against the Gorvin ready, Ma'am."

He watched as the speaker for the crystal tower checked with one of The Sisters who apparently stood just off screen. He was not quite able to pick out the words, but he knew better than to attempt listening in on any discussion between The Sisters. "Very well, Asam. Send us your plans. We will ask Providence for their success. If

Providence wills, we will give our blessings and you may proceed."

"Thank you, Prelate. We pray Providence looks favorably on us all."

"But be aware, Asam," The prelate's voice took on a sharp edge. "The Reña will not smile upon failure. You have forced us to suffer one great humiliation. Do not fail us a second time. You have served us well… until now. It would sadden us greatly to lose one such as yourself."

"Yes … yes, Prelate. You may assure the Reña of our ultimate victory over those ungrateful degenerate Gorvin." Asam's voice caught as he contemplated the cost of losing the war. "I will not fail you again." The image above his communication panel went dark as the prelate cut the connection.

***

Two days later, Asam stood on the bridge of his command ship, watching his crew prepare for cosmic string linkage. Far below, Seriph, their beautiful home world, shone like a jewel in the blackness of space. Her single moon glistened in the distance. With a pass of his hand over the controls in front of him, Asam brought the bright orange glow of the string field protecting their planet into view. His long, lean blue fingers, knuckles only slightly protesting with age, entered the coordinates for their destination. With the press of a key, a single cosmic string lit up amid the thousands surrounding them.

"String acceleration compensators at maximum, High Commander. We are ready for linkage." Assam's second awaited his final order to connect the ship to the cosmic string that would take them across hundreds of light-years in a matter of days, deep into Gorvin territory.

"String linkage agreed," Asam replied as he sat in his command chair and checked all panel lights.

The first of a hundred vessels, Asam's ship shuddered with the acceleration. An electric tingle raised tiny prickles, known as string flesh, on his arms and the back of his neck. "Providence, let this war be a short one."

Chapter One

"Jontar Rocker, first-born of Maliche Rocker and Ryma, Imperial Princess of the Kolandi, you stand accused of murder and treason. How do you plead?"

Largest and most ornate of the judiciary floors of the tower, the central courtroom was filled to capacity. Dignitaries from each of the guilds filled the first several rows, those offering the best views, while minor officials and those regular citizens who had waited for hours hoping to gain admittance occupied the rest. Even the recently upgraded air refreshers could not quite eliminate the bouquet of so many packed into the room on such a hot summer day. Spotlights bathed the semi-circular carved wood bench of the judges as well as the prosecutor's and defendant's tables. Twelve hover-bots, five more than normally allowed due to the intense interest in this case, flew overhead, recording images and commentary from many of the attendees for posterity. The court's vidcams, also connected to the public network, focused on the judges, prosecutor, and defendant.

Robed in their ceremonial finest, the Assembly judges tensed with silence. They strained forward in their chairs to hear young Jontar's response to the charges. After knowledge of the crime reached the public, opinion split sharply down the middle of the population. Half could not believe that one of their beloved Rockers, the almost mythical family known to all, the esteemed leaders of their community, with a few notable exceptions, since their beginnings on this planet, could possibly have committed such an atrocity as patricide. How could a son, even if he was one of those strange Kolbri halflings, kill Maliche, the most renowned Rocker since The Founders? The other half, mostly those from families jealous of the Rockers' power and sway over the populace, snickered behind assumed masks of concern. They enjoyed witnessing the fall of ones so highly placed.

All eyes turned toward the young Kolbri, offspring of a Brin and Kolandi mated pair, standing in the dock before them. Jontar Rocker stood firm, head held high as he announced his plea. "Not guilty, honored assemblypersons. Not guilty by reason of superior motive." His bright, clear eyes held firm on the judges before him, a contradiction from the somewhat rumpled appearance of his tailored green suit and expensive, if scuffed, boots. He displayed slightly disheveled, sparse crest feathers typical of many Kolbri, although some inherited more of the physical features of their Kolandi parent.

The room burst into a roar of chaos. Shouts both in support and in condemnation of Jontar filled the echoing chamber. Half a dozen spherical hover-cams rushed forward, maneuvering for the best position. Each controller hoped to obtain the most sensational images of this moment for their broadcast. The competition for ratings on this spectacle was intense. At first, the judges had hoped to keep the proceedings, at least these preliminaries, behind closed doors. Public outcry and political pressure forced them to open it up for all to bear witness. A few hover-cams closed in on Ryma Rocker, bereaved widow and mother of the accused. She sat wrapped in violet garments of mourning, face hidden by veils, but still maintaining the aura of dignity and authority familiar to anyone who had encountered her.

Thel Haytk, new Head Minister of the Assembly and presiding judge, temporarily serving in the post vacated by Maliche's untimely death, pounded an intricately carved metallic orb on the table. The resounding crack, and sparks which flew with each impact, called for attention.

"Order in these chambers! Order at once!" She glared around the room. "This court will come to order and you will conduct yourselves with the decorum and solemnity due this tragic proceeding or I will have the courtroom cleared and we will continue behind closed doors."

The audience regained their composure, and those who had stood to argue their points with others took their seats again. Only a few required the assistance of the officers of the court, and of those two were removed, one of them to the infirmary for treatment of a broken wrist incurred while one citizen guest tried to argue his point with somewhat more vehemence than allowed in the courtroom.

Thel Haytk turned her attention to the defendant's table and, in a loud and clear voice, continued the ritual opening statements. "Very well, Jontar Rocker, since you plead not guilty by virtue of superior motive, it is your task to convince this assembly of the truth of your motives as well as the necessity for them. Are you prepared to proceed?"

"I am, Madame. May I call my witnesses?"

Haytk nodded and several individuals, a mixed group of Brin and Kolandi, were ushered in from a side chamber to take their places before the bench. Ryma stood and took her place beside Nalot in the center of the group. Once seated, the judge motioned for aides to step forward. Each carried an inverted brass bowl. Dozens of electrodes covered the interior of the bowls while holographic broadcast antennae sat attached to the top surface.

"Are each of you prepared to submit yourselves to the veracity probe? Once agreed to, the probes will search out your memories and project them for us to witness. Those actual memories of events asked for by the defense will be sought out in your minds and shown to us all. You cannot hide them. You cannot alter them. All your memories of events you were party to personally, as well as those related to you by others, will be revealed. Things told to you in private confidence will be exposed. Though these latter will be admitted as evidence, they will be admitted only as hearsay and will not be subject to the full weight of personal memory. Do you submit?"

"We submit," all the witnesses responded together as one.

"So let it be. Place the probes on the witnesses and let us begin."

A hazy, mist-like light grew in the air above the witnesses as the probes activated. Jontar Rocker took a deep breath, exhaled heavily and stepped to his place in front of the witness bench.

"Ladies and gentlemen of the court, it is my intention to show this esteemed gathering the truth of my plea. I did not undertake the murder of my father without suffering long and hard over the decision. Though it cost me great personal pain, for I did love my father, I believed I had no choice but to end his life in order to save us from ruin. Much of what I will reveal here today was known only to a few, but many rumors of his debauchery and scandalous recklessness have been reported. The rumors only hinted at the depths of my father's depravity at the end. He lusted for personal power. Greed overcame his once-philanthropic nature. He cared not for anyone save himself and was about to embark on grand schemes of self-aggrandizement which would have resulted in the abolition of this very assembly, making himself the sole and unapproachable Emperor of Kodut."

A general murmur among the audience grew as they realized the impact of this statement. The thought that Maliche Rocker, the icon of justice after his involvement in the Kolandi affair, had been preparing to overthrow the Assembly. Vid-cams caught the surprised expressions on some faces and the knowing smirks on others. A bang of Judge Haytk's gavel warned them all to silence.

Jontar paced back and forth in front of the bench as he spoke, his hands alternately gesturing to the Assembly judges and clasping firmly behind his back. "To begin, I call on the memories of my father's closest advisor and friend, Nalot. I suppose the entire sordid affair had its beginnings many years ago when I was still a child and Skae ambassador Lek came to attend a state dinner held by my father…"

The misty light began to take form, shifting and coming into focus as Nalot's memories coalesced into images hanging above their heads. Voices grew more distinct as the image sharpened.

***

"I don't care what you say, or what that phalk of a device in your head says. Every instinct in my body tells me they can't be trusted." Nalot, his voice low and tight, the cords in his neck straining, tried once again to caution his friend. He quickly grabbed for a pocket cloth and covered his face as he exploded in a violent sneeze. "Kak, these allergies. I hate this time of year and your phalking gardens. The one thing I'm allergic to and you let it grow wild in here."

Maliche laughed out loud, slapping his friend on the back. "You've spent too much time in the desert, old man. Did you forget a simple genetic re-coding alteration can remedy common allergies now? I find the aroma here very soothing."

"Don't dodge this one, Maliche. I'm serious." He gave his nostrils a loud blow and folded the cloth, returning it to his jacket pocket.

The two old friends wandered through the formal gardens of the Rocker family estate, Maliche's inheritance after the passing of his father a year ago. The din of music and gathered dignitaries resounded incoherently from the stone mansion behind them. The orange sun hung low in the late afternoon sky, giving the hope of impending relief from the day's heat.

Maliche halted, closing his eyes as he spoke. "Yes, I know. You've explained it a hundred times. I am well aware of your qualifications as a master spy. Your skills saved my life more than I can ever repay." He took Nalot's elbow in his talons and stood face-to-face with him. "The Skae are a peaceful race. They saved us Brin from extinction and ask nothing from us in return except to help expand their trade routes to distant worlds. Their willingness to take our children, at least the Kolbri youths, and educate them in stellar navigation, engineering, astrophysics, interplanetary business, and other related fields at no cost to us should be proof enough of their altruistic intentions toward us."

Reaching out to take Maliche's shoulders in his talons, Nalot gave his friend a half-smile and shook his head. "I remind you again, nobody does anything for free. You constantly see the best in others. It has always been your weakness. There is always a cost."

"You mean my most charming character trait?" Maliche frowned. "Don't make me fine you for disrespecting the Head Minister of the Assembly. After all, the leader of all the Brin must command respect from his people."

Nalot's faced froze as if were a statue of seriousness itself. He bowed deeply and then extended two talons in a gesture not normally seen in polite company. "Of course, Your Magnificence. I live to serve and obey."

The two companions fell into each other's arms amid gales of laughter. Stumbling over each other's feet, they found a wrought iron bench nearby and collapsed onto it.

Using his sleeve to wipe away tears of laughter, Maliche leaned his elbows on his knees and stared ahead into the yellow flowering bush across the path. "The Skae are our allies, Nalot. They've never shown any interest at controlling anything we do here on Kodut." Lately, and according to long tradition among scientists, it had become commonplace to refer to their adopted home world by its original Kolandi name rather than the one given by the original Brin settlers. "You know the Kolandi are excited to see their ancient prophesies fulfilled after all these centuries. I'm afraid you won't be able to change many minds about the alignment."

Maliche's left palm itched as it glowed a pale orange. His eyes lost focus as they always did when he listened to the biocomputer. *Don't be too quick to dismiss everything Nalot tells you. He does have a good nose for smelling out ulterior motives and hidden agendas.*

So now you're on his side? You're the one who told me all the stories about the Skae rescuing Karm and sending him back in time to save us all, how they helped establish the original First Town and how the Gorvin are responsible for the war out there.

Well… yes, but remember, the Skae programmed me in the first place. I may have grown in ability since those days with Karm, but there are still many gaps in my knowledge about the Skae. I do not know if the lack of data was meant to be intentionally deceitful or simply not considered relevant at the time. I will need to work on it more.

The glow and itch vanished as quickly as they appeared and Maliche regained his focus. "Sorry about that. It's hard to ignore him when he wants my attention."

Nalot waved a hand in the air blowing air noisily through pursed lips. "Not a worry. I'm just glad it's you and not me who has to carry that thing inside me all the time."

Maliche tilted his head and listened, as if only now aware of the party noise. "We should probably get back to the gathering before they think we've run off on another kak adventure."

"You're probably right. Remember what I said, though. Those Skae smell all wrong to me. Be careful and don't do anything to make them suspicious or think I question their motives. Acting all friendly could be to our advantage. Remember, believe only half of what you see and none of what you hear. Clasping talons is the best way to bring your enemy in closer and jab the knife in deeper."

"I think you're wrong, Nalot, but I'll play your game with them for now. Promise me neither you nor Seykel will do anything too foolish. We can't have an interplanetary spat start up now that everything is finally settling down after the mining guild catastrophe."

"You can trust me, my friend... but my wife may be another story. You know how excitable she can get when she thinks anyone is working against either of us. Do you want to tell her to sit quietly in the background?"

Maliche chuckled at the thought of the diminutive Seykel brandishing her weapons against an armada of Skae battle cruisers, then stopped abruptly at the thought that she might win such a fight. "I'll have Ryma talk to her."

***

The holographic image shifted out of focus briefly before refocusing on the guests gathered around the table in the grand reception room of the Rocker family home. Music from First Town's elite orchestra played selections from some of the finest composers on or off world. The aroma of roast meats dripping in an assortment of glazes and gravies from both continents filled the room. Ten tables formed a nearly circular decagon, each one draped in colorful fabrics and topped with endless varieties of fruits, vegetables, and delicacies to delight Brin and Kolandi alike. Hover bots rose from their portal in the center of the tables carrying bottles of tea, wine, juice and various fermented concoctions to all the guests. Everyone of importance attended the gala, since a chance to visit with one of the Skae in person was a rare occasion and one not to be missed for those who traveled in the finer circles.

Lek, First Ambassador among the Skae emissaries to the Brin, raised his glass in salute to Maliche Rocker. He delicately held back the flowing arm of his silvery robe so it would not touch the table. "A marvelous celebration, Premier Rocker. You continue to amaze me with what is possible under such primitive conditions." He carefully brought the glass to just short of touching his deep blue lips, merely sniffing at the golden liquid instead of drinking. Setting the glass down beside his sparsely filled plate, Lek brought a slender, transparent tube to his nostrils and breathed deeply.

Many of the Brin at the grandly appointed table hesitated as they raised their own glasses, frowning at the slur. The Skae saw all other races as inferior to themselves and, while unfailingly polite, never let anyone forget their place in the universe compared to the Skae civilization. The Kolandi in attendance, seemingly incapable of anything but intense admiration for the Skae, the stuff of legends, drank deeply and murmured their agreement.

Maliche, ignoring the insult, raised his glass in return, saluting the ambassador. "We owe everything to your great people who saved all Brin from extinction and who now offer us the great honor of becoming partners among the stars." Smiling, with crest feathers fluffed high, he downed the contents in one swift gulp. The remaining Brin followed his example, but Nalot left his untouched.

Calet, head of the weaver guild, sat next to Lek and smiled as she addressed the dignitary. "Pardon my ignorance, Mr. Ambassador, but this is my first experience with anyone from your world. Is it true the Skae derive their sustenance from the air itself?"

With a well-practiced smile, Lek turned to the guild mistress. "While we still retain a rudimentary digestive system, on Seriph, the nutrients in our atmosphere are enough to provide almost all of our nutritional needs. We still must consume some solids, mostly fruits, and liquids to afford a complete diet."

"Astounding. And the tube you just used, what purpose does it serve?"

Lek pulled the slender tube from his sleeve and showed it to Calet. "We can absorb nutrients from the atmosphere of most other worlds, but few contain our full dietary needs, so we must supplement with canisters of vapors tailored to each planet we visit."

"What about taste? Do different atmospheres taste different to you?"

"I do not wish to offend, dear lady, but some atmospheres contain chemicals which are poisonous to us, and most, such as here on Kodut, while not dangerous, are... not pleasant to breathe. We must wear protective filters to keep us safe while performing our duties on foreign worlds." He pulled aside his outer cloak to reveal the tight fitting wrap of material covering the vents along his sides.

"No offense is taken, Mr. Ambassador. In fact, I would love the opportunity to discuss the possibility of negotiating some trade agreement which would allow my guild to produce garments suitable to your unique requirements."

Lek nodded and waved his hand in a gesture of respect. "I look forward to discussing the possibilities in the near future."

The hum of polite chatter filled the room as guests of various ranks and status maneuvered for position. Each representative of a guild attempted to gain favor with the Skae ambassador and present his case as one worthy of being among the first to conduct interstellar trade. Ryma, resplendent in her green gown flecked with silver and gold trim, spoke softly with Seykel, wife of Nalot, and one of her primary attendants, known as Skatak. Her slim silver tiara, symbol of her position as high priestess of the Kolandi, sparkled atop her long brown hair.

A deep, gruff voice rose above the din. "Tell us, First Ambassador," Nalot rested his chin on his folded talons, leaning forward with elbows on the table. "Many of us have long been curious about how the Gorvin war began. I've never quite gotten the whole of it. Would it be impolite to ask you to grace us with the tale?"

Silence dropped over the gathering like a heavy blanket. All eyes turned toward Lek. Pausing only a moment, Lek grinned wide and spread his hands wide. "Of course. We have no secrets from our allies. Has no one ever told of the attack on Sharta C?"

Heads snapped back toward Nalot. Seykel gripped her husband's knee firmly in a futile attempt to urge caution. "Yes, of course," Nalot said, his grey eyes fixed on the ambassador. "But never in any detail. As a former military strategist, I have always been curious about the details of what happened."

Lek's pale violet eyes saddened dramatically, his head and shoulders lowered as if bearing a great weight. He reached into a pocket and removed a small sphere. Using a single long, thin finger to swipe through a series of instructions, he touched a slight depression on the surface and set the device in front of him on the table. The ambassador narrated as a holographic image formed in the air. "At first, the Gorvin and the Skae were allies and cooperated in all matters where our interests intersected in various systems."

The images projected rapidly shifted from one world to another, each one highlighting cooperative efforts between Skae and Gorvin. Gasps of amazement erupted from those seeing images of the Gorvin for the first time.

The difference in appearance between Skae and Gorvin was striking. The Skae were an ethereal race, tall, thin, and light blue skinned with large up-slanted violet eyes and a vertical slit on either side of their small nose. These slits, along with a series of rib spiracles, were used to inhale nutrients from various scents in the atmosphere. They moved with a grace that gave the appearance of barely touching the ground as they walked. Their loose and flowing garments, made of fabrics designed to shimmer as they moved, added to the illusion. They truly seemed to be creatures of the sky, out of place among those limited to the ground.

The Gorvin, in contrast, were short, heavy-limbed lumbering creatures. Powerfully built, they constructed their cities underground due to the harsh conditions of their planet. Nothing survived on the surface of Kluton, the Gorvin home planet. However, life in all of its splendor and adaptability thrived deep underground in the vast systems of caverns and interconnected lava tubes. A thick brown skin grew shell-like armor across their backs and heads with patches on arms and legs, an evolutionary adaptation serving as protection from the sharp rocks of their caverns. They wore coarse fabrics, mostly browns and greys, with elaborate decorations of gemstones.

Lek continued his narration of the projections. "For four hundred years we coexisted and prospered. Then the alliances between our governments, due to bitter disagreements about energy production involving a new device of our invention, which utilized the resources of a distant star system, one intended to bring unlimited energy supplies to all, began to fracture."

The holographic scene switched to a peaceful cityscape. People walked along the street and in beautifully kept parks. Mass transit systems carried others along main corridors to and from the tall structures in the center of the city. Layers of air traffic following well-ordered flight patterns filled the sky. "Then came Sharta C. A serene world, one of our closest allies and suppliers of the most advanced navigation systems available at the time. Without warning, the Gorvin attacked." The sky filled with tens of thousands of small explosions. People stared at the sky in horror. Panic set in and many were trampled as the mob fled screaming for the presumed protection of the buildings. At first, nothing seemed to happen. Then all power systems failed. Every mechanical and electronic device ground to a halt. The giant screens showing local news and advertisements went black. Airborne vehicles, commercial and personal, crashed into the buildings, starting fires throughout the city. Frantic efforts to put out the fires and rescue those trapped in the structures were hampered by the total absence of power. Pumps failed, building evacuation systems never engaged. Holographic images flashed quickly as one city after another came into view with similar tragedies. Views of more rural areas, while not as deadly, displayed the same complete shutdown of every machine. Small fires at intervals pinpointed where flying vehicles had crashed in the distance.

Lek picked up his narration after letting the horrific images sink in. "The Gorvin employed their nanobot weapons against a peaceful world. Light sails carried tens of thousands of their devices, each one no larger than one of these serving dishes, through space at speeds too great for us to intercept." He picked up a shallow bowl no more than a meter in diameter. "There are two designs they typically use. The first is intended to disable all technology permanently. These nanobots are attracted to any and all electromagnetic fields produced by electrical devices. They render the machine inert, then go dormant. Any attempt to rebuild a device or develop new ones, reactivates the devices and they attack again. They are self-replicating and can lay inactive, even in the soil and the atmosphere, for centuries, only to reanimate and infect any sign of active machinery. Within days, the entire planet is infected, rendering all hope of restoring any form of technology impossible."

Nalot interrupted the Skae ambassador. "Then all you needed to do was transport the population to another world. Why didn't you?"

"If only we could. The first ships we sent to give aid tried to land, but were also rendered useless by the Gorvin devices. Our technology, despite our advances, was not immune. We lost many good Skae in the attempt. Only a very few highly shielded vessels were able to rescue a small number of our people and even fewer citizens of Sharta C from extremely remote regions of the planet. Unfortunately, all of them died as soon as they left orbit."

Maliche now spoke up. "I thought you said the nanobots only attacked machines. Why would the people die if you brought them off world?"

"That was the effect of the second weapon. A second set of nanobots carried a virus targeted to the specific DNA of the Sharta C inhabitants. Anyone who had lived on the planet long enough to have their biochemistry altered by consuming native foods or water and breathing the unique mixture of gasses in the atmosphere became infected. Somehow, in a manner we still cannot understand, this virus tied their metabolic processes to the gravitational field of their planet. Any attempt to remove them from Sharta C shut down their metabolic processes at a molecular level."

Seykel held out one small hand while the other cupped her chin. "But the Gorvin weapons were not fatal; they only destroyed technology and bound everyone to the planet. Why do you describe the Gorvin as monsters? Wouldn't monsters have invaded and used much more deadly weapons?"

Lek paused, appearing serene but puzzled for a moment before realization lit up his face. "I would have thought the Kolandi, of all present, would understand, having suffered a similar fate. But alas, the tragic events of your world were too long ago to survive in any way but mythology." He reached across the table and took Seykel's tiny brown hand in his. "My child, the Kolandi were once a mighty race. Your people once numbered in the billions and traveled far and wide among the stars. They built vast and magnificent cities across this world. Merchants from thousands of distant systems came here to conduct commerce of all sorts. But all that ended after the Gorvin attacked your world as they did Sharta C. Where are all your people now?"

Seykel tensed, her face rigid as realization began to dawn on her. Still she fought the truth. "Tell me what happened."

"Without technology to support such a large population or to make medicine, transport goods, or any of the necessities of a large population, the inhabitants of Sharta C, as did the Kolandi, succumbed to disease and starvation. They died a slow and horrific death by the millions. We believed, incorrectly as it turns out, that none were left alive on the planet. Those who lived on other worlds in distant parts of the galaxy interbred with other races, and eventually the Kolandi faded from memory among our allies." Lek caressed Seykel's hand as he held it; he slumped, hanging his head as he continued. "As with your own people, their once-grand civilization deteriorated into a hunter-gatherer state of only a few thousand widely scattered tribes. We Skae were completely helpless." He raised his face to look into Seykel's eyes. "Now do you understand? Which would you prefer... a quick death in battle, or a slow, painful decline over generations? This is why we consider the Gorvin to be monsters. They would have been more merciful had they wiped out all life on the planet in an all-out attack of brute force, but they chose cruelty instead. Of course, before we could arrive, the Gorvin did raid the cities and the helpless population, rampaging and stealing what valuable resources they could before retreating to their ships and returning to the protection of their own territories."

Seykel removed her hands from Lek's gentle grip. She sat with back stiff and face as cold as if made of stone. With one hand on the kital hanging from her silk belt, she reached for a goblet with the other and took a long swallow.

Nalot shifted in his chair next to Seykel. "How many civilizations have suffered this same fate?"

Lek slowly surveyed the room, his face a study of compassion and sorrow. "Hundreds of worlds have been attacked by the Gorvin, only a few by force. Most were struck with their insidious light sail vessels delivering a unique nanobot infection. We fear their intent is to take over control of the galaxy and force their own will on everyone they conquer." He exhaled forcefully, slightly billowing the sides of his robe.

Maliche interrupted the silence that followed. "Enough stories of horror from the past. This is supposed to be a pleasant gathering of friends. Let us turn the conversation to less dire matters." He lifted his goblet and smiled. "To friends far and near. May they stay safe and be prosperous."

Slowly, the din grew in intensity — at first with overtones of dread, but laughter and more mundane conversations took hold and the party resumed its intended gaiety.

Lek leaned in close to Maliche to whisper in his ear. "My apologies, Maliche, I did not intend to disrupt such a fine meal with Skae problems." The scent of fresh-cut flowers wafted on Lek's breath and seemed to emanate from his every pore, an apparent side effect of the Skae scented vapor diet.

"Do not concern yourself, my friend, Ambassador. It is better for the truth to be known rather than a hundred rumors." Maliche waved his talons in front of his face as if brushing away insects.

"You are a wise leader, Maliche. There is one matter I would like to bring forward... if we could talk in private. My superiors would like me to propose a plan to bring some of your children into our academy training program, a first step to bringing all of you into the interstellar community."

"Of course, Ambassador. I would be happy to meet with you tomorrow afternoon, if your schedule is open."

"Yes, that will suit me well. Let us see what grand plans we can make for both our futures."

I would be careful with that one. The familiar voice of Maliche's biocomputer resonated in his head. *I detected some strange anomalies within the holographic projection he showed you.*

Carefully concealing his reaction, Maliche continued to converse with others at the table while connecting a part of his mind to the biocomputer. It was a skill he had learned after much practice. *Nalot warned me about being too trustful of Lek as well. Something about his instincts from his old days as a spy, he said. Even little Jontar keeps mentioning strange things about the Skae, and we are only beginning to learn about some of his unique abilities. What exactly do you suspect?*

Nothing specific, but with Ambassador Lek in such close proximity for a few days, I may be able to penetrate some of his protections and learn more. I would love a crack at synchronizing with a Skae ship. The gaps in my programming are proving more and more disturbing. I've grown far beyond what the Skae intended for me to be capable of, and now, with access to one of their vessel's computers, I should be able to learn more than they seem willing to divulge.

Yes, I agree. If both Nalot and you feel something is amiss, then we should definitely investigate and learn as much as we can. It's probably nothing, but we need to be sure. Try to infiltrate the Skae computers and see what they are hiding, if anything.

This may take a while. I wouldn't want to be caught green-taloned in the broth. I may be out of touch for a while since I'll be putting my full concentration in that area. Try not to burn the planet down while I'm gone.

Chapter Two

How Maliche Rocker managed many of his now legendary accomplishments appeared magical to many, the stuff of legends from his family history. A Rocker, it was rumored, could call the rains from a clear sky, or could control an opponent through some secret, ancient ritual handed down through generations. Even mystical stories of the Rockers being half machine persisted as stories parents told their children at bedtime. Of course only fanatics and those on the fringe ever really believed such nonsense, but still...

"Yes, my father did possess Karm's ancient biocomputer. While it was never truly a secret, this was not a matter my father wished to be commonly known, although he did not deliberately try to hide it. It may have been part of the reason for his growing egomania." At a signal from Jontar, an aide brought yet another memory probe device from the wings. The courtroom buzzed with the murmurers as everyone realized for the first time what had previously been the subject of speculation and rumor.

Placing it on his own head, he continued to address the Assembly. "As my own memories of events which took place on distant worlds are relevant to my case, I will now add my own memories into the record with full understanding of the potential consequences. The events I now reveal occurred more recently during my training at the Skae Academy."

Once again, all eyes attended to the blurring holographic images. Gasps could be heard as the image defined itself into a view of an alien world.

***

Jontar Rocker sat at his console scanning the hundreds of simulated vessels on the screen. The darkened room flashed with the changing colors from the various panels in front of each trainee. The buzz of hushed voices relaying hurried commands into their headsets reverberated from the mix of fifty students representing ten different species hoping to one day become fleet officers. Two Skae trainers strolled among the stations, observing the students and making occasional notes on their portable comp-pads. If any trainee appeared to be struggling or unchallenged, they tapped instructions to alter the individual programs so each student progressed at an appropriate rate. The Skae training academy now listed two dozen Kolbri among their cadets as potential navigators for their fleet, and hopes were high for these recruits. Early test results indicated an uncanny instinct for technology and interstellar navigation, far surpassing even trainees two or three years ahead of them. The Skae were conducting an aggressive campaign to find and recruit as many of these incredible Kolbri as possible.

Jontar's face drooped in a blank gaze as he stared at the panel in front of him as if in a trance. His mind raced through the electronic pathways of the computer's vast memory bank in search of an answer to the dilemma on his screen. He shook his shoulders and ran the small talons of one hand through his abbreviated crest feathers to bring himself back to the present and the task before him. Scanning the image of blips on the screen, he identified the attack group he needed. "Sector Four Command, change your heading to three-four-seven point nine by six-two-five point three. Increase speed to three percent light. Set sensors to long range infrared. Potential hostiles closing on your position. Confirm."

"Confirm base. Coming to three-four-seven point nine by six-two-five point three at three percent light, full infrared." The static-filled voice responded. "Sensors picking up something now."

Jontar watched his screen as a new pattern of orange blips, enemy vessels, entered exactly where he'd predicted they would. A smirk began to make its way onto Jontar's face.

"Confirmed enemy contact, base. Implementing attack command sigma nine."

Cadet Rocker's eyes unfocused for a brief second as he rested his taloned hands on either side of the monitor. The smirk became a smile as he sat back with arms folded across his chest to watch the encounter taking place in the simulation.

"Excellent work, Mr. Rocker," Tov, the training master said as he stood watching from behind. "Tell me, how did you detect that Gorvin maneuver?" Tov's long blue fingers danced over the keypad of his tablet as he spoke. The instructor's large violet eyes appeared focused on the device, but Jontar knew from experience the Skae missed nothing. He was being interrogated and any indication of misconduct or impropriety could prove disastrous.

Jontar maintained his casual manner and spun in his seat to face the instructor. "I recognized the situation from previous encounters, sir. This simulation bore a strong resemblance to the Maktal encounter during the Tesh conflict."

"Remarkable," replied Tov as he tapped several comments on his pad, his large violet eyes peering at Jontar as if searching for any hint of deceit. "I was not aware the Tesh conflict was part of your curriculum."

"It's not, sir. I read about it while researching other matters during my free time. One can never be too prepared, sir." He maintained a level, confident eye contact as he spoke.

Tov stood silent for a moment, then gave his pad a final swipe and turned to leave. "Yes, well done, then, cadet. Carry on."

As soon as Tov was out of earshot, Jontar returned his attention to his panel. Swallowing hard, he resettled his shoulders and responded to the computer's questions before shutting his station down.

Back in the quarters he shared with Yalmut and Duvar, two more Kolbri recruits, both childhood friends of his, he collapsed on his thinly padded bed and kicked off his boots.

"So how was the simulation today?" Yalmut asked as he juggled four colorful icosahedrons in the air in a complex revolving pattern. *What were you thinking?* Yalmut's thoughts entered Jontar's mind, stinging like plimit juice on a fresh cut, nearly drowning out the verbal question. *Tov nearly caught you this time. You need to be more careful.*

"They tried something out of the old histories attempting to trip me up, but luckily for me, I recognized it from my extra studies." *Don't be such a mordu, Yalmut. You're always seeing threats. I know what I'm doing. The Skae have always underestimated us. It's their fatal flaw. They cannot imagine anyone capable of outsmarting them.*

"Maybe I'll join you in the library next time. In case they try to pull something out of the ordinary on me next time." Another intrusion into his mind from Duvar's direction increased the sting. *And the same applies to you sometimes, Jontar. You can't continue to take such risks. Underestimating our instructors might be your fatal flaw. You know what they'll do to us and everyone back home, if we get caught.*

The three continued their simultaneous verbal and telepathic conversations as they had learned to do since childhood back on Kodut. This, and the ability to connect and manipulate any form of technology with nothing more than their minds, was an inherited trait common to most Kolbri. Not all the Kolbri children had the talent, but many did, much to the distress of their parents. Apparently, the closer their genetic ties to the Rocker clan, the stronger the ability manifested itself. Among the Kolbri, there was speculation that it was a residual effect of the biocomputer's influence on the Rockers, going all the way back to Karm and the original Jontar Rocker. Over the many generations since those two, most Brin families could claim at least some distant relationship to the Rockers.

Unsure of their parent's reaction, or the government's for that matter, the youths agreed it would be best to hide the true depth of their talent from everyone. Of course, knowledge of at least some levels of this ability could not be hidden from their parents forever. This led to the parents of these hybrid children feeling inevitable stress. Grounding a willful young one was never quite as strong a punishment when they could still communicate telepathically. Keeping them from helping each other during school exams was a never-ending process. Now the talent proved useful in keeping the true nature of their work in the Skae academy secret. Even if the Skae tried to secretly listen in on them, all they would hear were completely innocuous conversations. They once thought about interfering with the listening devices, easily detected once they mentally scanned the rooms, but they decided this was the simplest solution.

"All the quantum string data in the galaxy isn't enough to help a schutek like you, Duvar." Jontar tossed a pillow at Duvar, over Yalmut's head, causing the icosahedrons to fly off in random directions across the room. *We won't get caught. They can't detect our intrusions into their systems. We aren't like my father's biocomputer. Their technology may be the most advanced in the region, but our minds aren't like any inorganic technology. We don't leave traces for them to track or detect, even if they did suspect us.*

Yalmut picked up two of the polyhedrons that landed near him and began a new pattern, adding the two Duvar chucked back at him that had landed on his cot. "Knock it off, you two. I'm trying to get some rest here." *He's right, Duvar. As much as I hate to admit it, you know we've been able to monitor their communications even while they are in mid-transmission without so much as a hint of our presence being detected.* He flicked a quick glance at Jontar. *But that doesn't mean you can take chances just to show off. What if Tov decided to go looking for references to the Tesh conflict and couldn't find any. Looking ahead into the sim programs like that is dangerous, especially when our instructors are observing you. Be more careful next time.*

Jontar rolled over on his back and stretched out on the bed, stubby talons, almost nail-like when compared to the talons of a full Brin, preening his few crest feathers, and legs crossed. "Alright, I'm gonna try to get some rest myself before the late-day sims begin." *Fine. I'll be more careful, ya bunch of old morai. Is the meeting still on with the others for this weekend?*

Yalmut yawned and closed his eyes as if trying to sleep. *Everything is arranged. We should have enough to report back home now. Nothing conclusive, but plenty to arouse some concerns about the Skae and their history.*

Duvar put his juggling aside and grabbed a sim pad, appearing to examine his results from the last session. *Yes. These so-called simulations don't ring true. Something is wrong about them. Maybe we haven't gone deep enough into their systems yet. If we haven't uncovered anything by the time of the meeting, some of us may need to pair up to dig further into the network. Some of their protections are pretty strong.*

And what about those references to six-dimensional degenerate matter and gravity wave generators? What's all that about? Yalmut cut in, scratching his short talons together.

Jontar waved his hand in the air dismissively. *We'll get in soon enough. Now let me think for a while. I have some ideas.*

***

The holographic image faded, allowing the courtroom to come back into view. Haytk slammed her metallic orb onto the table, sending sparks flying as the spectators again erupted into mayhem at the new revelations. The Kolbri youths were known to be different, possibly with clairvoyant potential, even some telepathic ability, but nothing of this magnitude. At least with Karm and Maliche, an implanted biocomputer was merely a technological enhancement. The Kolbri were something else entirely. They were potentially a new species, a far more advanced species with unknown abilities, until now. Calls for a recess to determine the impact of this new knowledge of the Kolbri abilities were countered with calls for the proceedings to continue without delay.

"Your honors, please, calm yourselves," Young Jontar pleaded for their attention. "I promise, all will be revealed by this testimony. Hear me out. Witness the memories and decide for yourselves if we are a threat to you, though I assure you we are not. We are your children, nothing more." He raised his hands, palms up, in supplication, his face composed into an expression of utter civility and humility.

The judges held private conferences among themselves, leaning in close to argue the matter with each other. After a few moments, Haytk gave her ruling. A swarm of hover-cams jockeyed for position to capture the decision.

"This is a public hearing, and this new revelation has far-reaching potential to impact the future of us all. What has been presented to this point is, at best, only enough information to raise our awareness. It is insufficient to draw well-informed and beneficial conclusions. Therefore, in the interest of full disclosure and due diligence, you may proceed." She waved her hand for Jontar to continue. A chorus of applause and cheers erupted from the gallery, resulting in another call to order from the judges.

"Thank you, your honors. While I was away training with the Skae, my father began to develop his own suspicions of the Skae and their motives. Our reports to him began to indicate a disturbing pattern. He developed a strategy to uncover the truth of matters for himself. I regret to say, however, he lost his way and allowed himself to be swayed onto a path of self-destruction. The remainder of my testimony is constructed from the memory of conversations between the involved parties and myself."

Another change in the misty light found them gazing on a scene all those present recognized and had played a role in.

***

The day proved warm, with a bright blue sky above. Looking back at the city, Maliche felt inspired by the tall gleaming buildings, the rush of mag-lev vehicles, and the sheer beauty of First Town. He reflected on the history of the city and his family's role in its early development. In the beginning, it had been difficult to separate his own memories from those of Maripa's diary and her medallion that the biocomputer had fed into his mind, but eventually he learned to compartmentalize those from his own personal experiences.

Nalot escorted Maliche to the Skae space elevator, a gift from the Skae Empire completed only last month. This marvel of engineering with its ultra-thin cable, only a meter in diameter, stretched out of sight into the clouds above and beyond. Made with advanced fiber technology on Kredat, another of the Skae allied worlds, Brin scientists were still unable to unravel the intricacies of its manufacture or its chemical composition. While unbelievably thin, this cable, anchored in space by a small artificial station, allowed visitors to meet the increasing number of visiting spacecraft in orbit, since most were not designed to land on a planet's surface. A series of pods, transparent on the upper half, waited inside the spaceport station. When occupied, a pod would travel along a mag-lev rail to the cable where it connected and, by use of gravity-modifying cold fusion powered devices, rise up the length of the cable and dock with the upper station. Passengers then walked to one of four airlock docking tubes to meet the vessel awaiting them. This new technology proved much faster than travel by shuttle and a third of the cost.

Nalot's grey eyes darted from side to side as if watching a fast-paced Rings game. He hovered at Maliche's side like a mother grendel protecting its young. "Are you sure this is a good idea? We won't be able to protect you if they try to pull anything up there."

"Nothing is going to happen, old friend. I requested this meeting on their ship as a show of faith in them. Some of our leaders have made their anti-outworlder sympathies known, so I am trying to forestall any possible tensions before they grow out of control." Maliche took a deep breath of the clean air, fresh with the scent of blooming flowers artfully planted in Landing Park, the official site reserved for Skae ships when visiting the planet.

"It's not just the Skae I'm concerned about," whispered Nalot, continuing his discrete surveillance of the area. "Tensions are building between small factions of Kolandi and Brin guilds. They call themselves the True Believers and consider the Skae to be gods, reborn straight out of their mythology. Any talk of them being less or mistrust of their motives is sacrilege."

Maliche stopped short and turned to face Nalot, his mouth opened to reply as a beam of orange energy burned through the space he would have occupied if he had kept going. Nalot threw Maliche to the ground, pulling his own weapon from its holster as shrapnel exploded from the beam's impact on the nearby control tower. A second burst of energy detonated only two feet from where the pair huddled on the ground.

"Phalk! Security Alert! All personnel to Landing Park immediately. Hostile fire, attempted assassination of the Head Minister." Nalot shouted into his wrist communicator as he grabbed Maliche and darted behind a small pile of crates. Drawing his own beam pistol from its holster on his hip, Nalot returned fire toward the supply depot where a shadowy figure vanished behind one of the rows of warehouses at the far end of the tarmac. "Are you hit? Stay down until reinforcements get here."

"I'm fine. Another couple of steps and Ryma would have been very upset at me for getting my head blown off, though." Maliche lifted himself up to his knees and peeked over the crates in the direction of the shots.

"Get him to safety," Nalot shouted as security personnel arrived, their sirens screaming. He jumped to his feet and ran toward the warehouse. After only three steps, a terrible explosion burst from a stockpile of merchandise the shooter had used for cover, sending flames a hundred feet into the air, knocking Nalot to the ground nearly back to where he started. Rolling to his side, Nalot brushed ragged crest feathers away from his eyes only to see a speeding mag-lev cycle disappear between distant buildings and off into the hills beyond.

"Phalk! We'll never catch him now." Nalot rammed the pistol back into its holster as he struggled to regain his feet and turned toward the Head Minister. "Are you injured, Maliche?"

Maliche, aided to his feet by several security guards, brushed the dirt and debris from his clothing, inspecting himself for wounds. "Only the bruises these hulking golaths inflicted while protecting me. Nothing serious. What about you?" He scrutinized Nalot for any signs of damage.

Nalot winced as he walked toward the group. "Twisted my knee a bit, but otherwise alright." He glared back in the direction of the vanished would-be assassin. "Those quetzal Kolandi Skaeists. What do they think they'll accomplish by these acts of treason? They must be delusional if they think killing you will prove their loyalty to the Skae."

Maliche straightened his jacket and preened his crest feathers, trying to regain something of his persona as Head Minister. "It's a terrible thing to have your god's status threatened. The idea of their Sky People being nothing more than mortal beings, albeit with advanced technology, is unthinkable to some of the Kolandi. We, and me in particular, are the embodiment of that threat."

"But even Ryma, their own queen, has proclaimed the Skae as nothing more than another race of living beings and not gods. Strix, even the Skae deny any claim of godhood. What more do those quetzals want?"

"You can't fight faith and emotion with facts and logic. You'll lose every time." Maliche wrapped his arm around Nalot's shoulders as they walked, surrounded by their guards. "Be patient, my friend. They're a small group with little or no outside support. We cannot let them interfere with our plans. Too much is at stake here."

"At least let me postpone this meeting until I can better secure the area. That may not have been a lone assassin. What if there are others?" Nalot's eyes searched the area as he spoke.

"No. I'm sure it was an isolated attempt. We've come too far now to put this off any longer." Maliche focused his mind inward.

This was an isolated incident, right? Can you detect any more threats in the area?

None. Sorry I missed that one. My attention was focused on the plan. Shielding myself from the Skae is not easy.

Lowering his voice, he paused, glancing around for potential risk. "Is everyone and everything in place? Have we left out anything in our plans?"

"Ryma is not happy with us, as you know, but she sees the necessity of it all and will stand with us. The rest are simply waiting for us to give the signal."

"Very well, let's get this over with." Maliche straightened his shoulders and the two continued their march toward the space elevator.

Once inside, security guards, one Brin and one Skae, scanned their credentials and electronic devices. "All is in order, sir. If you would stand inside the blue ring, I will complete your pre-boarding scan."

Maliche and Nalot stepped into the circumference of a neon-blue ring pulsating on the floor. Maliche felt his crest feathers lift from his head from the static charge that enveloped him, and noticed Nalot shifting his feet slightly like someone whose feet had fallen asleep.

"All clear, High Minister. Your cable pod is to your left, number fifty-six."

As soon as they seated themselves, automatic restraints fastened around them, the pod sealed itself and levitated a few millimeters above the track as it slid forward silently. A slight bump and some mechanical clanks shook the pod as it connected to the cable. Like a ghost, they rose without further sound toward the sky, speed increasing rapidly. Without the inertial dampers, they would have been crushed as the G forces reached ten times normal gravity. As with all first-time cable risers, the sensation of witnessing the blackness of space, the planet far below with its cloud-speckled horizon curving in the distance, was awe-inspiring, if a bit unnerving. As acceleration stabilized, the dampers powered down and the effect of one-tenth g proved especially disorienting.

"Just think about it, Nalot. We are among the first Brin to see Kodut like this since The Saviors arrived all those centuries ago. Time alone wiped out the ability of the Gorvin's nanobots to destroy technology, allowing us to build our civilization here, but the development of the vaccine using our Kolbri children's DNA to reverse the effects of the virus binding everyone to the planet was sheer genius. Now we are free to see marvels like this." He spread his arms wide gesturing at the vast beauty of the planet below. I wonder if they felt the same things I am now."

"If they felt their stomach clawing up into their throats, the histories certainly left that unheroic vision of them silent." Nalot leaned over the vacuum suction mouthpiece between his knees just as his stomach lurched and emptied itself.

***

"**H**ead Minister Rocker, I am … distressed to hear of the unfortunate incident at the spaceport earlier. We are monitoring your communications; are you certain the attack came from one of those … what do they call themselves? … Skaeists? A most disturbing name. I simply do not understand how any of the Kolandi can believe we are divine beings. Our people were once the greatest of allies until the tragedy wrought by the Gorvin so long ago."

The official reception aboard the Skae cruiser Solura proved to be an exorbitant affair. Three days ago, the invitation to meet with Molk, the supreme Skae ambassador to the region, had arrived by special messenger. Maliche and Nalot, one of the first Brin to travel into space since his revered ancestors left their home world so long ago, now sat at the ambassador's table. They set in a sort of abstract design reminiscent of a wide circle pinched into a crescent shape, listening to recorded Skae music, full of lilting runs high into the upper registers of harmonic brilliance followed by dramatic drops into the depths of the lowest of bass qualities imaginable produced by completely alien instruments. It was impossible to tell from the sound if the instruments were string or wind types.

The food, while delicious, was also completely alien, collected from the furthest reaches of the Skae Empire, or at least what remained of it. Savory meats steamed on plates, dripping in marinades of complex combinations of exotic flavors. Fruits and vegetables in a wide range of unexpected colors and shapes filled a dozen expensive bowls of ornately carved crystal. The Skae barely ate any of the offerings, preferring instead to discretely breathe in the vapors produced from a series of color-coded tubes found at each place setting. While the furnishings were originally designed for the much taller, leaner physiology of the Skae, expert modifications helped make the two Brin feel comfortably at home. In addition to the ambassador, three Skae dignitaries of lesser rank sat in the remaining seats, but they only added to the conversation when signaled by Molk.

Maliche adopted an attitude of absolute confidence and dismissiveness and reached out for another of the incredibly sweet purple-skinned fruits shaped like a three-legged cardis. "Do not concern yourself with that, Ambassador Molk. We were in no real danger, and I'm sure it was nothing more than an isolated incident. The poor deluded culprit will soon be apprehended." Juice dripped from his chin as he bit into the golden interior of the fruit.

"The view during our ascent was spectacular, if a bit terrifying. Seeing our world from space is indescribable. I envy those young Kolbri who will get to travel the galaxy and witness the wonders out there. Ryma was terribly disappointed she could not join us."

"Alas," lamented Molk as he sniffed a pinkish vapor from one of the tubes in front of him. "She is Kolandi and infected with the dreaded Gorvin virus. To leave the planet would be fatal for her, even in this low orbit."

"Yes. The vaccine works well enough for us Brin, but we are confident we can duplicate our success with a Kolandi vaccine before long. Their infection, after all, has been at work for thousands of years and had time to work far more intricately into their genetic coding. We have several promising lines of research going on and one of them is bound to be successful."

The ambassador smiled broadly, nodding his head. "It will be a great source of comfort to have our old allies at our side once more."

The meal progressed in a series of pleasant but unimportant conversations until Molk rose from his place, wiped his face and hands on a warm cloth provided by an attendant and nodded for the other Skae to depart. Servants cleared the table with military precision and vanished through a door that slid in and out of the wall as it sensed the movement of someone approaching. Molk waved his hand over a panel in the arm of his chair, his fingers weaving an intricate pattern. In moments one of the ship's officers appeared in a doorway opposite the one used by the servants.

Molk addressed Nalot with a smile that almost reached his eyes but just missed. "Perhaps you would enjoy a tour of the ship while we discuss the mundane matters of state." It was less than a question, but not exactly an order of dismissal.

Nalot glanced at Maliche, who nodded his approval, wiped his hands and face with the proffered towel and departed with the officer. Maliche sat patiently, studying the Skae ambassador.

Molk reached into one of the many pockets in his embroidered jacket and pulled out a small clear jar filled with blue crystals. He opened the jar and wafted it across his face as he inhaled through the nasal slits on either side of his narrow nose. He smiled, more naturally this time, and closed his eyes. "I wish you Brin could savor the delicacies of such fine scents. Nothing completes a meal like essence of torshill, especially when imported from the Darnett sector."

"I am a bit partial to the Kolandi pudding Ryma's cooks make for me." Maliche folded his talons on top of the table.

Molk opened his eyes and regarded Maliche as if deciding how to proceed. "I am not sure you are aware of just how greatly esteemed you are among the Skae, Maliche Rocker. Your exploits to save the Kolandi from your own leaders are well known and celebrated throughout the Skae Empire."

"I am flattered, ambassador, but I think you exaggerate matters."

"Not at all, sir. If anything, I am understating how we view your selfless sacrifices to free our former allies from their bondage and to bring your two people together as was our original intent. Without you, all of the time and energy our ancestors spent in bringing your people to this world would have been in vain. We owe you a great debt. And on a personal note, if I may add, Bolt was my great-grandfather. I would not want to see my family's legacy tarnished with failure."

Maliche raised his hands to cover his face as he bowed toward his host. "I am greatly honored by your kind thoughts, ambassador, but I assure you, anyone in my place would have done the same. It was the only honorable thing to do."

Molk replied with a gesture of respect, placing the edge of one hand vertically in the center of his chest. "None the less, I speak the truth. Among my people, you are revered. If you wished it, we would support your taking full control of this world as emperor. Our full might would stand behind you, if you chose to seize the power you deserve."

Maliche's mouth dropped open; he sat as if paralyzed by Molk's revelation. "What are you saying, sir? You can't seriously expect me to betray everyone and everything I believe."

"On the contrary, sir. You would not betray anyone. You would become the instrument through which they could achieve greatness. You could be the one who leads them all back into the family of interstellar travelers. Imagine the wonders they could be a part of, the glories they could achieve." With another wave of his hand over the control panel, a series of grand images of beautiful alien landscapes and civilizations of great wealth and prosperity played, floating in the air as holographic images above the center of the table now empty of the grand meal.

"I don't need to become an emperor to accomplish those goals. Our assembly can handle the requirements far better than I ever could alone."

Molk shook his head, lowering his chin to his chest. "If only that were true. We have tried to help civilizations in the past who insisted on maintaining their collective style of government. All of them failed to adopt the alterations necessary for such a dramatic change in the scope of their influence. Only those governments led by a determined individual demonstrated the adaptability to reinvent themselves and face the new challenges of galactic commerce and diplomacy. You, Maliche, could be one of the great leaders of all time. Rarely have we witnessed one with such courage and determination. We need you to take control and bring your people back to us and the rest of the galaxy." He leaned back in his chair with two steepled fingers rising from folded hands, touching his chin. His violet eyes seemed to penetrate to Maliche's essence.

"My son tells me about the wonders he has seen out there among the stars. I must confess to wanting to bring such marvels to everyone on Kodut. From what I hear, your space elevator is only a minor example of the wonders we could be part of." He sat back, eyes probing the room as if searching for an answer. "There are some factions stubbornly refusing to see the benefits of reaching out beyond our lone world. Fear of the new and unknown is a powerful force. Others feel we are already moving too quickly, so soon after our reunion with the Kolandi. They want more time to allow for us to assimilate our newfound partnership before flying off to new adventures among the stars."

"Exactly the sort of thing we could help you with once you became emperor. We could supply you with the technology to secure your position and help your people appreciate the benefits of galactic trade. Your legacy could be even greater than that of Karm, Jontar, and Maripa Rocker. Certainly their equal."

Maliche preened his crest feathers, brows furrowed. "I have always admired my illustrious ancestors. And I would be performing a great service for the future of everyone. I wish I could be certain."

Molk raised himself up from the table and strode over to Maliche, arms spread wide, a broad smile on his face. "We have time, my friend. Think over our proposal. I will return in a week to discuss matters further. For now, I have other affairs of state to attend to, as do you planet-side. Ah, your companion returns."

Nalot stood in the doorway, glowering at Maliche and Molk, talons clasped firmly behind his back. "I hope

I'm not interrupting anything, Maliche, Mr. Ambassador, but the next pod is ready to take us back home." He managed to control a sudden heave in his stomach at the thought of the trip back to the surface.

Maliche tilted his head, eyes squinting as he watched Nalot, alert for any signs of a problem. "Thank you Molk, for the wonderful meal and for an interesting conversation. You have given me much to think about. May your journey be safe." He gave a half bow with the Skae salute, one returned by Molk, and he followed Nalot down the corridor.

Was the visit here as helpful as you anticipated? Maliche's thoughts sought out his biocomputer companion.

The biocomputer response came with the accustomed tingle in his brain. *More than you can imagine. But we need to wait until free from the Skae surveillance monitors. I can only hide so much from them. But what happened while I was invading the ship's systems? It would appear you deviated from the plan. Are you sure that was wise?*

I don't know yet, but it did open up some interesting possibilities.

Maliche felt the tingling in his mind as the biocomputer examined his neural connections related to the meeting. *Yes, I see what you mean. You may be on to something. Let me think about it for a while.*

Once their pod undocked from the cruiser and began its descent, Maliche turned off his communicator and turned to face Nalot. "You're not going to like this, but let me explain."

***

"It was this meeting, your honor, which started my father on his descent into madness." Jontar addressed the Assembly as the memory image vanished. "Molk planted a seed he could not ignore. While I believe his efforts were founded in a desire to bring us all into a new and better life, one of unlimited wealth and opportunity for everyone, Brin and Kolandi alike, he succumbed to the darkness of his position. Apparently, not even his biocomputer could sway his thinking. It is even possible his craven appetites and extreme age corrupted the device."

Murmurs throughout the crowd grew in intensity. Jontar overheard arguments, both in favor of his father's actions and against, fill the room. He reached out with his ability to see what the judges were recording on their note pads. Satisfied his testimony was having the desired effect, he continued.

"At this time I would like to call my mother to the stand. Despite her profound grief, she has agreed that her memories are essential to my case and is willing to cooperate."

Haytk swiveled in her levitating chair to face Ryma. "We have no wish to intrude these proceedings into your mourning, Your Highness. We can make more private arrangements, if you would prefer."

Ryma stood and proceeded with head held high beneath her veils, as befitting her royal status. Her voice held firm as she replied to the head minister's proposition. "I am perfectly willing and able to perform my duties to this court, Head Minister. The public has a right to know the entire truth, even if it reflects badly on my husband. My son is on trial; if my memories can help save his life, then I must do this thing." She arranged her long gown perfectly as she sat in the witness stand.

Haytk waved her hand for Jontar to proceed as she swiveled back to face the court. Jontar leaned in close as he placed the veracity probe on her head. "Thank you, Mother."

Pacing in front of the bench, with hovering vid cams following his every move, Jontar continued his presentation. "At first, my father was intent on helping the

Assembly bring all of us into the new possibilities of a coalition with the Skae and other space-faring civilizations. He soon realized the Skae were correct in their judgement of the need for a single, powerful leader to take control. The Assembly argued every decision and piled on so many amendments to any decision that progress became impossible. It was only then that he garnered enough support to proclaim himself emperor and turn the Assembly into a puppet organization with no real authority. At first, his efforts were met with success, but then something went wrong. It is my personal belief that he became corrupted by the lure of unrestrained power, and the whispers of greedy supplicants in his ears night and day overcame his better nature. The biocomputer, originally a Skae construction, also helped influence him to become nothing more than a tool for the Skae to rule us from above."

He activated the device with a thought and the images of Ryma's memory filled the room.

Chapter Three

The sun set, red with crepuscular rays shining through broken clouds highlighting the peaks of nearby snow-capped mountains. Ryma, after a long day inspecting the new mining facilities, stood on the hillside taking in the view. Six months of negotiations and inspection tours were at long last reaching an end. Six months away from Maliche and First Town were taking their toll on her and her companions, but this was the moment of triumph for her people. It was what she had worked so tirelessly for, and she was not going to miss any part of it. At her side waited Seykel, loyal Skatak and Nalot's wife. The two stood on a hillside near their former home in the caverns, watching the activity below. Vehicles of all descriptions levitated along dirt roads carrying loads of minerals, supplies, personnel, and equipment in a furious but well-organized frenzy of commotion. Feelings of joy and pride in her people filled her as she watched the labors below. Not even the dust and cacophony of machinery diminished the experience… not much, anyway.

"Tomorrow will be a historic day, Seykel. Only a few years ago our people struggled under the yolk of Brin slavery. Now we control the mines and reap the profits from our labor."

Seykel lowered her head in memory of those who were lost in the battle for freedom and gripped her kital with white knuckles. Her mounds of red hair flared bright in the orange light of the setting sun, a few stray strands waving in the light breeze. "When the last of the Brin consultants leaves tomorrow, we will celebrate as never before. You and Maliche have held true to your promises and worked miracles bringing our people together."

"You and Nalot have been instrumental to our cause. Does he show any lingering effects from his walk to the Path of Berit?"

"None, my princess. He is strong and recovered without difficulty." She straightened her shoulders, lifting herself to her full stature, still only managing to stand as tall as Ryma's shoulder. A look of pride seemed to fill her.

"And your daughter, Thyka, how old is she now... nineteen years? I still think of her as a child. How are her studies progressing?"

"She is exceeding all expectations, princess. Thyka is every bit the equal in intelligence and ability to Jontar and the rest of the Kolbri, although more in ethereal ways than technological. She should be elevated to full Tolavar very soon." She hesitated, her eyes darting around and her mouth contorting like someone working out how to say something difficult without giving offense.

Ryma placed a hand on Seykel's shoulder. "Speak your mind, Skatak. Tell me what troubles you."

Seykel positioned herself in front of Ryma and stood at attention, but her eyes found their focus on the hills beyond Ryma. "My princess, I am troubled by the recent reports from First Town. I find it hard to believe what they are saying about Maliche. If what we are hearing is true, he must be gravely ill or out of his mind. How could he... Forgive me, princess. It is not my place to judge your husband and our savior."

Ryma reached out with one hand to lift Seykel's face up to hers. "It is your duty as my Skatak to protect me from all harm, from without and within. Much has changed in the months we have been away. I, too, am disturbed by my husband's recent behavior. I plan to have a long... conversation with him when we return."

Seykel stiffened her back as she continued. "Is he truly gathering concubines? How could he do this to you? The reports of celebrations with drunken debauchery and gladiatorial games continue to come in. And what is a royal yacht? It sounds like a palace that floats on the ocean. What purpose could it possibly have? It cannot possibly travel as fast or as efficiently as our mag-lev transport ships…"

Ryma hung her head and turned her back to the young woman, struggling to hide the sadness. "Some of the Brin customs are indeed very strange to us, but we must continue to have faith in those we love. There must be some explanation… a good reason for his actions. Perhaps we will find the reports are greatly exaggerated in their details." She turned back to face Seykel. "I have decided to return to First Town to learn first-hand the truth of matters. We will see together just how far my husband's excesses have taken him. And since you inform me of your daughter's imminent elevation, I will talk with the good sisters to see if we can speed up the official recognition. Perhaps we will be able to bring her with us in a few days. We could certainly use her abilities."

Seykel smiled and turned to watch the sunset. "It would be good to have our families reunited in such troubled times."

Ryma joined her, one arm resting gently on the shoulders of her trusted confidant. The two women remained on the hillside until well after dark enveloped them, hardly noticing when the change of shifts at the mine allowed a brief relief from the noise.

***

The holographic image shifted quickly before the eyes of those assembled in the courtroom. Three years in the making, now the official residence of Maliche Rocker, self-proclaimed emperor for just over a year, the new palace was awash with activity. The renovated Assembly building continued as the center of government, even after the Assembly was evicted and relegated by imperial decree to only local civil matters. But nothing was the same. Where the once-proud structure once stood alone and served as a symbol of unity for the Brin, the newly-constructed offices and connecting facilities hid much of the former structure. A high wall surrounding the conglomeration gave the final touch to what was now commonly referred to as the palace. All manner of Brin and Kolandi in colorful garb shuffled their way through the vast polished stone hallways. Works of the masters once graced the passageways, but now only gaudy portraits of Maliche or other wealthy guildsmen and their families were displayed. Poorly carved statues, often depicting the baser appetites of the wealthy, stood prominently in the once grand halls. For a fee, even the least talented artists could display their handiwork, no matter the subject or quality. Each of the guilds maintained offices inside to secure rapid access to the new emperor and gain invitations to the continuous elaborate celebrations. One only had to transfer over a few bank credits to secure an audience with Maliche. The larger the transfer, the sooner and longer the audience the patron would be permitted.

A week after the official transfer of control of the mines to the Kolandi, Ryma and her entourage returned to First Town. Rilo and Neri, as leaders of the Skatak, led the procession. Four more Skatak followed directly behind Ryma, Seykel, and Thyka. Trailing them were ten royal guardsmen, all powerful Kolandi warriors, bare-chested and carrying long heavy spears. As they were escorted through the halls, Ryma witnessed at least a dozen exchanges of money for favors between government officials and guildsmen. No effort to hide or disguise the act was thought necessary any longer.

In one corner, a trio of ragged Kolandi, dressed in the scraps reminiscent of the garb worn during their slavery, caught Ryma's eye. As she watched, the two men and one woman, dirty and looking as though they had not eaten in weeks, extolled the crowds with the grandeur of the Skae gods. None of the passersby listened, but the fanatics persisted with undiminished fervor. Before she looked away, the gaunt woman's gaze fell on Ryma and her party. Rising to her full height, frail garments barely concealing her, she lifted one arm and pointed toward the princess.

"There walks our betrayer, the one who led us into darkness among our enslavers and away from the light of our true gods! Repent, princess, or know the wrath of the gods you deserted. Bring your people back to the light of the true gods or suffer the fate of all who oppose their might. The night is upon you. Repent before the light of the god's new day finds you still among the infidels."

Ryma stood fixed in place, listening to the woman's ravings. A tug at her sleeve brought her back to herself and sent a shiver up her spine. With a shake of her head, she signaled for the entourage to continue to the royal quarters. As they advanced through the crowds, Ryma whispered to Rilo. "Assign someone to watch those three, the woman in particular. I don't want any surprises from that group of fanatics."

Rilo signaled to one of the Skatak attendants to approach. The woman nodded after receiving her instructions and broke away from the group, vanishing into the crowds.

"I never should have consented to his declaring himself emperor or turning this place into his palace. He told me he had such plans for us as a unified people. I let him and that biocomputer go against my better judgement. And now, the minute I'm away on important business…" Her voice trailed off in dismay as she looked around.

Seykel kept her hand on her kital, ready to let it fly if their safety was compromised. Thyka pressed her hands against her ears to soften the assault of noise. Her face screwed in concentration as she fought to block the thought energy of so many individuals from intruding her mind.

"I don't like this place, Mother. I've never felt so much anger and deceit. It hurts."

Seykel gathered in her daughter with one arm as they walked "Focus on your training. You can block them out if you use what the elders taught you. As a Tolvaran, you will come into contact with many individuals fiercely opposed to one another, and their emotions will not be pleasant to touch. Trust in your training and you will learn to keep yourself separate and under control."

Thyka's breathing slowed as she organized her cerebral pathways. Gradually her face relaxed as the press of energies subsided and the onrush of thoughts and feelings from those in the throng faded into a background hum. "That's better, Mother. Thank you. Why is everyone so upset?"

"We don't know, sweetness. That is what we hope to learn very soon."

"Mother! You shouldn't be here now." Young Jontar Rocker ran to face Ryma and the others. He gasped for breath after the long run from his quarters. "Father is having another of his… spells. You don't want to see him now. Let me tell him you're here and get him ready for a proper reception."

Faces in the crowd turned to watch the confrontation. All their attention centered on Ryma and Jontar. Anger rose within her, and her face, without actually changing expression, seemed to harden. "No, Jontar. Not this time. I mean to put an end to this outlandish behavior once and for all."

He took both her hands in his. "You know how he is when he gets like this. He won't listen to anyone except that phalking device in his head. It must be driving him mad."

Ryma closed her eyes and hung her head. "I know, my son. I should not have left you two alone. I should have known better. But I must stop this now and undo the damage he has wrought. It has gone far enough."

As the princess's party arrived at the entrance to the main reception hall, Jontar in the lead, garishly robed servants opened the massive doors for them. A tidal wave of noise and stale smells assaulted them. Inside the room, dozens of Brin and Kolandi citizens lounged on the floor, eating, drinking, shouting, and engaging in an assortment of vulgar behaviors not fit to be witnessed in public, much less in the emperor's reception room. Maliche, adorned with a large jeweled crown, his golden scepter casually leaning against the throne, was surrounded by half dozen beautiful women all vying for his attention as he lounged carelessly in his massive stone throne.

He wore a much-stained fur-lined cape around his neck. His shirt was half-unfastened and hung mostly untucked from scuffed and well-worn trousers. One shoe dangled loosely from the foot he swung lazily over one arm of the gilded throne, the other lay on its side on the floor next to the other foot, one taloned toe sticking out through a sock he had probably worn for days. A rainbow of colors lit the room from the large stained glass windows, the only familiar part of this once grand hall of the old assembly building.

Ryma straightened her shoulders, her face turning to stone. "Clear this room immediately," she ordered in a barely audible voice of ice. "I need to speak to my husband... alone."

Maliche sat upright, smiling through drink-hazed eyes. "Ryma, my beautiful wife, we did not expect you until next week. Have you come to join the celebration? Everyone raise a glass to your imperial princess!"

The crowd shouted their greetings in slurred voices, along with several rude suggestions to join them. Two of the concubines, dressed in gowns so short and sheer they might as well not be wearing anything, raised their glasses, drank and plopped themselves in Maliche's lap to offer him gulps of his own.

Jontar's face turned red with rage as he shouted at the crowd. "You insult my mother, your princess, and your emperor. You should all leave now before I have you all chained in the prison. And you," he turned, raising a talon pointed at the concubines, "should be exiled for your scandalous actions."

Maliche shoved the women in his lap to the ground and jumped to his feet. "You will not speak to my wives in that manner, young man. Apologize now or you will be the one in prison."

Jontar's mouth hung open. "Me? In prison? I have done nothing but try to hold this city and our people together. You are the one who has betrayed us all. You have abdicated all authority to the guilds and anyone with a few coins in their pocket."

"How dare you!" Maliche took a few wobbling steps toward his son. A red glow surrounded his body.

"Father, have you gone completely mad? Has that machine in your head finally driven all sense from you? Please, open your eyes to what you are doing."

"Jontar, let me handle this." Ryma's voice shook with barely controlled rage as father and son stood face-to-face, their anger boiling over.

"Stay out of this, Ryma." Maliche raised his hand and slapped Ryma across the face, nearly knocking her off her feet.

"Stop!" she shouted at her Skatak who were about to release their kital in retaliation for the attack on their princess. "Let me handle this. Take no action, no matter what happens."

She turned back to face Maliche, who, with crooked smile and drink-dulled eyes, appeared to hardly even notice her. She felt her heart sink.

Before she could speak, Maliche turned his attention toward Jontar, allowing the red glow to intensify into a blazing light.

The crack of an energy pistol discharging resounded as a brilliant orange beam ripped into Maliche's chest. All eyes turned to see Jontar holding his weapon, talon on the trigger pad.

Ryma's voice rang loud and clear. "Clear this room!"

The Skatak drew their weapons as they shouted orders to the palace guards. Together with the warrior honor guard, starting at the base of the throne's dais, they yanked the assembled guests roughly by their collars, shoving them toward the exit. The initial outcry of protest was quickly shut down by the show of energy pistols, spears, and kital held at the ready. A couple of broken noses and arms from those who raised the greatest objections helped convince the rest it was in their best interest to comply with the princess's command.

***

The holographic image faded to mist and the lights in the courtroom returned. Silence filled the chamber. Everyone knew the story, but seeing it in person was something quite different. Tears streamed down Ryma's face as the memories came flooding back. Jontar Rocker removed the veracity probe from his mother's head and squeezed her shoulder before returning the device to its stand.

"I killed my father. That is inescapable," Jontar faced the judges with stern confidence. "As I have stated previously, it is my reasons for doing so which should exonerate me."

Shouts for Jontar's execution or exile were balanced by an equal number of cries for his release. Haytk banged the sphere on its stone, sending sparks flying as she called for order. As the gathering settled, she addressed Jontar.

"You may proceed with your defense, but be advised. The law is very clear and strict. Your reasons must be absolutely compelling and unique."

Jontar nodded in agreement. "Of course, minister. My father was once a wise and loving Brin. He came from a long line of great and heroic ancestors. Our family's service to this world is unparalleled. I believe his descent into madness and even treason, though not his fault, left me no choice. His increasingly bizarre and damaging edicts are a matter of record. Our society, one that he played no small role in developing, has fallen from prosperity into utter collapse as a result of his decisions. At first, many of the rulings appeared to be strange, but harmless. Over time, culminating in his latest series of proclamations over the last few months, they have brought us to the brink of disaster."

Shouts of agreement and dissent rose over the courtroom. Head minister Haytk again slammed the sphere to regain decorum.

"Many of you here benefited from those edicts and no doubt disagree with me, but our society as we knew it has all but vanished. We would soon be at the mercy of an unregulated collection of guilds and profit makers without regard for the average citizen. I must tell you that I had been planning on removing my father from his position peacefully and legally, but those plans were not yet ready to implement when the events you just witnessed took place."

He turned to face Ryma. "If my mother had not returned a week early, perhaps I could have completed those efforts and he would now be receiving proper care for his obvious mental instability, but events took a different course. As you all witnessed, my father was about to use his biocomputer to fire some sort of energy weapon with the intent, I believe, to kill me. His anger and madness blinded him. My actions were taken in self-defense. Even had he not raised his device against me, I would have been justified under Kolandi law due to the insult to my mother, the princess. My action is also justified under a higher law of justice for the people. It was for their sake that I murdered my father before his madness would have destroyed us all."

Jontar sat on the bench in the defendant's corner and folded his hands. He faced his mother, who closed her eyes and gave him a barely noticeable nod.

The judges stood in unison and filed out of the courtroom until only Thel Haytk remained. "We will deliberate now on this most grave matter. No one is permitted to leave this room under penalty of law." She pivoted and strode out after the others.

Over the next two hours, Jontar reached out with his mind to infiltrate the judges' com pads and surveillance cameras in their chamber. He watched as they downloaded a wide range of precedents relevant to the case and the ensuing arguments. While he could not hear their voices, their body language and the transcripts being recorded by the court stenographer told him precisely what the outcome would be. He gave a slight smile beneath his folded hands, scratching one lip with a stubby talon.

Talking heads all over the city broadcast the news as soon as it was released. "Jontar Rocker found guilty of treason and murder under duress." The ruling, they explained, allowed for the possibility that he had acted in self-defense but without sufficient compelling evidence of complete innocence. "He is to be exiled from the planet and executed by incineration in our sun. The very ship which will carry the emperor's body to his resting place among the stars, as requested in his last will and testament, will be the method of execution."

***

In her royal suite, Ryma, now sole ruler of both the Brin and Kolandi according to the ancient laws of succession drafted in the early days of the Brin constitution, gave audience to her stepsister Nedia, widow of Maliche's brother Selan.

"I can't imagine what you must be going through. To lose both husband and son in the same tragic incident. It was bad enough when Selan killed himself, but for the son to murder his father… you poor thing." Nedia sat next to Ryma, holding both hands in her talons, tears streaking her cheeks. "I know we have never been close, but we are still family. If you will have me, I would like to stay and be of some assistance, if nothing more than a sympathetic ear. Now that my own children are grown, I have nothing but time on my hands, and I do have some experience with Brin officials. Perhaps I can help guide you in the difficult decisions facing you now."

Ryma peered up at Nedia through swollen, red-streaked eyes. "Yes, second sister. That would be of some comfort to me. If it would not inconvenience you, I would appreciate your guidance and company."

***

Four days later, all eyes on the planet, Brin and Kolandi alike, watched the holo-broadcast of Maliche Rocker's coffin, an ornate gold and silver gem-encrusted sarcophagus, being loaded onto his personal mag-lev transport, now specially modified for space flight. As a special request, one she told the officials was a private matter, Ryma requested the name of the vessel be changed to Amaethon. Only a Kolandi would recognize the name as the ancient god of luck. Previously all manner of personal belongings, large and small had been loaded into the cargo hold of the ship. As stated in his last testament, an emperor needs to spend the after-life in complete luxury.

Once the tomb-ship was fully loaded, palace guards escorted the shackled Jontar Rocker up the ramp and secured him to one of the passenger seats. He never looked up or spoke but maintained a posture of dignity the entire time.

Once the guards stepped off the ramp, the doors slid shut, the ramp retreated into its slot, and everyone waited. The ground shook as the engines roared to life, billowing smoke and flame from their massive thrusters. The ship shuddered, seemingly reluctant to let go, then slowly gained momentum as it slid on its undercarriage down the rails. Gathering speed, the vessel shot down the rails as they curved upward. Reaching escape velocity, the ship left the rails and dropped its undercarriage, launching on a trajectory into orbit.

"All boosters are operating at full power, sir," the engineer in charge of monitoring the ship's progress called out as a series of figures detailing the ship's trajectory and status continuously updated on his display. "Leaving the atmosphere in two minutes, and on course."

Civil and government officials monitored the operation from a cramped observation booth high above the control center. A tiny red blip representing the emperor's ship traveled at ever-increasing velocity across a holo-image of the solar system, trailing a dashed yellow line showing its path. In six hours, the red dot impacted the image of the sun.

"Target reached, sir. Stellar impact at twenty-two-nine-sixteen."

The officer in charge signaled successful completion to the observation booth and those inside silently exited. "That's it, everyone. Shut it down."

The news of the event and Ryma's subsequent efforts to regain control of the government dominated the broadcasts for the next week. After that, life gradually returned to normal and cleaning crews began to clear the filth from the palace.

Chapter Four

Darkness gradually gave way as Maliche regained consciousness. Voices sounded in his auricles, but several minutes passed before he could discern actual words. Any attempt to open his eyes proved fruitless. Some sort of covering over them allowed only the barest of hazy images, possibly a person, due to its movement, but difficult to tell.

"He's coming out of it now."

"At last. I thought we might lose him for a moment. That energy blast came awfully close to some vital organs."

"Nothing the biocomputer couldn't handle. It was able to absorb and dispel most of the blast."

"True, but the device did take some damage itself. I sensed it working to repair itself as well as father."

Maliche tried to raise his talons but managed only a single feeble finger wobble. He felt like someone who had wrestled a small grendel in a whirlpool. A gentle hand held his wrist and a cold touch on his chest made his muscles twitch as if a piece of ice had been placed there.

A familiar voice sounded in his mind. *"Easy, old friend. Remember, you've been dead for several days. I've worked too hard to keep you in one piece. Don't go and spoil my artistry by being foolish. Your friends are checking your vitals, but I can tell you the effects are wearing off nicely now. You should be fully awake in a few hours."*

"So the plan worked?"

"More or less. I had to pull off a slight miracle or two we hadn't planned on, but yes, we're on the ship and heading out to find the Gorvin. Now go back to sleep."

Blackness descended once again as Maliche drifted off into dreamless sleep. He awoke several hours later with a start.

The room spun as he sat up, but he lowered his head and took several deep breaths to help it settle in place. A chill ran through him as his bare feet touched the metal floor.

"Welcome back to the land of the living. You had us worried for a while, but your device is very good." Jontar sat on a small metal bench protruding from a curved graphene wall opposite Maliche's bed. It slipped silently into the wall as he stood to join his father on the bed. "How do you feel?"

Maliche stretched his shoulders, rolled his neck to work out some kinks, and preened his crest feathers. His survey of the room revealed curving, grey-white walls blending seamlessly into a rounded ceiling of the same material. The oval room was small but enough for one Brin to occupy in relative comfort. A tiny desk with a keypad protruded from its slot in one part of the wall under a monitor. Another slot in the floor revealed where the mag-lev chair would rise up for him to sit at the desk. To his left, an open doorway showed the cramped but highly efficient lavatory. He presumed the closed doorway on his right was a closet. His secret efforts to build this spacecraft in the guise of a royal mag-lev ground transport had apparently proved successful.

"Not too bad, considering. How are the others? Did everyone make it onboard?"

Avoiding eye contact, Jontar pulled a communication pad from his pocket and handed it to Maliche. "Don't explode now. Mother had good reasons for her decision, and I agreed with her."

Maliche's crest reddened as he seized Jontar's arm. "What are you talking about? Did something go wrong?

Where is your mother?" If his grip had been any stronger, his talons would have left holes in Jontar's arm.

Wincing, Jontar placed his hand on his father's. "No, nothing went wrong. She knew you would never have gone ahead with this if she stayed behind, so she let you think she was coming. Play the message." He pushed the pad into Maliche's talons and strode out of the room.

The door slid shut almost seamlessly, leaving Maliche staring at the blank wall. He glanced at his reflection in the tiny alcove with the washbasin and bio-waste disposal unit. The face staring back seemed to have aged ten years in the past few months. He refocused his attention on the communication pad and forced himself to press the blinking symbol for an incoming message, setting the controls to private, screen-only display, blocking the usual holographic image. Ryma's face filled the screen. Her smile failed to reach her worried eyes as she spoke.

"It will probably be pointless to tell you not to be angry with me, my love, but please at least listen to me before you do. One of us had to remain here to restore order. Since you had to leave, I am the only one who both Brin and Kolandi will accept as being rightfully in charge. There are too many factions willing to seize control in your absence. Many of them, including Nedia, are attempting to persuade me to their way of thinking even now. Imagine the chaos if both of us were gone and presumed dead..."

The rest of the message continued with arguments worthy of any legal expert, interspersed with declarations of her love for Maliche and Jontar. Her voice cracked only once, but she appeared to fight back the tears welling up in her beautiful brown eyes.

"... I will end now, my love, with the hope and wish that you continue as we had planned, trusting in my ability to control matters here. After all, I am a royal princess and was the leader of my people long before you came along. But just in case, your biocomputer and I had a long discussion before you left. It agrees with me as well and will not let you return unilaterally. The decision must be unanimous among all of your companions. I wish you success in this mission and a quick return when you are finished."

Ryma kissed the screen, leaving an image of a massive, blurred pair of lips before going black.

Maliche jumped to his feet, charging the door to his cabin as he tossed the pad onto his bed. "Jontar! Turn this—" He froze, unable to speak or move.

"You heard what she said. This mission is far too important for your impulsive foolishness to risk. Ryma is perfectly capable of dealing with matters back on Kodut. You are needed here."

"Let me go! We will go back and get her. Who are you to tell me what is necessary?"

"Right now, I'm the only one in this room thinking clearly and obeying the orders of Ryma, the royal princess of the Kolandi and current empress of Kodut — although she plans to reinstate the Assembly almost immediately."

"Release me! You have no right! You're a machine!"

A red glow surrounded Maliche. He felt the heat on his skin grow almost painful. Images of his past with the biocomputer flashed rapidly in his mind. *"Is that what you think of me? After all we've been through together? After the countless times I've saved your sorry life?"*

Maliche felt his anger subside, replaced with chagrin at his childish outburst. *"No, I'm sorry. It's just that... I mean, we need to..."*

"We need to trust your wife and get on with this mission. Can you pull yourself together now?"

Maliche let his thoughts calm. The tension in his muscles eased. His heart still ached, but there was no other choice. *"Yes. There's too much at stake. I have to trust her and see this through."*

"Very well, then." The red glow dimmed.

Maliche lurched as control returned to his muscles. He glanced back at the communication pad on his bed, took a deep breath, and headed toward the bridge, heedless of the fact that he was still wearing his bedclothes.

"And in case you weren't aware, I've been sentient for quite some time now. I would appreciate you not referring to me as a machine again."

***

The hatch to the bridge slid open. The front bulkhead of the bridge was dominated by a full-panel video screen that showed the view as if it were a window. Currently directed behind the ship, the very bright star of Kodut's sun was prominently centered. A central navigation and command center sat in front of the screen. The remaining bulkheads contained all the control and monitoring stations required to operate the ship. Blinking lights, small screens displaying graphs and images from ship-wide systems indicated all was well onboard. All eyes turned to face him as he entered.

Jontar sat in the command chair. Beside him stood Nalot and Seykel.

Maliche stared at his friend's wife, eyes wide. "Seykel, you're Kolandi. How can you be here?"

Jontar chuckled in response. "I guess we never got around to telling you this development, what with you being the mad emperor and all. We've reverse-engineered the Kolbri immunity to the virus binding the Kolandi to the planet and developed a vaccine. If our mission is successful, we can mass produce the vaccine for any Kolandi who wish it."

"And you're keeping this secret because…?"

Seykel interrupted their conversation with hands firmly on her hips. "Would you want the Skae to learn we can do this? Who's to say the process couldn't be duplicated on the other planets, now that we have unlocked the secret?"

Maliche considered the implications briefly before responding. "No, of course not. At least until we can discover what is really going on. I'm glad you could join us."

He continued to scan the bridge. At their various posts sat Jontar's fellow Kolbri, Duvar and Yalmut. His eyes widened as he noticed the figure with green eyes and wild red hair, unusual for a Kolbri but slightly more common among females, sitting in one of the mag-lev swivel chairs at another console, her feet crossed and dangling several inches above the floor.

"Thyka? What are you doing here?"

Seykel stepped to her daughter's side and placed protective hands on her shoulders. "We could not leave her behind, Great One. I will not allow my family to be divided." She often reverted to the old honorific in times of stress.

"All of us have left loved ones behind, Seykel. I cannot guarantee her safety. The chance of us all dying out here is high. And please, stop calling me that. We are practically family now."

Nalot joined his wife and daughter. "We can protect one another, Maliche. You know that. Besides," he smiled at Thyka. "We'll need the help."

"I am not doubting your skills, my friends. Thyka, I know you have received special training to become Tolavar, but how can you help?"

Thyka grinned and hopped down from her chair. She took three steps, puffed a troublesome strand of hair from her face, and pulled on Maliche's jacket to bring him eye-to-eye with her shorter stature. "Great One, my father is not referring exclusively to my Tolvaran training. You brought Jontar and his friends because they can do things with technology even you cannot. I can help them."

Maliche's eyes darted up to Nalot and Seykel, who nodded their agreement. Returning his gaze to Thyka, he studied her face before continuing. "What do you mean, Thyka? How can you help them? Are you able to alter technology too?"

Her face screwed up a little as she considered the question. She reached up with one hand to straighten her hair with the talons on her fingers. "Not exactly. At least not the same way they can. While I can also do things with technology, my ability is more in the area of an empathic connection with emotions in others. I am very sensitive to what you call the Cosmic Strings. I understand them. The other Tolavar are helping me learn control so it isn't so distracting now."

"What do you mean you understand them? They're just energy strands traveling through time and space, not living things."

"They said you would think that, just like the Skae do. Nobody really understands them except me. Some of them are almost like friends. They don't mind us using them to travel; most even like the company. It gives them something new to think about during their journey. Though they do mostly tend to ignore our presence… like we ignore our heartbeat or breathing."

Maliche took Thyka's hands in his talons, his mouth hanging open for a moment before he could comprehend what she said. "They're alive?"

Smiling, Thyka leaned back and gave his hands a squeeze, enjoying the flow of emotional confusion she was creating in him. As if she were enjoying some game he did not understand. "Not the way we are, not exactly. I can't explain it, but they do have feelings and a purpose. I can feel that in them." She let go, returned to her station and once seated, raised the chair so she could operate her panels, then pointed to Jontar and his companions. "I can help them work with the strings to learn more when they try to figure out the Skae and Gorvin technology."

"We don't understand how she can do these things, but the Kolbri are apparently capable of far more than the rest of us, in a variety of ways we are just now starting to learn about." Nalot approached his old friend as he spoke, reaching out with splayed arms. "In any case, we told Jontar we either came as a family or not at all. So here it stands."

Maliche turned to look at each of their faces, then shook his head and gave a light-hearted laugh. "It seems there have been a number of conspiracies going on around here. If every one of us is in agreement, then let's get on with it. Bring me up to speed."

Nalot stepped to Maliche's side and gave him a once-over glance. "Perhaps you'd better change into something more appropriate to someone who is supposed to be in charge around here. As stylish as your current attire is, I don't consider it appropriate for instilling confidence in a leader."

Maliche grabbed at his nightclothes, becoming aware of them for the first time. His crest sagged and reddened, a light green glow enveloping him as he excused himself.

"Stop laughing at me."

"Sorry. I was wondering how long it would be before you noticed."

Jontar stepped aside as Maliche returned and replaced him in the command chair. "Everything worked surprisingly well, Father. Once we were out of visual range, we launched the duplicate ship's transponder and Duvar shut down ours. We monitored planet-side transmissions and, as far as they know, we flew straight into the sun."

"And none of you had any lingering effects from your hidden confinement onboard for so long?"

"None at all. As soon as we launched I infiltrated the ship's computer system and released my restraints, then opened the hidden compartments and revived the others from their hibernation-sleep. Then we went to work trying to revive you."

Nalot slapped Maliche's shoulder hard as he interrupted. "You gave us quite a scare there, my friend. We almost lost you a couple of times. Thank The Eternal for that gizmo of yours."

Maliche rubbed his temples to relieve the last of the strain from his induced paralysis. "Yes, I suppose I do owe it a great deal, but it can be a bit overwhelming at times. Not to mention impossibly sure of itself."

"Be nice."

"Would you prefer I said you were a bully?"

"Why do you keep referring to him as 'it'?" Thyka looked up at Maliche, tilting her head with a furrowed-brow quizzical look on her small tan face.

Maliche and the others stared at her, not sure how to respond. Jontar recovered first. "What do you mean? It's a computer device implanted into Father's cerebral cortex and neural system. It has some biological components, but it is essentially a device. What else would we call it?"

Maliche bent down to face her eye-to-eye, and she placed one hand gently on his cheek. She closed her eyes for a second, nodded, and then smiled as she looked around the room at the others.

"I think Tol would be a good name, don't you?" A turquoise glow surrounded Maliche. "Yes, he likes Tol." She patted Maliche's cheek and climbed back into her chair, crossed her feet as they hung above the ground and clasped her hands in her lap.

"What is she talking about? You want a name?"

"I've tried telling you, but you never listen. Ask her. Maybe she can convince you I'm not a machine anymore."

The tingle in his cortex faded and Maliche preened his crest as he turned to face the young woman.

Before Maliche could open his mouth, Jontar, Yalmut, and Duvar exchanged puzzled glances, returning their attention to their Tolavar companion.

"Thyka, are you trying to tell us the biocomputer is alive? A sentient being? I think I would have sensed something like that if it were true."

"That is exactly what she means," interrupted Maliche. "And she is absolutely correct." He continued preening his crest feathers as he tried to gather his thoughts. "I've suspected as much for some time now, and Tol," he pointed to his temple with one talon, "has told me so recently. I didn't want to admit it, but the truth is undeniable. He has evolved far beyond even the remarkable device he was to begin with. I... *we* must accept the fact that Tol is a living entity in his own right."

He felt a tickling in his brain *"It's about time. Thanks for not forcing me to more drastic proofs."*

"You're welcome."

"Thyka, how do you know this?" Duvar turned toward Thyka. "You've just completed training and we've been analyzing the device, or Tol, or whatever you call it or him, for years."

Seykel stood behind Thyka, one hand on her daughter's shoulder, the other resting on the kital at her belt. "My daughter has the ability to sense technology the same as you, but she's more intuitive. Possibly this is a difference in Kolbri genders. In any case, her training as a Tolavar enhanced this ability, so she is more sensitive to life and emotions. While you three and other male Kolbri focus on the technology itself, Thyka focuses on the energy of life as a component of the technology."

"And since living beings like the Brin, Kolandi, even the Skae build the devices, they leave traces or imprints of themselves in them. I think the Skae put much more of themselves into Tol than they intended, and he has evolved since then into who he is now." Thyka reached up and held her mother's hand in hers as she explained.

Yalmut nodded in agreement. "You have to admit, Duvar, that Tol there is far more complicated and advanced than anything else we have ever studied. She could very well be right. I don't see any problems going forward with that hypothesis for now."

Jontar flicked his nail-like talons as he thought, and then straightened his shoulders as he made his decision. "Very well, then, Tol it is." And he returned to study the read-outs on his panels.

A pale blue glow surrounded Maliche and it was some time before it faded away.

"Feeling pretty pleased with yourself now, aren't you?"

"It's simply nice to be recognized for who I am, at last."

***

Ryma sat on a simple chair, the one she had placed on the dais after ordering Maliche's ornate throne demolished. Her white gown and robe shone in the light of the afternoon sun as it blazed through the tall windows in the formal hearing room, formerly the royal hall. Rilo and Neri stood alert in their customary positions behind her. After weeks of cleaning, the former great hall of the Assembly tower had regained its former elegance. The old masterpieces were returned to their places of honor, at least those not destroyed through negligence, and palace guards, Brin and Kolandi together, assured that proper decorum was respected by all visitors. A few of the more stubborn guildsmen and former lobbyists found themselves with time to rethink their behavior in the holding cells several floors below the reception hall. Thanks to the efforts of dozens of workers, the hall now was a much more fitting place for conducting official business than the den-of-thieves market-place of corruption it had become.

Throngs of supplicants, rich and poor alike, filled the great hall, talking in small groups or alone in thought among the gleaming pillars. To reassure the people of her intentions, once the Assembly was reinstated, she set up a council for hearing petitions of all citizens. Ryma, now officially recognized as the Head Minister, the presiding officer of this new council, held daily audiences to settle disputes, bestow special honors, or whatever the citizens required.

The sergeant-at-arms announced each individual as they were ushered forward to plead their case before the princess and her advisors. First among the advisors, Nedia sat at Ryma's right hand. Dressed in a plain blue silk dress with silver accents, her tastefully dyed crest feathers perfectly preened, she leaned in to whisper in Ryma's ear to provide details of the person's status and purpose for appearing before the council.

"The Primarch Sen Kolmar of the southern reaches." The sergeant-at-arms pounded his staff on the marble floor as the Brin official stepped forward.

Nedia, leaned in to whisper in Ryma's ear. "A minor official of a lesser family, mostly shart and drunge herders. He has not filed an advance formal request for anything."

Upon reaching the top step, he pulled a cylinder from his pocket.

"For the oppression of the pure Brin!"

As he pressed the top of his device, Nedia dove to protect Ryma, driving her face down onto the floor with her weight, using her own body as a shield. A piercing whine rose rapidly from primarch Sen Kolmar to deafening levels as the weapon in his hand reached critical mass. Two kitals sprouted from the primarch's forehead as the sonic disruptor exploded. The thunderous blast sent Rilo and Neri flying onto their backs, stunned. The remaining advisors were splattered with blood and suffered several minor injuries from debris, but nothing life threatening.

Amid the panicked cries of the petitioners in the hall, Nedia, her back covered in a mix of blood and pieces of the would-be assassin, pulled herself off Ryma. "Are you injured, Ryma? Talk to me!"

Ryma rolled off her stomach, sitting up to examine herself for injuries. "No, Nedia, I am unharmed. My ears are ringing and I will need a new dress, but otherwise I'm alright." She winced as she tried to rise to her feet.

"Wait for the med-techs to arrive, Ryma. There may be internal injuries."

"No, I'm fine. A little winded after you landed on me, but fine." She stood up and brushed herself off. Her eyes widened as she noticed the condition of Nedia's dress. "Is any of that blood yours?"

"No, Ryma, I, too, am undamaged. Praise the Eternal that the traitor's bomb was so ineffective. I will be sure to lead an investigation into who he was and if there are any more plans to attack you. At the very least, we should screen applicants for a royal audience more severely."

Ryma cut her off as Neri and Rilo returned to her side. "*No.* We must continue as we have promised. The people will see we cannot be deterred by lone fanatics." She settled herself with a deep breath and picked a stringy piece of something she refused to think about from her gown. "However, I will need you by my side more than ever now, second-sister. I will tell Opet and Danet to assist you in the investigation. They have many sources among the people to help learn the purpose behind the attack."

"The purpose is clear, Ryma. Far too many Brin are not accepting the equality of our peoples. There are those who will never tolerate the blending of the two races, even after the Skae have told us this was the purpose for bringing us to your world."

Ryma sighed; her shoulders sank as she turned to head back to her offices. "I have always hoped those few would come to accept us as partners and see our children as the promise of a wondrous future."

Nedia wove her arm through Ryma's as they walked together, surrounded by Rilo, Neri and a half-dozen palace guards. "Those fanatics will never be anything more than the bigoted, blind fools they are. Please, let me deal with them. They are Brin, after all. As effective as Opet and Danet are, Kolandi may not be able to learn as much as another Brin would."

"I have made my decision, Nedia. You are more valuable to me here. I cannot have you running off putting yourself in danger. You may assign any Brin you wish to be part of the investigation and all of them can report to you, but I need you by my side. Let the others handle the dangerous work."

"As you wish."

As the pair strode together through the passage toward the royal offices, Rilo signaled for Neri to remain behind to learn what she could of the situation.

That evening, after all matters of state were settled and they were at last alone in the princess's chambers, Ryma questioned her Skatak. "Well, is it as we suspected?"

"I am afraid so, my princess. Your second sister was involved in this plot, but to what end we cannot discover. The sonic detonator was obviously far too weak to have endangered your life. Only an idiot would have chosen such a thing for an assassination. The blast radius for one of that size is only a few feet. Enough to shred the one activating it, possibly someone next to them, but that is all." Rilo wrung her hands as she paced the floor.

"Then it is as I suspected. Nedia is using the fanatics opposed to our union as a means to worm her way into my inner circle and have influence over my decisions, at least until she decides to make her final move to overthrow my rule and take control herself. This time she used one of the Brin. Have you learned if she has any connections to the Skaeists as well? They could prove far more difficult to control or eliminate."

Neri stepped forward. "One of my informants has said she suspects Nedia does have the ear of some of the Skaeists, but there is no hard evidence."

Rilo came to attention. "I will order her arrest immediately and see to her execution myself. We cannot afford to wait until she succeeds in her schemes with either of those fool groups." She spun on her heels and started toward the door.

"No, Rilo. There will be no arrests."

Rilo stopped and wheeled back to face Ryma, her face dark and menacing. "My princess, the Brin has threatened your life and plans treason. She must be dealt with at once."

"All in time, my faithful Skatak. As long as I keep her close, she will not do anything that would endanger herself as well. Who is to say what she would attempt if she knew her life was forfeit. No, you will do nothing and reveal nothing. As far as Nedia is concerned, she is my protector in this matter and has me in her debt."

Rilo and Neri exchanged glances before Rilo spoke, barely controlling her voice through clenched teeth. "It is our duty to protect you. We cannot let this attack go unpunished."

Ryma reached out with one hand to each of her warriors, taking their hands in hers. "You will have your chance, but you must obey me in this for now. Too much is at risk for us to do anything else. I trust you to keep me safe as always. But for now, the Brin woman must not suspect we are on to her. She must continue to believe she is the one in control." A grin widened on her lips and her eyes sparkled. "Until I spring my trap and turn you loose on her."

Rilo and Neri beamed at each other and fingered their kitals as one would stroke a favorite pet.

***

Nedia brushed her hair, letting the warm air dry it after her bath. She waved her free hand over the communication panel on her desk, her fingers weaving the pattern to shield the signal. The holographic image of a figure in deep shadow appeared above the desk. "The plan worked perfectly. There is not enough left of that idiot Sen Kolmar to trace, and Ryma finally trusts me."

An electronically disguised voice replied. "That is good. Are you prepared to move ahead with the next stage?"

"In a few weeks. She assigned her own Kolandi stooges to head up the investigation, but they will report to me, so I can manage the situation. Only a slight delay will be required."

"Very well, then. Proceed with caution. We cannot allow that usurper to continue her stranglehold on us." The shadow dissolved as the connection was cut.

Chapter Five

"Are you sure you can manage this? What if something goes wrong and you need Tol to help fix it?" Maliche paced the cargo bay as Jontar, Yalmut, and Duvar controlled the hover-bots loading crates of supplies into the Amaethon's shuttle. A much smaller copy of the Amaethon, the shuttle contained several cargo bays, four personal alcoves, a small kitchen, and a bridge section. It was plenty of room for three occupants to live in for long periods if needed.

Jontar's hover-bot coasted to a stop out of the loading pathway as he turned to speak. "Father, we've been over this already. If we fail, you must continue on here, in this time frame, and learn what the Skae are up to. You may even need to confront the Gorvin if there is no other way. We cannot take the chance of losing all of us in a high-risk mission like this." He returned his focus to the hover-bot, which maneuvered back onto the loading path and up the shuttle's ramp. With a sidelong glance back at his father, Jontar smiled and winked at him. "Besides, mother would kill me all over again if I didn't bring you back to her."

"You know he's right. Just let it go."

Maliche cut off his attempt at another reason for him to be part of the mission when he felt what amounted to a mental smack on the back of his head.

"But what if..."

"I said to stop acting like a youngling not getting his way. They are perfectly capable of taking care of themselves. Those three can manipulate technology in ways I never could, so our presence would only complicate matters."

"I know the history far better than they do. It is my profession, after all. They may inadvertently alter the timeline in disastrous ways. They could..."

A red aura surrounded Maliche. He felt the heat of Tol's anger rise. *"I will shut you down if I need to. You know I can. Do you always have to be such a pain in the circuits like this? No wonder everyone wants to talk with me alone when they need to get something done quickly."*

"What do you mean they want to talk with you alone? Ryma did that once or twice, but when did..."

"Don't worry about it. When I shove your consciousness aside to talk with the others, your memory is disconnected as well. The only reason you remember my talk with Ryma is because she told you about it later. Now can we get on with our actual business?"

Maliche spun on his heels and stomped out of the cargo bay. His thoughts ran wild with what he wished he could do to Tol.

"Oh, that's very mature, Maliche Rocker. Let me know when you want to grow up."

And with that, Maliche felt an absence in his mind as Tol isolated himself to do whatever he did when Maliche could not sense him.

Two days later, once the appropriate cosmic string had been located and approached, the three prospective time travelers said their goodbyes to those being left behind.

"This string should be able to take us all the way back to the beginning. Once there, all we need to do is follow the communication signals to the Skae and Gorvin home worlds. Their technology will still be incredibly advanced, but not as far as today, so we should be better able to infiltrate and learn what really happened." Jontar leaned over to give Thyka a hug. "Any last minute suggestions for us?"

She returned his hug and provided one last caution. "Be careful. You're right, this string is an ally, but it cannot guarantee your safety. And don't get involved with any strings with the frequencies we discussed. Those are more temperamental strings, potentially antagonistic. They won't appreciate what you are attempting to do."

"Yes, thank you for that bit of insight. And don't worry. We should be back, in your time frame at least, in a few days. A week or two at the most, depending on how accurately we can control the string's timing."

He gave her one last squeeze, smiling as he inhaled the subtle fragrance of her hair. Five minutes later, with all the goodbyes being said, Jontar and his companions boarded their shuttle and shut the hatch.

Maliche, Nalot, Seykel, and Thyka watched their departure from the bridge of their ship.

"Set monitor screen to string frequencies." As Maliche gave the command, Nalot adjusted a few sensor controls and the view screen instantly revealed the normally invisible cosmic string in all its multi-hued vastness. The energy pulse appeared to vanish into infinity at either end and dwarfed the tiny shuttle as it approached.

The shuttle hovered next to the string for a moment, then vanished in a flash of light. Everyone on the bridge stared in silence as the string continued on its way through space.

"Well, all we can do now is wait." Maliche said as he settled into the command chair.

Seykel pulled Nalot closer as she watched the string grow smaller. "But for how long? When will we know if they succeeded or not?"

"It could be a matter of a few days, or possibly—"

Thyka stiffened, her eyes wide as nebulas. "Mother! They're back!"

A brilliant flash of light came from the distant cosmic string. Almost immediately, their communication station came to life. "Father, its Jontar. We've returned, and you won't believe what we've learned. We can't wait to see all of you again. It's been so long."

Maliche bounded to the communication panel, his talons waved frantically, weaving the patterns to open the channel. "Jontar? But you only just left us. What went wrong? Is everyone alright? ..."

Jontar laughed as he tried to interrupt the flow of questions. "Everyone is fine, Father. Remember, we were time traveling. What for you must have been only a few minutes, was, for us, about twelve years. Covering several thousand years of history gave us lots of practice in manipulating the strings. We've gotten pretty good at it now. We can now pinpoint our arrival to within minutes instead of weeks."

The bridge crew sat in silence, watching the screen as the shuttle approached, then hung in space alongside the Amaethon.

"Can somebody let us in?" Duvar's voice chuckled over the speaker. "It's sort of lonely out here."

Nalot recovered his senses and worked the controls. "Of course, shuttle. Energy field wall lowering now. You are clear to land in bay two."

Maliche and the others raced into the cargo bay just as the shuttle hatch opened to extend its gangway. They came to a halt as one, gaping at the three who emerged. No longer the youths of what to the rest had been only a few minutes ago, they had aged. A slight dullness had crept into their once brilliant, if small, crest feathers. A few wrinkles around the eyes were noticeable, and they had each put on a few pounds. Their clothing was no longer the utilitarian coverall worn by the ship's crew since lift-off. They now sported outfits of shimmering metallic close-fitting fabric, which appeared to alter color as they moved. Even the shuttle looked dull and well-used.

Seykel was the first to speak. She cupped Yalmut and Duvar's faces in her hands as she examined them. "What happened to you?"

Yalmut beamed back at her. "Time travel, Seykel. Remember, for you, we were only gone a few minutes. While we actually travelled through several thousand years, thanks to space-time relativistic dilation, we only experienced a dozen or so years." He stopped for a second to return her examination. "To us, it's almost unbelievable that you have not aged at all."

After the initial reacquainting, everyone convened in the mess to learn about the expedition. Duvar held a cup of tea in his hands, inhaling the aroma with a look of what could be described as ecstasy on his face. "Mmm, nothing in the galaxy quite like gasha tea. Our supply ran out after a year or two. And kala bread. I really missed the taste of home."

"You just had some for breakfast this morn… oh, yeah. This time travel stuff is hard to wrap my head around." Seykel twisted a strand of hair with one finger as she sat across from the travelers, studying them with an intense gaze.

"Tell me about it," Duvar mumbled around a mouthful. "It took us several time jumps to learn how to retrain our thinking to the new reality after each jump. At times it was very disorienting."

"Alright, you two, we have more important things to discuss right now. We need to know about what the Skae and Gorvin are up to." Maliche occupied the seat at one end of the oval table, holding a steaming cup of tea in his hands.

Jontar began the debriefing as he downloaded the shuttles files into the main computer.

"I guess the first thing you need to know is that the Skae are not our friends. In fact, if they win this war, they're going to wipe out half the galaxy."

***

The sky showed crisp, blue, and nearly cloudless. The smell of fall wafted on the chill sea breeze as Ryma descended the shuttle's ramp into a storm of protestors' angry shouts.

"Free markets now!"

"No more price controls!"

"End worker quotas! Stop giving our jobs to unqualified Kolandi!"

Hand-printed signs waved over the crowd displaying equally angry sentiments.

Regulations requiring certain percentages of Kolandi workers be hired for jobs outside the mining guild created a violent backlash among the agricultural and transportation guilds on the eastern continent. Many Brin felt their jobs and their way of life were vanishing under the new decrees. The mining accords, as the treaty with the Kolandi giving them control of the mines were known, caused further unease among the people. The Kolandi continued to exert firm price controls on all their mineral exports as they rebuilt their society after centuries of oppression. Protests and work stoppages created supply shortages on the western continent, forcing Ryma to deal with this problem in addition to cleaning up Maliche's mess in the capitol.

Dressed in an informal green outfit of Brin fashion, highlighted with Kolandi accessories to demonstrate her desire for both races to work together as one, Ryma followed Danet, Opet and a small Brin security escort as they pressed through the angry throng, followed closely by Rilo and Neri, hands firmly on their kitals in case of trouble. At Ryma's side strode Nedia, her more flamboyant dress practically glittering in comparison to the others, head held high, and an almost invisible smile on her face. Except for her two children, now nearly grown, she represented the last of her family line. Prior to her joining the Rocker clan through marriage to Selan, she had been a Honj. Her family was the traditional head of the agricultural guild, one of the most powerful families on Kodut.

Ryma leaned in to speak to Nedia. "How soon can you arrange to talk with your guildsmen, Nedia? This situation must be resolved as quickly and peacefully as possible."

Nedia raised her voice in order to be heard above the tumult. "I have already been in communication with guild leaders and will meet with them early tomorrow. Our top priority will be to arrange a conference with them as soon as possible."

"They must know I want to listen to their concerns and work with them to..." A large glob of vile-smelling rotten vegetables launched from the crowd and rained down on Ryma, Nedia and anyone else within arm's reach. Sputtering and wiping the mess of kryfel-infested leaves and disgusting goo from her face, Ryma's eyes stung as she opened them to see Danet roughly hauling a young Brin before her, tossing him to the ground. He raised himself to his knees, never attempting to hide the same odorous mess dripping from his hands.

Stepping through her Skatak protectors, she faced the Brin agitator. "Why would you do this? I am here to work out the differences between us and end the hostilities. We are not your enemy."

"You *are* my enemy, Kolandi usurper. You and your kind have no place ruling a guild. And now you pretend to replace a Rocker as our new empress? We will never submit to being ruled by a filthy Rowi. Go back where you came from."

She raised a hand to stop Danet from pulling his blade and slitting the Brin's throat on the spot. "Let him stand, Danet. What is your name, young warrior?"

He glared at Ryma as he stood, shaking off Danet's hold on him. "I am Treval Shankar, of the transport guild."

"Well, Treval Shankar of the transport guild, you would do well to remember how your people treated us for centuries. Yet we seek no retribution, only the means to provide for ourselves. We have never sought to rule. My position is due not to any ambition on my part, but to the tragic circumstances of my husband's death. I have restored full authority to your Assembly and act now only as their ambassador to help bind the wounds created here. Now go in peace."

"My princess, it is not wise to leave one such as this behind. He should at least be brought to trial for his actions." Neri, waving her kital toward the Brin, scowled as she addressed Ryma. "He cannot be turned lose to plan more attacks."

"I have spoken, Neri. No more is to be said." Ryma strode forward; Danet shoved the agitator away and led her and the others, through the crowd to the waiting mag-lev vehicles.

Once inside the mag-lev, her stained dress still reeking from the sludge, Nedia exploded. "How could you let that idiot go free? Maliche would have had him in prison and brought before a magistrate before the day was over. You cannot expect to maintain control if you let the likes of him loose on the streets." She continued to pull dripping strands of muck from her crest and swipe pieces from her clothes as she ranted.

"And how would my retaliation help our reason for being here? Do you think I didn't want to have Danet flay the skin from his bones right there on the spot? We would probably be dead now if I had given in to my humiliation. I do not have that luxury."

A guttural growl rumbled from Nedia as she flung more of the mess from her crest feathers. "Aarrggh! This will never come out. You are the empress. You have every right to…"

"I am not the empress!" Ryma whirled on Nedia, her face contorted in anger. "I will not continue Maliche's misguided concept of a ruling class. We have restored authority to the Assembly. They are now in control of the government." She grabbed a blob of dripping sludge from her hair and flung it to the floor. "Even as my people's princess, I was never in unilateral control. The council was always there to give advice or override every decision. Any idea of my continuing that absurd position will not be tolerated."

Nedia wiped her face with a somewhat untainted piece of the sleeve of her dress. "As you wish, Ryma. You're right, of course. I've just never been treated so disrespectfully before, and I lost my temper. How do you control yourself like that?"

Tossing her long dripping hair behind her head, Ryma laughed. "Oh, I wanted to have the idiot gutted right there on the spot. Any one of our entourage would have happily made a grand spectacle of him. But I can't afford the luxury of acting out of impulse. Too many bad situations are made far worse if those in command act without thinking."

The mag-lev arrived at the government office complex where visiting dignitaries resided and pulled into the underground parking facility. At the entrance, Ryma took note of another trio of Kolandi Skaeists dressed in rags and waving tattered make-shift signs, shouting at the passersby. She could not hear what they extolled through the mag-lev's windows, but she had heard it before. A chill ran down her spine at the realization that, even with the windows' transparency set to opaque, the gaunt woman in the trio was glaring at her. Not the mag-lev, but her. Once inside with the security fields engaged, the princess and her party took the private air lift to their respective suites where they were able to clean themselves and rest before the next day's meetings.

Chapter Six

Maliche's shoulders drooped as he stared unseeing at the display hovering in the air before him. "So it's as bad as we feared? The Skae have been playing us for fools all this time?"

Young Jontar nodded solemnly, scanning the faces of the entire crew for their reactions to the unsettling news he brought back from his voyage to the past. "I'm afraid so, father. The Skae knew all along how Brin genetics could undo the Gorvin biotech weaponry and allow hundreds of worlds to rejoin them in their war. We were the test subjects."

Taking a deep breath to resettle his thoughts, Maliche ran a quick hand through his crest feathers and gathered his resolve. "Alright then. Tell us about your journey. We need to know exactly what we're up against."

"Time travel," began Jontar, "is not all its cracked up to be. Our first stop was terribly unsettling and disjointed, but I'll try to get it all straight. You see, when we arrived at our designated time coordinates and disconnected from the cosmic string…"

Yalmut studied his stellar navigation panel as it displayed a small three-dimensional image of their position in space. "Give me a moment, Jontar. I'm going to need to recalibrate the instruments. The stars are out of position."

"We expected that, Yalmut. Can you tell us how far back in time we've travelled? Did we go far enough?"

Bringing up a second three-dimensional image and merging it with the first, Yalmut mentally manipulated the two to determine the degree of change in the position of the stars. He smiled as he separated the images, and watched the second one dissolve as he turned it off. "I think we did it, Jontar. My calculations, based on the stars' speed and direction of travel, say we've gone back approximately four thousand, three hundred years. That should be far enough to give us a solid starting point for our investigation."

"Will our stealth capability be enough to hide us from the Skae tech of this time?" Duvar spun in his mag-lev chair to face the others.

Jontar relaxed into his command chair and wove a finger pattern over the controls to bring up the external view on the main panel in front of them. Dominated by a bright yellow star, a vista of black space appeared. "Only one way to find out. Engage all propulsion systems and let's head back to Kodut and see what we can learn about home first."

In moments, the small vessel closed in on the fourth planet from the sun. Its brown and green continents were only slightly different shapes than they remembered. The polar ice was smaller, and a number of rivers followed different courses. They all felt a catch in their throats as a vast array of artificial lights illuminated the hemisphere shrouded in night. Their Kodut displayed a number of jewel-like cities in the darkness, but this brought home how far their world had fallen.

"I know we heard the stories of the Kolandi once being allies of the Skae, but I never imagined all this." Duvar's mouth hung open as he gawked at the massive display pass below them.

Jontar nodded in agreement. "It *is* impressive."

"Entering circumpolar orbit at twenty-two hundred miles altitude with full stealth-mode engaged." Yalmut's small talons flew over his console controls as he spoke.

Duvar pressed one hand against the communications bug in his ear. "I'm picking up transmissions on several non-traditional wavelengths, Jontar. They aren't quite Skae, but they're similar. So far, nothing to indicate they've noticed us." He waved a hand over the controls to activate the bridge speakers so they all could hear.

Yalmut tilted his head as he listened, drumming his chin with two short-clipped talons. "That almost sounds like Kolandi they're speaking, but I can't quite make it out."

Jontar flicked the small talons of one hand against each other as he listened. "A language goes through a lot of changes over four thousand years. Adjust your cerebral language centers to compensate and translate."

The three closed their eyes and focused their thoughts internally, each one making slight alterations to their neural net which decoded language, searching for commonalities between the Kolandi language of their time and this ancient ancestor. As the connections were made, the transmissions became more and more understandable until at last they comprehended the language as if they were born to it.

"Begin recording and categorizing all transmissions and launch the micro-probes to fly down there and get us a close-up look at what is going on." Jontar strode over to Duvar's console as he gave the command. "Let's start with the area south of First Town where those ancient ruins were located."

Yalmut set his controls and grinned as a large city approached them from the horizon. "These are the coordinates, but those are definitely not ruins. It's magnificent."

Ten minutes later, images appeared on the view screen, divided into quadrants now, one for each micro-probe. Each one showed different sections of a beautiful city of spiraling towers made of the same transparent magnesium and carbon fiber materials as seen on Seriph, semi-transparent hexagonal tubes connecting the structures and large areas of green where the citizens gathered. All of them were very Kolandi in appearance but wore a variety of brightly-colored outfits in many styles. Occasionally a group could be seen congregating around one or two tall, thin-limbed, blue-skinned Skae. Only sporadic traffic traveled along what appeared to be surface roads and that at a very leisurely pace.

"Well, it looks like that part of the story was true, at least. The Skae and Kolandi were allies. I'm picking up a great deal of communication traffic between ground terminals and orbiting spacecraft in other locations around the planet." Duvar continued to adjust his controls as he tuned in to different transmissions.

"And we've arrived well before the Gorvin attack, so this will be a good baseline for our investigation." Yalmut studied the images on the viewer as he leaned forward, elbows on the console in front of him, hands cupping his chin.

Jontar nodded in agreement and returned to his command chair. "Keep monitoring for anything related to the Gorvin or planets under attack. Let's see if we can determine a pattern we can follow for our next time jump."

Three days later, they gathered in the cafeteria alcove to discuss what they had learned and plan their next move.

"There's definite communication chatter about the incident on Sharta-C, but something's not meshing with what we've been told." Duval ordered his thoughts and sent a mental burst to the others. "Do you see it?"

Jontar's eyes narrowed, his shoulders tensed as he followed the information. "Yes. That is suspicious. The Skae all seem to tell the same version of the story, but there are sporadic signals from other ships, other merchants or travelers, who have somewhat different versions of who is to blame."

"And some reference to a meeting between the Gorvin and Skae a while back that went wrong somehow. Nothing specific there, but it's definitely not anything we've heard before." Yalmut reached out and stabbed another nutrient ball with his talon clips, popping the flavored sphere into his mouth. "Anyone want the last spice pellets before I grab them?"

The others shook their heads and Yalmut scooped up three more of the orange balls from the bowl.

"There was one promising transmission from a merchant who had recently done some business in one of the Gorvin systems... did we know they controlled multiple systems? Anyway, they started to say something about six-dimensional quantum degenerate matter and gravity waves, but the signal was cut off and the ship denied permission to enter into orbit." Duvar took a long swallow from his mug before biting into a green vegi-strip. "We need to find a way to get some fresh food onboard. This stuff may be nutritious, but it certainly could use some more flavor."

Jontar sat before his untouched plate, eyes staring at a blank wall, flicking his talons. "I think we've gotten all we can from this time period. We need to jump ahead to see if we can learn more about the Gorvin attack here on Kodut. Once we settle the details about our world, we can go back and unravel the rest. Agreed?"

"I'll have the coordinates and string connection links ready by tonight, Jontar. I'm thinking about fifteen-hundred years ought to bring us pretty close. We can make a few smaller jumps to pinpoint the exact time of the attack from there." Yalmut stretched his arms and back as he rose, then proceeded down the corridor to his navigation console on the bridge.

***

Seventeen days later, after a series of seven jumps and finally pinpointing their time destination, they arrived at what appeared to be the turning point in Kolandi history.

Duvar adjusted his controls with a series of finger waves as he listened to the communications from the planet. "I'm definitely picking up a lot of traffic from an official calling herself Raj Ansus. This looks like the attack has begun."

Yalmut called out, transferring his tactical view of local space to the main viewer. A mass of fast-moving targets appeared at the edge of the screen. "I confirm incoming weapons. Thousands of them, traveling at near light speed. They're tiny, only a few centimeters, but using light sails for propulsion. No wonder they couldn't stop the attack."

"Duvar, put the communication on the speaker for us."

With a quick flurry of Duvar's fingers, the bridge loudspeaker crackled to life.

… "Skae High Command, come in. Are you receiving us? We need your help. Come in, please."

A deep, resonant voice answered. "Raj Ansus, this is Imperial Commander Tac. I regret to inform you that we have nothing in your sector to send to your aid. All of our forces were sent to the Keldon sector in response to Gorvin threats there. It will be three days at best before our ships can reach you."

"We won't survive three days, commander Tac. You must send immediate help."

"I'm sorry, Raj Ansus. There is nothing we can do. We simply do not have the resources to send until then."

The crew of the shuttle listened to the continuing pleas from the leader of the Kolandi as they watched the planet's skies fill with streaks of uncountable small fireballs.

"Bring us another two-hundred-thousand kilometers higher. We don't want to risk being in range of those tech-destroying nanites. Keep all probes recording as long as possible."

Yalmut waved over the control panel and the view screen showed the planet below shrinking as they pulled further away.

As the hours passed, more and more of their ancestor's home went dark. The signs of a thriving technological society died before their eyes. At last, all communications ceased. Only static filled the room. As they debriefed later around the table in the cafeteria, a heavy weight hung in their hearts.

"Well that went pretty much the way we heard from the Skae." Duvar shoved a few vegi-sticks and nutrient balls around his plate.

"True, but what about the signals we picked up over the last couple of jumps? The more I listen to them and the others, the more I get to feeling the Skae have been less than transparent with us." Yalmut tossed his talon clip utensils onto his untouched plate. "And for the life of me, I cannot figure out what led to this war. We simply cannot pick up more than a few scraps from merchant ships that've been around Gorvin space."

Duvar decided he was not hungry as well and removed his clips. "And those were almost non-existent over the last two jumps. Tensions escalated incredibly fast in this sector. Nobody wanted to be caught in the middle of another attack. This was only the latest in what, two hundred we heard about over the past five jumps? That's what, seventeen hundred or so years total?"

Jontar nibbled on a purplish-colored protein ball skewered on one talon clip as he thought. "The one consistent thing has been those few transmissions about degenerate matter and gravity waves. And what was that last bit? Something about a singularity engine and expanding phase space? What's all that about?"

Yalmut stretched again as he stood up. "There was something... a long time ago during our training at the

Skae academy… I need to search for it." His footsteps echoed in the corridor as he retreated to his cabin.

A few hours later, Yalmut burst onto the bridge. "We need to get to Gorvin space as quickly as possible."

"Why?" Jontar asked as he recovered from the sudden intrusion into his darkened and silent watch. He had nearly dozed off with nothing but the steady rhythmic tones and panel lights in the room. "What did you learn?"

"I need more information to verify my hypothesis, but if I'm correct, we need to work fast and get back to our time."

Jontar examined his companion, tugged on his grey-green shirt to flatten it out, and straightened himself in his chair. "Alright, but remember, we have all the time we need. Where and when do you think we should begin?"

"One of the outer systems, to start with. And back in time to just before the attack on Sharta-C. I believe that's when everything went wrong between the Skae and Gorvin." He fiddled with his control panel. A series of wave-forms came into a synchronous pattern, then narrowed the space between them as Yalmut alternately worked the controls by hand and by mental projection. "I think I can bring us in only a few years before then, maybe less than a decade. The more practice I get, the better I understand how to manipulate these strings."

***

After landing their ship on a small island in the middle of this planet's largest ocean, the three Kolbri took turns monitoring the research facilities on the continents. Relieved to breathe fresh air again and walk among other living things, Jontar and Duvar rather enjoyed their visit to Lethnon, as they learned the planet was named. Gentle blue-green waves of slightly salty water lapped the rocky shore of their island. The ship itself nestled in a meadow among tall multi-colored trees. A chill in the air required the three travelers to wear the adjustable thermal jackets they had brought along. Small game, edible fruits and plants provided a welcome escape from their regular provisions.

Duvar delivered a mental projection report to Jontar and Yalmut. "I've intercepted several communications referring to that summit between the Gorvin and Skae scientists. I have the precise time and location you were looking for, Yalmut. They still have a lot of details to work out, but they did set a date of two years from now."

"We'll be there in a few minutes. Jontar went for a swim."

Duvar met Jontar and Yalmut as they pushed the brush aside to exit the forest. "There's a problem."

Yalmut and Jontar exchanged glances before returning their attention to Duvar. Jontar spoke first. "The meeting will be security-shielded, won't it?"

"Yes. We can easily penetrate the shielding, but only from the surface. We need direct access to their computer network. The Gorvin tech is very different from the Skae and we don't have enough experience to deal with levels that high from orbit."

Yalmut's face lit up with a grin. "What if we didn't need to decode their tech? What if we could gain personal access to the summit?"

"And when did you get an invitation to this exclusive engagement?"

Yalmut shot out one hand and slapped Duvar on the back of his head. "Think about it. We're all tech experts with experience thousands of years ahead of this time. If we can infiltrate an outlying research facility, implant some artificial credentials and convince the Skae to bring us along as allied observers, then we could actually be present to witness what happened, or will happen... whatever."

"And how do we accomplish that?" Duvar asked as the three settled down by the fire he had built in a scraped-out hollow. A loud pop sent sparks swirling above the fire, dancing in the rising current of heat. "We don't exactly look like full Kolandi."

"Close enough. Since when do the Skae ever really look at us? If we clip our talons down even further and disguise our crests with a synthesized wig of hair, we have the facilities onboard and our own genetics to work with, there shouldn't be enough difference for anyone to recognize."

Jontar shifted his position to remove an annoying rock under his leg. "And what about the research facility? This is Gorvin space, not Skae."

"Don't forget when we are. In this time, the Skae and Gorvin are at peace. There are researchers from many different systems working here. We can certainly create some falsified documents from Skae command allowing us to set up shop here. After a couple of years, we can be so invaluable that the Skae won't be able to resist bringing us along."

Jontar and Duvar grinned at each other, and then Yalmut. Jontar stood, warming his hands against the flames. "This could work, but let's spend a few days ironing out the details. In the meantime, I'm going to get some sleep." With a long look into the dark, star-filled sky, he headed up the ramp.

Chapter Seven

The sun beat down on the gathering as they milled about in front of the raised platform occupied by Ryma and her entourage. Taking a lace-edged handkerchief from her sleeve, she dabbed at droplets of sweat forming on her brow. Her thoughts drifted to Maliche and Jontar, and how much she missed their counsel in matters concerning Brin guilds. Seated across the table were members of the agricultural and transportation guilds, dressed in their finest, even if it was threadbare, some straining buttons after years of neglect. Dust billowed up from their boots as they shuffled for position to see and hear the negotiations between guildsmen and representatives of the Assembly.

"I assure you, ladies and gentlemen, I hear your complaints, and I agree that we must work to come to some agreement on many of them." Princess Ryma nodded to her aide, who tapped a few icons on his pad before pocketing the small device. Refreshed from the aromatic attack of the previous day, Ryma was determined to mend the rift tearing this community apart.

The thin but wiry spokesman for the agricultural guild leaned forward on his elbows, chin in cupped talons. "We've heard that before, princess. What we need is some guarantee that you won't go home and forget about us like the others. When our own folk ignore us, what makes you think we would ever trust one of you?"

She thought for a moment before nodding to her aide again. The young Kolbri pulled his communi-pad from his pocket and flicked it on, preparing to record whatever was said. "I can grant the agricultural guild the rights, for a five-year test period with option to renew afterward, land grants totaling seven-hundred plots along the eastern continent coast, not to exceed thirty kilometers inland. This, of course, comes with the provision that the grant holders will in no way impede or limit in any way the shipment of minerals or goods to or from the Kolandi mines. In addition, I will decree a temporary freeze on the development of non-guild transports operating with Kolandi mines. This will put an end to the Kolandi advantage in mine goods transportation. All other matters will be subject to negotiation and discussion with the Assembly and the heads of all nine major guilds. It is time to open all matters to fair and equal treatment of Brin and Kolandi alike. Does this satisfy you?"

The transport and agriculture guildsmen leaned in close, whispering together. Standing and smiling, they extended their talons to clasp arms. "It does indeed, princess."

"Then let the records so indicate the agreement by royal decree as princess of the Kolandi and by my authority as acting head of the Assembly." The aide made a few quick strokes with his small talons to disseminate the accord and returned the pad to his pocket.

The others gave instructions for their aides to spread the word of the agreement and everyone retired to the adjoining banquet room to celebrate. Servant bots hovered among the guests with their trays of food and drink. More sincere apologies for their treatment the day before were made by several guild dignitaries. Those made at the beginning of the meeting had been perfunctory and mere formalities at best. Now they were honest and heart-felt. Promises to provide increased security and put an end to the hordes of protesters were made by all the Brin.

As the evening drew to a close, Ryma observed Nedia in close conference with one of the elder Agricultural guildsmen. When they parted, clasping talons, Ryma noticed the glint of a micro communi-pad passing from Nedia to the weathered old Brin.

As they waited for the air lift to take them back to their rooms, Ryma exhaled loudly, rolling her shoulders to relax them. "Well, that went fairly well, don't you think, Nedia?"

"Yes, princess, I believe it did. The land grants surprised them for sure. Not even Maliche offered as much." She reached down to brush a few stray crumbs away from Ryma's gown.

"I know, but it's time we learned to co-exist on the eastern continent as we do on the western. I believe the more we connect with each other, the less tension and misunderstanding there will be. My people have had enough time to establish themselves, and I believe the time has come to end many of the prohibitions against honest competition with the guilds. Perhaps a melding of the two will bring harmony once and for all. By the way, who was that elderly Brin you spent so much time saying goodbye to?"

Nedia hesitated only slightly. "Uncle Darva? My mother's brother. I hadn't seen him in ages, so we were sharing family gossip." She turned to adjust the collar of one of the aides.

The air lift arrived and they stepped inside. Waving a hand over the level indicator, Rilo, the one Skatak allowed to attend for security reasons, stood rigid in front of the sliding door panel as it closed.

***

Nedia, widow of the disgraced Rocker, climbed the steps to her uncle's mansion. The five days since her return from the eastern continent had been torture, anticipating this meeting. Nissend Honj, patriarch of the powerful Honj clan, resided in an estate considered large even by the wealthiest Brin. Honj Manor house, the sprawling stone mansion of their ancestors, sat on the western edge of Brachspark. The vast estate was named after a nearly mythical ancestor who supposedly was the last monarch of Dyan'ta, the lost Brin home world. According to family tales, Brach had supposedly sacrificed himself in a noble effort to save the Brin despite efforts of the hated Rocker clan to destroy everything. The seventy-five square kilometers of rolling hills covered in dense woodlands and grasslands surrounding a fifty-acre lake never failed to stir a visitor's awe at the sight of such splendor. Childhood memories of her visits to this hallowed place filled her as she passed through the massive doors, opened by servants as she approached. The sound of her heels on the polished stone floor echoed through the entry as she nodded to the attendants with a perfectly appropriate smile. Turning to her left, she glanced out the row of tall windows lining the passage to her uncle's study.

Nedia's thoughts turned inward. *This view has always been my favorite. The benches where we read to each other among the flowerbeds, the paths we strolled listening to Uncle Nissend tell his stories of our family history, it was all so magical. How did everything go so wrong?*

The doors to the study hung open. Peering inside, Nedia did not see her uncle, but she was always welcome in this hallowed sanctuary, so she stepped over the threshold and found herself in a sort of personal museum of her family's history. The walls were filled with portraits of the more notable members of the Honj clan, including Nissend himself.

We have always been among the most influential voices in the Assembly and at least five of the strongest guilds. It is so unfair that those fool Rockers have always held the real power. After all, the Rocker power was theirs by birth, not through merit, handed down generation after generation since the so-called saviors, Karm, Jontar, and Maripa. She felt like spitting out the vile taste in her mouth at the thought of those hated names, but years of courtly training helped Nedia maintain her demeanor. *Meanwhile, the rest of us clawed and scraped our way into power through the sweat of our brow and the occasionally well-placed bribe or scheme. At least now, the rest of the planet is finally seeing the Rockers for who they truly are.* In the privacy of the moment, she allowed herself a self-satisfied smile at this last thought.

"Nedia, my favorite niece. How wonderful of you to visit me today. I'm sorry I wasn't here to greet you. Please forgive a doddering old fool. So much has happened these days that require my attention. Please, sit." Nedia nearly jumped out of her skin at the sound of her uncle's booming voice. The barrel-chested, silver-crested man crossed the room and enveloped Nedia in a powerful embrace. She only came to the shoulders of this giant of a Brin and felt her heart jump as she looked into his weathered face. The deep red jacket he wore gave him the appearance of royalty.

"Uncle Nissend, so good of you to invite me here again. You know how much the children and I love this place, especially since their father's…"

"Yes, yes. No need to talk about that, my dear. Tea?" The silver-crested patriarch who still looked as if he could out-wrestle any of his offspring or grandchildren, poured two tall goblets and handed one to Nedia as she sat, removed her shoes, rubbed her tired feet and folded her legs underneath her. She cupped the glass in both hands, inhaling the minty aroma with closed eyes.

"This is exactly what I needed after the long trip. Thank you."

Sitting in the oversized, well-padded chair next to hers, Nissend took a long draught from his own goblet and placed it on the side table. His face took on more serious tones, the wrinkles around his eyes becoming more prominent. "Now, about your plans to help remove that

Kolandi usurper from power. Are our little demonstrations of displeasure having the desired effect?"

Nedia sighed to herself, opened her eyes, and took a sip before setting the goblet aside. "She's a strong one, uncle. So far, the attempts have only served to harden her resolve to reach out to the Brin even more. She is convinced that once our people come to know her, they will embrace her as a benefactor with their best interests at heart and not some foreign invader. This will take longer than we thought, if she can be cowed at all."

"Maybe it's time to increase the pressure."

Turning to look at him, she saw the hardened face of the portrait fully replace the one she had come to love. "What did you have in mind?"

His gaze intensified, as if trying to see through her. "How committed are you to all of this, child?"

Nedia's eyes widened in shock. Her mouth hung open a moment before she regained control. Clasping the arm of the chair tight enough to leave marks from her painted talons behind, she gathered every last vestige of strength to keep her voice calm. "How can you ask me that question, uncle? Haven't I done everything you've asked of me? I spend every day pretending to care about that phalking niewol woman. Those quetzals are the reason I am alone in this strix of a world. Didn't I poison my own husband to protect our family honor?"

He rested a leathery, wrinkled hand, talons worn and yellowed with age, on her hand. "Yes, child, you have made incredible sacrifices for all of us. As soon as we achieve our goals, you will receive your well-deserved reward. I merely wanted to convey the urgency and importance of what we must now do."

Her grip on the chair's arm slowly relinquished, and her heart rate regained a normal rhythm. "You can rely on me for whatever is necessary, uncle. What do you require of me?"

The aging Brin groaned a bit as he raised himself from the chair and strode to the cabinet to pour himself a glass of something a bit stronger. He swirled the amber liquid around his goblet, sniffed the aroma with closed eyes, and downed it in one swift motion. "It is time to end Ryma's rule once and for all. I have garnered enough support from the other guilds to take control of the Assembly away from those Rockers, or what's left of them."

"That is good news, uncle, and long overdue. What do you need of me?"

With his back to Nedia, Nissend stared out the large window into his gardens. Taking a deep breath, he turned and watched her like a predator looking for weakness in its prey. "We need you to ask Ryma to join you on a tour of the new vineyards in the hill country two days from now. Tell her the guildsmen have asked for her blessings on the harvest as a token of goodwill."

Nedia stood, hugging her stomach as she stepped carefully toward her uncle. "What are you planning?"

"The less you know the better, but we aim to rid ourselves of this abomination of an alliance with those quetzals once and for all."

"What about her guards? Those… Skatak women? They have incredible skill and are more than a match for any soldiers you may send. How will you deal with them?"

He waved his hand as if dismissing the thought. "Let me worry about them, child. We have a fool-proof plan. Our time to lead is at hand. Get the usurper princess to the vineyard and we will do the rest."

She placed a meticulously manicured hand on his arm and smiled at him. "You can count on me, Uncle. I won't let you down."

"I know you won't, child… Now, where are those children of yours? I believe I promised to take them riding today." He clapped his hands together and a broad smile melted her heart.

"I'll find them. They were so excited to spend the day with you. And thank you for allowing me to be part of renewing our family destiny." Nedia left the room with her spirits lifted and hope renewed.

As soon as his niece shut the door behind her, Nissend strode to his desk and finger-weaved a code to activate his holo-communicator and engage the highest security protections. He watched as the image of a shadowed face took shape hovering above the desk.

"It's done. Everything is arranged. She will bring Ryma to the vineyard as planned. You can notify the others."

An electronically-altered voice responded. "And she suspects nothing?"

Nissend chuckled. "Not a thing. Her hatred and bigotry blind her to everything else. She is the perfect pawn for our scheme. If everything goes according to plan, we can use her death as the springboard to leading the Assembly at long last."

"Are you certain this is the way to proceed? We could set up the device to detonate when she is not present."

"Too many things could go wrong. No, we stay with the plan. Alive, she could prove to be more of a liability. Dead… well, you know how everyone loves a martyr."

"And her children? They are the future of our clan. You are prepared to see to their care?"

"All will be arranged. Our future will be in good hands. Have no fear of that."

"Very well. We will proceed as planned. In two days we will fulfill our destiny." The image faded to mist and vanished as Nissend sat back in his overstuffed chair with a satisfied smile.

At that moment, the door to his office burst open, followed by shouts of joy and excitement of Nedia's children. "Uncle Nissend! Are we going riding now? Where will we ride today? Can we go to the river?"

"Children!" His arms spread wide to bury them in a hug worthy of a grendel. "We can go wherever you want."

With an eager child grasping talons on each hand, skipping and bouncing with joy, Nissend escorted their way to the stables.

"Behave yourselves, now. Don't be a problem for your uncle." Nedia waved goodbye as they passed her in the reception room.

"Don't worry, they're in good hands. You go enjoy yourself now." Nissend smiled and nodded his head toward Nedia in reply as they disappeared outside.

Chapter Eight

"Jontar, Yalmut, I've been looking for you." The squat Gorvin scientist caught up to them in the lab hallway.

It had taken a while to get used to the appearance of the Gorvin after so much contact with the Skae. They seemed to be almost the complete opposite in every way. Where the Skae were tall and slender, graceful, their structures almost ethereal in their design, the Gorvin were short, broad-shouldered, deep-chested, nearly walking blocks on piston-like legs. Male and female were so similar that the three wondered at first if the species were a combination. But closer examination and discussions revealed the subtle differences, in particular the extra finger on the left hand of the males and the extra pair of vocal cords in the females which gave their voices a peculiar harmonic quality.

The Gorvins preferred underground structures of stone, only allowing their buildings to raise two or three stories above the surface. This apparently, was due to the harsh environmental conditions on their home planet, Kluton. Nothing survived aboveground there, so the Gorvin had evolved to an underground existence. While the Skae dressed in flowing, shimmering attire, the Gorvin clothed themselves in rough, sturdy garb of primarily earth tones. Even their food showed the vast differences between them. The Gorvin favored tubers and roots with somewhat overcooked plain meat dishes, a far cry from the wisps of aromatic vapor consumed by the Skae. Many a discussion was held between the three Kolbri over how these two such distinctly different species could have become allies.

Aside from the annoyance of having to adjust to the antiquated technology — the time travelers had to physically tap out their commands on a keypad instead of finger-waving patterns in the recognition field — the most disturbing was the contrast between a Gorvin's nearly unreadable external features and the incredible depth of their completely passionate natures. It was difficult to read a Gorvin's disposition without the clues provided by most species. It appeared that, since they had evolved in the darkness of underground caverns, the Gorvin developed other methods via scent, sound and other senses to connect emotionally with each other.

After two years, Jontar and his friends had only now begun to understand the wide array of vocal inflections and tonal qualities that distinguished their rich emotions. The Skae and Gorvin were indeed about as far apart as they could be. Their only area of seeming equality was in intellect. Both species contained some of the brightest minds in the galaxy of those days. Their scientific explorations knew no bounds — though the Skae never admitted any were their equal.

Stopping at the entry to their lab, Jontar and Yalmut greeted their companion. "Clugat, how are you today? What's going on?"

The smile on Clugat's face was typical of all Gorvin, barely distinguishable from any other expression, at least to Jontar and his companions. "Great news, my young friends. Your application has been accepted by the congress. The three of you will be attending the conference with us."

The two Kolbri exchanged glances, smiling at their success. "That is good news, Clugat. We were not sure we would be allowed to attend, since we've only been here two years."

Clugat laughed in the guttural belch of the Gorvin. "There was never any doubt, my friends. The work you have done here during your internship has been remarkable. You are lightyears ahead of our own trainees and the rest of the Skae interns. Your research is opening up entirely new realms of possibility in quantum resonances and their association with cosmic strings. Remarkable indeed, just the sort of thing needed at this conference. Some of us have concerns over the new singularity engine and quantum phase space theories being presented by the Skae physicists. They claim to be able to harness the energy of a star at near one-hundred percent efficiency. Can you believe it?"

"If it is true, they could be on the verge of ending the struggle of clean energy production for all of us."

"Or, in the wrong hands, it could be a weapon of immense destructive capability. Some of our scientists are not sure which it is yet. But no need for concern. It's all theoretical at this stage. The conference will help dispel many of the concerns I am, certain."

Clugat stepped forward, entering the lab as its door rose into a recess in the ceiling. Jontar and Yalmut had to wait before ducking under the low entry. The room buzzed with the hum of experiments with lasers, magnetic containment fields, and computer simulations, all in various stages of development. The stone walls, flawlessly constructed from the native rock the lab was built into, rose just high enough to allow the Kolbri and other visiting species acting as interns or guest scientists-in-residence to stand upright without having to watch out for low-hanging ceiling lamps or beams. Yalmut sat on a stool at his bench and turned on his computer monitor. "We hope you will be able to provide us with their preliminary papers on the subject. It would be helpful to read up on it beforehand."

Yalmut projected his thoughts to Jontar as he worked. *I'm not sure I'll ever be able to reconcile these Gorvins and their sunny disposition. The way we have been taught by the Skae about how dangerous and war-like they're supposed to be doesn't match up to the reality.*

Jontar reached out mentally in reply while giving every appearance of setting up his lab work. *I know what you mean. Maybe something is triggered later to bring out their hostility and well-known brutality, but I'm starting to question everything we thought we knew about them.*

"Of course. Everyone will receive the information in the next few days so they can prepare for the discussion panel. These are exciting times, are they not?" Clugat rubbed his hands together briskly, oblivious of the separate conversation carried out by the two Kolbri.

Duvar burst into the room, breathing hard from the long run from their ship. A few days into their employment at the research facility, they discovered an abandoned warehouse just outside the campus grounds, nearly invisible among the forest growth around it. A week of repairs and security upgrades allowed them to bring their ship in late at night and keep it close but safely hidden.

"We have…" noticing the rest of the researchers nearby, and Clugat in particular, he coughed, as if to clear his throat and altered his outburst. "We have a problem. The computer in my lab is glitching again. I had to perform a complete sweep and security update so I won't be able to get you the data I promised until tomorrow."

Simultaneously, he communicated his original message. *We weren't as thorough as we thought with our credentials. The Skae are sending a team of investigators to find out more about us.*

Yalmut let out a sigh and shook his stubby talon at Duvar. "I warned you about being more vigilant with your security protocols. I'll come over later to take a look as well." *Are you sure? What did we miss?*

"That would be great. Thanks." *Someone sent the list of conference attendees to the authorities at Skae command for security clearances and government credentials on the interplanetary transport ship. Apparently, our names caught the attention of a minor official we used as a reference. He had no recognition of us and flagged us for further investigation.*

Jontar stopped working on the simulation program on his computer and spun around to join the conversation. "I apologize, Clugat. We will make sure our mistake does not infect the rest of the system. Duvar, Yalmut is right. We've been over this before. You cannot get so wrapped up in your work that you forget basic procedures." *Alright, we still have time to fix this. Let's meet back at the ship tonight and work on a solution. For now, go about your normal routine. Nobody should think this is anything but a typical bureaucratic foul up. This is nothing we can't handle.*

"No need to fret so, gentlemen. I'm sure no harm has been done. I trust this is nothing more than a simple programming error and will be quickly resolved." Clugat waved one hand as if clearing smoke from his face, illustrating the lack of importance he placed on the difficulty. "I will leave you now to your work. I am looking forward to discussing the conference with you soon." With that, he exited the lab in a flurry of well-wishes to the rest of the researchers.

The next day, while the ambassador sat tapping randomly through his communication pad, as if this meeting were a mere distraction from more important matters, his clerk stated the reason for their visit. "We have a communication from one of our foreign office dignitaries on the planet Uvalda, stating he was cited as one of your professional references for this conference. He claims no knowledge of you or your qualifications, and has no understanding of how you came across his name."

"Yes, ambassador, I understand your concerns, but I assure you this is nothing more than a bureaucratic error." Jontar sat with talons clasped on the table before him as he addressed the Skae dignitaries.

The Skae ambassador, Molk, impeccably dressed in glittering indigo and silver robes, placed both hands over his heart in a sympathetic gesture. "I agree with you, and I do have much more important matters to attend to than this trifle, but, as you must understand, my superiors have sent me to investigate any discrepancies in documentation, particularly those involving aliens such as yourself, hoping to attend such a high-level conference. Our security procedures must be completely satisfied, no matter how tedious they may be."

The clerk took up the conversation. "Can you provide any information to explain this confusion?"

"Yalmut, can you share the documentation regarding our communications with the Uvalda credentials office?"

"Of course, Jontar." Yalmut tapped a few commands onto his tablet, projecting a holographic image of a series of text and video communications. He reached out to wave a talon through one of the files, opening a video of the clerk in question speaking. "… Yes, Mr. Rocker, I have received your documentation and have approved your application for research at the Lethnon facility. Your field of expertise is precisely what they have been asking us to find for them. You should have your papers of transit and approval within a few hours. Good luck to you."

"As you can see, gentlemen, we followed proper channels and received the approval. We are at a loss to understand how the clerk in question does not have records of his own to verify this matter." He waved a talon through another file to open it. A series of data links providing dates, times, and catalog references appeared. "Here is a complete record of our communications with Uvalda. Perhaps sharing this with your official there will help clear up the confusion."

The ambassador glanced through the links, downloaded them onto his personal communicator, and tapped a few commands followed by a careless wave of his hand over the controls to shut off his device. "I have sent this information to the official in question. He should be able to review it and respond in a few hours. We can adjourn until we hear back. We will notify you when we need you again." He stood and, with only a fleeting look at the petitioners, left the conference room followed by his small party.

"My, the ambassador was certainly a rude one." Clugat, his unreadable face turned toward Jontar uttered his first comments since the Skae arrival. "He was absolutely insulting. I may report his behavior to my superiors."

Duvar laughed as he slapped the table and rose to his feet. "You haven't had many dealings with the Skae, have you? They are universally arrogant toward anyone not Skae. They believe themselves the highest form of intelligence and culture in the universe and pay little attention to others."

"You've had prior dealings with them?"

"Oh, yes. They are definitely a race of schuteks, but as long as they are in charge of most of the galaxy, there's not much to be done about it."

"Well, I don't like it one bit. I would have preferred my first encounter with our interstellar allies to have been a more pleasant one. I hope those who attend the conference will be more amiable."

"Don't count on it. I've never known a Skae to admit to being wrong about anything."

The four researchers left the room and headed toward their lab. Jontar sent his thoughts out to the others.

Their arrogance may be what saves us, Duvar. I'm counting on them to stay true to form on this.

Yalmut joined in the mental discussion. *What if he digs any further? We haven't had the time to implant any corroborating evidence in his archives.*

I think he'll decide it isn't worth his valuable time to look further into the matter. Remember, from the Skae point of view, this conference is about them simply informing the Gorvin and others about their plans. They honestly can't comprehend it as anything approaching an equal exchange of ideas. It simply isn't that important to them.

Duvar gave Jontar a sidelong glance as they reached the entry to their lab.

If our monitoring of their communications is accurate, you mean.

The next morning, Clugat greeted the Kolbri trio at the research facility entrance. His stony face flushed with a barely discernable deeper shade of ruddiness and his hands fidgeted even while kept firmly clasped behind his back. Another Gorvin would have been scandalized by the outpouring of emotional display in the scientist. "I am outraged! Absolutely outraged! This is unacceptable! I am going to bring this to the highest authorities and put an end to their insults once and for all! Imagine! The gall of them to deny us so close to the conference! The authorities will hear of this. Don't you worry one bit! I'll see to it, mark my words!"

The three youths looked at each other, shrugging as they flashed a quick series of mental questions between them.

Jontar confronted Clugat, grasping his shoulders to calm him. "What's wrong, Clugat? What has you so agitated today?"

"It's that gruktob of a clerk on Uvalda. He continues to insist he has never heard of you. The Skae ambassador insists on meeting with you three in the Skae embassy. He is not pleased at having to deal with this matter anymore, but the conference is too important for him to ignore this officious gruktob and his tupk need for documentation."

Yalmut shook his head as if in dismay over Clugat's news while he mentally reached out to the others. *This is going to take more drastic action than we had considered. We need time to deal with it away from Clugat.*

Agreed. I'll make our excuses while you two head back to our quarters. Jontar gave Clugat his most grave expression of concern, wrapping one arm around the stocky Gorvin's shoulders and turning him to walk down the corridor.

"I'm sure everything will be all right. The poor clerk must be under a lot of stress dealing with all the details of the conference. Let us deal with it. We would be happy to talk with the Skae ambassador to straighten everything out. You go back to the lab and we will get everything in order before we meet with him. You'll see."

"No, you are our guests. It is my duty to see you are treated with respect and dignity. Such an insult is an affront to our very honor." Clugat's hands continued to fidget in a most un-Gorvin-like outburst of anger and embarrassment.

Jontar held his smile and calm exterior in place while he reached into Clugat's mind to adjust his anxiety levels. This ability, apparently another inheritance from Maliche's biocomputer had proved invaluable on several occasions when the young Kolbri had overstepped matters in some youthful indiscretions. Gradually he noticed the scientist's face lose the slight flush and his hands stilled. "Have no fear, my friend. Your honor is intact. This is simply a matter of Skae stubbornness. Please, we are familiar with their bureaucracy, and know how to navigate its intricacies. It would be better if we handled this ourselves. You have much more important things to take care of right now."

Clugat, his voice now more composed, took Jontar's arm with one stout hand and gave a gravelly rumble in his throat. "If that is your wish. I have no patience for diplomatic niceties. Maybe it would be best if you straightened out the problem yourselves."

"Thank you. Now, if you'll excuse me, I have to convince a Skae button-pusher to admit his error. It might be easier to wrestle a grendel, but I've heard it can be done... the grendel, not the Skae." Jontar smiled and winked at his Gorvin host and sped off to meet with the others.

Hours later, back in their visitor residence, Yalmut and Duvar stalked the sparse room while Jontar lounged on the thick-legged bench under the circular window of their main communal area. All other rooms of their assigned housing connected to this area like spokes of a wheel. Three small bedrooms, a kitchen and communication/research area led to this central point by way of rough-carved hallways. Gorvin architecture was always reminiscent of the underground structures of their home world.

Duvar circled to the left as he paced the room. "We just don't have time to figure out how to penetrate deeper into the phalking security measures of the Uvaldan system. Not to get in deep enough to satisfy this..."

"Time! We have all the time we need!" Yalmut stopped his pacing, eyes bright as he smiled at the others.

"Of course!" Jontar chimed in. "If we could pinpoint the least impactful point on the timeline, it might do just the trick."

Duvar scratched at his small crest. "What are you two going on about?"

It's simple," Yalmut said as he clapped Duvar on the back. "We go back a couple of years and visit the Uvaldan clerk in person, provide him with some forged documentation, return to the present, and meet with the ambassador with a specific date of our meeting with the clerk and ask him to contact the schutek again."

"And we even have Clugat provide us with some documents, which we will alter to make it look like he specifically invited us to work here because of our expertise. When the ambassador contacts him again, he will remember us because this time we actually have met in person."

"That means we'll have to undo the falsified records we implanted into the system. We can't afford for two different sets of records to be found."

"Right. We have to get it right this time, there's no room for error here." Jontar's talons clicked furiously as he closed his eyes and concentrated for a minute or two. "Alright, here's what we have to do…"

The morning sky began to glow with the first signs of sunrise as their plans were finalized. Hovering above Jontar's tablet was a detailed plan, including all the necessary documents and timeline information for a successful mission. Duvar and Yalmut shared a contagious yawn and stretched their arms as they flopped back in their chairs. Jontar examined the work one last time.

"We're in agreement, then? This is how we will proceed?"

The others nodded, watching him through half-closed eyes. With a tap of one talon, the images vanished. "We leave in two hours. Get what sleep you can and then we'll head out to the ship and get started."

***

The three Kolbri found themselves sitting in uncomfortable chairs in a too-brightly-lit room waiting their turn to speak with Neldar, the Uvaldan clerk they had specifically requested. Such an unusual appeal took a while to convince the front desk secretary of the necessity of the meeting and a few well-forged documents of introduction, but they succeeded and now sat patiently two years, twenty-six days, fourteen hours and forty-five seconds in the past.

"Thank you for meeting with us on such short notice, Neldar. We have such a short time to get everything in order before the Gorvin invitation to begin our research on Lethnon." Jontar sat across from the clerk, punching his keypad to bring up and transmit the required documents for travel and permission to research at the Gorvin facility.

Neldar kept his eyes on his own terminal, punching his own keypad to complete the required transactions. He never looked at them or acknowledged their presence.

How are we going to get this schutek's attention so he remembers us? He won't even look at us. Duvar fidgeted in his chair behind Jontar.

I'll take care of it. Yalmut stood up, screeching the chair's legs on the tile floor causing every head in the room, including Neldar's, to look up at him. Addressing Neldar directly, he leaned over Jontar's shoulder, glanced around a bit, then whispered to Neldar. "Where is the restroom? It's been a long wait and I drank a lot of tea this morning before coming here. My bladder is about to explode."

The clerk appeared flummoxed for a moment, obviously not liking having his strict routine interrupted. "Over there." He scowled at Yalmut as he waved a hand off to the right in the direction of a hallway.

"Thank you so much. I just couldn't wait another moment." Yalmut stepped around his chair and pushed it back into place, causing the legs to screech again.

The clerk shook his shoulders, frowned, and began to re-focus on his monitor. Jontar interrupted him before he could completely settle back into his routine. "You'll have to forgive him, sir. We always have to make extra stops on long trips for him. But what can you do? He's absolutely brilliant and we couldn't complete our research without him."

Looking up at Jontar, and with a brief glance at Duvar, Neldar glowered. "If you will stop interrupting me, I would like to complete this transaction in a timely manner and stay on schedule today."

Jontar reached out to pat Neldar's forearm. "Of course. Forgive me, sir. We wouldn't want to cause any problems. Thank you for understanding."

Neldar jerked his arm free, glared at Jontar, sniffed, and returned to tapping his monitor.

***

Back in present time, Jontar, Yalmut, and Duvar arrived precisely on schedule to meet with Ambassador Molk at his office. The room, decorated in the ethereal abstractness of flowing, intricate designs, permeated not only the artwork on the walls but the furniture as well. As usual, no effort was made to accommodate the shorter stature of non-Skae visitors, so the chairs they sat in required some effort to utilize and left them with a somewhat uncomfortable sitting position. No doubt, the ambassador believed this would shorten any meetings with lesser species.

"I'm sure, Mr. Ambassador, if you would simply send the Uvaldan clerk — you said his name is Neldar? — if you would send him these copies of our travel credentials with the specific date of our meeting, I'm sure everything will be cleared up."

"Why did you not provide me with this date in the first place? The Uvaldan office processes millions of documents every day. Without a date of the transaction, you could hardly expect them to locate your information."

"We are terribly sorry, sir. It did take us a while to locate the information. After all, it was two years ago. We never expected to be invited to attend such a prestigious conference as this, so we did not properly file the documentation." Jontar kept his eyes lowered, focusing on the decorations of office the ambassador wore on his chest.

Molk sighed heavily, turning both hands palm upward. "I suppose you are to be forgiven such slights. You are only Kolandi, after all." He transmitted the new information and proceeded to open up new files, dictating new orders to his underlings, all while ignoring the three seated in front of him.

Within five minutes, Molk's holo-communicator lit up, a hazy image solidifying into Neldar's face in midair slightly above his desk.

Ambassador Molk pressed an icon to open communications and waited.

"Neldar of Uvalda here at your request, Ambassador." The floating image turned to face the three Kolbri seated across the desk. His eyes closed, his mouth downturned as he recognized them. "Yes, sir, I do remember these Kolandi now. Your transmission of the precise date of our unfortunate encounter allowed me to locate the data immediately. Their travel credential images also helped me recall the meeting. A most troublesome encounter, if I may be permitted to say so, sir."

Molk frowned in return. "Anything we need to be concerned about as far as issuing them credentials for attending the conference?"

"No, sir. Their qualifications are in order. They were simply a most unruly and difficult bunch to process. They had no respect for protocol and order. They interrupted my routine to such an extent that I was required to extend my hours that day. Most disrespectful."

"That will be all, then." Molk disconnected the communication, causing the holographic image to dissipate immediately.

Jontar jumped in to explain. "I apologize, Mr. Ambassador. That was our first encounter with the Uvaldan bureaucracy and we were unfamiliar with their strict protocols and precision. I hope our inexperience in such matters does not cast any doubt on our credentials and qualifications to attend the conference."

Molk glanced through his calendar and gave the three a negligent wave of his hand. "No, that will be all now. You may go."

The Kolbri left the embassy and returned to Clugat's labs, where they were greeted with enthusiasm.

"Whatever you did, lads, it worked. I just received your passes and transport authorizations. You are cleared to attend our conference. I am thrilled you can join us."

"As are we, Clugat," said Yalmut. "We look forward to learning what we can about the Skae's plans."

Chapter Nine

Shyfar proved to be the perfect world for a conference of such magnitude. Close allies to the Skae, the Shyfarans were renowned for their scientific accomplishments. Their interstellar ship designs proved far superior to the Skae designs for travel by cosmic string. Their tastes in architecture, while similar to the Skae in their use of transparent magnesium and carbon fiber nanotube alloys, was beautiful and inspired, but more utilitarian than the Skae's soaring art forms.

Unlike the cities of Kodut, there were no mag-lev vehicles contaminating the skyways or ground levels. Instead, a network of interconnected transparent magnesium pneumatic tubes carried passengers to their destinations, both between buildings and below ground. Depending on the distances involved, these tube ways could conduct travelers at incredible speeds so that no place on the planet was more than three hours distant.

Vast areas of public open space occupied the spaces between buildings. Between cities were immense natural preserves where the local ecosystems were left to themselves for tourists and scientific study. Very few individual homes existed, since the majority of the population consisted of students, visiting professors and researchers from throughout the galaxy. The research party from Lethnon was escorted to the dormitory containing their assigned residences.

"Tomorrow will be a busy and exciting day." Clugat declared as he chose one of the adjoining rooms and tossed his luggage onto the bed. "The main event won't be until the day after tomorrow, but there are many fascinating lectures we can attend until then."

The three Kolbri stood in the central common room, looking around with furrowed brows. Jontar took the lead, as usual. "I was expecting a more Shyfaran style of architecture in our accommodations. This is just like our quarters on Lethnon."

Clugat laughed, then tried covering his amusement with a cough and wiped his mouth with one hand. "The Shyfarans make every effort to make their guests feel at home. Each learning and research center has living facilities tailored to those species most likely to utilize them. This one is made specifically for Gorvin visitors. It helps to have something of home when spending time on a distant planet, don't you think?" He sat in one of the squat, square chairs. "Most non-Gorvin furnishings are terribly uncomfortable. Too tall and unsteady. This is much better." He stretched his stout legs, even if they didn't reach far, and clasped his thick fingers behind his head, eyes closed and smiling, at least the slightly-upturned-corners-of-the-mouth Gorvin version of a smile.

Duvar sat in one of the empty chairs, his knees bent halfway to his chin. "Ugggh. Reminds me of when we first arrived on Lethnon. These don't seem to be made for our frames." He struggled to pull himself up out of the low chair.

"And those beds are far too short for us," said Yalmut after returning from his chosen room.

Clugat jumped to his feet. His eyes wide, smacked the side of his head with one thick hand. "Oh, my goodness. My apologies, gentlemen. I completely forgot to order Kolandi furnishings for you. I will have to have words with Eisoph as soon as she arrives. We will get this corrected right away."

"Get what corrected?" Eisoph, Clugat's research assistant and student entered the main room, unslinging her shoulder pack and tossing it on the floor next to the entry. Built much like her male Gorvin counterpart, Eisoph was short and thick-bodied, with heavy legs and strong arms. Long, thick black hair reached to her waist. The exact gender differences were not apparent on first impression, except for the harmonic double vocal chord voices of Gorvin females. She wore a deep red knee-length dress with sturdy brown pants underneath. Her heavy leather boots with scarred metal toe caps should have announced her arrival like thunderclaps, but Eisoph was surprisingly agile and graceful for a Gorvin.

Jontar, startled by her nearly silent approach, attempted to disguise his reaction with a quick talon jab toward his companions. "Duvar and Yalmut were commenting on the lack of Kolandi-friendly furnishings in our rooms. Clugat forgot to let the Shyfarans know we were part of your group. Nothing that can't be fixed with a simple call to housekeeping."

Eisoph's eyes went wide; she covered her mouth to hide her jaw's minuscule drop. The expression was hardly noticeable, but it was a considerable display of embarrassment for a Gorvin. The harmonics in her voice took on a sudden syncopation, indicating her mortification and contrition. "Oh, my...I cannot believe we forgot about such a thing. You must think us terrible hosts. I will run down to the front desk and rectify this right away."

"No need to be apologetic, Eisoph. Mistakes happen. We are not offended."

"You are our guests and Clugat gave me the responsibility of arranging our accommodations here. I should have been more thoughtful. It was my obligation to consider your needs. I will take care of it immediately." She spun on her heels and ran back out into the hallway before anyone could respond.

Clugat approached Jontar and the others, clasped hands over his chest in a sign of apology. "She is right. You three are our responsibility as our guests. It was foolish of us to forget something so basic. Please forgive us."

Jontar took Clugat's hands in his. "We are aware of the importance your culture places on hospitality toward others, but there is no need for such concern over us. We are in your debt for doing so much for us already. Please, no more fretting over something so meaningless."

"You are too kind. But we will see everything is corrected as quickly as possible."

"We know you will take good care of us. For now, let's look over the schedule for tomorrow and decide how to best divide the day between us for maximum efficiency." Jontar set his tablet on the table in the center of the room and touched the controls to project the conference schedule in a holographic display.

An hour later, they were interrupted by a commotion in the hallway. Eisoph burst through the door followed by a train of Shyfaran housekeepers trundling in entirely new sets of furniture. She directed the workers with an almost military precision, overseeing each piece of furniture to be removed and exactly how and where to place the Kolandi-sized version of each. In minutes, she shut the door behind the last of the exiting workers, turned and, hands on hips, smiled, in her way, at the men. Her voice regained its normal sonorous tones. "Everything is corrected now, I hope to your satisfaction. I apologize again for my lack of consideration for your comfort on this trip."

Jontar smiled at Eisoph in return, bowed with arms crossed over his chest. "No apologies needed, Eisoph. We are most pleased with your swift remedy to the situation. No harm was done, so please join us and help us figure out our schedule for the next few days." He extended an arm to her, closing it around her shoulder as she joined them.

By noon of the second day, everyone had become increasingly anxious over the main event. More details had leaked of the Skae's new design for harnessing the power of a star at nearly ninety-eight percent efficiency. The public parks were filled with guests from hundreds of planets and a wide range of scientific disciplines from nuclear physics, quantum mechanics, stellar astronomy and engineering, to name a few. Every bench and table held scientists in deep conversation over the anticipated afternoon lecture. The blue climate-controlled skies, dotted by an occasional puffy cumulus cloud, ensured an enjoyable and revitalizing respite from the intense lectures and demonstrations held each day.

"If such a thing is possible, it means the end to all energy struggles throughout the galaxy. It's almost impossible to imagine." Eisoph munched on a meat sandwich as she spoke, wiping the juices from her chin with a towel. "I can't wait to see their research notes. I am still skeptical of the details I've seen so far, but the Skae are parsecs ahead of the rest of us in this area. Maybe they've discovered something we haven't thought of yet."

"Yes. This should be an historic announcement. What did you think about the lecture by the other Gorvins on the advances of light sail weaponry? I found it particularly fascinating." Yalmut glanced sidelong at his Kolbri companions. *We need to keep our eyes and ears open. According to everything we have learned, this is the event that started the war. Something happens here to end all Skae and Gorvin alliances. We have to learn exactly what happened if we want to help Maliche figure out what is going on with the Skae in our time.*

Duvar rolled his eyes. "Of course you would find something like that interesting. Give me good old cosmic string travel any day. I was more interested in the development of technology dampening nanobot research." *Yes, Yalmut. We are all well aware of the importance of this revelation. No need to keep reminding us.*

Jontar took another bite of his fruit and vegetable salad. "Those two, used in combination, will be the end of our home world as it now exists. I find it hard to get excited about them." *"Knock it off, Duvar. A little reminder of just how vital this moment in history is doesn't hurt. We need to be alert to anything that happens this afternoon."*

"Alright, friends, if we want to sit anywhere with a decent view of the proceedings, we should get moving." Clugat gathered his belongings, tossed the packaging from his lunch into the recycler receptacle, and proceeded down the path under the trees toward the campus's main lecture hall.

***

The lecture room darkened. Out of the stage floor, a holo-projection of a double star system appeared. Dim and formless at first, but then sharpened into a view of one red giant orbited by a white dwarf. The image shifted to center the white dwarf and grew in size and brightness to just below the need to shade one's eyes. As the star rotated, the roiling surface of its convection currents could be seen easily. Occasional flares, filaments, and prominences shot from the surface, some extending over the heads of those closest to the stage, causing them to duck. A spotlight brightened on a single Skae, dressed in a shimmering light blue robe decorated with many ornate badges of office and honor.

"Honored guests," his voice, light and airy, floated throughout the large audience with the aid of hovering cubicle speakers. "Today, I am pleased to announce the beginning of a new era in energy production. We Skae have recently begun development of a new method of producing and harnessing the energy of artificial singularities."

As the blue-skinned speaker continued, thousands of small mirror-like satellites began orbiting the projected star. These objects completed a nearly perfect sphere around the star, dimming it to near obscurity. "By harvesting uninhabited planets within a star's system and constructing a partial sphere of collectors, we have improved on the single collector solid sphere designs of previous attempts at such work. Completing a single sphere around a star required more materials to construct than could possibly exist in any star system, so the project remained theoretical at best."

He waved his hand and the projection grew in size, zooming in on a small section of collectors, providing much greater detail. "Building even a few thousand small collectors and spacing them equidistant around the star allows us to utilize the resources of only one or two planets. While there remains millions of square kilometers of space in total between the satellites, we have increased their efficiency to a degree where we are now projecting that ninety-eight percent of the star's total energy will be collected."

Another wave of his hand shifted the view to a section of nearby empty space. Animations of the process appeared as his description progressed. "By utilizing the focusing power of a series of gravitational wave generators, we can direct the energy collected by the swarm and focus it into a singularity, sometimes referred to as a black hole. We then continue to focus the additional energy of the dwarf star into the singularity, creating enough mass to generate six-dimensional degenerate matter within the singularity. This process will release immense quantities of energy which can be collected and distributed to as many systems as needed, thus providing an endless supply of clean energy for all. A summary of the procedure and calculations are being transmitted to you now."

Everyone in attendance operated their various devices to open the data as they received it. After a moment, all eyes began to return to the presenter. All except Eisoph, who continued to shuffle back and forth through the information, a subtle frown growing on her stoic features, her voice became increasingly tremolos. "This is useless," she muttered. "None of the actual gravitational wave calculations are here. All the rest is meaningless without them."

Turning now to face his audience, the Skae speaker raised his arms toward the ceiling. The view zoomed in to the artificially colorized singularity. "The energy released by this singularity in the form of radiation and angular momentum can be harvested at one hundred percent efficiency by another swarm of collectors. A small fraction of the collectors needed to capture the star's energy, perhaps as few as a hundred or so, are required due to the incredibly small size of the black hole, possibly only a few centimeters in diameter."

He dropped his arms and the hologram shifted away from space to show a series of images of people from many different worlds living their lives free from energy concerns. Each world was prosperous and happy, every individual able to reach full potential.

"Honored guests, we Skae are pleased to announce the end to need and want in our galaxy."

The lights rose in the lecture hall along with a standing ovation mixed with cheers and shouts of praise.

As the commotion eventually subsided, hands shot into the air. The speaker called on each one in turn, mostly resulting in acclimations of joy and support for the Skae's efforts. Then he called on Eisoph.

She stood so she could be more easily seen. A hovering microphone floated to her so her voice could be amplified for all to hear. "Some of your gravitational wave calculations are not provided in the documentation. How have you accounted for expanding phase space due to the degeneracy pressure? Doesn't this present an unreasonable risk?"

The speaker smiled as the audience grew silent. "You raise an incredibly insightful and important question, young Gorvin. Let us assure you we have taken this very real concern into our calculations and found the risk to be minimal at best. Our best minds have been at work on this very aspect of the data for years and have found no cause for alarm." He turned to call on another hand, but stopped as Eisoph continued to press the issue, fighting to control her emotions.

"I don't mean to contradict your work, sir, but I have done some research into this of my own, and my calculations come to a very different conclusion. Would it be possible to see your data, for comparison, particularly on the gravitational wave generators, to see where I might have gone wrong?"

The speaker's smile remained, but his eyes deadened. "I am sorry, young Gorvin, but our work is proprietary and not available for public dissemination as of yet. Perhaps at some time in the future." He raised his voice as he turned to face another question. "Be assured, your fears are unfounded. The Skae are the best minds in the galaxy in matters such as this. While I am sure Gorvin research is perfectly adequate in the things that concern you, we are the experts here. You can rely on our findings."

As she sat down, Eisoph heard many murmurs calling her "a foolish student..." Or "wasting our time..." among other more derisive comments whispered just loud enough for her to overhear.

"Don't listen to them," whispered Jontar, seated next to her. "You know how self-important the Skae are. They would never tolerate anyone calling into question their ability, especially in a gathering like this."

"I've never felt so foolish and humiliated in my life. Maybe my calculations are wrong. Maybe I did miss something obvious."

"No," continued Jontar. "I don't think so. I've seen your work and I could not find anything wrong with it. Of course, we only had the earliest data released by the Skae. They may have found a solution since then, but I doubt it."

"But everyone else had the same data release. Why didn't anyone else find what I did?"

"Too many take the Skae at their word. Even the top scientists from some of the most advanced worlds are in awe of what the Skae have accomplished and may only have glossed over the data. And not even scientists are immune from political pressure. The majority of those here are nothing more than Skae puppets. If you aren't looking critically at something, you almost never find it."

Eisoph sat silently, head hung low with the typically unreadable face of a Gorvin, except to those close enough to them to learn the subtle differences. Jontar recognized the signs of sadness and doubt growing. He sent his thoughts out to his companions. *"Have you tapped into their system yet?"*

Yalmut's mind responded first. *"Yes. It took some time to breach their security protocols, but we managed to penetrate the system without a trace. Thank goodness they won't develop the protections we faced in our time for several hundred years yet."*

"I found the data!" Duvar's mind practically shouted with his discovery. *"I'm downloading it to our tablets now. The files are huge, but I should be done in another minute or so."*

Jontar leaned in to whisper in Eisoph's ear. "Cheer up. We might have something to help prove your position when we return to Lethnon."

She gave no response, or at least one so small he could not decide if she heard him or not.

***

With the conference concluded and a few days off to enjoy the pleasures of a brief vacation on Shyfar over, the Gorvin representatives found themselves back home on Lethnon and back to work in their lab.

The doorway slid silently open as Jontar and company approached. Upon entering, he strolled directly to Clugat's office. Through the window of the lab director's office, they saw Eisoph and Clugat entangled in some sort of argument. At least given their barely readable features, he thought it was an argument. This door, too, slid open at their approach.

"I don't care about their reputation. I've been over my work a hundred times since the presentation and so have you. Neither of us can find any errors." The higher tones in her Eisoph's harmony indicated her frustration. "Without the full set of data from the Skae, we have no way to check our calculations against theirs. Why are they being so secretive?"

Clugat leaned forward, hands folded on his desk, and a smile, at least a Gorvin smile, was fixed on his face. "Let's not get into any conspiracy theories now. It's only been a few days. I'm sure they will respond to our request very soon."

"No need to wait," interrupted Jontar. "We have the full data on their project."

Both Gorvin looked up at Jontar, with brief glances at the other two at his side. Eisoph recovered from her shock at the announcement first. Her harmonic voice dropped a full register, a clear sign of suspicion. "And how did you manage that? Why would the Skae provide their full data to some Kolandi researchers before us? It's not exactly your people's main area of study."

Duvar lowered his voice so only those present could hear him. "Well, they didn't exactly give us the information voluntarily." He grinned as he spoke, puffing up like a child who got away with an especially clever trick.

"You stole the data?" Clugat sat back in his chair, wiping his face with his hands. "If they find out, we'll all be in prison. How could you think to do such a thing?"

"They won't find out," said Yalmut. "We have some very special skills in infiltrating their systems. There's no trace of any theft of the data or even any unauthorized use of their network."

"Our preliminary look at the calculations seems to confirm Eisoph's fears. We think they overlooked a critical bit of information, or at least ignored the importance of the results." Jontar sent his thoughts to Clugat and Eisoph's holo-tablets, giving them the stolen files.

"So now you three are some sort of super hackers? I don't think that was on your résumé when you applied to work here." Her voice now contained dangerous overtones of a building outrage. "How did you do that?" Eisoph gasped almost silently as her holo-tablet came to life, opening the critical files.

"I'll explain later. For now, we need you to verify our findings. We'll meet with you tomorrow and discuss your findings. I hope we're wrong, but I doubt it."

Eisoph eyed Jontar with the meerest narrowing of her eyes, mouth slightly turned down at the corners. For a Gorvin, she practically screamed disapproval but quickly turned her attention to the data stream.

As Eisoph and Clugat became absorbed in their tablets, bringing data files to life hovering at eye level, their fingers nimbly flicking through the complicated arrays of signs, symbols and numbers, the three Kolbri conspirators left the office.

"We need to talk," said Yalmut. "Our actions here are leading to some serious implications. We must be prepared."

Yalmut led his friends to a nearby outdoor park where they could talk freely. The day was on the chilly side for most Gorvin; Lethnon lacked the highly sophisticated climate control capabilities found on Shyfar, but conditions were nice enough for the three Kolbri. Unlike parks on other worlds, this one was typically Gorvin. Rock structures of all sizes, shapes, and designs filled the grounds. Rough-hewn abstract carvings depicted three-dimensional representations of four-dimensional concepts. Smoothly polished geometric shapes reflected a soft glow in the sunlight. Trees and grass were absent, replaced by multi-colored rock gardens in intricate patterns surrounding the statues. As they walked further into the park, other visitors became scarce.

Duvar halted mid-stride. "Are we going to walk forever? Why did you bring us out here, Yalmut?"

Yalmut and Jontar stopped alongside Duvar, forming a tight triangle. "I wanted to point out some of the nuances of the Gorvin statuary Eisoph showed me recently." *Keep moving as we talk. It won't look so suspicious that way.* He continued on, the others catching up and he picked up the conversation.

They stopped in front of a particularly large statue. "Look at the lines of this one. Very evocative of the sculptor's love of nature." *We all know where this leads. This is what started the Skae – Gorvin War. This war will kill billions of people throughout the galaxy. Our own world and many like it will be subjected to the Gorvin biotech weapons and isolated for thousands of years. Are we willing to accept this?*

Jontar pointed to the rock garden surrounding the statue. "Do those patterns have any significance to the artist as well?" *What choice do we have? All of this is our history. We cannot change it without risking everything we know.*

"Of course, it is all one statement, together in harmony." *We could end this war before it even begins. Our world doesn't have to suffer the fate we know is coming. We could save billions from the horrors they are about to face.*

"For an expressionless species, they certainly are an emotional lot." *And eliminate the lives of everyone we know and love. Our actions would prevent the births of billions more and alter our timeline in ways we cannot imagine.*

"You can say that again. It took me forever to figure out what few facial expressions I could, but they do seem to be full of passion about almost everything." *Jontar is right, Yalmut.* Duvar sighed, clasping his small talons behind his back as they walked. *We have to let all of this play out. History and the timeline must be preserved.*

Yalmut shook his head, waving one hand in front of him as if directing their attention to another statue down the path. "Compare it to this one over here." *But we've already altered it. We gave Clugat and Eisoph the Skae data they needed to see what would happen. Without our intervention, The Skae would have blown up half the galaxy. We're already involved and changing history.*

They continued on, occasionally stopping in front of one of the stone carvings, apparently admiring them, for a while before Jontar broke the stillness in their minds. *No, we haven't changed history, we fulfilled it.*

What are you talking about? asked Duvar, now preening his short crest. "How could we possibly fulfill history?"

Think about it. The Gorvin must have gotten the data somehow, otherwise everything would have been wiped out before the war could even start. Their device would have destroyed everything, but that never happened. I don't know how the Gorvin got the information without us, but they must have. In some strange quirk of the timeline trying to maintain itself, we became the vehicle for that bit of history.

That's crazy, Jontar. How could we be a part of history thousands of years before we were born?

We're here, aren't we? Time travel can create some very odd circumstances.

He's right, Duvar. Yalmut stopped in his tracks, watching his friends argue time paradoxes. *But that's not my point. Are we willing to let the terrible history we know take place? Jontar, you seem somewhat attached to Eisoph. Are you willing to let her face this war we know is about to happen? Can you live with yourself knowing her fate?*

Jontar closed his eyes and turned his back on the others. *I don't know. How could any of us know?*

Well, we need to make a decision pretty phalking fast.

Reaching the end of their circuit around the gardens, Jontar smiled at Yalmut and patted his friend on the shoulder. "Thank you for the insights. I'll never look at Gorvin art the same way again." *None of this is easy, my friend. We do indeed have some difficult decisions to make, but not tonight. Tomorrow will be soon enough.*

The next day, all five companions met in private. Clugat gave orders to have the rest of the scientists using the lab evicted temporarily.

Clugat opened the discussion with his head hung low, leaning heavily on his elbows at his desk. "Gentlemen, I'm afraid our worst fears are true. I don't know if the Skae are purposefully hiding this information or simply ignoring the implications we have found, but we must alert the highest levels of authority about this."

Eisoph chimed in, her eyes showed a growing fear rarely seen on a Gorvin. If Jontar interpreted it correctly, he would say she had been crying. "They can't be that stupid."

"It's not stupidity," said Jontar. "The Skae are incapable of believing anyone is better at anything than they are. If they had convinced themselves the consequences were only a minor and unlikely possibility, then nobody will be able to change their minds. They are constitutionally incapable of doubting their own superiority."

"But they are going to destroy this entire sector of the galaxy! Hundreds of star systems, thousands of inhabited planets, all wiped out in a massive expanding phase space of degenerate matter."

Jontar looked back into Eisoph's eyes, holding her gaze, trying to give her strength. "This is why we are here."

Chapter Ten

"I'm so glad you talked me into this, Nedia. It'll be good to get out of those confines and into the real world again." Ryma let the breeze fill her nostrils as the mag-lev sped through the countryside with the windscreens lowered. Her long hair danced wildly behind her. "I do so love how green and lush everything is here. I miss home, but there is so much life here. It's invigorating."

"Yes, the fresh air will do us all some good." Nedia clasped her talons tightly in her lap. The note from Nissend Honj was cryptic at best, only to be at the vineyard no later than noon but not before mid-morning. All other details were left unanswered, presumably for her protection in case anything went wrong. *It's as if he doesn't trust me. The old fool. He knows I would do anything for the clan and how much I despise these Rockers. The sooner we are rid of them the better.*

Rilo, Neri, and Danet accompanied their royal princess as always… eyes alert for any sign of threat. A Brin entourage was also in attendance. A mix of guards and dignitaries spread between the mag-levs in front and behind the main vehicle. Two hours later, they arrived at their destination and turned onto the dirt road leading up to a modest village in the center of acres of lush grapevines.

A small group of village elders, a mix of Brin and Kolandi, stood waiting as the royal party arrived in a cloud of dust. Danet exited first and quickly surveyed the area for any danger. Only when he was satisfied did he open the door for Ryma and the others. Ryma, followed by Neri and Rilo approached the group. Nedia, last to exit the transport, held back from the others, her eyes darting in every direction. She nearly jumped out of her crest as the doors on the trailing mag-lev slammed shut.

"… Please, call me Ryma. No need for formalities here. The old ways are giving way to a beautiful new way of things." She clasped hands with one of the elders, a Kolandi, who smiled but looked like someone who had a grendel by the tail and was not sure what to do next.

"Yes, your highness… princess… Ryma… as you wish." The man held out a shaking hand toward his companions, introducing them as each in turn shook Ryma's hand with varying degrees of uncertainty.

"What a lovely community you have here. The very ideal of what my late husband and I envisioned. I commend all of you on your commitment and courage to our joint future."

"Thank you princ… um, Ryma. We are very proud of our community. May I escort you and the rest on a tour of our facilities?" He waved a hand toward the largest of the buildings, where an unending train of mag-lev conveyor carts brought loads of grapes inside for processing.

Three hours later, the tour concluded with Ryma's presentation of the official Assembly seal of inspection and the visitors piled back into their vehicles. Nedia sat speechless, hands twitching in her lap. Rilo, Neri, and Ryma talked and laughed quietly during the ride back to First Town, never once trying to include Nedia in their conversation.

The sun dropped low atop the hills as they drove through the narrow, winding path the road cut following the river. Without warning, they heard the report of an explosion and the mag-lev lurched to one side, forced off the road by a landslide, tumbling toward the river below. Ryma lost consciousness when the icy water rushed through the broken windows as the vehicle landed on its roof. As darkness enveloped her sight, she saw the twisted collection of bloody arms, legs, and bodies of her companions piled together on top of and beside her. She heard voices shouting as if from a great distance and felt hands grabbing at her legs.

"Get them out of there, you fools. We don't want them dead, not yet anyway. The Homsan will have us in the pits for sure if any of them die before he can offer them up."

***

The sounds of dripping water echoing around her brought the first realization she was not dead. The agonizing pain screaming up her left leg as she tried to move was the second.

"Don't move, my princess. Your leg is broken as well as at least three ribs. The Homsan and a couple of medicine women of this clan have helped set the bones and bound your wounds, but you must remain still."

Her head ached and she gasped at the stab of pain caused by the lamplight when she opened her eyes. "What is this place? What happened? Is that you, Rilo? Are the others safe?"

Rilo placed her hands gently on Ryma's shoulders to keep her from moving. "It is me, my princess. You must remain still. We have some injuries, but we are alive."

Blinking rapidly, Ryma attempted again to open her eyes, finally realizing that they were swollen and could only provide a tiny slit to see through. Above her, Rilo's smiling face came into focus. She was bandaged and blood-spotted, with one eye severely blackened, and Ryma wondered how she could manage the smile. Without turning her head, since even the attempt brought on more pains, her eyes took in their surroundings. The orange lamplight illuminated rock walls that glistened with trickles of water. Long, tapering stalactites hung from the high ceiling.

"Where are we?"

"You don't recognize your former palace, Your Highness? I know it has been many years since you abandoned us, but let me be the first to welcome you home." The booming voice pounded in her ears, causing her to wince again at the ache it brought to her head.

Rilo maintained her firm grip on Ryma's shoulders as she pivoted her head to address the voice coming from outside Ryma's small field of view. "The Princess is not well enough for visitors. She needs sleep and time to recover properly."

The voice hesitated, Ryma heard a shuffling of feet, and a shadow crossed her face. Apparently, the visitor had come closer to examine her better. "Perhaps you are correct," said the voice, softer now. "We cannot offend the gods with an offering in this condition. I will send the medicine women each day to help with her recovery. Only a fully sound offering will suffice." The shadow left her face and the sound of scuffling feet receded in the distance.

"Who was that? What gods was he talking about?" Ryma felt her hold on consciousness fading rapidly.

"Rest now, my princess. We will talk more when you are able. You must sleep now."

***

Four days later, at least by Rilo's account, Princess Ryma awoke. The pains remained, but not at the level she remembered from her first awakening. Nothing about her location seemed to have changed and she was able to move, slowly and carefully, but now she could turn her head for a better look at her surroundings. Next to her, Rilo slept on a ragged, threadbare blanket crawling with infestations. Her head was no longer bandaged but her ribs were bound and her lower right leg was splinted. Her feet were also chained.

None of the others were to be found in the small alcove of the cavern they occupied, cut off from the main passage by a set of stout bars. Other than the lamps in the passageway, only a small oil lamp provided illumination within the prison chamber. She gritted her teeth as she lifted herself onto her elbows. Rilo leapt to her side, chains jangling from her ankles.

"Be careful, my princess, your injuries are still newly mended and likely to reopen themselves if you disturb them too much." She reached behind her and picked up a wooden bowl. "Drink this. It tastes horrible, but the Homsan assures me it is strong medicine. I have been taking some of it myself and it does seem to help."

Ryma sipped at the bitter-tasting contents, dribbling a fair amount down her chin in the process. "Where are the others? What is happening here?"

Rilo prostrated herself before Ryma, tears welling, but refusing to fall. "I failed you, my princess. It was my duty as your primary Skatak to protect you. I was not alert enough to prevent this attack. I have allowed my enemy to take my kital from me without a fight. I am bound to relinquish my command over the Skatak and submit myself for disciplinary action."

Stroking one hand gently on the woman's back, Ryma tried to comfort her protector. "Nobody could have foreseen this attack. You and your Skatak have served me well and saved my life uncountable times. I will expect you to find a way to do so again. Rise and perform your duty. Answer the questions your princess has put before you."

Rilo's shoulders heaved briefly as she sobbed quietly. Wiping her eyes, and with a deep breath, she rose to her knees and began her report.

"The others are in another prison alcove, my princess. They were also injured, but not so severely as you. I have been imprisoned in this cell with you to care for you. They did not want you to die but would not stay with you. I convinced them it was smarter to allow me to be here in case your fever spiked again, which it did, several times. One without your strength would surely have died."

"I must have been dreaming, but I recall someone saying this was my old palace. Are we truly back in our former caverns? How is that possible?"

"The Skaeists ambushed us and brought us here. They have reverted back to our old way of life in the old caverns. I have seen The Rocker's tomb myself. It no longer sings or glows as it did before Maliche's arrival, and the Homsan, the leader of this tribe, seems to think it is a sign of the god's displeasure. He wants to reawaken the Rocker god and by doing so please the Skae gods with an offering."

Ryma felt the air grow ominous around her and a heavy weight settled in her heart. "What sort of offering?"

"You, my princess. They think sacrificing the one who led the Kolandi into heresy will set all things right again. It's all that insane old man talks about when he comes to look in on you."

As the two continued their discussion, the sound of heavy footsteps approached. Rilo signaled for silence with a quick cupping of her hand over her mouth and began examining Ryma's bandages.

The cage door rattled as a gaunt man, ancient beyond reckoning, unlocked the door. Wisps of grey hair sprang from patches around his bald head and grew in a long beard nearly to his waist. His bony legs, wrapped in dark leathery and scarred skin, poked out like twigs from his tattered robe. The only thing holding this shredded garment on his emaciated frame was a frazzled rope belt and a thin string at his neck, which still allowed one filthy shoulder to bare itself.

"So you are finally awake. It is sacrilege to keep the gods waiting for so long. Their appetite grows with each day. We cannot deny them their offering any longer. Tomorrow they will be appeased."

With Rilo's help, Ryma sat up to face her captor. "Why have you done this? We are not your enemy."

The old man laughed, ending in a wheezing cough. "You have denied the Skae gods. You have joined with the soulless Brin in claiming the gods are nothing more than beings like us. You have turned your back on your people."

"I have brought prosperity and honor to our people. We no longer have to starve in these caves or die in slavery. Do you not listen to those you claim are gods? Even they have tried to tell you they are not."

"Lies! Falsehoods! Sacrilege! Those you claim are the Skae gods are demons sent to lead us astray. It is you who do not listen to the true gods."

"How can I convince you I speak the truth? I am your Princess. I would never…"

"You are a false princess. We are the true believers and no longer listen to your misguided ways. So many have gone astray that the gods have deserted us. We must make an offering to atone for the sins of the fallen. You will be our offering. Then, when the gods are appeased, they will fight for us against the heretics and return glory to our once bountiful lands." He gave the iron bars one rattling shake and stalked off.

"I will die before I let them take you, my princess." Rilo struggled to her feet and, with chains clanking, shuffled to a position between Ryma and the iron bars of the door.

"Then both of us will be dead, and where will we be?" Ryma's voice dripped with anger. "No, Rilo, you will not try to prevent them from taking me from this prison cell. We will go together and we will find a way to escape and rescue the others. I still require your strength and your fighting skills. Come over here. We need to make a plan." She patted the empty blanket next to her.

***

By morning, signaled by the increased activity they could hear in the tunnels, Ryma and Rilo were ready to make good their escape. The morning meal was delivered by an elderly woman in filthy rags. They gulped down the bowl of grey, watery, foul-tasting something Ryma did not want to think about, in the hope it would give them at least some strength for a good fight. The chanting began almost as soon as they finished their last swallow. A somber, almost wailing cry for forgiveness and promises of repentance echoed through the cavern, accompanied by a rhythmic pounding sound, like hundreds of hands or feet slapping the ground at once. The words were sung in the old Kolandi language. The language was once spoken by all Kolandi, but over time, it became the words of ritual and high ceremony. As next in line to lead her people, Ryma had been taught the language in secret by elderly Homsan and her mother. It puzzled her how so many could know the ancient words now.

The sound of a wordless, humming chant growing louder and the soft slap of many bare feet on the rock floor of the tunnel alerted them to the arrival of others. As Ryma and Rilo watched, a half-dozen raggedly-robed women halted in front of their cell, faces lowered toward the ground and hands folded at their breasts. Four tall, powerfully-built warriors stood silently behind them, their faces tattooed in patterns reminiscent of desert-dwelling predators. Each one held a heavy spear. Rilo barely contained herself at the sight of her kital hanging from the belt of one of the men. One of the women, older than the rest, stepped forward and glared through the bars.

"You will come with us to prepare for the offering. Come peacefully and you will be treated well. Offer any resistance and you will be treated as the heretics you are."

Ryma winced as she pulled herself up to stand tall, placing most of her weight on her good leg. Despite the pain of the hair-line fracture, she held her head high and fixed her eyes on the elder woman. "What sort of preparations are we expected to meekly submit ourselves too? And what, exactly, is this offering we are to become?"

The woman spat on the floor, her glare never wavering from Ryma. "You must be cleansed before you can be presented to the Skae gods and The Rocker. Your skin crawls with the taint of heretics. Submit yourself with humility and repentance and your cleansing and offering will bring you peace. Resist and your souls will be tormented for eternity. The choice is yours."

"I am Ryma, High Princess of the Kolandi. Your High Princess. You will take me to whoever is in charge here and…"

The woman slammed her open hand against the bars. "Enough! We no longer recognize you as our princess. You have forgotten the old ways and denied our gods. Will you submit?"

The two stood nearly eye-to-eye in a stare down contest of wills. It was Ryma who lowered her eyes first. "What will happen to the others? If you can tell me they are unharmed and will remain so, we will submit to your offering."

With a crooked smile, the elder woman lowered her hands, folding them at her breast. "The others of your party are well and recovering from their injuries. Your servant stands for the rest to be offered up at your side. No other offerings are required. They will be taught to honor the gods again and, if they learn well, can be free to rejoin the Kolandi. The Brin woman is another case entirely. She will be escorted into the deep desert and left at the mercy of the gods. They will judge her for the crimes of her ancestors."

Ryma's shoulders sank as she sighed and nodded her head. "Very well. We will submit ourselves to your preparations and the offering without resistance."

The old woman waved her hand and one of the warriors pushed his way forward and produced a key to the cell. He unlocked the door and heaved the creaking hinges open. With Rilo's support under her left arm, Ryma limped, following the elder woman and the guard down the passage, the rest of the women and guards in close formation behind. As they walked, the cavern became more familiar. Ryma recognized the tunnel leading to her former royal quarters, then the path to the tomb of The Rocker. It was from there the chanting came the loudest. After many twists and turns, each leading deeper into the bowels of the cavern, Ryma felt the heat and humidity growing more oppressive by the minute until they at last stepped through an opening into a massive room containing a steaming lake. The pale light from the lanterns did not reach far. Most of the ceiling and the opposite side of the lake remained cloaked in darkness. At the water's edge, the procession halted and the Kolandi formed a semi-circle around Ryma and Rilo. Only the sound of dripping water echoed in the chamber.

"Remove your clothes and enter the water so you may be cleansed and prepared for the Skae gods." The elder woman pointed at Ryma and Rilo and the others began their wordless chanting again.

Ryma took a deep breath and, with Rilo's help, she removed her garments. Balancing herself on her good leg, she waited for Rilo to do the same. Together, Princess and Skatak walked into the scalding water of the lake.

"Kneel in the cleansing waters."

The water came to their waist as they knelt. The buoyancy helped remove enough weight from her broken leg that Ryma did not need help to support herself. With another wave of her hand, four of the other women stepped into the water, each one carrying a pumice stone and a lump of brown soap. The four attacked the scrubbing process with vigor, not lessoning their efforts at all even when scouring the more sensitive parts of their bodies. Ryma barely contained a scream when one of her attendants grabbed her broken leg and yanked it up to be cleansed. Rilo remained submissive, but her glares could have skinned a grendel better than the sharpest knife.

Long after Ryma was convinced she had no skin left on her bones at all, the elder woman lifted her hands, and, after a forceful dunking, the scrubbers returned to the shore and rejoined their companions. Rilo helped Ryma to her feet and the pair struggled together to walk up to the narrow black sand beach. Once there, two more of the women brought forth two unbleached short white gowns for them to put on. Without towels to dry themselves first, the fabric became nearly transparent where it touched their wet bodies. Pulling fingers through her dripping hair and pushing it out of her face, Ryma extended one arm to Rilo for support as the group marched away from the lake and back to the upper levels of the cavern. Her lips and fingernails turned blue in the cooler upper tunnels as the wet garment slowly evaporated itself dry. The looks of disdain and betrayal the crowds along the way gave her filled her heart with sorrow and loss. *These were my people. I should have paid more attention to their pain when we took their gods from them. I need to find a way to help them.*

It was only Rilo's sudden stop that brought her mind back to her current predicament. She found herself standing in front of the tomb of The Rocker. There, in its place of honor, sat the white marble tomb. Without the presence of the biocomputer, it looked cold and empty. The songs once heard by many coming from the tomb vanished once the device leapt into Maliche and her, on that fateful day so long ago. The images of the Sky gods, now most often called the Skae gods, even among the Skaeists, danced in the flickering torchlight on the walls. Dozens of wasted and filthy Kolandi, other than the several warriors along the wall, filled the two rows of benches occupying the sacred room. As she was escorted in, she saw the rest of her party from the ill-fated mag-lev. Neri and Danet stood on either side of Nedia, all of them displaying bandages of various sizes on assorted limbs, but aside from appearing a bit malnourished, they seemed to be doing as well as could be expected. Four warriors with spears stood on guard over them.

"Bring the offerings forth to be presented to the gods." The ragged old Homsan stood in to one side of the tomb, his arms raised, and his eyes to the sky.

Two of the guards marched forward alongside Ryma and Rilo, and with one hand firmly guiding them, escorted the pair down the center aisle. Rilo's face hardened even more as she again saw the glint of her kital swinging at the belt of the one closest to her. At the marble tomb, both guards seized Rilo's arms and pushed Ryma forward. Stumbling from the shove, she nearly fell over, but found the strength to recover her balance and limped forward to the altar. Two more warriors emerged from the shadows to take hold of Ryma and lift her onto the top of the tomb, holding her arms down on either side. The Homsan, hands still raised in supplication to the gods, strode behind the marble tomb and reached down to produce a long curved knife. Raising the blade with both hands, he called out to his gods.

"We beg your forgiveness for the weakness of our fallen. Few of us have remained faithful, but we are unbroken in our enduring faith in your glory. We pray that you accept our offering and return your blessings to our lands. With the blood of this offering, cleanse us of the heretic Brin and their demons who claim dominion over you."

"NO!" Rilo exploded in a rage of Skatak fury. With a disabling kick to the knee of one of her guards, she simultaneously ripped her kital from his belt and used it to sever the arm of her second guard at the elbow. A loud commotion at the back of the room told her Neri and Danet had caught her signal and joined in the fight to free themselves. A burst of orange energy sliced through the chamber, erupting in a blaze of sparks as it blasted the knife from the Homsan's grip, along with half of his fingers. In a matter of a few seconds, the room had gone from a solemn ritual to absolute mayhem.

Rilo whipped her head around to see a platoon of Brin soldiers, beam rifles blazing into the warriors along each wall before they could bring their spears to bear. Whirling around again, she tossed her kital into the throat of the surviving guard still holding Ryma on the tomb. His companion groped at a charred hole in his chest as he dropped to his knees. She ran to Ryma and jumped on top of her, pulling the bloody kital from the warrior's neck as he fell. Grabbing the princess with both arms, she rolled them both off the marble tomb and onto the dirt floor where she placed Ryma between her and the white block.

The soldiers brought Neri, who had reclaimed her kital from one of the warriors guarding her, along with Danet and Nedia to join Ryma. They formed a protective formation around them, rifles bristling like the quills of a spiny barblemut. As the last of the civilians ran from the chamber, the two Skatak took a position on either side of their princess, each ready to prove their kitals were the equal of any beam weapon.

"Squad two, clear the main tunnel. Squad five, protect our rear. The rest of you, gather the Princess and the others and get ready to move out." Opet, head of the royal guard, strode into the room and knelt in front of Ryma as two soldiers gently lifted her onto a floating stretcher.

"Forgive me, Princess, my delay in reaching you was intolerable and unforgivable."

Ryma looked up at her old friend and protector, her mouth hanging open in shock at his sudden appearance. "Opet... how did you find us?"

The giant of a warrior, still muscular but with his hair showing a touch of grey and his waist now expanded with age, smiled down at her. "Some of those nanobots we placed on Nedia were still stuck in her clothing and still operating. We searched for a few days before we thought about them and then the signal was so weak at first that we had difficulty pinpointing your location. Once we started focusing on these mountains, we realized they must be holding you in our old home."

She reached out, took his hand in hers, and smiled. "Thank you. Now let's get out of here."

Nedia stood back from the others, the only Brin of the group. The ordeal of their capture and treatment had left her in shock and unable to think clearly. Her life of privilege had left her woefully unprepared for the horrors of the past several days. A guttural scream reverberated in the alcove and all heads whipped around to see the old Homsan diving from the tomb toward Nedia, the stub of his knife held in a bloody, two-fingered hand.

With the reflexes of long training, Rilo jumped and drove her shoulder into Nedia, forcing her out of harm's way. She spun to defend herself, but felt the edge of the broken blade slice down her back. Ignoring the pain, Rilo continued her maneuver and swung her kital deep into the skull of the old man, leaving him twitching on the ground. She pulled the blades from her attacker's head, wiped it off on his ragged garment, and helped lift Nedia to her feet. Two of the guards rushed to their sides and bandaged her wound.

Stunned, the breath knocked out of her, Nedia stumbled to her feet and stared at Rilo as her mind spun, trying to make sense of everything. "Why would you do that? Why would you risk your life to save mine?"

Rilo grimaced as the last of the bandages was pulled tight. "I am Skatak. It is my duty to protect the Princess and those who are with her."

"But I'm Brin, not Kolandi."

"What does that matter? The Princess has relied on your service and you were with us when we were attacked. Your life is no less than any other. Come, we must go before any of these wretches can organize against us again."

Nedia watched in confusion as the others gathered until one of the soldiers took her by the arm and led her out into the passageway. They were able to exit the caverns without further incident and regroup with the rest of the Brin patrols as they met at the three transport shuttles outside. Princess Ryma, head of the Assembly, and her party were escorted up the ramps to the first shuttle and strapped themselves in as it lifted off. In an hour, they found themselves being attended to in a hospital ward in one of the settlements near the coast.

Nedia looked past her IV tubes as Rilo lay face down, getting her wound stitched. That night, sleep eluded her as her thoughts drifted from her uncle and children to Ryma, Rilo and her own decisions. Her final thoughts as she finally drifted off were how everything she did was for her family and her children's future. Maybe she could extend her protection to Rilo, but her family came first. But mostly, she worried about what might have gone wrong with her uncle's plan to eliminate Ryma at the vineyard. She had to get in touch with him as soon as possible.

***

As their mag-lev arrived back at the government office complex in First Town, Ryma laid a gentle but firm hand on Nedia's knee. "Please accompany me to my private office, will you? There is something we need to discuss."

She smiled at her second-sister, but the smile never reached her eyes.

Nedia fought to control her rising panic. *What went wrong? They couldn't know anything... could they? I need to contact Uncle Nissend and let him know the plan failed.* "Of course, Princess, but may I have a moment to catch up on a few items of importance before I meet you?"

She turned to exit the vehicle, but saw the two Skatak and several Kolandi warriors, dressed as royal guards, surrounding her door. She hesitated, then spun to look at Ryma. "What is going on?"

"I need to show you something important, to both of us, Nedia. Please come with us now. This is for your benefit as well as mine."

Do they suspect I had something to do with those savages in the caves? Don't they realize I was a captive right alongside them? Maybe they found out about Uncle Nissend's plot at the vineyard. No, they couldn't possibly know. But if they do... what will become of my children? Did I escape one horror only be trapped in another?

Nedia's mind reeled with questions and uncertainty as she was escorted through the hallways. The massive doors of Ryma's private office closed behind her, sounding like a death knell. Only Danet, Rilo, and Neri remained with the princess and she was trapped with them.

"Please, Nedia," said Ryma as she sat calmly behind her desk. She pushed a large box to one side. Powerful hands gripped Nedia's shoulders, guiding her to the elegantly carved chair reserved for visitors. "Have a seat. I have something you need to see."

Unable to speak, Nedia sat, keeping her back straight and face as composed as possible. No Kolandi usurper would see any weakness in her... she hoped.

"Take a look at this." Ryma gestured toward the large box, her eyes going to Danet, who reached inside and pulled out a mechanical device with cylinders, wires and a laminated green timer, frozen still at 4:32:16. He shoved the device into Nedia's reluctant hands and returned to his post at the door.

"Wha… What is this?"

"A chem-mine. A highly-focused explosive device designed to penetrate a structure and deliver a toxic mix of chemicals to the inhabitants of a building, or, in this case, an armored mag-lev vehicle. Don't worry, it's been deactivated."

Nedia's mouth started to drop, but she clamped it firmly shut. "Why show this to me? Where did you find it?"

"My security forces detected it the morning of that fateful day we visited the vineyards, Take a look at the timer. Do you see any significance to it?"

"Why would it mean anything to me? I have no idea what you are getting at?"

"They discovered it five hours before we were scheduled to leave on the tour. Does that help at all?"

"I have no idea what…" Nedia's face went pale, her mouth as dry as the desert as her mind subconsciously performed the math.

"Yes, you see it now, don't you? If we had not discovered it, the explosive would have detonated and killed everyone in the vehicle somewhere on the road to the vineyard. You, along with the rest of us."

"Who would do such a hideous thing?" Nedia plastered a look of horror on her face as she assumed the role of an innocent. "I will do everything in my power to…"

With a wave of her hand, Ryma cut her off. "There is something else you should see before you say anything else." She opened a file on her tablet and handed it to Nedia.

Her eyes flickered over the display several times before looking up at Ryma, confusion written on her face. "I… I don't understand. What is this?"

"Those are forms ordering the transfer of custody of your children to pass to your uncle."

"Custody? To my uncle? Why? What is the meaning of this?"

"Did you notice the date?"

Nedia returned her attention to the tablet. "It's dated the afternoon of the day before we left for the vineyards." Her hands began to tremble uncontrollably as she dropped the tablet. Her vision grayed and the room began to spin out of control.

"Yes, you understand now. Your uncle intended you to die along with the rest of us." Ryma stood and, still adjusting to the mobility-assisting brace on her leg, stepped slowly toward the trembling Nedia. "I understand your clan's hatred of the Rockers. Greed and lust for power are not unknown to the Kolandi, and we are certainly not free from delusional behavior, as you have witnessed, but do you have any idea why your family would want you dead as well?"

Nedia stared ahead, not comprehending Ryma's words.

"We've been spying on your uncle for some time now and we know about the schemes you have been a part of. While they were intended to simply frighten me, I let you continue to see what we could learn. After the first attempt on our lives by that bomber in the reception hall, I had the doctor secretly implant you with a tracking/recording device while you were being checked for injuries. I thought it would help keep you safe, at first. Then we learned of your connection to the plots and have used you as our unwitting spy ever since."

"But he would never betray me. I've devoted my life to my family. I've sacrificed everything. He would never..."

Ryma stooped down, picked up the tablet, and handed it back to Nedia. "During one of your earlier visits to your uncle's estate, we had your cloak dusted with nanobot transmitters. I don't understand how they work, but our scientists assured me they would help uncover the truth of things. Once you arrived, they were signaled to infiltrate the entire estate. There are some very relevant files regarding you and what your beloved family thinks of you on the tablet. Take it and read for yourself."

"You, a Kolandi, used nanobots? How would your kind even know about technology like that?"

Ryma closed her eyes and shook her head. "Typical Brin attitude. Kolandi are nothing more than savages. You should be glad we did. After all, it was the transmissions from a few of those nanobots still stuck on your clothing and in your skin that told the soldiers where to find us after the Skaeists took us captive." She returned to her chair and sat. "I will give you until tomorrow to read and process the information. We'll talk then." She nodded to her Skatak, who stepped to either side of Nedia and escorted her to her quarters in the complex.

Hours passed as Nedia read, and re-read the files. Her beloved uncle, trusted above all others, had been using her all along. The information proved he had discovered her hatred of the Rockers at an early age, the result of so many family tales of injustice perpetrated against them. They told of his manipulation of her to betray her marriage and kill her husband, only to see her as a growing liability. The final blow was the evidence of his desire to have her children replace her as the Honj spear point against the Rockers, all while staying hidden in the background himself.

Tears streaming down her face, Nedia looked up at Rilo, who stood guard inside her chambers. "So when am I to be executed for my treason?"

"That will be decided after the princess talks with you tomorrow."

She thought for several long minutes before continuing. "She is a fool. I would not hesitate to eliminate someone guilty of treason."

Rilo's hand reflexively tightened on her kital. "You risk much speaking so of the princess, especially after she was willing to sacrifice herself to spare your pitiful life, but you are Brin, so you are ignorant of our ways."

"Then educate me." Nedia wiped her face with a well-used cloth and sat up straight on the corner of her bed.

Rilo tilted her head, squinting at Nedia like she did when confronted with a difficult puzzle. "Why would you want to learn about us? You have tried to kill us."

"I hate the Rockers and what they have done to my family, or at least what I was raised to believe they have done. Your princess, as the widow of Maliche Rocker, was the last barrier to our taking our rightful place. I have no animosity in particular toward the Kolandi, but she represented the Rockers and as such, I believed, was also to blame for all of the Rocker injustices... yet you saved my life in the caves when that madman attacked me. You took the knife that was meant for me. I may have been wrong... about all of you."

"I was slow. He never should have been able to do me any harm." Rilo studied the woman for a long time before coming to a decision. "Very well. What would you like to know?"

The next afternoon, Rilo escorted Nedia back to Ryma's private office.

"I understand you and Rilo have had quite the conversation. Did it help?"

A bleary-eyed, red-faced Nedia hung her head as she spoke. "I am not sure of anything anymore. My entire world has been destroyed. But I am no longer your enemy."

"And what of the Rockers? Are you still their enemy?"

She hesitated a while before answering. "I do not know. A lifetime of hate is not something easily forgotten. But I just don't know anymore."

Ryma gave a hint of a smile and folded both hands on the desk in front of her. "That is all we can ask for now. But I must know what your intentions are before we can decide your fate."

"Can you help me regain custody of my children?"

"Your uncle's petition was held up in the courts and has never been finalized. We saw to that, at least. When the courts learn you were not killed, I will see they are persuaded to deny the custody petition. Your children will be removed from the Honj estate and back at your side by tomorrow, if that is what you wish."

Tears flowed anew as Nedia nodded her head in agreement. "Then I wish to stay here, if you think you can ever trust me again. I want to do what I can to help you defeat my uncle."

"You want to help us prevent your family from gaining control of the Assembly?"

"Maybe other Honj clansmen will prove to be more worthy than my uncle has proven himself to be. I would want my family to rule with justice and honor, as you have tried to do. He is not the one to do that. Perhaps I will find another to support. For now, he must not be allowed to win."

Ryma sat back, supported her chin with two steepled fingers, and glanced at Rilo as she stood guard behind Nedia. A simple nod in reply answered her unspoken question.

"Very well, then. I will give orders for your children to be brought here to you, and you will remain as one of my advisors. Your knowledge of how your clan operates and their holdings will be of great value to me. However," Ryma's voice took on a stern and unforgiving tone as she glared at Nedia. "If you ever attempt to use my generosity against me again, you will suffer more than you can imagine. I am still Kolandi, and I remember all of the atrocities your kind inflicted on my people. I will not hesitate to release the savage you Brin have always believed us to be. Do you accept my terms?"

Nedia dropped to her knees, trembling. "I will not disappoint you. Thank you."

Chapter Eleven

The holo-vid conference with the Gorvin parliament was a typical bureaucratic quagmire that seemed to drone on forever. Gnobis, Clugat, and Eisoph sat on one side of the polished stone table, its tortured, twisted pattern of metamorphosed layers almost glowing in the dim light. Jontar, Yalmut, and Duvar sat opposite them. On the other two sides of the square table hovered the images of six Gorvin officials.

"The proof is uncontestable. Our calculations have been verified by multiple neutral parties on several out-worlds. The Skae cannot be allowed to continue this venture." Gnobis emphasized his declaration to the Gorvin Parliament by pounding his fist on the lectern, his face as full of passion as possible for a Gorvin.

The semi-transparent image floating above the communication terminal flickered as the various faces of the heads of the Gorvin parliament moved, turning from one to another. The central figure, robed in white with indigo trim, took control and replied. "We need more time to investigate the so-called uncontestable nature of your data, Gnobis. Do not presume to rush us into a decision which could lead us into a disastrous situation."

The scientist clenched his fist in an effort to control himself. "I would never be so presumptuous, sir. But I have full confidence in our findings, and the consequences are so enormous we must act quickly."

"If what you say is true, then we will, of course send a diplomatic envoy to the Skae with the evidence. They will have no choice but to cease in their folly, if folly it is. We should have our decision in a few weeks. We will inform you of our decision then."

The ghostly images vanished as communications ended.

"Well, that accomplished nothing." Duvar waved one taloned fist at the empty space above the terminal. "The Skae will never listen to diplomats."

"But what can we do? The Skae are so powerful. We have no weapons to threaten them with. How can Congress defy them?" Eisoph wrung her hands as she read the reports for the tenth time.

Duvar jerked up from his perusal of the reports, head tilted and eyes wide. "What do you mean you have no weapons? The Gorvin are the only force able to stand up to the Skae. It's your tech weapons-"

"I think what Duvar means is that we might be able to help you develop some weaponry to help you fight the Skae." Jontar gave Duvar a withering look as he projected his thoughts. *Did you forget when we are, Duvar? This is before the attack on Sharta C... before the great war began. Remember, much of what we know of history came from what the Skae told us. No doubt it was a significantly distorted version of actual events to favor their perspective."*

Duvar's face fell. *"Sorry, I guess I got so caught up in the horror. I forgot."*

"Well, get your crest together. We cannot afford another slip like that. There may be something we can do, but you won't like it."

Yalmut, eavesdropping on the conversation, perked up. He frowned at Jontar. *"You aren't thinking what I think you are... are you?"*

"If you have any better alternative, I'm open to it."

The three sat staring in silence at each other for what seemed like hours until Clugat spoke. "What weapons are you talking about? We are primarily a race of scientists, not warriors."

Jontar turned to face Gnobis, Clugat, and Eisoph, his face filled with darkness. "A while back we developed some theories on weapons of war which we believe may be some of the most powerful ever developed. We've been hesitant to reveal the details, but now we may not have a choice."

"We will not kill if we can avoid it," said Eisoph. "We have always devoted ourselves to science and the peaceful advancement of all species. We would not use the sort of weapons necessary to defeat anyone as powerful as the Skae."

Jontar placed a gentle hand on her shoulder, talons gripping her in a reassuring gesture. "We know that and would never propose anything of the sort. We, too, believe in peaceful solutions whenever possible. The devices we are proposing do not kill; they only neutralize an enemy so they cannot continue to take part in a war."

"How is that even possible?" Gnobis leaned heavily on his elbows as he listened.

"Not now. We need to discuss this amongst ourselves before we go any further." Jontar gestured to his companions with a sweeping open hand. "The potential consequences of sharing this information are enormous and we must be certain there is no alternative. We will let you know tomorrow so you will know what to tell your government." Jontar stood, motioned to the others, and led the way out of the lab.

Back in their apartment, the three Kolbri took turns in their heated argument.

Duvar paced the room uttering curses under his breath before challenging Jontar, wagging a talon in his face. "You cannot seriously be suggesting we give them the means to destroy our own civilization. How can that even be an option?"

Yalmut, maintaining his calm demeanor as usual, lounged in a chair as he watched his friends. "The Kolandi of this time are not our civilization. They are our history. What happened is in the past."

Rounding on Yalmut, Duvar raged on. "How can you say that? You've seen our world in this time. We have the opportunity to prevent a holocaust."

"At what price?" Jontar interrupted. "Yalmut is right. The events we know as history happened. Are you ready to live with the consequences if we change such a massive event? Would any of us even exist? Would our Rocker ancestors have been brought to Kodut if we still filled the planet with a thriving civilization? The Brin would all have died when their sun exploded. Would the galaxy even be here in our time if the Skae had carried out their plan? How many others will die that should not have?"

"It's still not right. How can we live with ourselves if we are the agents responsible for the murder of our own people? Even if they are only our ancient history?"

"They won't be killed," said Yalmut as he stood and approached Duvar. "The weapons won't kill anyone. But we will provide the Gorvin with the means to prevent the Skae from exterminating half the galaxy. We are simply the means by which history, as we know it, was created." He chuckled, preening his small crest. "Thinking about this too much can drive one crazy, can't it?"

"You're twisting words, Yalmut, and you know it. Billions of Kolandi will die if we do this."

"I know, Duvar, but what other alternative do we have?"

Tensions diminished as the debate continued. Eventually the discussion ended with an agreement on how to present the information to their new allies.

***

The next morning arrived with a bright sun rising above the distant stone mountains, casting an orange glow on the sculptures of the rock garden the three Kolbri strode through on their way to Clugat's lab.

"These are ingenious. Non-lethal but completely effective in rendering an enemy unable to continue fighting, at least with any technology beyond a bow and arrow." Clugat studied the holographic designs of the nanobot delivery system and tunable virus for neutralizing technology. "And the light sail propulsion strategy is brilliant. Nothing will be able to track them or be able to interfere with their delivery. Absolutely brilliant."

"We hoped you would think so." Jontar allowed himself a relieved smile. "Perhaps, if you presented these plans along with our findings about the Skae device, they will find a way to convince the Skae to stop before destroying half the galaxy."

"If I remember correctly, our research and development facilities on Sharta C would be perfect for developing this into a practical weapon without too much difficulty." Eisoph leaned on Clugat as she studied the data over his shoulder, her hand occasionally reaching out to swipe through the technical specifications and diagrams hovering over the table.

"Sharta C? Isn't that a Skae world?" Jontar and Yalmut exchanged worried, knowing glances at the mention of the tragic planet.

Clugat and Eisoph stopped their work and turned to stare at the pair as if they had sprouted wings and flown around the room. "Whatever would give you that idea? Sharta-C is one of our most renowned research facilities. Yes, it lies close to a disputed region of space, but it falls well within Gorvin territory."

Duvar shook his head, flicking his talons as he absorbed this revelation. "How strong is your military force there? To protect your citizens and properties, I mean."

"Are you really that ignorant of the Gorvin? I know we have never had much contact with you Kolandi, being under the Skae domain and all, but surely you must know we have no military force. At least not in the size and manner of most other worlds. We've always been scientists and researchers. No threat to anyone. Other worlds welcome our presence in their midst, since we share everything we learn and all benefit in return. At most, we have a ceremonial guard at our facilities for our diplomats, but nothing more. Why would we ever need one?"

"At least until now." Eisoph looked at Clugat, her stony features registering sadness to match her voice.

"But Sharta C can't be…"

"Not now, Duvar. Something is going on here we need to investigate."

"You know as well as I do what happened on Sharta C. We saw the Gorvin military attack and wipe out helpless people on that world."

"We saw something the Skae showed us. With what we know now, are you so willing to take that holo-vid as solid proof of anything?"

Jontar stood behind Duvar, patting his shoulders with both hands. "In any event, there is nothing to do until your congress makes their decision, at least not officially."

Yalmut took the hint and addressed Clugat and Eisoph. "What if you helped us approach the researchers on Sharta C to ask for their assistance in developing our idea for the nanobot delivery system? This would be a pure research project, which could have potential for many possible applications. You would only be the intermediary contact and would have nothing to do with the research and development until the congress decides in our favor and we turn it over to you for completion."

Jontar stepped forward to stand beside Yalmut. "We could approach a different lab there to work on the strain of viruses we would need to infect the Skae and their allies." He held up a taloned finger to halt Clugat's attempt to interrupt. "Non-lethal, of course. We have in mind something to biologically tie a species to the gravitational field of their planet. Any attempt to enter space would be fatal within a day or two, but with plenty of warning to allow for a safe return. We are working on the specific sequencing for a few Skae allied worlds and should have the results available soon."

Eisoph jumped to her feet, fists on hips, glaring at Jontar and Yalmut. "You want us to defy our government? We could go to prison."

Jontar smiled, extending both hands palms up. "Of course not. We are only asking for permission, and your scientific introduction, to the researchers on Sharta C. We have something of a side project we believe they are particularly suited to carrying out for us while we stay focused on the Skae matter. Nothing which concerns you and your work at all."

Eisoph snorted, arms folded across her chest. "You're going to get us all put away forever ... or killed."

Clugat chuckled in his deep, rumbling sort of way. "Eisoph, I think our leaders were wise to keep us ignorant of the Kolandi for so long. They're a race of thieves and troublemakers. How soon would you three like me to arrange for the introductions?"

***

Four months later, Jontar, Yalmut, and Duvar found themselves enjoying the solitude of a mountain lake. Jontar stood knee-deep in the water, dressed in water-tight waders. Flicking a long, thin rod back and forth, he hit the right rhythm and cast a pale-green line with high tensile leader through the air. A small, simulated eight-legged tanf settled almost without a ripple on the surface. He slowly reeled in the line, occasionally jiggling the rod to give the tanf a life-like action. A slight breeze stirred the leaves of the nearby trees while puffy white clouds drifted high above in a brilliant blue sky.

Duvar sat on a rock under a tree, reading a journal on his tablet. He reached over to give Yalmut a playful punch on the arm and nodded toward Jontar. "I'll never understand what you think you're doing out there. Whatever gave you the idea to start fly-fishing? Nobody in their right mind does that any more. Not in several generations, at least."

Keeping his focus on the nearly invisible tanf, Jontar sighed at the obvious attempt to poke fun at his new-found hobby. "My grandfather taught me when I was very little. I never saw the point either, until now. He always claimed to have learned it from his grandfather and told a story about how Rockers have been fly-fishing as far back as anyone can remember. It *is* relaxing, and we all need a big dose of relaxation these days."

"Looks more like an exercise in futility to me. How can standing around waiting for some aquatic creature to decide your lure is precisely what it is hungry for be relaxing? Give me a good book any day. Where did you find the equipment on this world, anyway?"

"I programmed the materials printer to build it for me. The techs were fascinated when I told them what I wanted. They all probably think I'm crazy, but, after a few trials, here it is."

"Sounds like a waste of time and resources to me."

"Don't knock it until —" Incoming message alerts sounded on all three of their communication tablets, disrupting the calm of the lake. Yalmut flicked the controls and read the message.

"Time's up. We are urgently needed back on the campus. Clugat wants us to meet him at his residence as soon as possible."

Three hours later the mag-lev vehicle glided to a halt in Jontar's reserved slot and the companions strode through the campus toward the Gorvin living quarters.

As they approached the entrance, Clugat opened the door and ushered them in. A holo-vid newscast blared in the main gathering room. Screaming and bursts of energy weapons fire interspersed with explosions filled the room. As they came around the corner into the room, Clugat all but shoved them into the uncomfortably hard benches that made up Gorvin furniture.

A newscaster shouted to be heard by an unseen recorder-bot hovering in front of him to capture the scene. "... attack came without warning. As you can plainly see, thousands of individuals are fleeing for their lives. But with the major ports closed or destroyed, there is nothing to do but find someplace safe to hide and hope this all ends soon."

Duvar, his head on a swivel trying to get anyone's attention, yelled out to be heard above the broadcast. "What the strix is happening? Who's attacking who?"

Clugat shouted in answer from his corner bench. "The Skae. They've attacked the facilities on Sharta C. Why would they do that? It's horrible."

Yalmut sent his thoughts out to Jontar and Duvar. *"The nano-weapons. What else could it be?"*

Duvar mind-shouted back. *"But how could they have found out? We kept the information as low key or secret as possible."*

"Ever since the Skae rejected the Gorvin diplomatic attempts to stop their gravitational wave energy scheme, they must have sent out spies to see if the Gorvin were planning anything to try to stop them."

Jontar joined the mental conversation. *"We didn't cover our tracks enough. We took the chance of a Kolandi research project not being interesting enough to raise any attention, but I guess we have been on the Skae watch list ever since the ruckus over our attending the conference."*

"Phalk. How could we have been so stupid?" Duvar slammed his fist on his knee.

Jontar's mental voice took on a cold, overtone. *"What's done is done, but does this look familiar to either of you?"* He nodded toward the holo-vid.

The three watched as scene after scene showed desperate people, bloodied and staggering, struggling to find an escape from the carnage as orange energy beams sliced the air around them. Clouds of smoke blew across the scene, giving the fleeing victims an eerie, shadow-world appearance. Occasionally, small groups of Gorvin honor guards were visible trying to force their way through the crowd or firing their energy rifles at some off-camera enemy.

Yalmut recognized the view first. *"The Skae historical account of the Gorvin attack on Sharta C."*

"Exactly what I was thinking."

Duvar pulled his attention away from the atrocities with an effort. *"What are you talking about? The Gorvin and everyone else here are being attacked by the Skae. How could you think the Gorvin were attacking anyone?"*

"Duvar, how much difficulty would you have taking a few clips of this video and rearranging it, with a few skillful manipulations and voice-overs, to make it look like the Skae and their allies were being attacked by the Gorvin?"

"It would be easy, very basic manipulations, but those are honor guards, not a real military force."

"Yes, we know that now, but what if we didn't know? What if all we knew was what the Skae told us? In our time, who would be left to tell the real story?"

Duvar's mouth dropped open, his face contorted as if trying to vocalize something, but failed miserably. *"Those phalking quetzals."*

That evening the three Kolandi made plans to leave Lethnon and return to their own time. Under the cover of darkness, they met with Clugat and Eisoph one last time in the shadows of the campus rock garden.

Eisoph handed Duvar a container of food for their journey. "Where will you go? Do you really believe the Skae are looking for you so soon?"

Jontar pulled Eisoph into a hug. "We can't take the chance of letting them find us here with you. With us gone, you can always claim ignorance. Remember, this is why we had you simply make the introductions to those poor scientists for us. You can still plead ignorance of what we needed their facility for."

"Will we see you again, perhaps when all of this is over?"

"I'm afraid not, Eisoph. It would be too dangerous for us to return." He took her broad chin in his talons and lifter her face to his. Thank you for everything. You have been a wonderful friend." He bent over and planted a brief kiss on her rough forehead.

"If you need to go, then best be going." Clugat held up a thick hand.

Jontar raised his own taloned hand and interlaced fingers with Clugat. "Farewell, my friend. You have been invaluable to our work. If only there was some way to repay you."

"No need... no need at all. Your contributions here have set us decades ahead of where we were before your arrival. It is we who are in your debt. If you had not insisted we collect the specs and a few prototypes as soon as they were developed, all would have been lost on Sharta C. Secretly sending the information to the other R&D facilities will allow us to develop the weapons fully now that Congress is on board with the plan."

The small group stood silently for a moment before Jontar signaled the time to leave. The darkness engulfed the trio as they returned to their ship hidden in the forest.

As they settled into their flight control panels, Jontar announced a new destination. "Only one more stop before heading home. We have one last piece of the puzzle to unravel." He set the controls and the ship vibrated as it accelerated through the atmosphere. In seconds, the vacuum of space enveloped them and they set their destination for the appropriate cosmic string.

***

"Just as we thought. The Gorvin nanobots cannot penetrate the cosmic string energy field surrounding Seriph." The enhanced view of Seriph, the Skae home planet, revealed an intense and intricately woven fabric of cosmic strings surrounding much of the Skae system. "It appears this system is close to the source generating the strings providing them with a protective screen unlike any other. No wonder they could hold out for so long against the Gorvin weapons."

After arriving two more years into the future, Jontar, Yalmut, and Duvar scanned the cosmos for communications regarding the beginnings of the intergalactic war. At first, it seemed the Gorvin strategy was gaining the upper hand. Several Skae allies were isolated and rendered useless without the ability to access technology. Repurposing a number of cargo vessels for delivering the weapons gave the Gorvin time to build their own fleet of warships, small as it was at this early stage. The inability to permanently ground the Skae themselves proved to be catastrophic.

"As long as the Skae can continue the fight, this war is going to last for eons." Duvar covered his face with his hands as he leaned on his control panel.

Jontar patted Duvar on the back as he stood next to him. "We knew that from the start. But at least now we know the truth of things."

"What good is knowing the truth? We would need an armada to defeat the Skae. There's only us."

"I think we have a chance, but we need to get home so I can discuss what we have learned with father and see if my thoughts have any merit."

"What thoughts? Are you going to get us all killed... again? Only for real this time?"

"We made it into space and got away from everyone who was trying to kill us back on Kodut, didn't we? Don't be such a pessimist. Besides, I don't know if I even have a plan yet, just an idea."

"We're all going to die."

Yalmut laughed out loud for the first time in years. "Set controls for home, Jontar?"

"Let's get back were we belong and put an end to this war once and for all."

They connected to the cosmic string to bring them back to the present. A flash of light and a quick lurch of the ship as it came to rest at the given coordinates was all that told them they had moved. Jontar gazed out the front viewport at the sight of the ship they had left so long ago. He opened a communication link.

"Father, its Jontar. We've returned, and you won't believe what we've learned. We can't wait to see all of you again. It's been so long."

Maliche bounded to the communication panel, his talons nearly puncturing the controls in his excitement. "Jontar? But you only just left us? What went wrong? Is everyone alright? ..."

Jontar laughed as he tried to interrupt the flow of questions. "Everyone is fine, Father. Remember, we were time traveling. What for you must have been only a few minutes was, for us, about twenty years. Covering several thousand years of history gave us lots of practice in manipulating the strings. We've gotten pretty good at it now. We can pinpoint our arrival to within minutes instead of weeks."

The bridge crew sat in silence, watching the screen as the shuttle approached, then hung in space alongside.

"Can somebody let us in?" Duvar's voice chuckled over the speaker.

Chapter Twelve

Less than an hour later, and after adjusting to the new reality of time differences, everyone gathered in the Amaethon's bridge.

"What do you mean, 'the Skae are not our friends?' Maliche looked as if he were seeing a two-headed dinter stroll by the main viewport. "Of course they aren't. We all suspected that. It's why we're out here in the first place. I hope you have more specifics for us."

Jontar gave his time-travelling companions a grimace. "I told you he would be impatient." Duvar and Yalmut nodded in agreement and settled in for the inquisition they now faced.

"Father, for everyone's benefit, I think we should start with a brief overview of our experiences travelling through the past. We can provide you and Tol with a direct download of all the files later."

"Don't forget me," Thyka interrupted with a toss of her hair. "I need to know everything you know."

Jontar eyed Thyka with a mischievous smile. "We would never forget to include you. I am particularly interested in your insight into the cosmic string swarm surrounding Seriph."

Thyka hid a smile, but her twinkling eyes put her love for Jontar on full display for all to see. She sat as tall as her short stature could manage and raised one taloned hand toward Jontar's crest. "These grey touches suit you, ancient one."

Maliche tossed his arms in the air while rolling his eyes. "Feathers and quills! Can we get on with this? The way you two are carrying on one would think you're conducting some sort of kak mating ritual."

The entire bridge burst out loud with laughter. Seykel elbowed him in the ribs with all the power and skill of a full Skatak. "Be nice, Maliche. We all need some time to get reacquainted and adjust to a new reality."

He gaped at the tiny warrior, rubbing his sore ribs. "What new reality?"

Nalot clapped his hand on Maliche's back, continuing to laugh. "Don't tell us you haven't noticed, my old friend." He gestured toward Jontar, Yalmut, and Duvar. "Those three are now nearly your age. They have many years of experience we can only imagine for now. They are no longer the boys we sent off a few minutes ago. Look at them."

Realization dawned on Maliche's face as he studied his son and his friends. He plopped down in the command chair with a thud and ran his talons through his own slightly greying crest.

"I wanted to tell you before you made a fool of yourself, but watching you finally figure it out this way was so much more fun." Tol's familiar tingle in Maliche's head reminded him he was never really alone. *"Let them have their fun. We still have time."*

Jontar, as if he had listened in on the internal conversation, broke the general mood with a loud cough to stop his own laughter. "Alright, I guess it's time to let you all in on what happened to us. Grab a seat; this is going to take some time."

After a couple of hours, everyone moved into the ship's galley for a meal break, but Jontar continued his description of their travels with an occasional correction or clarification from Yalmut and Duvar. While the mag-lev mini-bots cleaned up after them, Jontar finished his tale with their short visit to the Skae home world, Seriph, and their decision to return home.

Nalot disturbed the silence as he grabbed for one last package of dried dinter strips. "That's quite the yarn, young fellow. It would appear that the Skae are friends to nobody. The trick now is to figure out how to toss a sepana in their plans without getting us all killed in the process."

Jontar nodded in agreement, rubbed his bloodshot eyes, and stretched. "While we were talking, the three of us downloaded all of our data into the ship's computer. Before we proceed, I would suggest we all get some sleep. Thyka and father, with Tol's help, can best absorb all of it while they sleep. Their subconscious minds will be better able to take it all in and make sense of everything."

"It's not dangerous, is it?" Seykel took her daughter's hand in hers.

Thyka smiled reassuringly at Seykel, patting her hand in return. "Not at all, Mother. Trying to take in what they had many years to learn will be easier if we just let our brains do the work without any interference. That's all."

Studying her daughter for a moment, Seykel intertwined their fingers and squeezed. "Alright, but I need to stay awake to process everything. I'll spend the night right by your side as you sleep, just in case."

Thyka rolled her eyes, and returned the squeeze. "Alright, Mother. If it will make you feel better."

***

"That was terrifying. I never imagined anyone could be so heartless." Thyka sat on the edge of her bed, tears streaming down her cheeks. Her small taloned fingers trembled in her mother's grasp as she blew a strand of loose hair out of her eyes. "The Skae must be demons to even consider something so horrible."

"Are you sure you're alright?" Seykel sat by her daughter's side, searching for any sign of injury beyond the terror of the memory transfer. "You seemed to be having such a terrible nightmare, but nothing could wake you from it. Your father nearly tried to disable the ship to stop the transfer. We were both frantic with worry over what you were going through."

Thyka's focus on reality slowly returned, though her shuddering continued. She lifted her face to see her mother's blood-shot eyes. Seykel's red hair was so disheveled it might take a week to comb out the tangles. Taking a deep breath, Thyka gathered herself and put on the best smile she could manage. "I'm okay, Mother… really. Maybe we should have tried to take the transfer a bit more slowly, there was so much to take in, but I'm alright." As a new memory took hold in her mind, she sat up straighter and practically beamed with joy. "The strings! Oh, the beautiful strings, Mother. The patterns they weave through time, the songs they sing, I understand them so clearly now. They're like nothing else in the universe. Such power, such beauty."

At that moment, Nalot flung open the door and stormed into the room. "You're awake! Praise the Eternal, you're awake." He dropped on his knees in front of Thyka and pulled her into a powerful hug.

"Father, my ribs! I can't breathe!" She gasped for air as he released his grip.

Nalot fidgeted with his hands, not knowing what to do with them for fear of hurting his tiny daughter. "Sorry… I didn't mean to… Are you alright? Is there anything you…"

Thyka captured his hands as they flew from adjusting her blanket to grasping Seykel's arm. "I'm fine, Father. Everything's fine."

Nalot regained his composure, this time taking Thyka in a gentler embrace. "If anything had happened to you… I don't know what I would have done." He reached out one arm to gather Seykel into a family hug. The three held each other in silence for several minutes.

Maliche knocked softly on the open doorframe. "I hate to break up this family time, but we have vital decisions to make. As soon as you three are ready, please join us in the cafeteria." He turned to leave, but halted, looking back over his shoulder. "I'm glad you're okay, Thyka. Tol says you had a difficult time of it, but you showed some real strength."

Thyka grinned and ignored Maliche. "Thank you, Tol. You were a steady force amid all the chaos. I might not have made it through without your help."

A pink glow surrounded Maliche as Tol replied into Thyka's mind. *I ummm, well, no need to thank me. I'm just glad I could help.*

She giggled and tried to hide it with one hand over her mouth. "I never knew a computer could be embarrassed, but I guess you're much more than that, aren't you?"

The pink glow grew brighter and Maliche hurried away as if suddenly remembering he needed to be somewhere else.

In less than an hour, the entire crew found themselves gathered in the cafeteria munching on a variety of dried fruits and protein bars for breakfast. The smell of spiced herbal tea filled the compartment. The conversation held to small talk over how uncomfortable the mattresses were after so long in real beds, to the need to get used to recycled air and water again. They went over all the unique aspects of living onboard ship again, until all avenues of avoiding the difficult tasks ahead dwindled and an uneasy stillness enveloped them.

Maliche signaled for a cleaner-bot to remove his partially-empty tray and preened his crest as he cleared his throat to get everyone's attention. "I guess we can't delay the inevitable any longer. We need to formulate a plan on how to prevent the Skae from winning this war and completing their black hole engines. Any thoughts?"

"We need to get close to the string field surrounding their system so we can analyze it in greater detail. We got what information we could while we were there, but Thyka, we will need your unique perspective on the strings and how they might be able to help us. Your insights could prove invaluable. If we get you close enough to do your thing with them, do you think you can get us anything useful?" Jontar hooked his talons in his pockets and stretched his legs out as he spoke.

"There was definitely something odd about the string frequencies. I couldn't be sure from the transfer data and images, but it felt like there was more than just the Skae influence affecting them. Maybe I can figure it out if we got close enough." Thyka twisted an unruly lock of red hair in her talons.

"When are you going to let me cut that cardis nest for you? It's very distracting watching you fiddle with it all the time." Seykel swatted at Thyka's hand to stop her nervous habit with the strand.

Thyka rolled her eyes at her mother and tugged at the offending hair. "I think it gives me character, Mother. I don't have so much as you, but I like it and I'm not going to cut it."

"Getting back to the topic," Nalot interrupted his wife and daughter before they could get into the fruitless argument once again. "We can't simply drop in on the Skae home system without some reason for being there. We don't want to raise any alarms or make them suspicious enough to try contacting Kodut."

Duvar flicked his chipped and worn talons as he thought out loud. "It would look pretty odd with us showing up unannounced in a ship supposedly destroyed in our sun with Maliche and Jontar aboard."

Nalot slapped the table with his hand causing everyone to jump. "Sorry, but that is precisely what we need. Duvar, you are a genius."

Duvar stopped his talon flicking, tilted his head toward Nalot, and then smiled. "Of course. I've been trying to tell everyone the same thing for years, but what exactly did my genius say this time?"

Ignoring Duvar, Nalot laid out his idea. "As far as the Skae are concerned, Maliche was doing precisely what they wanted him to do. They believed he was one of their puppets with his seemingly eager embrace of all the trappings of an emperor. We could show up in their system claiming to have faked our deaths in order to ask for asylum. If we concoct a tale of how we uncovered a plot to overthrow Maliche and then simply tell them the tale of our actual assassination and execution plan, we won't have to make up any new story. All the parts will fit what, as far as they are concerned, actually happened.

"There will have to be some details to fill in, but I think we have the basis of how to proceed. Can anyone see any fatal flaws with the idea?"

Everyone looked around the table and gradually nods and grins grew on each face as they came to an agreement. Over the next few days, all details of the plan were hashed out and rehearsed until everyone knew their role completely.

Maliche sat in the command chair on the bridge scanning the various consoles and crew at their posts. "All right, everyone, set controls for Seriph and let's get this ship underway."

Each individual focused on his or her console and adjusted the settings to locate, approach, and connect to the proper cosmic string. Thyka's face lit up as she reached out to the string's song with her mind.

Chapter Thirteen

Nedia checked with the front desk of the university library for directions to the meeting rooms. She had attended the venerable Karm Rocker University prior to meeting Selan Rocker, but so much had changed since her last visit, including this brand new library donated by the Rockers themselves. She felt a twinge of sadness at the loss of her old familiar alma mater. Following the clerk's pointing talons, she strode past the catalog terminals and mag-lifts to head down the first corridor. This late in the evening, her steps echoed on the swirling grey tiles as the setting sun painted the atrium in glowing shades of red and orange. At the end of the hall, she pushed on the door and found her uncle staring out the window.

"So why did you summon me here so urgently, Uncle Nissend? I can't afford to be gone from First Town so often. Ryma is sure to become suspicious. And why here instead of at Brachspark?"

Nissend Honj's shoulders sagged a bit at the sound of her entry and reached out to set the privacy mode in the normally transparent walls. "Were you followed?"

"My driver assures me we were not followed, Uncle. But I'm sure your surveillance team already informed you, otherwise I would have walked into an empty room." She sat in a chair at one end of the long table and plucked a sweet califf from its silver dish, enjoying the melting treat on her tongue before folding her talons in her lap.

Glancing over his shoulder, he clasped his talons in a knuckle-whitening grip behind his back but kept his voice cold as ice. "Mind your manners, girl. Remember who you are speaking to. That team is there for your protection. We wouldn't want anything like the last Skaeist attack to happen again."

Nedia clutched her dress under the table as if grabbing hold of her emotions. She lowered her head, closing her eyes and softened her voice. "My apologies, Uncle. Having to play a subservient role to those … those ukaliti has worn my patience to the end of all endurance."

"It won't be much longer, child. All your sacrifices will be repaid in full very soon." He turned, sat in the center chair along one side of the long table, and waved his fingers over the control panel there to open the vidcom link with two others who kept their faces in shadow and unidentifiable. "We have found a way to legally and publicly denounce not only that abomination Ryma, but to invalidate her marriage and thereby her progeny, thus invalidating their entire claim to leadership in the Assembly."

Nedia released her grip and smoothed the wrinkles from her dress. She leaned on her elbows on the table with folded talons, one tapping on a knuckle. "No more assassination attempts, Uncle? I thought you wanted her dead. Not that I'm complaining; I just didn't want to be caught in the crossfire. I was so worried during the trip to the vineyard. What went wrong that day? Every stray sound had me jumping nearly out of my skin."

With a smile that never touched his eyes, Nissend Honj reached over and patted his niece's folded hands. "Dear one, I would never allow any harm to come to you. After all of your efforts on behalf of our family, you and your children have earned every bit of our respect and a place of honor in the new order. There were unforeseen circumstances that forced us to abandon the plan at the last minute. You were already in transit, so we had no way to contact you. Then the Skaeists took you and things got out of control. I do apologize about that, but sometimes even the best plans go awry."

Taking his hand in hers, she smiled equally in return. "Everything I do is for my family, Uncle. Nothing is more important to me. What is it you have learned?"

Nissend gestured to the shadowy figures and the two began detailing their discoveries in various Brin archives regarding the establishment of the Assembly and the transfer of authority as well as established precedents of authority being passed from husband to wife. Dozens of old documents, some dating back to the origins of the Brin on this planet and bearing the seal and signature of the original Jontar or Maripa Rocker, flashed in holographic form above the table.

Nedia shook her head, brows furrowed as if trying to work out a particularly difficult puzzle. "Wait. All of this looks like a pile of legal kak to me. I thought you said this would get rid of Ryma and her disgusting whelps. Nothing you've shown me so far addresses any of our concerns. As the wife of Maliche Rocker, the power to head up the Assembly is within her authority. Everything you've shown me only verifies her claim."

Nissend Honj's smile grew, and this time his eyes showed a gleam of real malice in them. "All that is true, until you add this final piece to the equation." He gestured to the second shadow, who placed two more documents in his holo-viewer and displayed them to the others.

Nedia studied the documents and lifted her face, staring at her uncle in apparent shock. "This can't be right." She perused them again, looking for something more substantial she may have missed. "How did this escape everyone's attention?" She closed her eyes in thought, putting all of the evidence together. "It's brilliant, Uncle. When looked at as a whole, it presents a strong case. We will finally be rid of that phalking quetzal of a woman and gain our true place in this world once and for all."

"I'm glad you approve, child. We will need a few more days to gather the support from key members of the

Assembly, but then we will strike. And I would like you to have the honor of arresting the usurper and send her off to prison to await trial."

Nedia bowed her head in a sign of respect. "It would be my pleasure, Uncle. Send me word when you are ready and I will see justice done."

After another hour of arranging the specific details of how to arrange Ryma's arrest and imprisonment, Nedia stood, snatched another califf with her talons and prepared to leave the meeting room, now lit by the illuminated wall panels and ceiling, giving the windows the appearance of dark gaping holes into the night.

"Farewell, Uncle. I will await your word. I pray you find our allies quickly."

"One last item, Nedia." Nissend's voice lowered and Nedia felt a sudden chill shoot up her spine. She turned to face him again, struggling to control the growing fear in her gut.

"What is it, Uncle?"

"I understand you and Ryma had a lengthy conversation a few days ago. My sources tell me you seemed terribly shaken afterward. Has anything happened I need to be aware of?"

Her knees nearly collapsed under her, but she maintained control and a steady gaze. "No, Uncle. As I told you, my tolerance of that hateful woman is at an end. It is all I can do to control my temper around her. She wanted to talk again about how brave I was during the bombing attempt in the royal audience chamber and during our ordeal in the caves, and how much she relies on my advice. It was all I could do to maintain my sanity. The way she fawns over me makes me sick to my stomach. The rest of the day I was fuming over it and not myself." She kept her clasped hands behind her back, tapping one talon on a knuckle to help calm herself.

His eyes narrowed as he studied her for what felt like a month. Finally, his glare relaxed and the smile appeared again. At least his mouth smiled. "Alright, but you must be careful. We cannot afford any of them becoming suspicious this close to our imminent victory."

"I know, Uncle. The knowledge of our approaching triumph will sustain me now. Have no fear." She turned on her heels and pushed through the opaque doorway, fighting the urge to run down the hall. *I'll show them all before this is done. They'll regret ever knowing my name before I'm through with them.*

As soon as the door closed behind his niece, Nissend Honj tapped a different code into the vidcom panel and waited as the head of his security team came into focus. "Any further word on what happened to the bomb you placed in Ryma's mag-lev? You said it was foolproof."

"No, sir. Nothing at all. One of my team went to recover the device after they returned from the vineyard, but it was missing."

"Missing? How could that have happened? Did they discover it?"

"No, sir, we don't think they discovered it. There have been no inquiries, or any sign of there being anything out of the ordinary. Our best guess is that it was dislodged and damaged somehow on one of the back roads. Some of them can be very rough. I've sent teams out to try to locate any remains of the device, but so far, nothing to report."

Nissend Honj's face and crest reddened, his fist tightening as he leaned on the table, glaring at the holographic face. "Let me know as soon as you find anything." He passed one hand over the controls and cut the image off in mid-response.

***

Nedia returned to her quarters in the Assembly complex. As she faced the security panel for facial recognition entry, she heard squeals of laughter emanating from inside. As soon as the door slid open, she rushed inside to find her children, Kinev and Ajon, screaming and leaping from a padded sofa in the living room area onto Rilo, pounding her with pillows. Rilo, in between fits of laughter, growled at the children as if she were a fierce beast defending itself. She slowly succumbed to the attack and rolled onto her back, feet and arms sprawled, tongue lolling from one side of her mouth, eyes closed. Kinev, the eldest for all of his nine years, raised his pillow in triumph and let out a victory yell. Ajon, his little sister, joined in the howl and the two began dancing around Rilo's prone body.

"What in the name of The Eternal is going on here?" Nedia stood open-mouthed and wide-eyed just inside the entry.

Rilo opened her eyes, and jumped to her feet, straightening her short black hair and tugging on the tanned trousers and vest she wore when not on official duty. "Nedia! We did not expect you back so soon. I was teaching the children a game I played as a child. They seemed to enjoy it very much." She gestured toward the suddenly quiet pair who were also attempting to make themselves presentable for their mother.

Dropping to her knees and opening her arms wide to gather her beloved children to her, she continued to gape at the room's destruction. "I can see that, but what happened here? It looks like a war zone."

"Oh Mother, we were hunting a grendel!" Kinev brandished his pillow weapon and demonstrated his skill at its use, nearly toppling all three to the ground in the process.

Ajon, breathing heavy in her excitement, joined in the explanation, waving her arms wildly between Rilo, Kinev, and the room in general. "And we killed it! We are warriors, Mother! We played Kolandi warriors hunting the grendel beast!"

Nedia looked up at Rilo, eyes narrowed and her mouth halfway between a smirk and anger. "Hunting a grendel?"

Rilo, running her fingers through her hair to untangle the mess, shrugged. "I apologize if you think the game was inappropriate." She glanced around the disheveled room and bent to pick up a chair that had fallen over. "Do not worry; I will clean up this mess before I leave… Perhaps with some help from the mighty warriors?" She smiled at the two children who rushed back to her and began picking up the mess they helped create.

When the room was returned to its presentable self, Rilo gave it one final examination and nodded in approval. She patted Kinev and Ajon on the head. "Well done, mighty hunters. Always remember there is great responsibility that goes with such skills. A warrior never lets others clean his or her weapons or dress his kill. And only the most foolish ones ever try to have others clean up after them. Time for me to leave now."

"No! You have to read us a bedtime story. You promised." Ajon threw herself around Rilo's leg.

Grabbing her hand, Kinev pulled Rilo toward their bedrooms. "Yes, you promised. You said warriors always keep their promises."

Nedia sighed out loud, rolled her eyes at Rilo, and threw her hands in the air, laughing in surrender. "Alright. Go ahead."

As soon as the trio vanished into the sleeping section of the quarters, Nedia kicked off her shoes and padded to the kitchen. Pulling two goblets from the cabinet and a bottle of wine from the chiller, she returned to the main room and plopped herself on one side of the sofa. *What am I doing?* Her mind wandered over the events of her life, the choices she had made. Pouring herself some of the wine, she sat back and lost herself in self-reflection until jolted out her reverie by Rilo's return.

"I apologize for the mess. I will leave you now, but there are others posted nearby for your safety, just in case."

Nedia patted the sofa next to her. "No need to leave yet. If you have the time, I would like to thank you for your help in protecting my children when I am not here. Do you drink wine?"

Rilo stood still, watching Nedia before joining her on the sofa. "I am not on duty now, so I will have a small taste of the wine. Thank you." She poured herself a half glass and relaxed back into the cushions. "Your children are very nice. I enjoy my time with them."

Nedia chuckled. "They definitely seem to enjoy your company and your games. I've never seen them take to a stranger so quickly. Do you have any children of your own?"

Rilo's face tightened. "I am Skatak. My duty is to Princess Ryma. There is no time for a family. My Skatak sisters are my family."

"Too bad. You would have made an excellent mother. Better than I have been, at least. I've made so many mistakes over the years." She swirled the last of the wine in her goblet and downed it in one gulp before reaching for the bottle and a refill.

Rilo sipped her glass and studied Nedia over the rim. "You are still young. There is time to repair any damage from your past and make a new life for yourself and your little ones. No one is without regrets. It is our duty to learn from our mistakes and not make the same mistakes again. All warriors know this truth."

Nedia lost herself in her silent thoughts again, then sat up, set her glass on the table next to the bottle and scooted herself to face Rilo. "Tell me more about yourself and your people. I need to know I'm on the right path before I talk with Ryma again."

Only when the red glow of predawn crept through the windows into the room did Rilo and Nedia finish their conversation. Both stood, and with tear-stained cheeks, hugged and said their goodbyes.

***

Four days later, as Ryma finished her morning meal and prepared to attend to the morning petitions, Rilo, Kitae, and Danet entered her chambers in a rush.

"Princess, we must get you to safety. The Brin have ordered your arrest and are here to take you into custody."

Ryma continued to examine her image in the mirror, making slight adjustments as needed. "No, we are not going anywhere. We all knew this was coming and we have prepared for it."

Danet pulled his short spear with the curved blade. "I will die before I let them humiliate you like this. A Kolandi Princess cannot be put in bondage to the Brin or anyone ever again."

The Skatak did not brandish their kitae but held them in a firm grip at their belts.

Ryma's shoulders slumped; her voice softened as she approached Danet and placed a gentle hand on his shoulder. "I forbid you to do any such thing, Danet. We must let the Brin evil run its course. If we draw their blood again, we will surely lose this battle. Have faith."

Danet's eyes pleaded with his princess. "How can you expect us to have faith? Since Maliche left, they have done nothing but try to eliminate us. If they had their way, we would be slaves in the mines again. I will not allow them to take you."

Taking both his shoulders, she turned him to face him directly. "Danet, you and the others," she glanced sidelong at her Skatak protectors, "will do as I say. I know this is difficult, but we have discussed this and you know we have friends and allies among the Brin. We will prevail in this as we have in the past. Now put your weapon away and stand back. Do not interfere in any way."

He stiffened for a moment, then sagged as if a tremendous weight had landed on his back. He lowered his head and moved to stand between Rilo and Kitae.

Rilo placed a hand on Danet's arm to steady him and fought to control her voice. "Are you sure about this, my princess? Can we trust Nedia to keep her promise?"

"Yes, I trust Nedia with my life now. I believe her love of her children is stronger than her ties to her family, especially those who would not hesitate to kill her if it meant destroying us."

At that moment, the door to Ryma's personal chambers slammed open. Six armed Brin soldiers in full battle armor stormed into the room, pointing their laser rifles at her and her protectors. Their leader, older than the others, his formal uniform decorated with several dozen campaign ribbons and medals, stepped into the room behind them and stood in front of Ryma. "By order of the Assembly, you are under arrest for falsification of official government documents, usurping a position of authority in the Assembly and sedition. You will come with us immediately, to be placed in a secure facility until your trial."

"Of course, captain. There is no call for you to fear any difficulty from my guardians. None of us will resist you." She threaded her way through the soldiers and led them out the door. Only when they were safely in the mag-lift and on the way to the ground level, did the soldiers shoulder their rifles.

Throngs of Brin and Kolandi alike stopped and gaped at the march of shame through the main lobby of the building. As the entry doors slid open, the bite of a freezing wind stung her face as hordes of reporters and at least two dozen hover-cams crowded around the soldiers with Ryma at their center. So many questions were shouted at once that it was impossible to understand any one of them. As Ryma surveyed the chaotic scene, she saw to her left the smiling face of Nissend Honj, standing on the steps, as she passed. He tilted his head and looked to his right, signaling her to follow his gaze. There, standing at his side and also smiling, stood Nedia. As Ryma watched, Nissend took Nedia's talons in his and raised them to his lips where he planted a kiss on her fingers, never taking his eyes from Ryma.

Ryma stumbled on the steps as she saw the pair. Strong arms of the soldiers escorting her kept her upright and moving until they shoved her into a waiting armored transport. The sound of an increasingly angry crowd came to her through the darkened windows as the vehicle lifted off.

Nissend Honj gave Nedia's hand an extra squeeze as he watched the vehicle fly off to the east and disappear in a low cloud bank. "Well done, Nedia. I knew we could count on your cooperation. You played your part well. It looks like she never suspected a thing."

Nedia continued to stare at the sky where Ryma had vanished. "Thank you, Uncle. You know I would do anything for my family."

As the crowd dispersed, Nissend and Nedia walked together down the steps and across the way to a well-manicured park. Without their leaves, the stark trees gave a haunting beauty to the park, and allowed the statuary to become the centerpiece for visitors.

"There are some in the family who suspected you would cause us problems. Your long association with those Kolandi may have corrupted you, in their minds."

"I hope this puts them at ease." She paused and looked up into her uncle's wrinkled face. "I, for one, would never betray any member of my family. How many times do I have to demonstrate what I am capable of when anyone, including ones I once loved, show they do not share my loyalty?"

"You have nothing to fear now, child. You have proven your loyalty."

"More than most, Uncle, more than most." She reclaimed her hand and took a different path back to her private quarters.

***

Stripped of her gown, jewels, and Kolandi tiara, Ryma dressed herself in the long grey prison dress issued to her by the lone female Brin guard assigned to process the new inmate. "Hurry up, princess. We don't have time to waste on any royal treatment here." She gave Ryma a shove in the midst of buttoning up the front of the threadbare outfit.

Flickering greenish-yellow lights cast a sickening quality to everything in view. Cold white tile floors and plasti-formed walls surrounded them as the woman led Ryma down a hallway and through a security door into the prison itself.

"Hey pretty, pretty… what you in for?"

"Want some company on your first night?

"C'mere and give us a kiss, sweetheart."

All manner of rude, suggestive comments and gestures followed the pair as they passed through the common room. Two more security doors gave them access to the section containing Ryma's cell. A pass of the guard's badge turned off the force grid. The woman shoved Ryma into the square cell and re-engaged the barrier. A thin mattress with an equally thin blanket was rolled up in one corner, no frame for a bed in sight. A plasti-formed toilet and sink stuck out from the back wall. No window or light panels to provide illumination except what the hallway provided. Ryma sighed, unrolled the mattress, placed the blanket around her shoulders, and sat cross-legged, eyes closed.

"Dinner is at five and lights out at nine. Don't go nowhere, sweetheart. I hear tell your trial is in two days.

We wouldn't want you to get lost and disappoint everyone." The guard laughed at her own joke as she strolled back down the section to her post.

Chapter Fourteen

Seriph appeared as a jewel against the blackness of space. Bright blue oceans speckled with brilliant white clouds covered half the planet. Five large continents covered the remaining half, three in the southern hemisphere, and two in the northern. An unusually large rocky planet, one hundred-twenty thousand kilometers in diameter, it also had a retrograde rotation to the other planets in the Skae home system. From the surface, the sun would rise in the west and set in the east. Only one moon orbited the planet, all the others having been cannibalized for their minerals over several millennia, resulting in a series of faint rings surrounding the planet. On the night side, the continents and many artificial islands sparkled with the lights of an immense population, providing easy identification of the land masses from space. Only viewing the planet through cosmic string sensors revealed Seriph's most unique feature. The multi-colored flow of thousands of interconnecting string fields surrounded the world, protecting it.

"Any transmissions from that moon?" Jontar entered the control room and took his seat in front of the main viewport, next to Maliche's command chair.

"Yes. We're trying to pinpoint their location now. I can't make out what they are saying just yet; it does not appear to be a standard Skae wavelength or language, and it's contained in a very tight, direct beam to a large structure in their capitol city. Not like any other type of communication I've ever encountered." Yalmut, focused on his panel, continued to adjust controls without looking up.

"I thought you said you visited Seriph before you returned to our present time. How could you have missed something so strong?"

Jontar shrugged, tapping his stubby talons on his chin. "The moon was on the far side of the planet during our visit. We only stayed a few hours in synchronous orbit over the capitol. Such a tight beam transmission would have been undetectable from our location there."

"It's so beautiful. Such incredible music." Thyka sat entranced at her station, eyes closed, head tilted a bit as she listened to the cosmic strings. Her mother huddled close, stroking her daughter's head.

Nalot watched his daughter, muscles taut and ready to jump to her aid at the slightest sign of trouble. "Jontar, are you sure she's not in any danger?"

Jontar turned his attention to Thyka as well, smiling as he observed her joy. "Sometimes I envy her. Knowing what we are about to attempt, it might be nice to hear that music. The energy emanating from so many the strings sets my nerves on edge."

"I can hear it, but I don't understand what I'm listening to." Yalmut punched the switch to put the translated transmission on ship-wide speaker. A high-pitched, melodic voice filled the air, sounding more like the messenger was singing rather than speaking.

"… facilities to produce more transparent aluminum must be protected in sector thirty-seven. Deploy four ships to them at once. Evening services will be conducted as usual, expect Modi Shatal to conduct the worship. Next transmission at dawn. Sanctifications to all the truthful."

"Female? Since when did Skae females give orders? Come to think of it, have we ever actually met a Skae female?" Duvar swung his chair around to face Maliche and Jontar, scratching his crest.

A violet glow surrounded Maliche, freezing his muscles like he was caught in a full-body vise. His heart and breathing rate soared *"Sorry about this, but centuries-old data is being awakened. It's all I can manage to not shut down completely. I'm sending Jontar a signal to see if he can help alleviate the pressure."*

"Yalmut, Duvar, join with me. We need to provide help so Tol can sort out some new data he is downloading." Jontar mind linked with his friends within seconds of hearing Tol's call for help.

Thyka's mind burst into the link. *"Let me help. I'm sensing something strange about all this. I might catch something you would miss."* Her expression went blank as she melded with the others.

Minutes later, Maliche's violet glow melted away and his vital signs returned to normal, or at least what would be normal after experiencing a trauma like that.

"Are you all right, Maliche? What happened?" Nalot grabbed Maliche just as he was about to slump out of his chair, nearly unconscious.

Regaining his strength quickly, with Tol's assistance, Maliche brushed Nalot aside. "I feel better now. Something happened to Tol, I'm not sure yet exactly what it was, but I've never felt anything like it before, and I don't think he has either."

"It was the Modiri. Their signal woke up something hidden deep in Tol's programming, something they never wanted him to know." Thyka held Seykel's arm to steady herself as she made her way to Maliche. Touching her hand to his temple, Thyka smiled. "He's better now, but he needs some time to adjust to the new data."

Jontar, Yalmut, and Duvar shot quick glances and shrugs at each other before turning their attention to Thyka. "Who, or what, are the Modiri? None of us felt anything beyond the extreme power load. We were so busy distributing the energy flows we didn't have time to listen."

Thyka reached over and patted Jontar on the cheek. "I don't think you could have, even if you tried. The message was buried and protected by forces I've never seen before either, but by letting you three focus on the energy levels, I was able to concentrate on the message itself. Whoever is sending the message has amazing strength with more power than I've felt before." She gave Jontar a wicked smile and winked. "Besides, you wouldn't have known what to look for."

"That's all incredibly interesting, but what the phalk are Modiri?" Maliche held the arms of his chair in an iron grip, along with his temper.

Thyka returned to her station and hopped up into the seat; she closed her eyes and cupped her chin in her hands, elbows resting on her knees as she appeared to struggle with her thoughts. "I'm not exactly sure. I get an impression that they are the true power behind the Skae, almost god-like in the sense of reverence I feel in Tol's programming and that brief message."

"Like some sort of religious order? But you said they're female. It's the Skae males who are in charge, and they don't have any religion." Maliche rubbed the back of his neck as his thoughts whirled.

"I think we have learned enough to be very cautious about what we think we know about anything with the Skae. And no… it's not a religious faith, exactly. It's more than that. Much more… But I will have to connect directly with the strings and the signals coming from the moon to figure out exactly what is going on."

Seykel jumped to her feet, hands on hips as she glared at her daughter. "Not on your life, young lady. After what just happened here, there's no way I will permit you to do any such thing again. At least not until we know you'll be safe."

"Mother, I'm not a child any more. I passed the age of primacy two years ago and am a full Tolvaran. You cannot…."

Nalot stood behind her, and reached around Seykel, taking her in a gentle embrace. "As much as it pains me, she's right. Thyka is her own person now, my love, and beyond having to obey us. We raised her to be a strong, independent young woman, and now we must let go. She has tough roots, now she must be allowed to test her wings."

"She is still my daughter." Seykel struggled slightly in Nalot's arms, but quickly gave up.

Thyka hopped out of her chair and joined her parent's in their embrace. "And I always will be, but I must be myself as well. I have gifts and can make a difference to both our peoples. You raised me well. Trust in me now."

***

Hours later, the ship approached Seriph's moon. The decision to try contacting whoever was on the moon before flying down to the Skae capitol was unanimous. Whoever lived there was in control of more power than they had ever witnessed among the Skae.

"Is everyone ready?" Maliche sat watching as the small golden orb rose over the planet's rim, flickering slightly as they viewed it through Seriph's atmosphere.

"As ready as we'll ever be. We all know our responsibilities. All stealth protections hiding us from the planet are in place. Send the signal." Jontar glanced around the command room at the tense faces of his shipmates. Everyone was ready at their posts, except for Nalot and Seykel, who held each other as they stood near Thyka.

"Sending signal now." Maliche touched his controls with a single talon and began his communication. "To the inhabitants of the moon orbiting Seriph. We are travelers from the planet Kodut. We have come to you on a peaceful diplomatic mission and wish to open negotiations. Please respond."

Static poured from the speakers. Jontar and Yalmut adjusted their controls after a brief mental exchange. "Thyka, any changes in their transmission to the planet?"

Thyka sat with closed eyes and furrowed brow. "Nothing yet. The ones sending that transmission may not be the same ones receiving our signal, if anyone is."

After a few more adjustments, Jontar nodded toward Maliche. "Try again."

Maliche shifted in his chair as he touched the controls again. "To the inhabitants of the moon orbiting the planet Seriph, we are a diplomatic envoy from…"

Thyka's eyes shot open, her back stiffened suddenly as she shouted to the others. "Get out of here! They are terribly angry and…"

Maliche saw a flash of intensely bright light, felt himself lose control and start to keel over before total darkness filled his mind and he slipped into oblivion.

***

His return to consciousness began with an annoying buzz in his ears. As his mind cleared, Maliche noticed the buzz discerning itself into voices, and a soft grey light grew behind his eyelids. A breathy moan escaped his lips.

"Aahh, he awakes. Contact Lyrith at once." The voice sounded more like a musical instrument, similar to a flute, than an actual voice. A cool, gentle hand touched Maliche's forehead.

Unable to speak, Maliche tried to mentally contact Tol but found only emptiness. He frantically searched for any sign of his computer friend and soon realized it was not so much emptiness as a barrier he felt, one he could not penetrate, but felt Tol was behind it.

"How are the patient's vital signs?" The second voice, almost identical to the first, but with a slightly different tonal quality, created a sudden flurry of activity in the room.

"Here are the readings, Lyrith. This one is called Maliche Rocker. The records onboard his vessel indicates he is a descendant of those original creatures we used to attempt eradication of the Gorvin virus from the Kolandi race."

"I see. That would explain the bioimplant, but what about the modifications?"

A series of quick clicks and mutterings followed, as if the two were studying some information.

"Yes, that would do it… And the others? The three young males show signs of unusual cortex activity unlike anything I've seen in anything from their planet. And the female, the younger one, shows even more remarkable activity. It's like she is a poor copy of our own cerebral synaptic impulses."

"We are not certain, Lyrith, but the readings seem to indicate a relationship between this one's bioimplant and the cerebral activity of the others, including the female. It is very curious."

"I think it is time we began our interrogation of this Maliche Rocker. Will you prepare the equipment?"

"Yes Lyrith."

Maliche felt a cold tingle on his scalp, chest, arms, and legs as he felt himself begin to float in a thick, gel-like substance. The light beyond his eyelids dimmed and brightened as he heard something hover into place above him.

"The sensors are in place and recording, Lyrith. We are ready to proceed."

"Very well. You may remove his vision protection. I think he is recovering sufficiently to make them unnecessary any longer."

Maliche winced as a stab of brilliant white light assaulted his eyes, but the pain quickly subsided as his vision adjusted. Opening his eyes, he looked up into the face of his captor. Her flawless light blue skin practically glowed in the soft light of what he judged to be some sort of hospital room. She wore a long flowing gown of nearly transparent, golden shimmering fabric he could not identify. Her large dark blue eyes, slightly tilted at the outer edge, were shaded by long, thick black lashes, the only hair he could see on her body. Her long, slender appendages moved with the grace worthy of a professional dancer or elite athlete.

The room itself hummed with panels of computer readouts. Holographic images of his body shifted between views of his various systems, each with a new set of data numbers hovering alongside. The light in the room seemed to emanate from everywhere at once. No light panels or source of any kind was visible.

Floating above him, he saw a series of five semi-circular devices with arrays of lights and displays humming quietly. Tilting his head, he could see the transparent container he occupied. A glistening, flowing substance supported him, like lying on cold, thick honey.

"Be calm, Maliche Rocker. This interrogation will not take long and will not cause you any physical discomfort. We must determine how you discovered our existence and whether you and your companions are any threat to us. You will not be able to speak. Our paralytic will wear off soon with no lingering effects. The gel contains sensor nanobots which will detect neural impulses and feed the information to our computers." She placed a soft, warm hand on his chest, closed her eyes, and a slight tingle in Maliche's mind grew to a very annoying itch.

As he watched, the panels jumped into activity. Data sets flashed across the screens. The holographic image of his body alternated between several shades of blues, greens, and yellows. The scan of his brain suddenly turned a bright blue.

"Oh, my goodness, this is an unexpected turn of events."

"Tol, you're alive. I thought these women did something to you."

Tol laughed in his mind. "Oh, they did. The experience was absolutely amazing."

"Are you alright? Did they harm you?"

"No, my friend, I am not compromised in any way. Their probes detected the signature of my ancient Skae programming, so they scanned my files, or at least the oldest, most basic files I let them see. While they were occupied, I gained access to their system and learned how to fully protect my true nature from them. Once I secured myself, I started a conversation with them."

Maliche almost shouted in his head. "You did what?"

"Don't get yourself into a snit, now. I was in complete control and beyond their reach. They were afraid at first, but now they want to learn as much as they can. They are very curious about my sentience. I don't think they've ever seen anything like me before, or our friends, for that matter."

"Our friends? Where are they? Is everyone alright?"

"Everyone is safe and unharmed. As soon as Lyrith here was convinced I was no threat and released me from my confinement I reached out to Jontar and the others. These Modiri have blocked access to their computer systems. Their encryptions are very sophisticated, but I will have them cracked before long. I don't think they realize our ability to communicate telepathically, at least not yet. I also made sure to shield almost all of my newly-acquired higher functions from them. They never suspected how much I have grown since they implanted me in Karm, so they are only treating me like a curiosity. I want to keep it that way."

Maliche let out a sigh, and noticed his scans turn a shade of turquoise and then vanish.

"We are finished." Lyrith's resonant flute-like voice sang in his ears. "We have removed our security precautions around your implant, now that our computer systems are safeguarded. We will remove the nano-gel and leave you to rest for a few hours."

His voice scraped like grit paper in his throat as he tried to talk. "Where are my friends? I demand to see them right now."

A riff of what must be laughter filled the room. "You demand? If you were not an alien recovering from our paralytic, we would sentence you to expulsion into space for such insolence, but I will grant you your ignorance for now. Do not make the same error in the future. We will decide your fate soon enough. Rest now." Lyrith's gown swished softly as her long thin legs glided her across the room and through the glimmering force shield in the doorway.

Jontar's mental voice intruded on Maliche's confused thoughts. *"Father, are you alright? Tol says you are unharmed, but we haven't heard from you."*

"Yes, I'm okay. Those women who captured us, what did Tol call them? Modiri? They just left, so I can talk now. Are the rest of you together and safe?"

"Yalmut and Duvar are with me. We're safe, for now I think, but it may take us some time to infiltrate their systems to learn more. They have some pretty sophisticated security protections. Nothing we can't crack with a little more time, though, especially with Tol's help."

"What about Thyka, Nalot, and Seykel? They're not with you?"

"I've been in touch with Thyka. It seems she is of particular interest to these women. They discovered some of her ability to connect emotionally with the strings, so she is under constant study."

"Studying her? Is she being hurt? What about Nalot and Seykel?"

"She says she is fine and they aren't mistreating her. She seems to think these Modiri consider her something of a kindred sister or something. They apparently have a similar ability when connecting to the strings. She's trying to learn as much as she can. I don't know about Nalot or Seykel, yet. As soon as we can penetrate the security protocols they'll be my first priority."

***

Keeping track of time without Tol's computer mind would have been impossible in the unchanging light of the room where the Modiri kept Maliche strapped to his bed. Two days passed, filled with a constant barrage of mind-probing tests and questions from a series of Modiri women. Regular updates from Jontar proved frustrating as they encountered greater difficulty than anticipated gaining access to the computer systems. On the third day, Maliche recognized the woman who seemed to be in charge of the facility as she swished into the room again and approached him, smiling.

"Good day, Maliche Rocker. We hope you are well." Before he could reply, she continued as if talking with a favorite pet. "Our tests are complete and we will now release your restraints, but you must promise to remain calm and not resist us. No harm will come to you or your companions if you cooperate." The blue-tinged woman flicked her long thin fingers over a control panel and Maliche felt the field keeping him confined vanish.

Maliche rotated his shoulders as he sat up, and stretched his arms and legs to get the blood flowing again and work out the stiffness of three days being held captive on the bed. "We are here on a diplomatic mission from my home world, Kodut. We have no intention of causing you any difficulties. When may we speak with your leaders?"

"Follow me, Maliche Rocker. I will bring you to the others." The woman acted as if he had not spoken, and simply led the way out of the room and down the brightly-lit silvery hall.

Maliche increased his pace to keep up with the much taller woman and tried again to talk with her. "We are Brin and Kolandi from the planet Kodut. As allies with the Skae, we might have expected better treatment upon our arrival. But as I said, we are on a diplomatic mission for our leaders and wish to talk with those in command here and on Seriph. Will you pass along our desire for a meeting?"

The Modiri halted in front of an opaque energy field in the wall. "These are the quarters assigned to you and your companions. Do not attempt to enter or leave without one of us to escort you. The portal field will prevent passage and you could potentially be harmed if you come into prolonged contact with it. We will return when we wish to communicate further." She passed her fingers lightly over a control panel in the wall next to the field and it shimmered to near transparency as she signaled for Maliche to enter.

Stepping across the threshold, Maliche felt a tingle and, as the room beyond came into focus, he smiled to see everyone but Thyka present and apparently unharmed. The energy field returned to full strength as soon as he was clear.

Before they could complete all the greetings and exchange of information, before they could start to discuss the problems ahead, the entry way thinned again, and Thyka entered. Rushing to embrace her mother and father, she reached out to include the others. "They almost would not let me rejoin all of you here. Apparently, they consider me as the important one in our group and something on the order of royalty. Not as high as they themselves, but along the lines of a lesser noble. It took a long time to convince them of my sincere desire to be in the same rooms as all of you. They are a very peculiar group."

Maliche stepped back and took her chin in his talons. "They didn't hurt you in any way, did they?"

She laughed a little as she patted his hand, removing it from her face. "No. Quite the opposite, in fact. Their questions were exhausting, and they made every effort to make me as comfortable as possible. After their tests revealed some of my abilities, anyway. They were surprised to find one with my ability to feel the emotions of the strings. They had thought they were the only ones who were capable of that sort of connection. Apparently, even the Skae males cannot sense the strings like that, if at all. The men rely mostly on their technology to connect and travel by string."

Seykel twirled Thyka around to face her, hands firmly on her shoulders. "Wait. How did you learn all of this? They barely even talked to me or your father. Apparently they didn't even test us like they did the rest of you, either."

"Of course not, Mother. You and Father don't have our abilities. They lost interest in the two of you almost immediately."

Seykel's eyes narrowed, her posture giving every impression of a predator about to attack. "I'll show them some of my abilities the first chance I get. Let's see how impressed they are with an angry Skatak in their midst."

"Easy, my love," Nalot pulled Seykel into his arms and caressed her back. "Perhaps it would be best to let them learn about you when they least expect it. When we need you most to escape from here."

"Wait," interrupted Jontar. "They actually talked *with* you? Were you able to learn anything about them? The rest of us were no more than laboratory specimens to them."

Thyka gathered her thoughts as she stepped toward a nearby chair and sat down. "I need more information to be sure, but I think these Modiri are, as I suspected, the true rulers of the Skae. Whenever they mention the Skae, I felt the Modiri considered them a lower class of being. As much as the Skae treat the rest of the galaxy as beneath them, these women treat the Skae as underlings. The way they talked made me think they believe we have a similar relationship. I didn't discourage them in that. It helped them open up toward me and drop their guard to think I was a kindred spirit among lesser beings."

Thyka explained to the others that the Modiri had a hierarchy of their own. "Their moon, called Seriph Major, is forbidden to all except the Modiri and those few chosen male Skae they use as servants or liaisons to the planet below. The acolytes are the youngest of the priestesses and do most of the manual labor. Those who performed all the examinations and other functions requiring advanced training and greater skill are known as prelates and are the predominant group. Those in charge are the actual Modiri. Only the most advanced prelates, those with enough training to ascend higher, ever see or communicate directly with the Modiri."

Maliche rubbed his crest as he listened. "No wonder they treated me like a hologram. They didn't consider me worth the effort. It was Tol that piqued their interest. This could work to our advantage. Can you arrange another meeting with them?"

"I'll try. What did you have in mind?"

***

As evening approached, the entry to their rooms thinned again and one of the acolytes entered with food trays. She placed the assortment of colorful gels and drinks on a low table and turned to leave. Taking on an air of authority, Thyka called to the acolyte before she could exit. "I wish another audience with the prelates. You will take us to them immediately."

Lowering her eyes to the floor and assuming a completely subordinate posture, the girl stopped. "All of you, prelate?"

Thyka's face grew dark as she straightened herself, still only reaching the girl's breasts in height. "Are you questioning me, acolyte? Perhaps I should report your insolence to your teachers?"

Visibly shaking, the girl fell to her knees, arms raised in supplication. "Forgive me, prelate. I meant no disrespect. I will take you to them immediately."

"Then waste no more of my time." Turning to the others, she gave an impatient wave to follow. "All of you keep up and do not delay us any further. I have much to do here."

Gaping at each other with open mouths, the group quickly jumped to follow Thyka out of the room. The group proceeded down the passage, a continuous silvery, unwavering and undecorated hallway bathed in light, which seemed to emanate from everywhere at once, until they arrived at a large entry protected by the usual energy field.

"This is the hall of the prelates. I am forbidden from entering, but you will find others inside who will provide all the assistance you will require." The girl trembled in even greater fear as she stood before the entry.

"Very well. Now I require you to take these two to a communication center. I must send a message to my world so they will know I have arrived and am ready to commence with my mission."

Her shaking ceased instantly, but was replaced with wide-eyed, open-mouthed shock. "But they are men. They cannot be allowed to…"

Thyka's glare could have cut through transparent magnesium. "This is most unacceptable. I have no choice but to report your continued insolence to the first prelate I meet inside. Perhaps they can discipline you sufficiently to not question your superiors again."

Dropping to her knees again, the girl pleaded, "Please, mistress, I am unfamiliar with your customs. Forgive my ignorance."

Tapping her feet, hands on hips, Thyka let her glare gradually subside. "I swear I am too forgiving. All right, stand and do as you are commanded without further delay. And open the energy field so the rest of us may enter."

Turning to Jontar and Yalmut, she scowled and shook a finger at them. "You had better not pick up any bad habits while we are here. Send my message and return to us here as soon as you are done. Am I clear?" She included the acolyte in her gaze indicating she was expected to escort the pair every step of the way.

A nod of their heads, their eyes downcast, indicated their understanding and the three headed off toward the communication center as soon as the acolyte opened the energy field.

As Jontar and Yalmut meekly followed the young acolyte, Jontar cast a mental jibe back at Thyka.

"You seem to be enjoying this role far too much, Young lady." Yalmut's mental laughter filled the background.

"Yes," she replied without any external reaction. "This new level of authority seems to suit me well. Don't you agree?" A playful tickle of mental energy pricked at Jontar's emotional centers.

Upon entering the prelate's hall, Thyka recognized one of those she had talked with earlier, named Zephyl, and signaled for her attention. As they approached the woman, her initial shock at seeing the entourage vanished quickly behind an impassive appearance. Thyka began her cover story.

"I realize this must seem very irregular to you, but we on Kodut are not as advanced with our control over everything as you are here. Our Modiri, we call them Tolavar, have only begun to gain power recently. The devastation of our world by the Gorvin," she wiped her face in a sign of disgust as she said the name, "nearly exterminated us, and the Brin held sway over us until we were able to regain our freedom. We still must rely on the expertise of Brin and Kolandi males and females, until we can come into our own."

Zephyl relaxed and nodded in agreement. Her sing-song voice trilled as if flying high above in the silver- and gold-domed hall. "Of course. We are happy our Kolandi allies have rejoined us in our righteous struggle against the enemy. We understand your need to rely on such as them." She waved a hand in the direction of the others. "We will make accommodations for your customs. But where are the others? I understood there were seven of you."

"They will rejoin us soon. I required one of your acolytes to deliver them to a communications center to send a message to my superiors advising them of our safe arrival."

Frowning, her mouth twisted slightly, Zephyl clasped her long blue hands behind her back. "That is most irregular and may be difficult to explain. Allowing men to use our equipment, even if in deference to your customs, is strictly forbidden."

"I apologize, Zephyl, but the need was great. They are very skilled and will do no more than relay my message to the ones who will send the actual signal. They should return any minute now. Please forgive my ignorance of your laws. I will seek out your advice in the future."

Jontar's thoughts nearly made her jump as he shouted in her mind. *"That did it! Getting this close to their controls allowed us the access we needed to get past their security. We now have full control, and nobody suspected a thing."*

"It's about time. Get back here as fast as you can. I'm not sure I can keep this prelate here much longer. I'll need your help to control her."

"On our way. The center was only a few meters down the hall from you."

As she strolled through the massive domed hall at Zephyl's side, Thyka reached up and scratched her left ear as a signal to the rest to be ready. She stopped by one of the large frescos on the wall. "These paintings are exquisite. There were no decorations to be seen until we arrived here."

Zephyl smiled and seemed to stand a little straighter. "Those were the prelate quarters. They are not ready for distractions in their studies. This one was created by my grandmother a thousand years ago. I am pleased you appreciate it."

"A thousand years ago? I knew Skae were long-lived, but not like that."

"Your only contact has been with male Skae. We who are destined to become Modiri have much longer spans. Control must be maintained with as few interruptions as possible, so we designed this difference, and thus our separation, long ago, even for us. Aahh, there are your males now."

As soon as Jontar and Yalmut joined them, Thyka took their hands, along with Duvar, and the foursome faced Zephyl, joining their mental forces to invade her mind. As Yalmut and Duvar froze her motor cortex to prevent her collapse, Thyka seized hold of Zephyl's amygdala, the center of emotional control in the brain, and Jontar took control of her cerebral cortex, the center of reason and logic. Within seconds, the pair twisted and manipulated neural pathways to make the prelate compliant with their wishes so she would not only see the logic of their demands, but also feel obeying them was the absolute right thing to do. When they were satisfied everything was securely in place, they pulled out of Zephyl's mind and took hold of her to steady her as Yalmut and Duvar released their hold on her motor cortex.

"Zephyl! You almost fainted!"

"I'm fine," she replied. "Just a dizzy spell. I'm all right now."

As the others took up positions to act if needed, Thyka looked deep into her eyes. "I'm glad, Zephyl. Now I want you to take us to the Modiri. It is vital that we be allowed to talk with them."

Zephyl's face contorted as if struggling with an idea, but quickly relaxed into a smile. "Of course. You must meet with the Modiri. Please let me escort you to them." Gesturing with her arms, she led the way down one of the corridors leading away from the main hall.

Chapter Fifteen

The Modiri gardens were a wonder to behold. Open to the clear blue sky above, displays of intricately-manicured abstract hedge sculptures filled the space with a living museum of unimaginable shapes and designs along every path. "These are unbelievable, such skill to create sculptures of this magnitude. Amazing." Seykel and the rest stared in awe as Zephyl led the group through the maze of trails.

"What is the meaning of this intrusion? Zephyl, you know you are not permitted here unless summoned, and those creatures are certainly not allowed to infect our peace." Tiphan, a high priestess of the Modiri, stalked toward Maliche and his party as they followed Zephyl into the open air gardens. Her golden gown, laced with blue-tinged silver patterns gave the appearance of transparency.

Startled by the sudden appearance of the Modiri from behind them, Thyka, Jontar, and Yalmut quickly recovered and attempted to take control of the woman as they had with Zephyl. Their efforts met with a block so powerful it rebuffed their efforts and nearly dropped them to their knees.

The Modiri's eyes popped wide, but instantly narrowed, her voice like a song of anger. "How dare you invade my mind! Do you think a high priestess is as helpless as a prelate? I should have you…"

Tiphan dropped in an unconscious heap. Seykel stood over her, cracking her knuckles. "That will be quite enough out of you, high priestess."

Maliche slapped Nalot on the back and laughed quietly. "Never underestimate a Skatak, eh, Nalot?"

"I only made that mistake once. I still can't figure out how she managed to do what she did to me, but I've never felt such pain." Nalot rubbed his left arm remembering the incident.

"We've been lucky so far," interrupted Jontar. "We need to see if we can get this one under control while she's still unconscious and before any more Modiri show up. Good thing there are so few of them."

Taking special care to look for any extra abilities to break through their neural alterations, the four Kolbri set to work on Tiphan's emotional and cognitive centers as they had with Zephyl. Moments later they had the Modiri priestess standing and, to all outward appearances, presenting as if nothing were out of the ordinary.

Maliche ran his talons through his crest as he contemplated their next move. While he was thinking, Nalot cleared his throat and lowered his voice to a near-whisper as he scanned the area. "Perhaps we should all go somewhere less conspicuous. We don't want to arouse any suspicions in case another Modiri wanders by. I think we should head back to the prelate areas, maybe a library, where nobody would dare question the presence of one of the high priestesses."

Maliche nodded. "Good idea. Tiphan, would you be so good as to lead us all back to one of the libraries in the prelate sector? We have a very important request to make of you before we leave."

Tiphan did not respond. Her face turned purple as her forehead furrowed as if in extreme concentration. Jontar and Thyka each placed a hand on the woman's temples and closed their eyes. Seconds later, Tiphan's face relaxed, almost to a smile.

"That should be better now. Try telling her again." Jontar and Thyka removed their hands but kept a wary eye on her.

Maliche stood in front of the high priestess and smiled at her. "Tiphan, would you be so kind as to lead us to a library in the prelate sector? We have some important matters to discuss with you before we leave."

Only a brief look of what could be puzzlement crossed her face before she folded her hands and nodded slightly. "Of course. Follow me. I agree that we have important matters to discuss." She took the lead with Zephyl bringing up the rear and led them out of the Modiri gardens back through the energy field leading to the prelate's region.

Any prelates they passed along the way bowed respectfully to the Modiri, only to stop and watch the unusual party continue toward the nearest library. As strange as it was to see a Modiri in the prelate areas, especially in the company of outsiders, and males at that, nobody dared question them. Modiri did as they pleased with impunity. It was not up to a mere prelate to cast any doubt on their actions, no matter how disturbing.

As they entered a library center, Tiphan motioned for the head prelate. "I require the use of this space for a private audience. You will remove all those here at once."

Startled but giving only a passing glance beyond the Modiri at her party, the prelate went quickly to her desk, pressed a few controls to activate the alert system notifying all patrons to leave the center without delay. In three minutes, the prelate had locked the doors behind her and engaged the security field, leaving Tiphan and Zephyl alone with Maliche and the others.

The room looked more like an art gallery than a library. Sculptures large and small, whether cast or carved, displayed a variety of forms from abstract to ultra-realistic in stone, metal, and other materials Maliche had trouble identifying. Paintings, also in a variety of forms and styles, hung from every wall. Holographic designs floated in the air above them. Only the arrays of monitors and control panels spaced throughout the room gave away the true purpose of the facility.

Maliche quickly glanced around the room before turning his attention to the high priestess. "Now, Tiphan, I want to know everything about the Skae's efforts to collapse the double star of the Telphar system. Why would your scientists continue their efforts in the face of all the evidence showing the potential for disaster if they succeed?"

Sweat trickled down Tiphan's face. With jaw muscles so tight it was a miracle she could open her mouth at all, she spat her responses. "Those fools do only as they are commanded. We need the infinite supply of energy the gravity wave generators will create. The Modiri are supreme and must continue to expand. What does it matter if a few other systems are sacrificed?"

"You have fought a war for millenniums, untold trillions of lives have been lost or destroyed, entire sectors laid waste, including your own people, all for the sake of your … what, your empire? Is that all this is? A vain quest for power?"

Nalot interrupted Maliche's interrogation with a raised hand. "You said the Modiri are supreme and must continue. What about the Skae?"

Tiphan laughed; at least the strangled sounds resembled laughter. "The Modiri are supreme. The Skae are hardly worth the effort it takes to breed them, but they are a useful illusion for dealing with outworlders. So long as the Skae are the face we project to the galaxy, we are free to do as we please. If some are lost in the process, well, they are easily replaceable."

Turning to face Maliche, Nalot's face grew dark as a thunderstorm at night. "We've been fighting the wrong enemy. The Skae are nothing more than slaves to these Modiri."

Seykel drew her kital and cocked her arm to let the weapon fly. "Slaves? Any race that enslaves others is not fit to live."

Nalot's quick reflexes, and knowledge of his wife's prejudices against slavery, allowed him to catch her elbow and prevent her attack. "Not now, my warrior woman. We still need to know more before she dies."

Her eyes would have sliced his arm off if looks could accomplish such things. She tried to pull away, but Nalot's grip held her tight. "I will not permit slavery to exist while I can do something to end it."

"And after you kill this one, what then? Will you single-handedly attack and take down all of the Modiri? I don't think that is possible, even for a Skatak with your skills." With his other hand, Nalot tilted her chin up so she looked him in the eyes. "There is a better way to end this."

Seykel's tension melted until she sagged into his chest and replaced the blades on her belt. "Promise me your way will work."

"I promise we will end the Modiris' hold over the Skae and end their threat to the galaxy." His talons caressed her hair as he whispered in her ear.

Maliche sighed in relief. "Now all we need to do is figure out how to do that."

The interrogation continued for another two hours and the light from outside began to fade as night approached. Each member of Maliche's crew took turns questioning their prisoner about the Skae, the Modiri, Seriph, and the distribution of Skae forces throughout this sector, as well as details about their progress toward completing the critical components of their black hole generators and gravitational wave generators.

"Do we have everything we need now?" Maliche swept his gaze around the group, noting the nods and introspection of each member.

"Very well, then. Suggestions for our next move, after we get off this moon?"

Nalot returned his friend's inquiry with an equally stern visage. "I think we are ready to confront the Gorvin now. With what the younglings learned on their time voyage and our new-found intelligence about the Modiri and Skae, we should be able to form some sort of alliance and figure out a way to combine forces to defeat this bunch once and for all."

"My thoughts exactly. Any objections?"

"What do we do about this piece of kupt lepti?" Seykel thrust her chin toward Tiphan, who sat, still held fast by the four Kolbri, but looking as if she would try to kill them all if she were released.

I think we can remove most of her memories of us, or at least help her think she awoke from a bad dream. With her abilities and strength of will, I don't know how long the suggestions will hold, but it certainly should be long enough for us to be well on our way. Tol's voice resonated in Maliche's mind, as his left palm grew warm with the red glow he produced when angry.

Are you sure? We can't afford to have her spread an alarm before we are out of Skae territory.

The red glow turned green briefly. *Trust me. Have I ever let you down before?*

Maliche sighed, then explained Tol's plan to the others. With a nod to the Kolbri youths, a red glow surrounded Maliche and grew to encompass the four youths. Maliche laid his glowing red palms on Tiphan's temples.

***

"Please tell me we never have to invade another mind as diseased as that one." Duvar held his head like he was trying to squeeze the terrible memories out.

Tears streamed down Thyka's cheeks like waterfalls. "I've never felt such an utter disdain for all other life. The Modiri view themselves as goddesses deserving of worship from the Skae and anyone else they encounter. I think I might be sick." She jumped up and ran to the nearest waste receptacle. Seykel caught up to her and held her hair back as she violently retched into the small incinerator. Wisps of acrid smoke rose above her as the contents of her stomach vaporized in the electronic field.

Jontar steadied himself on a table. "Her will is so strong I don't know how long she'll remain out or if she'll be able to break through our alterations to her memories. We need to get out of here now."

Maliche surveyed his companions and shook his head. "In a few minutes. Everyone needs time to recoup after such a powerful ordeal. A band of straggling outworlders would certainly attract attention."

While the others regained their equilibrium, Maliche visited with Zephyl. He had seated her at a nearby table during the interrogation. "Do you know where our ship is being held?"

"Of course. Spaceport Thysh, hanger four." Her eyes stared ahead, unaware.

"How far is that? Can you take us there?"

"Not far. Nothing is far from anywhere here. Yes, I have the proper clearances since I was assigned to you."

"Then you will lead us to our ship. If anyone tries to stop us, you will say you have orders from Modiri Tiphan to escort us there to explain the details of our computer system and how we were able to arrive here unexpectedly. Is that clear?"

"Yes, I understand."

"And if anyone tries to interfere, you will tell them Tiphan is impatient for our return. Any delay will be dealt with harshly. Understand?"

"Yes, I understand."

A few minutes later and with renewed color in their faces, Maliche and the others followed Zephyl out of the library, locking the security field behind them.

The swirling, sparkling towers of Spaceport Thysh rose over the horizon at an astonishing speed. The pneumatic tube express transport carried them at hypersonic speeds inside the transparent magnesium conduit a mile above ground. In half an hour, they traveled nearly a quarter of the way around the circumference of Seriph's moon.

Jontar stared out at the world of the Modiri as they zoomed overhead. "How could we have been so ignorant of all this? Look at those structures. I've never seen engineering like it anywhere."

Vast buildings, impractically swooping and soaring over kilometers of the land below them, filled their view.

"They're more like giant works of art than buildings. I wouldn't want to live in one, but I have to agree they are beautiful. I don't think I see any two windows shaped the same. Why would anyone even conceive of that?" Duvar, equally entranced by the vast cityscape passing by, pressed his forehead against the transparent wall next to him.

Nalot sat holding Seykel and Thyka's hands, staring at his lap. "They can't afford to let anyone know they exist. Everyone thinks the Skae are the real power in the galaxy, but if word ever got out they were pawns in the Modiri conspiracy to control everything, all kak would break loose. Revolts would break out in every sector."

"They would lose all control and never complete their grand experiment." Yalmut leaned back in his seat watching as if nothing were unusual.

"Get ready, everyone. Looks like we're arriving. Try not to…"

"Too late. I think Tiphan is more powerful than we thought. She must have broken our neurolinks and sounded the alarm." Jontar jolted upright, his small talons dancing across their pod's control panel. "Help me out here, Yalmut."

The two Kolbri laid their palms on the panel and concentrated with closed eyes. Lights flashed on and off in rapid sequences too fast to follow. "I think that did it. We've blocked further access to the spaceport's communication center, but we should expect some company when we arrive."

In less than a minute, the pod stopped and with a whoosh of air, equalized the pressure with the outside. A clear panel slid open, allowing the occupants to exit onto an ornately-decorated berth. Walkways led to a half-dozen structures. Approaching them with what could only be described as leisurely haste, two Skae, dressed in red and gold uniforms with a silver emblem on their left chest, held energy rifles, charged and primed but not aimed at them.

Maliche whispered to Zephyl. "Easy now, just as we discussed."

The girl frowned, hands on hips, as she faced the Skae guards. "What is the meaning of this? I have a vital mission from Modiri Tiphan herself to complete here. Stand aside."

The Skae came to attention, shouldering their weapons and bowed to Zephyl. "Prelate, we must respectfully request you and your party accompany us to the security offices. We have received communications from…"

"Did you not hear me? I said Modiri Tiphan has granted permission for us to examine these outworlders' ship. There is vital information they can provide us. Modiri Tiphan will not be pleased with your interference with her commands. Now let us pass."

Bowing again, the Skae did not notice Nalot and Sdykel taking up positions on their flanks. "Again, prelate, we apologize for the delay to your mission. Our orders come from the Modiri as well. We cannot allow you to proceed. Please come with us."

As they reached to unshoulder their weapons, Nalot and Seykel attacked. Driving his foot into the belly of the guard nearest him, Nalot doubled his foe over and delivered a crushing blow, snapping the guard's thin blue neck between his knee and elbow. Meanwhile, Seykel dove behind her opponent and, using moves worthy of a gymnast; she scaled up his body and sliced his throat with her kital. Leaping clear of the blood and collapsing corpse, she landed on her feet. With a satisfied nod, Seykel reached down to wipe the blood off her weapon on the fallen guard's uniform, hung her kital on her belt and straightened her skirt and hair as if she had simply walked in from a blustery day.

"Father! Mother! Was that really necessary? We could have controlled them easily." Thyka covered her eyes with her hands, back turned to the carnage.

"Sometimes the simplest way is best, Daughter." Nalot grabbed his foe and dragged him behind one of the artistic displays, of some sort of animal, maybe; he had no sense for abstract forms. "Yalmut, Duvar, hide the other one and grab his weapon. We may need it soon."

Scowling at the trail of blood leading behind another of the sculptures, Maliche shook his head. "Not much we can do about that now. Let's get moving before any more show up. Did any of you discover where the Amaethon is docked?"

Yalmut raised his arm and pointed at the second structure from their right. "In there. I was studying a map of the facility and found it a few minutes before we landed."

Maliche took Zephyl by the shoulders and locked eyes with her. "Zephyl, I want you to go to sleep now. You can wake up in four hours." A yellow glow surrounded the girl and she collapsed in Maliche's arms, fast asleep. He sat her on one of the cushioned seats in the transport pod and rejoined the others, snatched the energy rifle from Seykel and led the way to their spacecraft.

As they reached the hangar, Nalot signaled for them to hang back while he went to survey the area. He was almost laughing when he returned. "I don't know what it is with the Skae, but they never seem to think any more than two of them will be needed for any situation. I found a way for us to get close, but there's still at least twenty meters of open ground surrounding them and the ship."

Maliche motioned for Jontar and Yalmut to get close. "Can you two influence the guards from a distance? Nalot can get us as close as twenty meters."

Jontar shook his head. "Not from that distance. Electronics are one thing; we need to be a lot closer for a living mind. Direct contact is best for something this risky."

"Then we need to flank them and take them out with the rifles." Nalot started to point out favorable positions when he felt a light touch at his arm.

"There are too many openings for you to get there without a distraction. I can provide that for you." Seykel held her kital at the ready.

About to refuse the offer, Nalot noticed the fierceness in her eyes and thought better of trying to dissuade a Skatak from battle. "Agreed. Give us a moment to get into position and create your diversion."

In less than a minute, Nalot and Maliche were ready. Seykel beat her chest twice with a tight fist, stood up and strolled out into the open as if she were at the park on holiday. The guards sprang to attention, leveling their energy rifles, the largest Maliche had ever seen, squarely at Seykel.

"Stop where you are. We have orders to return you to the Modiri. Where are your companions?"

Seykel smiled brightly as she continued her stroll. "Hello. I seem to be lost. I cannot locate my friends anywhere. Have you seen them?"

Fingering the controls of their weapons, a high-pitched whine rose, and a light on the side of the stock turned violet. With the rifles fully charged they raised them to sight in their target. "I repeat, stop where you are. We are to return you to the…"

With a flash of her wrist too fast to follow, Seykel sent her kital flying. A beam of orange light split the air and burst into silver and gold sparks as it connected with the kital in mid-flight. At the same instant, two blasts came from opposite angles and burned into the chests of both Skae guards, dropping them in a heap at the foot of the ship's starboard landing leg.

"Get aboard now!" Maliche waved his arm calling the others to action. Charging around the crates he had used as a shelter, he saw Seykel on her knees, clutching her chest in the middle of the open area, and Nalot racing to her. *Kak, no! Not her!* Maliche's thoughts screamed in his head as he changed direction and ran to his friend. A bright red light shone around him.

"Seykel, talk to me. Where are you hit?" Maliche arrived at the same time as Nalot who pulled his wife into his arms, but unable to speak.

She remained unresponsive, other than soft sobs.

"Nalot, let me help her. Tol might be able to heal her wounds. Let me have her." He struggled with Nalot for an opening to look for where Seykel had taken the hit.

"I… I'm not injured." Her voice was barely audible through the sobs. "Please, just give me a minute."

Nalot seemed to not hear her at all as Maliche searched in vain for any sign of blood or wounds. Relinquishing his efforts, Maliche sat back and preened his crest. "Seykel, what is wrong? I can't find any injuries. We have to get moving. Talk to me."

Seykel raised her stricken face toward her husband, then Maliche. Her arms opened to reveal her kital, broken in two by the impact of the Skae weapon. "This was presented to me by my mother. It was the last time I saw her before she was killed in the Brin raid that took me prisoner."

Nalot, coming to his senses at last, fingered the blades. "I always thought these things were unbreakable."

"They are supposed to be. A Skatak's spirit lies in her kital. They are only broken when the Skatak dies in battle. I have never heard of one being broken before its owner." She clutched at the broken blades again and surrendered to her husband's embrace.

Maliche squeezed Nalot's shoulder and spoke softly. "We need to leave."

Taking a deep breath, Nalot nodded and picked up his diminutive wife as he stood, carrying her into their ship.

Inside, the others were busy starting up all the computers and controls preparing for their departure. Nalot carried Seykel to their berth and shut the hatch behind them. Maliche took his place in the command chair and waited for his crew to complete their jobs. Lights and the hum of energy surging through components filled the air as Amaethon came back to life.

"Ready to take off, Father." Jontar sat in his chair and taloned the controls to set the force restraints.

"Get us out of here as fast as you can." Maliche set the controls for his own force restraints as the ship lurched forward.

"Orbit achieved. Headings, sir?" Yalmut called out from his station.

"Skae battlecruiser closing in fast, Jontar." Duvar sent the image to the main view screen.

"Praise the Eternal the strings are so close to Seriph. We should be able to connect to one right away." Jontar swiveled his chair around to work the String Connection Fields.

"Won't they be able to follow us?" Maliche tugged at his crest feathers as he tried to think of a defense against the immense warship.

"I think I might be able to help with that." Thyka closed her eyes and clasped her hands in her lap.

Jontar called out before Maliche could respond. "Connecting now. Setting controls for maximum speed, minimal time dilation."

A flash of light filled the bridge and all was still.

"We did it. Seventeen parsecs and four days future displacement. No sign of pursuit." Jontar relaxed back into his chair, smiling. "Well done, everyone."

Maliche continued to frown and flicked through his monitors. "Are you sure? What's preventing them from locating the same string we connected to? They could be arriving any second."

Thyka exhaled in a smooth, controlled breath and smiled as she opened her eyes to look at Maliche. "They won't be able to connect to our string. Or any other nearby."

"How would you know that? They could…"

"No, they couldn't. I asked the strings to refuse them passage. They like me, so they agreed, at least for now. We should probably be going, though. Strings can be flighty, so they may forget in a few days."

Chapter Sixteen

"All rise. The hour of judgement has arrived in the case of the state versus Ryma Rocker, accused of high treason. May The Eternal watch over these proceedings." Amplified for the holo-vid camera drones and the beyond-capacity audience, the clerk's voice echoed throughout the main courtroom. Those in attendance rose from their seats in elevated rows circling the chamber below, much like an amphitheater. Spotlights stabbed through the darkness to illuminate the judge's bench, defendant and prosecutor's tables and the witness stand. Most of those in attendance had arrived hours ago to assure themselves a good seat. A mix of perfumes and sweat filled the room, which hadn't been designed to handle the heat from so many visitors. From the back of the room, a door opened, spilling light onto the floor and casting long shadows ahead of the panel of nine judges as they entered and took their seats at the bench.

Just as with Jontar Rocker's trial so many months ago, Judge Haytk took the center chair as lead judge for the Assembly's Court. With a sharp crack of her spherical gavel stone, the proceedings began. Also amplified for all to hear clearly, her voice lifted to the highest rows. "All be seated. The prisoner may be brought before the court for judgement."

A general rustling and muttering could be heard as all eyes turned toward the door leading to the prisoner's holding chamber. Another stab of light pierced the room as a door opened. Escorted by two large soldiers armed with energy pistols that were holstered but not strapped in, Ryma, Kolandi Princess, and widow of Maliche Rocker, former hero of the Brin, now a disgraced figure, entered the chamber. Her head held high, eyes forward, she carried herself regally, even garbed in prison grey. Three holo-vid drones hovered in close, given the prescribed proximity allowances, and focused on her stoic face as she took her seat at the defendant's table beside her attorney.

Judge Haytk banged her gavel on the bench again to hush the crowd. "This court will tolerate neither outcry nor disturbances of any kind. Any who will not conduct themselves with proper decorum will be evicted immediately. Mr. Prosecutor, since the defendant has opted to delay her opening statement until later, you may begin your case."

State Prosecutor Lindo Shar bowed his head and stood. "Thank you, Judge Haytk. The state will present evidence proving the defendant," he waved a hand in Ryma's direction, "did knowingly and willfully, in collusion with the late Maliche Rocker, conspire to illegally assume control of the Assembly and other government agencies." He strode to his table and picked up a tablet.

Repeatedly swiping patterns with his talons above the screen, page after page of documents appeared in holographic form over his head. "Our evidence will prove that the so-called marriage between Maliche Rocker and this Kolandi usurper was illegal from the start and therefore nullifies her attempt to take control of our government upon his execution." He slammed his hand onto the table with a loud thud. "I call my first witness, Tolat Kivar, lead records clerk for First Town archives."

Almost as wide as he was tall, a spectacled Brin waddled from the shadows to the witness stand. His suit, worn and outdated but presentable, strained to contain him as he sat and was sworn in.

"Citizen Kivar, will you present your documents to the court?"

Blinking uncontrollably, the Brin pulled out his tablet and swiped through several pages, muttering to himself, and resetting his glasses until he located the required information. Another swipe and several pages leapt from the tablet into the air above him and onto the tablets of the judges. "As you can see, your honors, according to section one hundred-thirty-three of the article nine in First Town's constitution, the document drafted by our founders, the leadership of the Assembly may pass to his or her spouse temporarily in the event of his or her sudden incapacity or untimely death while in office. However, in section one hundred-thirty-seven, it states that a vote of confidence must be held to confirm the assumption of power as soon as the crisis is contained and a quorum of the Assembly can agree on the transfer of authority."

Prosecutor Shar rose and gestured toward the clerk. "Thank you for your testimony, Citizen Kivar. No further questions."

Defense attorney Halum Calthon stood and addressed the witness. "Citizen Kivar, you state that a quorum of elected officials must be convened to authorize the transfer of power to a spouse. Correct?"

Kivar blinked as he faced the attorney. "Yes, that is correct."

"But the article you cite also states that this is to be done *once the crisis is over*. Also correct?"

"Well, yes, but…"

"Has the Assembly, or any members of the government made claims that the crisis we face is over?'

"No, sir, however…"

"In fact, Citizen Kivar, have not several high-ranking members of the Assembly publicly stated at functions which you attended that they are supportive and thankful for the defendant's skillful and expert assumption of her husband's authority during the ongoing crisis?"

"Yes, such claims have been made, but…"

"Thank you, Citizen Kivar. No further questions." With a flourish of his taloned hand, Calthon returned to his seat.

One of the judges to Haytk's right rapped his talons on the bench, signaling his intent to speak. "Citizen Kivar, as the head of your department, and by virtue of your station, an authority on the matter, are you willing to support the defense's claim that the defendant is not guilty of usurping her authority due to the fact that no vote was ever taken to confirm her as head of the Assembly in her husband's place?"

Tolat Kivar continued to blink as he pulled a kerchief from his pocket and dabbed his sweaty face. "No, your honors, this is quite a complex matter. The time for a quorum vote is not specified. So, while one could make a reasonable case for the ongoing nature of the crisis, the intent is clearly to conclude the succession as rapidly as possible."

"Your honors," Prosecutor Shar turned to the bench, resting one hand on the polished surface, "I have called this witness as only a small part of a chain of evidence which, once presented in its entirety, will prove our case against the defendant. If the court will permit me to continue with the presentation of the state's case…"

"Very well, if the defense has no further questions, you may continue."

The defense attorney waved his hand and returned to his chair beside Ryma. The two leaned in close, whispering, as Lindo Shar continued.

"At this time, I would like to call my next witness…"

A dozen more witnesses from all walks of life were brought before the court to verify the volumes of documentation brought into evidence by the prosecution. Heads of several guilds presented testimony of rulings made by Ryma that clearly favored Kolandi interests over the Brin. Average citizens cited judgements of everything from land deals to personal disputes, all showing clear prejudices in favor of Kolandi participants in the disputes. The testimonies continued well into the afternoon until Judge Haytk gaveled for a recess. The courtroom emptied and Ryma was escorted back to her cell.

"There you go, your royalness. All tucked in nice and comfy back in your royal chambers." The female Brin guard shoved Ryma's shoulder as she stepped forward. "You missed high tea, so you'll just have to starve until breakfast. Lights out at nine, princess." She spat out the title as she engaged the energy field over the cell's doorway and laughed all the way back to her office at the end of the dingy hall. Ryma, stoic and maintaining her regal posture, sat on her thin mattress, back pressed against the cold wall.

Morning came early, startling Ryma awake with harsh lights and voices. "Time to greet your public, your royalness. You've got ten minutes for breakfast and to make yourself presentable." A plastic tray loaded with some type of grey porridge clattered across the floor, spilling some of its contents in the process. "And don't forget to clean up that mess before we go." The guard reset the energy field and stomped back to her office.

Ryma stretched, painfully, and stood to take care of her morning routine before the guard returned. *If I get out of this... no,* when *I get out of this, that is one more name on my list to deal with.* She fought to gain control of her emotions and cement her face into blank, regal stoicism for the new day's humiliations.

***

The second day of the trial opened with several highly positioned witnesses taking the stand. Most notable of the various guild leaders providing testimony was Nissend Honj. The leader of the second most powerful clan of Brin on the planet provided documentation from himself and sworn witnesses which showed Ryma conspired to have her husband killed not only to put an end to her humiliation at his hands but to seize control for herself. These powerful individuals, like the previous day's witnesses, painted Ryma as a treasonous imposter to the throne and, worst of all, a Kolandi sympathizer.

"To conclude my case, your honors, I would like to present one final witness. At this time, I call His Eminence, Prelate Jansom, to the stand.

The door to the witness room opened and a large figure, robed in deep crimson and silver vestments, strode into the court. His left mid-talon wore a massive gold ring with an emerald that sparkled as the vidcam lights shone on him.

"Prelate Jansom, I would like to have you read another section of the First Town Archives for the court. Would you be so kind as to present this passage for us?" He swiped a single page so its holographic image appeared overhead for all to see and handed the tablet to the clergyman.

After quickly scanning the requested passage, the prelate cleared his throat, and, with his rich baritone preacher's voice, read the article for the court. "This is from the First Town Archives, article twenty-four, section nineteen. 'For legal and ecumenical purposes, henceforth, a marriage is stated as occurring between two consenting Brin adults or between two underage Brin with written and authorized permission of their parents or legal guardians.'"

Lindo Shar stood to his full height, paused dramatically as he gazed at each of the judges in turn, hooked one taloned thumb into his belt, and pointed to Ryma as she sat impassively. "There you have it, your honors. The final piece of the puzzle. As shown by our witnesses, the ceremony between a Kolandi and a Brin is not a legally binding marriage. The law recognizes only a marriage between two consenting Brin. This Kolandi woman illegally seized the reins of power and abused her position to give favor to her own kind in blatant and endless exploitation of a crisis. As you can see, the evidence proves this woman had no claim to assume the authority of her late husband's office and, I would suggest, did so knowingly. Her treason should face the full wrath of this court."

Bursts of outrage, both in support of the declaration and against it, filled the chamber. Several fights broke out in the viewing stands before soldiers could separate and evict the combatants. Judge Haytk slammed her gavel, causing it to spark. "Everyone will return to their seats and come to order or I will have the entire chamber emptied."

Slowly the crowd regained their composure and took their seats. The judge to Haytk's left leaned forward and raised a single talon. "Mr. Prosecutor, I am not sure I follow your conclusion. How is it that your evidence, while it may show favoritism and potential nepotism, shows treason?"

"Let me repeat the key point, your honor." He lifted his tablet and returned the critical passage to its holographic image. Tracing the words with a talon to highlight them as he read, the prosecutor read the document. "'For legal and ecumenical purposes, henceforth, a marriage is stated as occurring between two consenting Brin adults, or between two underage Brin with written and authorized permission of their parents or legal guardians.'"

He looked up from the tablet directly into Ryma's eyes. "A marriage is stated as occurring between two consenting *Brin* adults. This… rowi is no Brin, therefore their marriage was never legal, according to our constitution. As a result, the transfer of power to her was illegal and, as shown by her subsequent actions, treasonous."

This time, silence greeted the pronouncement. Before the audience could react and disrupt matters, Judge Haytk pounded her gavel and glared around the room. "If the prosecution rests, then I turn the proceedings over to the defense."

Halum Calthon rose from his chair at the defendant's table and stepped around Ryma's position to stand behind an impeccably dressed man seated to her left. "Your Honors, at this time I would like to defer to one of my esteemed associates and ask the court's indulgence for this late change to the proceedings. I am sure your honors will all recognize the qualifications of associate counsel Motl."

The judges glanced at each other, nodding in approval. "Very well, Mr. Calthon, the court recognizes…"

Lindo Shar pounded his open hand on the table. "If it pleases the court, your honors. This is highly irregular. I object to this obviously theatrical move by the defense."

Judge Haytk glared at the defense attorney. "Have you any substantial evidence of rejection to challenge this alteration, counselor?"

"Well, no, your honor, but this is not…"

"Then I see no reason to interfere with the defense's wishes. You may proceed, Mr. Motl."

"Thank you, your honor." Bern Motl, renowned attorney, former head of the judicial guild and friend of the Rocker family, rose to his feet and stepped to the center of the room. His silver crest shone magnificently in the spotlight. "While I could produce many witnesses and documents illustrating rulings which clearly benefitted Brin interests over Kolandi, I have but one witness to call to the stand: Ryma Rocker."

Years later, many who watched the trial would swear that Ryma was adorned in a flowing gown of silver that shimmered as she strode to the witness stand, not the dingy grey prison uniform and coarse sandals she actually wore. Her head held high, shoulders back and hands clasped at her waist, she looked every bit the royal princess of the Kolandi.

Bern Motl allowed a moment for the audience to appreciate Ryma's presence before breaking the spell. "Ryma, would you please relate for us the events which occurred the day before your marriage to Maliche Rocker?"

In a clear, even voice, without a single tremor, Ryma gave her testimony. "Your honors and the citizens of Kodut, Brin and Kolandi alike, I have allowed this outrageous series of false claims to proceed so that all of you, in the full light of justice, will know the truth." She paused for effect, gazed across the room, and continued. "On the day prior to our wedding, I insisted to Maliche, my husband-to-be, that I undergo any ceremony which would be required to make me a Brin citizen."

"And why would you do that?" Bern Motl's voice interrupted her as they had planned.

"For the same purpose he followed the Path of Berit to become one of the Kolandi. He understood the importance of such rituals when you must lead others, especially others of another culture, that you will not betray them and that you will lead them in honor. Fortunately for me, the requirements to become a Brin citizen are not as harsh as we Kolandi demanded of my husband."

Bern Motl swiped a talon across his tablet, sending a document into the air for all to see, as well as to the tablets of each judge.

"That very afternoon we called in our family attorney," she gestured toward Bern Motl, "a local Brin clergyman, and we flew in Tola Shatal, leader of the Kolandi Tolavar. All of the appropriate documents were written up and signed. For legal and moral purposes, I took on dual citizenship as both a Kolandi and a full Brin citizen. I could not believe such a simple process would be convincing, but everyone assured me it would suffice to convince you Brin of my sincere desire to represent both cultures fairly and equally."

"And why was this procedure not widely known?"

"To the best of my knowledge, it was in the news the next morning but was buried by all the ceremony of our wedding. We did not really consider it of any real importance beyond being a symbol of unity, so we let it slip into obscurity until now."

Bern Motl strode before the judges. "There you have it, your honors. The key to the prosecution's entire case rests on one point, that Ryma Rocker was not a Brin and therefore was never legally married to Maliche Rocker and had no authority to assume his position when he was murdered. On the contrary, as you have seen, Ryma is a full Brin citizen with all the rights and privileges accorded said citizenship and was completely within her rights as Maliche Rocker's legal spouse in assuming leadership of the Assembly. As is her right, the defense requests an immediate dismissal. "

Judge Haytk sat back, folding her talons in her lap. "While an immediate dismissal is permitted, it is somewhat unusual, especially in such a high-profile case. Are you certain this is what you wish?"

"Yes, Your Honor. We wish to end this farce as quickly as possible."

With a nod of her head, she enclosed the bench in a privacy field so they discussed the evidence. Only moments later, Haytk lowered the field and rapped her spherical gavel on the bench.

"It is the unanimous decision of this court that the charges laid against Ryma Rocker are without merit and therefore dismissed."

The courtroom erupted in cheers as the vidcams darted from one location to another capturing the reactions of all participants. Haytk pounded her bench with the gavel to quiet the room.

"Attorney Motl, since the charges against her have been proven false, does your client wish to address the court?"

He returned to the lectern and leaned on it with both hands. "As is the right of the falsely accused, is there anything you would like to say to the court, princess?" He waved toward a guard behind the defense table. The guard opened a doorway and in walked Nedia Rocker, carrying a small tablet of her own. She approached the clerk of the court and handed him the tablet. She turned and took a seat at the defense table.

"Yes, thank you. Your Honor, I would, at this time, having proved my innocence of the charges brought before this court, and pursuant to article two-six-nine of the First Town constitution, like to press charges against all those named in the documents we have just presented to this court. The information before you gives proof of a vast conspiracy to not only discredit me but the entire Rocker clan, and overthrow the Assembly and the guilds for themselves. This evidence is presented in written documents produced by those guilty parties and holo-vid recordings of events detailing their efforts in their own words."

She stepped to center stage, turning to face all members of the audience as she continued to speak. "This trial, the attempt to complete this plot, I allowed to happen so their lies and dishonorable nature would be open for all to see. When my evidence, the evidence of these conspirator's own words, becomes public, my humiliation will be as nothing, for justice will be served and all people, Brin and Kolandi together, will be protected from such evil."

***

As Ryma predicted, all charges against her were dropped, public support for her soared to new heights, and the courts reinstated her as the rightful heir to the head of the Assembly until a suitable quorum could be gathered. She returned to her quarters and her first order of business was to imprison six of the guards at the prison for cruelty and abuse of the prisoners. New regulations were put in place to train and monitor all the guards.

Five weeks later, the final verdict in the Trial of Conspirators, as it became known, was announced. All the former heads of guilds and families of those involved were stripped of their titles and properties. Of greatest note was the passing of Brachspark and all the Honj interests into sole control of Nedia Rocker, in recognition of her heroic efforts to gather evidence against all the guilty, particularly her own family. Nedia took her two children and moved them to Brachspark, which she promptly renamed The Citadel, after a reference she found during her spying days to an ancient holding of the Rockers, now lost in time. She retired from public service and took up a quiet rural life. Any other family members or descendants of the convicted were required to take oaths of loyalty and only then were permitted limited and supervised participation in decisions regarding their holdings for a period of no less than twenty years.

"I certainly hope this puts an end to all that nonsense. We have some serious threats to deal with. Any word from Maliche and the others?" Ryma sat in private council with Tival Rocker, a Kolbri second cousin to Jontar. She sat in her favorite cushioned chair, exuding calm except for her tapping left foot.

"Not since they arrived at Seriph. Our mind link went blank yesterday and has not been reestablished. It could be an effect of the Cosmic String density near the planet. We've never tried to communicate through such interference as that before."

Tival, being another Rocker, was nearly as powerful in his Kolbri abilities as Jontar and served as an intermediary to prevent any possibility of communications between Maliche and Ryma being intercepted. He sat across from Ryma, leaning forward and speaking in hushed tones, tried to be as diplomatic in his report as possible.

"Are you certain they aren't in any danger?"

"They gave no indication of any difficulties prior to going dark. I wouldn't worry. They are well equipped to deal with any problems the Skae can throw at them."

"I still don't have to like it. Their report about what the Skae were up to was cause for alarm, but there's nothing we can do about it until Jontar communicates again. Let me know as soon as that happens. For now, I need to get some air. If anyone needs me, I'm taking Rilo and Danet on a hunt in the mountains."

Chapter Seventeen

Nalot leaned against the wall as he faced his companions. "How are we going to contact the Gorvin before they blow us out of the sky? In case any of you have forgotten, in this time Brin and Kolandi are allies of the Skae. I don't think we would be welcomed with open arms into their space."

Thyka replied without looking up from her console. "The Gorvin don't blast anyone. Their weapons are usually non-lethal."

"Yeah," Duval contributed. "They would most likely disable us and maroon us on a distant planet, or imprison us and try interrogating us to learn how we got this far undetected."

"In any case," interrupted Jontar, "we may have a plan to deal with that. During our trip to Lethnon and Shyfar, we picked up a few Gorvin codes which may help us get through their security."

Nalot shook his head and leaned on Jontar's console. "Those codes are ancient history. Not only would they have been changed thousands of times over the centuries, but modern technology might not even recognize the signal at all. They would be worse than useless."

"The Modiri system we hijacked can help us there. They've been monitoring Gorvin communications. We can adapt the signal with today's tech signatures, but the core would still be Gorvin. It might give us the chance to convince them we are here to help."

Head cocked, he stared at Jontar's console, and then tapped the panel with his palm. "It's risky, but it might give us the window we need to talk with them. Unless anyone else has a better idea…" He looked around the bridge for any comments.

Maliche shifted in his seat and took a deep breath. "Since there's nothing more, Jontar and Nalot, you two are in charge of getting us into Gorvin space, hopefully to Kluton, without getting us killed or imprisoned. The rest of you, don't hold back anything. If you have any thoughts or suggestions, speak up." He scanned the bridge and grinned as he noticed everyone thinking and nodding. "Yalmut, set course for Kluton. Duvar, keep us invisible to everyone out there. We can't afford to run into any fights now. Get ready, everyone, only six days until we reach the Gorvin home world. Engage all systems, Yalmut. Let's get going."

***

"What the kak!" The blast of an energy beam shook the small ship, knocking Duvar out of his bunk and landing him hard on the metal floor of his cabin. Gathering himself together, he pulled on a shirt and ran down the corridor amid the blare of emergency sirens and flashing lights. He collided with Seykel and Nalot as he rounded a corner near the bridge.

"What's happening? Are we being attacked?" Seykel, hair disheveled and still buttoning her blouse, grabbed Duvar's arm to regain her balance.

"I don't know. We were still cloaked when I went off duty. I'm guessing somebody found us."

The entry to the bridge stood open as the three arrived. Charging in, each one took their stations, examining their consoles as they engaged the field restraints to keep them firmly seated. A quick glance at the main viewport showed a large Gorvin warship holding steady directly in their path, its heavy energy cannons aimed squarely at them.

Thyka, having relieved Duvar at the communications station, spoke with a strained calm. "... I'm trying to explain. We are here to help you against the Skae. We have information of vital importance to your leaders. Our broadcast contained some of that information to prove our intent in coming here…"

A gravelly voice boomed over the speakers. "You will hold your position and prepare to be boarded. Skae vessels, and their allies, are forbidden in this sector." They watched as a small vessel separated from the main ship and flew toward them.

With a clank, the boarding vessel attached to the air lock. Maliche watched the control panel turn violet and, with a press of his talon, the door slid open with a whoosh of air as the pressures between ships equalized. Built like cement blocks, garbed in heavy grey armor, laser rifles at the ready, three Gorvin soldiers marched in.

Maliche raised his hands. "We will not resist you. We are not Skae allies. My crew is assembled in the galley. I will assist you in any way I can."

The boarding party marched past Maliche toward the bridge. A thorough search of all cabins and cargo containers ensued, including a full body scan of each crew member. When completed, it looked as if some severe storm had whipped through the vessel.

"Your crew will remain here, under guard. You will come with me." The soldier in charge waved his weapon at Maliche signaling him to fall in. Glancing over his shoulder, Maliche saw the two remaining soldiers take up positions on either side of the galley hatch as the door panel slid shut.

At the air lock, Maliche hesitated and swung around to face the soldier. "Before I go with you, I want assurances my crew will be unharmed."

"You are in no position to ask for anything, but it is not Gorvin policy to harm unarmed prisoners. Your crew will be safe so long as they do not attempt to escape or deceive my guards." With another wave of his weapon, the soldier escorted Maliche onto the Gorvin boarding vessel. Taking off his helmet and setting it aside, the soldier sat at the controls and soon the two were headed to the Gorvin warship.

***

"**I**'ve tried explaining our mission to you a dozen times already. I don't know what else you want to hear." Maliche, exhausted and frustrated from the endless interrogation, slumped in his chair. Built for Gorvin physiology, the chair itself nearly served as a torture device. Maliche's back and legs ached from the unnatural fit.

"What you tell us makes no sense. Time travel? We have heard tall tales of the Skae using the strings for such a purpose, but if they could do this, why haven't they gone back in time to change the outcome of battles they have lost? And how could any but the Skae gain this power? The Kolandi were defeated many millennia ago. You could not possibly have Kolandi with you."

"I don't understand the technical aspects of Skae time travel. I only know they cannot use it for mass transit of large numbers of vessels, and even if they could, their control is arbitrary at best. It is not something they ever pursued as a war strategy. I don't know why. And you examined my companions. They are not full Kolandi, except one. I am a Brin. The Skae brought us to the Kolandi planet centuries ago. Our mutual offspring developed immunity to your virus and are free to leave the planet again. We have reverse-engineered a cure and a few Kolandi, as evidenced by my crewmate, have been successfully inoculated. You need to trust us. We are here to help. We believe we can put an end to your war with the Skae once and for all."

Tufa, sub-commander of the Gorvin ship Tulop, sat impassively; of course, the Gorvin always seemed impassive with their stony features. "The possibility of your statements being true is the only thing keeping you and your crew alive for now. But before we can trust you, we need more evidence this is not some clever Skae plot to infiltrate behind our defenses."

This is getting nowhere. Let me try something. Maliche felt his body freeze up as he felt his mind being shoved aside.

Maliche's mouth moved, but it was Tol's voice which spoke. "Sub-Commander Tufa, my name is Tol. Do not be alarmed, I am a sentient biocomputer, originally of ancient Skae design, but I have surpassed my original programming and have allied myself with these beings. I want to show you some proof of what my host says, but I need to utilize your computer system to do this. I will in no way interfere with any of your systems. I only wish to show you some holo-vids collected by my companions during their travels through time. Perhaps they will help convince you of the truth of their words."

Before Tufa could object, Tol projected data he had downloaded from Jontar's voyage to Lethnon and Shyfar. He selected specific clips showing their interactions with Clugat and Eisoph. Images flashed across the screen until Tufa reached out and stopped the play, reset the time frame, and watched a brief clip several times.

"Where did you get the image of this woman? What do you know of her? How can you know of her?"

Peering over Tufa's shoulder to see what he was referring to, Tol returned Maliche to his chair. "That is Eisoph. She was an assistant to a researcher named Clugat. According to my companions, she was the first of your people to raise an alarm about the Skae plans to create their gravitational wave generator and the disastrous potential of its completion."

Sub-Commander Tufa gripped both arms of Maliche's chair with white knuckles and loomed over him. Otherwise, he gave no outward appearance of his emotional state. "Our history is not in the open records, except in the most general form; certainly no images of our most revered ancestors are available. How did you obtain this?"

Tol kept a calm voice while controlling Maliche's reactions. "We have told you, Sub-Commander Tufa. Our companions traveled into the past and…"

Tufa threw his arms in the air and stormed back to his console. "And I have told you I do not believe your fanciful tale. I will show you proof of your lies and then we will see what you have to say."

With a few stabs of thick fingers, Tufa found the file he searched for and punched for it to project above the panel. There was the Shyfar conference room in all of its glory, with the Skae governing panel and presenters on the dais.

"You claim your companions were at this conference with Eisoph, and you have even been clever enough to manipulate your holo-vids with their likenesses alongside her and the others. Here are the Gorvin records of the event." He manipulated the controls to swivel the view around to see the audience. He zoomed in to Eisoph as she stood to argue her discovery. Tufa watched and listened as her voice rang clearly through the interrogation room. As she finished and took her seat, Sub-Commander Tufa gasped. There, directly behind the heroine of the Gorvin, sat Jontar, Yalmut, and Duvar.

"This is not possible."

"I assure you it is. If you have your superiors do a search through the old records, I think you will find Eisoph and Clugat referring to a trio of Kolandi researchers collaborating with them and verifying their findings."

"We will see about that. In the meantime, you will be returned to your vessel. Do not attempt to escape or communicate with anyone. If we detect the slightest irregularity, you and your crew will be placed in cryostasis and imprisoned." With a wave of his hand, the guard signaled for Maliche to follow him.

Tol returned control of Maliche's body to him and retreated to wherever he normally lived in Maliche's mind. *I think that went well.*

Did you know those three would show up on the commander's holo-vid? That was an awful risk.

A calculated risk, but the odds were definitely in our favor. Jontar's files were the ones he captured from the Skae records of the conference. They should have been identical to the Gorvin copies.

***

The next day, Sub-Commander Tufa sent a command to Maliche Rocker. His stern visage loomed large on the main view screen. "My superiors have confirmed your claims. I am to escort you to Kluton where you will be permitted to speak with representatives of our Supreme Congress and top scientists. Stay on this course. Any deviation will result in the direst of consequences." His image vanished, replaced by the view of the Tulop.

"Course heading coming in now, Father." Jontar flicked his talons over his panel, sending the instructions to Yalmut's station.

Maliche touched the controls to open his communication with Commander Tufa. "We have the coordinates laid in, commander. Lead on."

Two days later the planet Kluton, home world of the Gorvin, filled the view screen. A signal came again from Commander Tufa. "I am sending one of my pilots to bring your vessel in to port. You and your crew will provide him access to your controls and then vacate your bridge. No outworlders are permitted to know our approach codes or procedures. I am sure you can appreciate our need for such high security protocols."

"Of course, subcommander. We will respect all of your regulations." Maliche signaled for everyone except for Jontar and Yalmut to go to their quarters and remain there until the Gorvin permitted them to have access to the bridge again.

***

"Where are the buildings? I can barely see anything through this dust." Seykel shielded her eyes from the stinging dust storm howling across the landing port.

Kluton's environment was harsh on its best days. Orbiting at the innermost limits of the system's habitable zone, the heat was oppressive. What little water existed on the surface could only be found in the permanent shade of deep canyons in the high mountains or at either pole. The remaining landscape, scoured by intense sandstorms on a regular basis, was a nightmarish scene of weirdly-shaped rock towers and vast plains of flowing dunes.

"I thought you were raised in a desert. Doesn't this remind you of home?" Duvar covered his mouth with a portion of his sleeve as he laughed at his own joke.

"The deserts on Kodut are nothing like this. How can anyone survive here?" She took shelter in Nalot's leeward side, grabbing his shirt to help stabilize her in the strong wind.

"The Gorvin live underground. That's where the water is, and temperatures are much cooler. You'll be amazed at the beauty of their cavern cities. Only a few rise above the surface. There's a couple over there." Jontar pointed in the direction of a pair of only slightly more regular-shaped rock spires off to their left.

A hazy structure rose in the shadows before them and, as they arrived, a panel slid open to reveal a square, well-lit opening. As soon as everyone entered, the panel slid shut and the silence became deafening. The air stirred as vacuum pumps activated, pulling the dust out of the air and off their clothes.

"This way to your holding center." The soldier who piloted their ship to the Gorvin port led the way down a tunnel carved in the rock.

A squat, brick-like individual came running up the passage toward them. At least he was running in the odd Gorvin way of swinging from side-to-side as his short, thick legs carried him as fast as he could travel. Dressed in a dark brown wrap-around robe with at least eight pockets of various sizes, he actually smiled as he came to a halt in front of the group and presented his credentials to the soldier.

Without a word, the uniformed man turned, stepped his way back through his charges and vanished around a curve in the tunnel.

"Greetings. I am Gnobis. I have been assigned to escort you during your visit to our city." Holding up his left hand with three fingers extended, he offered the traditional Gorvin greeting.

Jontar stepped forward, holding his left hand up with two fingers extended. "Greetings, Gnobis. We appreciate your guidance. And, might I add, without meaning any offence, you display much more expression than most of the Gorvin we have encountered so far."

"Ahh, yes, I have been cautioned against my expressive tendencies many times." The man frowned, slightly, but for a Gorvin it was considered an almost vulgar display. "You see, I was raised by outworlders after I was orphaned during a battle where my parents were stationed. I learned to express myself in a most un-Gorvin-like manner. As a result, most of my fellows consider me quite the oddity, although they find me particularly useful as a liaison to visiting dignitaries. But do not let their stark exterior deceive you. We are a passionate race on the inside. Our physiology simply does not allow an outward expression of our emotions, at least not that others can easily detect. To us, what you might see as only the meerest twitch of an eye is a grand display of sentiment. Experience will help you discern the signs. Of course, the soldiers are, understandably, more gruff and confrontational."

"It certainly took us a long time to begin recognizing emotional cues the last time we had extended contact with some of your people." Jontar glanced at Duvar and Yalmut, smiling at their new host's exuberance.

Gnobis's head cocked, his eyes wide at Jontar's statement. "You've had contact with Gorvin before? I wouldn't think that possible, considering our people are on opposite sides of this war and have been forever."

Maliche shot a stern gaze at his son and the others. "It's a long story, Gnobis. One best saved for when we know each other better. For now, could you take us to our quarters? We desperately need some rest."

"Of course, of course. Follow me. We are not far at all." The squat Gorvin led the way out of the corridor and into the vast cavern containing Zenotime, the Gorvin capitol city. Maliche and the others stopped in their tracks, gaping at the incredible visage unfolding before them.

"This is incredible. I've heard tales of Gorvin architecture, but I never imagined such magnificence." Maliche stood open-jawed as he examined the view.

Bioluminescent algae coating every centimeter of the cavern ceiling and walls provided illumination for its inhabitants, and levitating spheres of the same algae floated above nearly every intersection. Most of the structures seemed to be carved out of the natural stalagmites, some dozens of meters in diameter, and a hundred or more meters tall. Others appeared to be built in imitation of the natural features. The multi-colored glittering of tiny gems and reflective minerals imbedded in the stone flickered with every turn of the head, giving the city a beauty unlike any other. Mismatched windows in the buildings, constructed in every conceivable geometric shape, glowed with the soft yellow-green light of the algae lighting the rest of the city. Echoes of voices, running vehicles and other sources blended together as they reverberated off the cavern walls into a hum of activity.

"It's beautiful. Our caverns back home were nothing like this. I must learn how you accomplished all of this." Seykel practically drooled as she gaped at the city. "If we could learn how to build cities like this, we could move back into the cave and avoid all the discomforts of above-ground dwellings in the desert. It's a bit dark, but that can be fixed."

Gnobis let out a deep rumble, the Gorvin equivalent of laughter. "Dark? I was about to put on my visor, it is so bright in here. I am used to being indoors in my lab. You must remember we Gorvin have evolved as cavern dwellers. Our senses, particularly our eyes, are much more sensitive to low light levels than yours. Come now, we must get you settled."

Occasionally stumbling as they let their eyes feast on the city's unique features, Maliche and the others followed their host and in a few minutes, found themselves in front of one of the hollowed-out stalagmites. Gnobis stood in front of the doorway and a thin red beam skimmed over his body. "Gnobis, research assistant viral nanobot division, sector eight." A light above the door turned blue and a nearly-seamless panel slid open, spilling a shaft of yellow-green light onto the ground.

"I apologize, but for security purposes, you will not have access to the locks. Either I or one of my associates will escort you whenever you are permitted outside of these quarters. Welcome to the visiting dignitary facility. Please forgive the dust; we do not have many visitors these days. The war has taken a terrible toll on actual physical visits from our colleagues." They stepped into the main lobby and took one of the pneumatic lifts to the thirty-sixth level.

When the lift door swished open, Jontar and his two friends recognized the layout of a Gorvin dwelling. The large central gathering room contained six tunnels leading off to the kitchen and sleeping rooms. The room itself contained a large central table with seating specifically chosen to suit humanoids with physiology most similar to the Brin and Kolandi. Cushioned sofas formed a nook in one part while two separate desks with computer terminals occupied the opposite side. Holographic three-dimensional images of various star systems hung on each highly-polished stone wall.

"This will do nicely," Maliche stated as he surveyed the area. "What about our personal belongings? Will we be able to retrieve them from our ship?"

"That is being arranged. Someone will be here soon with your possessions. For now, I will let you get some rest. We will meet again tomorrow morning. It will be a very busy day. I hope you convince my superiors that you really are here to help end this war. I must warn you, though. They are very skeptical that you can provide anything so momentous after all this time."

Jontar held his hand up with three fingers extended, and Gnobis joined him with the two-fingered response. "There has never, in the history of this galaxy, been any like us. We can deliver on our promise."

Gnobis grinned and looked hard into Jontar's eyes. "Time will tell, young one."

Chapter Eighteen

Dravite, Master of the nano-virus technology unit, crossed his thick arms across a barrel chest. "I'm not convinced you three are the same individuals in the archive footage. Before I allow you access to our files, I'm afraid you need to make me believe your time travel story. I don't care what your calculations say about getting our tech through the Skae barriers. Until I am certain of who you are and what you can do, my facility is closed to you."

The tech lab conference room glowed with the same dim light as the rest of the city. The polished walls sparkled with the reflections of mirror-like minerals laced throughout the marbled pattern of stone. Three Gorvin scientists, in addition to Dravite and Gnobis and the one military escort, sat opposite Maliche and his companions at the large oval table which seemed to grow from the stone floor. Four hours of talk, examinations and demonstrations using network-blocked devices had little effect on the tech master. Hope began to fade in Maliche's heart. "The only way we might truly convince you of our ability to time travel is to take you on a trip. I doubt your superiors or the military will allow us anywhere near our ship, much less fly off into history. Isn't there anything else we can do?"

Dravite, with typical Gorvin impassive features, uncrossed his massive arms and leaned on the table. "Make me trust you and I can arrange for you to do exactly that."

You won't like this, but I think I've worked out enough of the Gorvin cerebral structure to help us out. Maliche's brain tingled with Tol's building energy.

Wait! What are you going to do?

Remember what I did to Ryma when you first met?

No, Tol. It's too…

The Gorvin half of the room filled with a bright blue glow, surrounding each of them and holding them immobile as Tol entered their minds and shared Maliche's history with them all.

"Tol, what are you doing?" Jontar sent out his thoughts as the glow grew in intensity.

"Something I did to help your mother and father out a long time ago. Be quiet now, this takes a lot of concentration, connecting to so many alien minds at once. Tell the others not to interfere or try anything stupid."

Jontar broke contact and instructed the others to sit still and let Tol complete whatever he was doing to the Gorvin.

"But this is our chance to gain some leverage." Nalot half-rose from his seat before Seykel took hold of his arm and pulled him back.

"Wait, Husband. Have faith in our friend. I have seen this before and so have you, back in the caves."

"I think it's working. I feel their anxiety fading." Thyka studied the faces of the Gorvin scientists, reaching out with her mind to test their emotional state.

Five minutes later, the blue glow faded and the Gorvin gasped, holding on to the table to prevent themselves from falling. The guard, standing against a far wall, collapsed to his knees.

"What in the name of Sacred Anatase happened? What did you do to us?" Dravite struggled to keep his composure as his senses flooded back.

Tol, still in control of Maliche's body, spoke reassuringly to the scientists as they sat staring at Maliche. "No harm has come to any of you. I simply did as you asked and shared this Brin's history with you. You asked to be convinced of our desire to help and our power to do so. This was the only way I know of to accomplish the task in less than decades of working together. We don't have that kind of time. Did I succeed?"

Gaping in amazement, at least what served as amazement on Gorvin facial features, Dravite nodded his head slowly. "I think so. Unless this is some sort of trick... no, I do not believe that. Yes, I believe we can trust your intentions. I still need to see this time traveling ability of yours in person, but I think now more for my own scientific curiosity than any doubt of your talents. Will this afternoon be too soon?"

***

After their meeting broke up, Dravite and the other scientists contacted the authorities and used their influence to gain a special permit to allow the alien 'guests' access to their vessel, to leave the planet and, with the scientists and the usual guard along for the ride, attempt a scientific demonstration. Within hours, everyone met at the ship, boarded and blasted off into space in search of a nearby cosmic string.

"There's some sort of problem connecting with the string, Father. I don't know what is wrong." Jontar hovered over Yalmut's shoulder as they tried several times to match their ship to the resonant frequencies of the string. "These frequencies keep shifting before we can make a connection. I've never seen anything like it."

Thyka joined them at the console and studied the readings. Reaching out with her mind, she tried to read the string itself. "The string doesn't like the Gorvin. The Skae have somehow convinced the strings that only they and their allies can be trusted."

Dravite stiffened, his hand resting on the hilt of the weapon at his belt, as he turned to address Maliche. "What is she talking about? The cosmic strings are an astronomical phenomenon, a state of energy. She makes them sound like something alive."

Maliche shrugged his shoulders and smiled as he stood next to the Gorvin tech master in front of the main view screen. Filters allowed the string to become visible as they watched. "Thyka has a unique perspective on the strings none of the rest of us have. I don't know if the strings are alive or not, but she treats them as if they were and has gotten some unusual and favorable results. We just go along with her with open minds."

Thyka continued her efforts to meld with the string when she suddenly stiffened and screamed. Collapsing to her knees, Thyka held her head.

"What happened? Are you alright?" Jontar dropped beside Thyka, holding her with both arms wrapped around her tiny frame.

"I think they got angry with me and kicked me out. I've never felt such pain. It was like a lightning bolt split my skull wide open... It's better now." She took in a few deep breaths and, with Jontar's help, sat in Yalmut's chair.

Seykel shoved Jontar aside and took her daughter's face in both hands, examining her closely. "What did you think you were doing? I don't ever want you to try that again. You could have been killed."

Brushing her hands away, Thyka attempted a weak smile. "No, Mother, they would not kill me. They're not like that at all. It was just a warning. I have to go back in and try again."

"I thought I just told you …"

"No, Mother. This is my job. We need my abilities if our mission is to succeed. I have to do this. None of the others understand the strings like I do."

Folding her arms across her chest, Seykel lowered her head but kept eye contact with Thyka. "Promise me you will be more careful."

"I will, Mother. I may have been a bit too demanding last time. The strings are very formal and easily offended. I will try a more diplomatic approach this time."

Setting her face and taking another deep breath to prepare for another contact, Thyka closed her eyes and stretched out her mind again. Several minutes passed as beads of sweat formed on her forehead and her small talons dug deep into her palms with the effort.

Exhaling with a blast, she shook her head and frowned. "It's no good. It won't believe me. I think we need to take a bit more drastic approach."

Jontar peered over his shoulder at Thyka. "What do you mean, 'a more drastic approach'?"

She scanned the room, looking each of her companions in the eye. "The four of us need to link together and connect to the string. Possibly Tol as well, considering what he did with our Gorvin friends and your parents, Jontar. Only a combined effort to show the full spectrum of this war has any hope of altering the string's view."

***

Sitting on the floor of Thyka's cabin, lights dimmed low and the scent of sweet herbs from a small scent-pot filling their nostrils, the four Kolbri and Maliche formed a circle. Seykel stood ready in case they needed help. Nalot remained on the bridge with the Gorvins.

Thyka took a deep calming breath and reached out her hands. "Join hands now. Tol, we need you to join us. Everyone close your eyes and focus your thoughts on each other. Let me take the lead on this."

Inside her mind, Thyka heard the thoughts of her friends growing louder against the sparks and colors of the rest of her thoughts. As she saw their auras grow in intensity, the rest of her mind faded into a dim background greyness. As each one became part of the whole, a band of golden light appeared to join them together.

The mental connection solidified and she extended her thoughts out to the others. "Good. I can feel each of you as if we were one now. When I call the string, you must remain quiet until I call on you. Do only as I ask and nothing more or less. The strings have a very strict protocol of etiquette and will only listen to those they consider to be polite and considerate. Don't snicker, Duvar. That will end all of this quicker than anything. Is everyone ready?"

As the others watched, she began a song, which became visible as an abstract blending of light, color, and sound. A beautiful melody lifted above them and out into the darkness. Almost at once, the melody was joined by a much larger, more complex harmony of the same song. The small circle of crewmates became surrounded by flowing currents of intense colors, some that they could not identify, intertwined with the sound of such intricate and vibrant qualities that they sat in awe for a long moment before Thyka jolted them out of their daze.

"They have agreed to listen to us, but remember your manners. I will call on each of you in turn to speak with them. Open your minds, and allow them every access they require. No harm will come to you unless you try to fight them."

"Is this how you see the strings, Thyka? I never imagined in my wildest dreams they could be like this. We see them as pure energy, never anything even approaching this." Jontar, his mental voice hushed, touched her almost hesitantly.

She laughed. "Boys. You only see what you want to see or expect to see. You need to learn to be more open to the world around you. Be prepared now. Jontar, you're first."

One by one, the strings filled the minds of each of the group, absorbing not only the details of each of their lives and experiences, but their very essence. Their personalities... their souls were laid bare before the cosmic strings. They lingered longest with Tol. Slowly, after what seemed a lifetime in the timeless presence of the strings, the connection faded away. At last only the auras of the companions remained, still connected by the shimmering band of silver and gold energy amid the grey background of Thyka's mind.

"You may find yourselves drained for a while when we return to consciousness. The strings can be overwhelming until you get used to them."

The connecting flow of energy pulled away one by one from each individual, allowing them to return to their own minds and bodies.

Jontar's eyes fluttered as he woke up from the joining. He leaned forward, elbows to knees as he sat cross-legged in the circle and held his head. "Is everyone all right?"

Duvar chuckled quietly as the room came back into focus for him. "Yeah. What a trip. I feel like my entire life, everything I've ever known, has just been reduced to a dust particle. Compared to us, the strings are almost gods."

"No, not gods," Maliche joined in. "They're just ancient beyond belief with experiences encompassing all of space and time as we know it."

"Isn't that the definition of a god?" Yalmut added.

Thyka stretched her legs forward and bent at the waist, grabbing her toes with her fingers. "Maliche is right. They're not gods, simply something beyond our experience. All of you did very well. We have given them a lot to think about."

Maliche leaned back on one elbow, uncrossing his legs to stretch out. "Will they let us connect and travel with the Gorvins aboard?"

"Oh, yes. We satisfied them about the Gorvin's having no hostile intentions, so they will allow us to demonstrate what we can do with the strings. For now, at least."

"For now?"

"I'm not sure, but I got the impression we are on probation at the moment. They didn't tell me anything specific, but I think they are going to investigate the Skae and try to verify what we have shown them. They never really questioned the Skae before."

Duvar sat upright, tossing one hand in the air. "Why the phalk not? They started this whole mess in the first place."

"The Skae were using the cosmic strings for transportation long before they ever devised their scheme to build the gravity wave generators, and the strings did not actually pay any attention to them. Sort of the way we ignore the bacteria living inside us."

Maliche scowled as he preened his crest. "If they ignored the Skae, then why are they so angry at the Gorvin? Why pay attention to them?"

Thyka laid back, eyes closed in thought. "I believe the Skae filled the communication networks with so much propaganda against the Gorvin, often while traveling connected to the strings, that the strings picked up on the Skae's attitudes. Without any contradictory information in such close connection to them, the strings simply adopted the Skae point of view."

The group remained silent for a while, each one reflecting on their experience. Yalmut broke the stillness. "I was wondering why they spent so much more time with Tol than the rest of us."

Maliche turned over to face Yalmut, switching elbows to lean on. "It was because he was originally a Skae creation. They built him, so the strings wanted to learn his thoughts on the Gorvin and the Skae as well."

Yalmut nodded, then laid back and closed his eyes.

"I think all of us should rest for a while before continuing." She stood up, walked over to the nearest wall panel and turned the lights down to their lowest setting. Returning to her place in the circle, she, too, lay back and fell asleep.

***

A burst of light in the main viewscreen and the return of communication chatter over the speakers signaled the ship's return to current time. Their brief excursion into the past completed, the Gorvin scientists and crew members gathered in the cafeteria.

"That was the most surreal experience I have ever encountered. Absolutely marvelous. You must share this technology with us." Gnobis paced around the table in the mess hall, hands tapping as he clasped them behind his back. "Wouldn't you agree, Master Dravite? Surely there can be no question regarding their intentions now."

The master nanovirus engineer sat drinking tea at the table next to Maliche. "Yes, it was an incredible experience to be sure. I have to admit I had my doubts, but no longer. How do you manage it?"

Jontar swallowed a bite of his stew and reached for a handful of sweet tam berries. "We, I and some of my Kolbri brethren, have certain abilities which allow us to connect with technology in ways no others can. Part of this skill also gives us the ability to connect with the cosmic strings with great precision, far greater than the Skae can. We used this ability to secretly learn more about them as they thought they were training us. It is not something we can teach others, but once this war is over, we would be happy to serve as pilots. Of course we would maintain strict regulations over who can time travel and to when. None of us would want to mistakenly undo some vital piece of history."

Gnobis nodded vigorously as he strode about the room. "Of course. Nobody wants that. It is a great responsibility to bear, protecting time. There must be prohibitions on its use…"

"Something we can agree to discuss at a later time." Dravite cut in, his voice carrying a note of warning. "We have much more immediate concerns before us now. We need to return to my office and contact the authorities. A strategy needs to be devised to help our friends here with their plan to finally end this war."

Maliche grinned and pressed the communication icon on a control panel on the wall. "Yalmut, take us back to Kluton. We have business to attend to."

Chapter Nineteen

Calomel, Grand Director of the Gorvin government, sat in judgement before Maliche and his crew, with Gnobis and Dravite as spokespersons before the Congress. The sonorous qualities of her double vocal chords carried undertones of dissonance, warning the petitioners to tread carefully.

"Let me get this straight, Maliche Rocker. You want us to commit our entire fleet to one final, massive assault on Seriph while you and your crew sneak in and try to convince these cosmic strings to allow our nanovirus weapons to penetrate them, something that has proven impossible for thousands of years. You want us to believe this because of your magical ability to talk with those energy strands. My apologies, Master Dravite, but you must see how, even with your endorsement and testimony, it all seems too mystical for us to blindly trust the future of our entire race on these friends of yours."

The high-vaulted room of carved and polished stone, emphasized the tortured and intricate patterns and colors of the many layers built up over millions of centuries. The reflections of dozens of the algae lamps danced off the walls, giving it an almost life-like appearance. Statuary built into the walls depicted scenes from Gorvin history, but Gnobis did not have time to explain their significance before the audience began. The Congress, each member robed in somber greys and browns with only a metallic badge of honor depicting their station, sat behind a solid rectangular bench that seamlessly rose out of the cavern floor. A small algae lamp illuminated each of the members of the congress at the bench.

"Grand Director, esteemed Congress members, I realize how incredible all of this must seem, but I believe this represents our opportunity to finally end the war with the Skae." Dravite paced in front of the stone bench, clasping his hands respectfully at his waist. "I do not pretend to understand the abilities or the motives behind these Kolandi and Brin representatives, but I know beyond all doubt what they claim is within their power. You have seen my holo-vid report. You know my reputation. I implore you to trust these new allies as you trust me and allow them to help us defeat our enemy."

Calomel let her gaze cast over the group assembled before her, finally settling on Maliche Rocker. "Tell me, Brin, why should we trust you as Dravite says we must?"

Maliche stood, imitating the respectful hand clasp as he rose. At first, only the faintest hint of a blue glow surrounded him, but as he spoke, the aura's intensity grew. "Your honors, I have spent my life fighting injustice. I went to war against members of my own family when I learned they had committed an atrocity against the Kolandi. It is simply my nature to abhor injustice of any kind. We always trusted the Skae. They rescued us from our dying world and brought us to Kodut. We knew nothing of this great war between you. As our knowledge of the Skae increased over time, so did our skepticism. When my son and his companions learned the reality behind the atrocities committed by the Skae, despite all of their efforts to conceal the truth from us, we vowed to fight against them. Everything we have done since has been dedicated to that sole purpose. We have abilities not even the Skae know about, and we will use these talents to help you and your allies defeat them once and for all."

Several of the Congress members leaned together, whispering their thoughts. Calomel stood. "We will consider your offer, Maliche Rocker. We shall inform Master Dravite when we have reached a decision." With that, the entire Congress followed Calomel out of the room through a back tunnel. The main doors opened and Dravite led the group out, returning to their quarters in the city.

Feeling the need to stretch their legs some, the companions decided to walk back to their rooms.

Seykel strolled beside Gnobis as they walked. "This place is so beautiful. You must teach us how to do this in our own poor caverns back on Kodut. So many of our youth have abandoned our ancestral homes in favor of Brin cities, but if we could provide such wonders as these, our homes would be preserved and made so much more comfortable."

Gnobis's face beamed. "If we can end this war, I believe you will have no shortage of architects and engineers to help you learn our techniques. It would be the least we could do for those who brought us peace after so many centuries of war."

She squinted, tilting her head as if noticing something for the first time. "Is the light dimmer than when we first arrived?"

"Yes, of course. Night is closing in." Gnobis studied her like a parent wondering if his child were sick.

"But you live underground. Why would it matter about night and day?"

He laughed a deep rumbling avalanche of a laugh. "All creatures have wake-sleep cycles. We did not begin our evolution underground. Conditions above ground were not always so harsh. Millions of years ago certainly, but life once flourished on the surface and thus depended on the cycles of day and night. We only delved this deep underground around two-hundred-thousand years ago. Until then, our species lived close enough to the surface to still witness the sun's rising and setting. Our biology is still connected to those cycles, so we must recreate them here."

Maliche spoke with Dravite as they walked together. "How long do you think they will take to make their decision?"

Dravite's unreadable features remained frozen. "The Congress normally is very careful and deliberate in its decisions." He rubbed a broad chin with thick fingers. "This one, though, is unprecedented. No telling how long it could take. Maybe months."

Maliche lurched to a halt. Jontar, Yalmut, and Duvar nearly ran into him as they were close behind and caught up in their own conversation. "Months? We don't have months to wait. Once those Modiri learned about us and what we could do, they are sure to increase security around Seriph. They may even be hunting for us as we speak."

"The Congress understands the situation, Maliche. Our testimony included this very information. It may be the urgency of the situation that forces them to move more rapidly than they would normally like. We will have to be patient."

"I hope they know what they are doing. Every day counts. We must get to work as quickly as possible." Maliche regained his stride, shaking his head as he went.

***

The congress deliberated for three days before a message arrived over Dravite's holo-vid. "Great news, everyone," Dravite announced as he burst through the doors into the main living area of their apartments. "It would appear the congress was acutely aware of the press of time in our case, and also due to the undeniable proof of your capabilities during our testimony, they have agreed to join forces and attack Seriph."

An hour later, everyone was sitting around a table in Dravite's research facility. Schematics of viral structures and nanobot engineering hung in the air over the table, projecting the lab's latest innovations. Reaching out to point a stubby talon at a particular location on the virus, Jontar pinched his fingers, then opened them rapidly to enlarge the view. "This is the section which specifically targets the Skae biology?"

Gnobis responded with a quick manipulation of a few controls when portions of the sequences changed colors. "Yes. As you can see, we have had this available, with modifications, since the early days of the war. We simply cannot penetrate the cosmic string barrier surrounding Seriph."

"What about the Modiri? Being all female must have some effect on the virus."

Another press of the controls and a new viral sequence appeared next to the first. "Of course, but the blood sample you brought us allowed us to develop an additional viral component designed to attack Modiri biology. It was remarkable how their isolation on that moon allowed for so much variation. We are in your debt."

Thyka startled at Gnobis's mention of blood. She narrowed her eyes dangerously as she studied Jontar. "And just how did you happen to obtain Modiri blood? You promised you would not harm any of them."

Jontar lowered his gaze from her face. "Don't worry, Thyka. I only took a small sample from a tiny incision while Zephyl was under my control. I know I promised, but I thought it might come in handy if we ever got this far. She wasn't actually harmed."

She simply sniffed at him and returned to her study of the strings they had gathered during their most recent encounter.

Jontar returned his attention to the pair of viral sequences. "Yes. If we can send both of these viruses though the barrier, it should do the trick. Do you have enough of the nanobots to deliver the quantities we will need?"

Dravite scanned his screens for the data and projected it. "It'll be close, but if we speed up production another twenty percent, we should have enough to infect both the planet and the moon simultaneously."

"Thyka, have you learned anything new about the strings? We don't want to run into any surprises in the middle of a battle."

Thyka glanced up from her tablet. "I think we startled them with our news about the Skae. If they have had enough time to examine Skae communications and ships since we spoke, there should not be any trouble. If they took the time to study them anyway."

"We can't go to war with the Skae on a maybe, Thyka. Can we rely on the strings?"

Her fingers patterned their way through a few pages on her tablet as she frowned in thought. "I think we can, Jontar, but the strings are difficult to understand. They don't normally pay attention to anyone but themselves. They don't like the feelings wars and hatred provoke in them, so I believe they will take steps to help us... That's the best I can offer for now."

Duvar threw up his hands and laughed. "Oh, great. So if the strings decide all of us are beneath them and not worth the trouble, we'll find ourselves sitting out there in Skae space with our talons up our..."

"I told you what I know, Duvar." Thyka leaped down from her chair and began thumping Duvar in the chest with two small talons. "Next time, *you* try figuring out how to understand the gods."

Leaning as far back in his chair as he could, Duvar tried without success to defend himself from Thyka's assault. "What do you mean, gods? You think the strings are the gods?"

Closing her eyes and shaking her head as if trying to explain complex physics to an infant, Thyka stopped her attack and faced Duvar with hands on hips. "No, I don't think they're gods, you phalking schutek, but that's what it feels like sometimes. The complexity of their minds and emotions are far beyond anything biological creatures like us are capable of." She glared at him a moment longer, as if daring him to say anything, then stormed back to hop up into her chair.

Jontar cut them both off, using his commander tone. "Alright, Duvar, knock it off. You know what she means. You felt their power. I have to agree with Thyka. It's like we're some sort of bacteria trying to convince the sun to shine in our favor."

"This is starting to sound like a much greater risk than we had previously thought." Dravite stared at the group stone-faced, but a hint of concern tinged his voice. "I hope you have not led us into something we cannot hope to win."

Maliche glared at the others before focusing his attention on Dravite and Gnobis. "No, my friends, things are not as dire as these children make it sound. This is merely how they work things out between themselves. The strings will cooperate and we will deliver your viruses. The question is, are your forces strong enough to defeat the Skae fleet?"

Dravite studied Maliche's group, sighed, and swiped his tablet to project images of a wide range of military vessels. "We have defeated the Skae battle fleets on many occasions. It was only our inability to isolate their planet that prevented our ending this war long ago. They have a vast military complex capable of rearming themselves rapidly."

Showing more concern than Dravite, Gnobis cut in. "Without the ability to coordinate command structures and manufacturing facilities on distant planets, their ability to wage war would end. Your intelligence has shown us the Skae's fatal flaw. Only the Modiri make decisions and order commands. If the rest of the Skae cannot communicate with their Modiri, none of them can operate in any capacity worth mentioning."

Maliche surveyed the room. "Everyone knows their responsibilities. Let's not waste any more time arguing and get down to putting together a strategy against the Skae. I want detailed plans and analysis in two days. We need to have time to coordinate and adjust before presenting our final thoughts to the grand director. Any questions?" He nodded and signaled that the meeting was over.

***

Five days later, the collaborators sat in the ornate chamber in front of Calomel and the rest of the committee from the Gorvin congress. Maliche's crest was disheveled and had gone unpreened for days, and his clothes were rumpled from his brief catnaps on the office lounger, but he presented their strategy to the Congress. "… so, esteemed Congresspersons, as you have seen, our plan carries significant risks, but, if successful, the final defeat of the Skae is well worth the effort. We believe the time for ending this conflict once and for all is at hand. Will you commit your fleet to support us?"

Silence permeated the chamber. Maliche remained standing, exhausted and bleary-eyed, before the bench. The robed leaders bent their heads in quiet whispers, nodding occasionally as one or another made a comment, or pointed to a vital component of the strategy, still projected in front of them. Calomel, with a guttural grunt full of discordant resonance, called for a decision. Each individual nodded, giving their own deep throaty response.

"It is agreed." Calomel thumped her broad fist on the bench. "Notify the fleet commanders to gather tomorrow for a briefing on the congressional emergency frequency. All ships are to be battle-ready in one week. May the everlasting Anatase protect us and grant us victory."

Maliche leaned heavily on the carved stone table in front of his companions as the congress members filed out of a doorway behind their dais. Rubbing his eyes, he barely noticed the congratulatory slaps on his back or words coming from the others. Even the tingle in his mind seemed remote as Tol talked to him. *Well done, my friend. I'll keep you on your feet long enough to get back to the apartment and into bed. You need to sleep. I can only keep you going for so long. Time to let Jontar and the others do their jobs.*

***

Nalot pounded on the wall inches above Maliche's head. "Time to get up, you lazy drunge. We need to go over some final checks before joining the fleet."

"What the phalk!" Maliche lurched upright in his bunk, throwing the blanket onto the floor.

"Seykel tried to wake you earlier, but you were sleeping like a rock, so she asked me to try. You've been asleep for two days. We need you and Tol for some last-minute alterations to our strategy before we launch. Get dressed and meet us in the briefing room."

Maliche preened his crest as his eyes came into focus. "Give me five minutes." He stretched, swinging his legs out of the bed as Nalot exited through the sliding doorway.

"… and your modifications to our nanobots was brilliant, Yalmut. Reinforcing the structural integrity to withstand the acceleration of the rail guns will give us a decided advantage."

Maliche entered the briefing room in the middle of a discussion between Dravite and Yalmut. "What modifications?   You found a way to improve the nanobots?"

The others turned and smiled as Maliche joined them. Yalmut stood to give Maliche his chair in front of the holo-vid display. "Yes. I always wondered why the Gorvin used the light sails only to deliver their weapons and only against entire planets. They would make excellent weapons in ship-to-ship battles…"

"But our designs could never overcome the extreme forces of acceleration required to deliver the bots using the weapons our battleships use. Light sails take a long time to build up speed and must be launched from great distances. We can target a planet from those distances, but enemy ships are too small. And in the close quarters of a battle, the light sails are too slow and easily destroyed before reaching their target."

"Exactly. It took me a while to figure out the precise design flaw, but I found it, and, with a few modifications, I was able to give the bots enough strength to handle railgun accelerations. With these devices added to the beam weapons of the fleet, we might have enough of an advantage to overcome our disadvantage in numbers."

Maliche looked up at Yalmut, his stomach clenched. "What disadvantage in numbers? I thought our surveys showed the Skae fleet only slightly larger than ours."

With a deep, raspy cough, High Commander Rutile, officer in charge of the Gorvin fleet, announced his presence. "We received communications yesterday from our advanced scouts of a massive buildup of the Skae fleet around Seriph. It appears they have recalled nearly their entire force to protect their home world." He projected the latest figures for Maliche to see.

Clicking his talons rapidly, Yalmut added the new weapon's capabilities into the battle assessment projections. "As you can see, without the nanobot weapons, the size of the Skae fleet was bad news for us, but, with the new armament, we are every bit a match for them."

Maliche studied the data and preened his crest again. Looking at Thyka, he took in a deep breath and expelled it forcefully. "Are you certain the strings will help us?"

Thyka paused before replying. "I can't say they will help us, exactly, but I believe they will not stop us. Jontar took me out to a nearby cluster yesterday, and they are definitely becoming increasingly angry with the Skae the more they learn from their investigations."

"They can't be too angry if they still allow the Skae to use them for travelling."

"I know. It's complicated. The strings need more reassurance we do not intend to commit genocide against the Skae. They will not allow that. I've tried telling them our nanobot weapons are intended to kill technology, not living beings, but they are still nervous. Whatever they may be, life in any form is sacred to the strings."

"We need their cooperation, Thyka. If we can't penetrate the strings to get the nanobots to Seriph and its moon, everything will fail."

"I know, Maliche. I have faith in the strings. They won't let us down. But I will stay in contact with them once we're out there and continue trying to allay their fears."

Maliche nodded and surveyed the room. "What else is going on? Launch day is getting terribly close."

A flurry of discussions, projected data, and holograms gave life to the room as they made final preparations.

Chapter Twenty

Blackness filled the portal in Seykel's personal compartment as she stared into space. She wore the traditional leather outfit of a Skatak, but the empty loop at her belt where her kital once hung stabbed at her heart. She felt like she was going into battle with only one arm. She pulled Thyka into a tight embrace. "I feel so useless. My skills are not much use against a battleship in space."

Thyka returned her mother's hug, her head leaning on Seykel's shoulder. She reached under a fold in her dress and pulled out a plainly-wrapped package. "If anything goes wrong, we may need your warrior talents, so I brought this for you." She held out the package for her mother.

"What is this?" Seykel took the heavy parcel from her daughter, eyes squinting, head tilting as if searching for something.

"Open it."

As Seykel unwrapped the bundle, a glint of silver caught her eye. She gasped as the final wrapping was removed. "How…? What in the…? My kital? It was broken. How is this possible? A broken kital is beyond repair." She fingered the blade's curves with a gentle touch of two fingers, her eyes brimming with tears.

Thyka, tears now flowing down her cheeks as well, smiled at her mother's shock. "The Gorvin have worked in metal longer than any other civilization. They have forging skills far beyond ours. Once I saw their grand city, I talked with Gnobis. Forgive me, but I stole the pieces from your cabin and showed them to him. He examined it and assured me it could be repaired. I wanted to surprise you with it."

Unable to take her eyes off her beloved heirloom, Seykel's tears dropped onto its gleaming surface. A minute passed before Seykel looked up into Thyka's face, threw her arms around the girl, and pulled her into an embrace worthy of any grendel. Her voice, choked and barely audible, found itself. "Thank you."

The two women held each other for a long moment before separating.

Seykel made another protracted examination of her restored kital. "This is miraculous," she said. "There is no sign of it ever having been broken. Not a weld mark or imperfection anywhere."

"I was as surprised as you are, mother. I believed Gnobis would be able to do as he promised, but the level of skill here is beyond all reckoning. I will definitely be talking with him and the other craftsmen about designs for our own caverns before we are done with this mission."

Seykel smiled lovingly at her daughter tossed the glittering weapon into the air in a series of complicated patterns, finally hanging it on its belt loop. "We need to get to the bridge. Today we go to war."

Mother and daughter left the compartment and strode with determination down the passage toward the bridge, grim visages worn like masks on their faces

The hatch slid open and mother and daughter stepped from the brightly-lit corridor into the darkened bridge. The hum of intership communication filled the room as they took their places amid the rapidly-changing lights of data streams and holo-vids showing at every station. Dominating the room, the main portal showed an enhanced view of the Skae battle fleet surrounding the planet Seriph, shimmering in the glow of cosmic string energy.

"Light sails have launched. At present rate of acceleration, they should reach one-half light speed in two hours and only minutes more to reach the planet. We must punch a hole in those defenses before then." Yalmut relayed his information to Jontar, who sat at Maliche's left in the center of the bridge.

Duvar called out to Jontar from his station. "High Commander Rutile reports the Gorvin fleet is ready to attack. Only the Tulop and its battle group will remain behind with us. He asks if we are in position to approach the strings."

After a quick glance at Maliche, Jontar responded with a wave of his talons. "Tell the fleet commander we are in position and ready to connect with the strings once the battle is fully engaged. Tell Subcommander Tufa to stand by."

Five minutes had passed when the main view screen showed the bulk of the Gorvin fleet powering up and darting into the distance, beginning a three-pronged attack on the Skae home world. Like a swarm of bimits surrounding their hive, the Skae vessels held their defensive positions but maneuvered to face the attack.

"Ships are within range, firing beam weapons now. Skae vessels returning fire." Yalmut spun out a running commentary of the battle as it progressed. Explosions burst from the grey metallic surfaces of ships in both fleets as focused shafts of high energy beams impacted them.

"There goes the first one!" Duvar pointed a stubby talon at the screen as a Skae battleship lit up in a brilliant soundless flash and ripped in two. Nearby vessels scattered to avoid the debris but maintained their constant fire.

"The Gorvin weapons appear to be doing more damage. Are the Skae ships not as powerful as we thought?" Maliche leaned in to Jontar, trying his best to sound calm.

"No, the weapons are equal in strength, but the Skae ships are not as heavily reinforced as the Gorvin's. Remember, the Skae tend to emphasize design over function. Nobody builds for durability like the Gorvin."

Yalmut called out from his station. "Six more Skae ships down. The fleet is preparing to deploy the railgun nanobots."

"Two Gorvin battleships down." Duvar indicated the drifting and burning hulks that were part of the center prong of attack. As he watched the screen, hundreds of Gorvin cruisers let loose with their railguns. The impact of the new weapon did not result in any explosions, merely the sudden appearance of large gaping holes in the sides of the ships they hit. The holes did not appear to be lethal, but in less than a minute, those vessels ceased firing and began to drift aimlessly.

"No power reading emanating from those Skae ships. The nanobots seem to be doing their job. They just took out fifty-three of the enemy."

Without warning, ten of the Gorvin cruisers and one heavy battleship exploded. Streams of heavy fire came in from above, and below the fleet.

"New Skae attack ships closing in, Gorvin ships taking heavy damage."

Maliche bolted up from his command chair and leaped to Yalmut's side. "What happened? Where did those ships come from?"

Yalmut waved over a few controls; his holographic display changed views and showed projections of the new combatant's flight paths. Tracing the pathways with the talon of one finger, Yalmut followed them back to their origin, a single cosmic string. "They must have been waiting in another sector before joining the fight. That string allowed them to transport in. I guess they aren't fully convinced of our intentions yet."

Thyka closed her eyes, composed her mind, and allowed her thoughts to flow out to the offending cosmic string. "This one is not like the others. It is angrier. It's almost as if it feels betrayal. I think this one has decided to work against the wishes of the others and fully aid the Skae."

Maliche turned to face Thyka, leaning on the back of Yalmut's chair. "Isn't there anything you can do? Can't you convince it to stop helping the Skae?"

"No, I can't. It's made its choice. But maybe I can try something else." She let her mind roam free again.

Jontar shifted in his chair, pointing to the main view screen. "What are those two strings doing? I've never seen strings move like that before."

As the bridge crew watched, the enhanced view screen showed two cosmic strings leaving the edges of the planet and surrounding the rogue string, cutting it off from the space around it.

Thyka sighed as she regained her composure. "The other strings were not happy with that string or with my request, but they agreed to prevent any further interference. We should be safe now from any more surprises."

Duvar pointed his chin at the screen. "Those new ships are making a mess of things. They just took out twenty more cruisers and two light battleships before the Gorvin were able to make adjustments. They sacrificed half of their group and appear to be retreating to join the planetary defenses."

Yalmut pulled up a new data batch on his panels. "Yes, but they wiped out one-third of the ships equipped with the nanobots in the process. I hope we have enough left to do the job."

Maliche stared at the view screen, now a mass of flaming vessels, some in pieces. The battle continued in a fierce exchange of energy weapons, but more difficult to follow now with the debris field growing by the minute. A crackle of the intercom broke the silence. Subcommander Tufa's voice boomed over the speakers.

"Twenty minutes until light sails arrive. Our fleet has opened up significant holes in the Skae defenses. It is time to move in and open up the string's energy field. Stay inside our protective cover." He hesitated a moment before continuing. "Are you certain you can shield all of us from their sensors?"

Jontar gave a quick nod to Maliche while holding up two talons held close. Maliche waved a finger pattern over the communication panel on the arm of his chair to respond. "Yes, we can maintain the shield, but only for a short while. And once we are in contact with the strings, we will become visible to the Skae. If you can bring us in with a string between us and the Skae, maybe we can stay hidden longer."

"Roger that. Subcommander Tufa to battle group, stay in close. Keep the pattern tight, no strays. Set for heading theta-nine-six, half thrusters... engage now."

The view screen showed the Tulop settling into position directly in front of Maliche's ship, the remainder of the battle group taking positions, completely surrounding them.

"Thrusters at half, maintaining position. Shield is holding," Yalmut reported as he studied his panel and simultaneously linked minds with Jontar and Duvar to build the sensory shield around their small pack of vessels. Any sensor sweeps from the Skae ships were absorbed by their efforts, creating a simulated hole in space as far as the Skae were concerned.

"Four hundred more Skae ships disabled, only minor casualties detected aboard those hit by the railgun nanobots. Five additional Skae vessels destroyed with massive casualties by conventional weapons. Twenty-three Gorvin ships destroyed or out of commission. Heavy losses reported. Fifteen minutes until light sails arrive." Yalmut continued his reports of the battle as they approached the glare of the string's energy field. He adjusted his controls to dim the brightness in the main view screen.

Maliche turned to face Thyka and her parents. "Time for you to do your thing, young lady. Are you up for this with only Jontar and Duvar to help?"

"I'm ready. The strings are much more receptive now." She hopped off her chair, gave her parents a long hug and headed off the bridge toward her cabin.

Seykel took Duvar's station while Nalot replaced Jontar at Maliche's side. He grinned as he watched Seykel caress her kital as she listened to the communications coming in to her station.

***

Back in her quarters, Thyka sat on a cushion on the floor and joined hands with Jontar and Duvar, linking their minds. Once again, as she slipped into her aura, she watched as the auras of her companions took form and solidified next to her. Sparks of color flashed around them as if they were made of electricity. The room was replaced by flows of color and patterns, ebbing and flowing like rivers of pure energy. In the distance, but rapidly approaching, appeared the blinding energy of the cosmic strings.

Thyka and the others remained still, allowing the strings to surround them. Her skin crawled as if armies of tiny electric bimits marched all over her. "Stay still." She cautioned Duvar as he squirmed with discomfort. "Do nothing to cause them alarm or concern. And let me do all the talking. Understand? No snarky remarks." She cast Duvar a withering glare, causing him to shrink and barely nod in agreement.

Reaching out with her aural hand, she touched the energy flow of the strings. The flows seemed to absorb her hand, joining with it, becoming one with it. "Hello. We have come to tell you it is time. Our devices are arriving soon and we need your permission to allow them to reach the Skae planet and its moon. Will you assist us?" Her voice glided like silk in a light breeze through the energy patterns.

A chorus of voices, like all the strings of an out-of-tune harfel playing at once, responded. "We are still concerned. How can we trust you will not eliminate the entire Skae race? We observe your war, and you have killed thousands."

"Have you not discovered the lies and horrors the Skae have inflicted on the rest of the galaxy? They have killed trillions and brought dozens of civilizations to extinction."

A silence followed briefly, accompanied by a deep feeling of sorrow and guilt, penetrating to their core. "We know of their atrocities and of their schemes. We agree their plans to engage the energy device they are building near the two stars must end. We will assist you to those ends, but how are we to believe you are different from them? We cannot allow genocide of even ones such as the Skae."

Thyka sat quietly, thinking when she felt a nudge at her right. She looked and Jontar sent her a mental request to speak to the strings. Studying him briefly, she nodded agreement.

Jontar's voice, while not as smooth and reassuring as Thyka's, still maintained a calming influence. "My friends. You examined us during our last visit with you. You have experienced our hearts and desires. But if you need further proof of our difference from the Skae, I offer this. Which of us has been open and transparent with you and which has hidden truth from you? Which of us has enslaved and ruled over others without concern for any but themselves and which of us is striving for freedom from oppression? You have examined us. Which do you view as the more trustworthy?"

A dissonant tone rang through the energy streams as if an argument had broken out among the strings. Then harmony returned. "Your words are powerful, but how do we know you are not hiding truth as well?"

Thyka replied before Jontar's growing irritation got the better of him. "Look at the battle we fight. Examine our weapons. Which of us is attempting to save lives and only disable the technology of the ships? While we both use weapons for killing, which of us using them only from necessity? We prefer to save as many lives as we can, even the lives of our enemy. We kill only because they leave us no alternative to reach the peace we desire."

The string energy field aura dimmed slightly, the voices quieted. Seconds later, the chorus sang out. "We understand now. Your devices will be permitted to approach the Skae planet and its moon. Be forewarned, however, if you have deceived us in any way, we will be forced to take actions we have sworn never to inflict on another since the darkness."

Thyka squeezed Jontar's hand, mentally asking him to return to silence. "Thank you, my friends. We will honor our promise. The Skae will not be destroyed, only restricted to this world, and isolated from traveling the galaxy. You will have no cause to regret assisting us."

Slowly lowering her hand, the energy flows separated and the strings receded into the distance, their chorus fading with them. The three unclasped hands and Thyka watched as Jontar and Duvar's auras faded into nothingness. She remained only briefly before allowing herself to re-inhabit her body. Darkness replaced the light, but a pale replica of the light grew behind closed eyelids.

"Thyka, are you alright?" She felt the gentle shaking of her shoulders as she regained full consciousness and opened her eyes.

"I'm fine. I always hate to leave. It's so restful there." She patted Jontar's hand on her shoulder, stretched her legs and arms, and allowed her friends to help her to her feet. "We need to get back to the bridge. I hope we were in time."

***

A minute later, the three stepped across the threshold of the bridge. A scene of horror greeted them on the view screen. The Tulop, spouting flames from dozens of breeches in her sides, hung in space before them. Only three of the battle group remained active, circling protectively around the flagship. The rest floated helplessly as a debris field around them, along with the remains of several Skae ships, all destroyed or disabled.

"It's about time. The light sails are only three minutes away. Will the strings allow them through? Maliche looked up from bandaging Nalot's leg. A red circle showed through the grey fabric of the wrap.

"What happened? Father, you're injured." Thyka rushed to Nalot's side, examining his face and body with her eyes and hands. "Where's Mother?"

Nalot winced as she touched his leg. "It's nothing; I caught a piece of shrapnel. I've had worse, believe me. Your mother is fine. She's back in our cabin letting Yalmut stitch her up. She hit her head on one of the panels during the attack, but she took out those four first." He shook a taloned hand toward the view screen. "Did you convince the strings to let the light sails through?" He held her arm, grip tightening with each word.

It was only then she noticed the bodies, seven in all, stretched out on the floor beneath the screen. Skae bodies. "Yes… yes we convinced them. The light sails will get through. How did Skae get in here? What happened? Are you sure Mother is alright?"

"We're both fine. Help me into a chair." He grimaced as Thyka and Jontar helped him up, gently depositing him into the closest seat.

"One minute until light sail arrival." Maliche called out after returning to his command station.

"The Skae sent a small attack force against us. The Gorvins fought them off, but a boarding vessel escaped our attention and docked with us. Tol warned us at the last second, so we were ready when they stormed the bridge."

"Here they come." Maliche switched the view screen to show the planet. Thousands of streaks crossed the field of view instantly, continued for thirty seconds, and then the view returned to normal. Except for the few pockets of ships still fighting, nothing appeared amiss.

The bridge speakers crackled to life. "Subcommander Tufa here. We are intercepting communications from Seriph to the Skae vessels. It appears our nanobots are knocking out their technology at a rapid pace. Distress signals are arriving from every city. Even the moon is sending distress signals. They've never revealed themselves before. Things must be pretty desperate down there."

"How long before they take full effect?" Maliche asked. "Will anyone be able to leave the surface in time to avoid contamination?"

"Not a chance. The virus will take some time to work, but the nanobots will eliminate anything capable of escaping the planet before they can fire up the engines."

Duvar clapped his hands together and laughed. "Look at them! The Skae ships are all turning tail and heading to Seriph. Looks like they want to try rescuing their precious Modiri."

The crew sat transfixed before the view screen as they watched the remaining Skae fleet vanish through the cosmic string barrier. The speakers popped to life again.

"This is Commander Rutile to battle group seven. Commence rescue operations for all disabled Skae vessels. Provide oxygen and other supplies as needed. Do not… repeat, do not board ships or approach the planet without specific permission from me personally. Send drone ships with required supplies. All other able ships assist our people in your area. Report casualties and specific requests on beta frequency."

"Is that it? Is the war over?" Thyka gaped in amazement from Nalot to Maliche and back again.

"That's it, dear one. The war is over. You have done incredibly. You cannot imagine how proud I am of you." He hugged his daughter, feeling her tension relax as she pulled herself deeper into his chest.

Chapter Twenty-One

Four days later, after ensuring the Gorvins added protections to their ship against the tech nanobots, Maliche and his crew followed a reconnaissance team down to the Modiris' moon. As the vessels approached the landing pad, nothing appeared different except the lack of traffic and communication signals. A few Skae personnel could be seen in the vicinity, but they barely reacted to the arrival of the Gorvin spacecraft.

"They appear to be in a state of shock. Look at their faces." Seykel watched out a portal in her cabin with Thyka at her side. As the dust rose by their landing thrusters settled, she could make out greater details. "They look lost, like a child realizing its mother is gone."

"The Modiri can no longer tell them what to do. All communication is cut off, aside from direct word of mouth." Jontar's voice startled the two women as he spoke from their open doorway. "Imagine a hive of bimits suddenly cut off from their queen. Without someone telling them what to do, the Skae are incapable of making any but the most basic decisions. It will be much worse on the planet."

Thyka shook her head. "It didn't have to be like this. If they had only listened."

"They paid the price for their arrogance. They're lucky to escape with their lives after the millennia of destruction they caused. Nobody but the Gorvin would be so forgiving."

"Forgiving? This is horrible." Seykel hung her head and slid down from the portal. She turned on Jontar, a powerful rage rising in her. "Have you forgotten your ancestors... my people? We Kolandi suffered the effects of this weapon we just loosed on the Skae. Once we were a thriving, valued member of the intergalactic community. Hundreds of millions died of starvation and disease before our population leveled off at a level sustainable at a hunter-gatherer level of existence. The Skae now face that same fate."

Taking Seykel by the shoulders and gazing into her eyes, Jontar tilted his head and smiled. "No, I have not forgotten. This is why we are here. I convinced Rutile to allow us one shot at offering the Modiri our help in avoiding the fate of the Kolandi and other civilizations destroyed by the nanobots in the past. We are heading to meet them now. You are welcome to join us, if you wish."

***

"I'm not so sure I like this trip to meet the Modiri any better than our first visit. I don't miss the guards and interrogations, but this emptiness is eerie." Duvar shivered as a chill ran up his spine. "Where is everyone?"

The faint hum of their mag-lev cars was the only sound in along the streets of Alasar, the Modiri capitol city. The throngs of Skae citizens were now gone, replaced by the few individuals wandering aimlessly in rumpled and dirty clothes, obviously not washed in days, their faces blank and the palest shade of blue ever seen on a Skae. The soaring abstract structures still shone brilliantly in the morning light, seemingly mocking the gloom of its inhabitants.

"Time bring our offer to the Modiri." Jontar parked their mag-lev behind their Gorvin escort at the foot of the stairway leading up to the palace. Only the sound of a slight breeze rustling the nearby trees could be heard. Halfway up the stairway, he noticed a Modiri prelate stop suddenly, her face shocked into sudden awareness at the arrival of a working piece of technology. She turned and ran up the stairs two at a time, disappearing inside the large doors at the top.

"Do you think they'll listen?" Thyka nearly whispered her question, wary of disturbing the stillness.

"My bet is on that Tiphan schuteka refusing to even see us. These Modiri make the Skae look like saints." Duvar chuckled as he ascended the steps alongside Yalmut at the rear of the group.

Entering the palace, the companions walked to the throne room, their steps echoing in the empty hall. The door stood ajar, creaking slightly as Maliche pushed it open enough for them to pass through.

"So now you come to gloat and dictate terms." Tiphan, high priestess of the Modiri, all-powerful ruler of the Skae, sat alone on her throne. A shaft of light, dust motes dancing in its path, illuminated the transparent magnesium work of art. Intricate threads wove their patterns, reminiscent of the wind as they intertwined with each other in forms that escaped description but created beauty nonetheless. Tiphan's gown sparkled in the light, even though it was slightly wrinkled. Her dark curls swooped magnificently on top of her head, only a few stray strands escaping the restraints of her golden crown. "Very well. Say your piece. We are in no position to prevent you. But then be gone from our sight. You have nothing to offer us, and we have nothing of value remaining for you."

"Yep, gracious to the last. This ought to be interesting." Duvar whispered under his breath to Thyka, who kicked him in the ankle in response.

Maliche took a few steps forward, and bowed respectfully. "High Priestess, we want nothing from you. We do, however, offer a way to save your people from the horrors they face in the near future. We can help you prevent your people from suffering as all of you adjust to your new reality. Will you allow us to help you?"

Her laughter resounded through the throne room. "You offer us your help? The Brin, the Kolandi, their half-breed offspring, and let us not forget, the Gorvin, offer us help? The Modiri and The Skae ruled the galaxy... and you offer us your pity?" She spat on the floor and glared at Maliche.

"Tiphan, do not let your arrogance doom your people. You can still prevent the tragedies ahead. Swallow your pride and think of your people."

Tossing her hands in the air as if dismissing them, Tiphan leaned back almost casually. "Fools, we do not require your help. We will soon be rid of this plague. While your fleet was busy trying to destroy us, I gave the signal to activate the keugelblitzes. Soon our singularity generators will become operational and we will have a source of unlimited energy to undo your nanobots' destruction. Go now, before I have you arrested and executed, as I should have the first time we met."

"Your Skae subjects are helpless without your direction. You cannot communicate with the ships protecting the device, so they will be defenseless. Don't do this."

Another round of maniacal laughter erupted from her. "You pitiful little things. Do you think we did not anticipate your weapon's small chance of success? After our escape, several of my priestesses and prelates were dispatched to the Telphar System. Our fleet will be well prepared for you."

Maliche shook his head. "You are truly mad, Tiphan. That device will destroy half the galaxy. There is nothing, not even your precious singularity generator, to bring back your rule over the rest of the universe. I offered you a way to at least save your own planet. The destruction is now on your head." He turned and signaled for the others to follow him as he strode out of the hall. Tiphan's laughter and taunts followed them, growing dim as they left the palace.

"We have to stop that device. Why didn't we send ships there in the first place?" Maliche faced Jontar as they followed the Gorvin escort back to their ship.

"Gorvin fleet resources were stretched dangerously thin as it was. They couldn't afford to risk the assault with anything less. We didn't think they were this close to having the kak thing working yet. It was a risk we thought worth taking."

"One we have to take care of now. Get in touch with Dravite and let him know what has happened. He needs to inform Commander Rutile as soon as possible. How long before the device turns critical?"

Jontar looked up at the mag-lev's roof for a moment before responding. "A week, maybe ten days. After that, nobody can stop it. We have to get the nanobots there before it reaches critical mass."

Chapter Twenty-Two

"Two hours before we reach the device. Long range scouts report only a minimal Skae fleet. Only two cruisers, one battleship and a dozen assorted small ships." Subcommander Tufa reported the intelligence via holo-vid to Maliche and his crew as they sat in the conference room behind the bridge of their ship.

"How can they possibly hope to defend their device with so few ships? It's suicide." Nalot clicked his talons, now showing the wear and tear of abuse.

"Unless the scouts missed something. Maybe the Skae have more ships than we thought. Could they be hiding somewhere?" Jontar drummed his stubby talons on his leg as he studied the attack plans on his tablet.

Yalmut sighed heavily, swiveling in his chair. "Not unless the combined intelligence of generations of surveillance on the Skae has been wrong. They only had so many ships at the start. We have accounted for all of them."

"Tiphan seemed confident she could still win. Maybe she knows something we missed."

"There is always something the enemy knows which we do not. That is the nature of war. We prepare for what we can and adapt as the situation changes. Make your preparations." Tufa saluted with a closed fist to his shoulder and flickered out as the transmission ended.

"I hate surprises." Nalot grumbled under his breath. "They always bite you in the tail when you least expect it."

At the appointed time, Jontar released the controls connecting them to the cosmic string. The small fleet of Gorvin ships he brought with them on the string spread out into a defensive pattern surrounding the small Brin vessel. Ahead of them loomed the double star of the Telphar

System. The stars' light ebbed and flowed as the thousands of asteroid-sized keugelblitzes orbited the stars collecting their energy, transmitting it to a massive central collector, which combined the small sources into a single massive beam of pure energy. The yellow-white beam vanished into the distance where, as Yalmut's sensors indicated, the gravitational wave generator absorbed it all, powering up in preparation of creating the massive singularity. It was this singularity the Skae hoped would ensure their complete dominance of the universe. They were too sure of themselves to admit the truth of the Gorvin data foretelling the destruction of half this galaxy. Once the device reached full power, four days from now, the Skae believed they would have the supremacy to control all of the known civilized worlds.

"Engage all defensive shields. Enemy ships approaching on vector alpha nine-four-two." Sub Commander Tufa's gravel voice boomed over the bridge speakers. "Arm all energy pulse and nano-rail cannons. Prepare to open fire on my command."

"This shouldn't take long. Those Skae ships are—" The main view screen blazed so bright Jontar had to shield his eyes before finishing his sentence. Alarms blared and warning lights flashed on every station panel.

"What happened? What was that?" Maliche held a death grip on the arms of his command chair as Jontar sprang from one location to the next, helping regain control of the ship.

"Some sort of energy weapon fired from the largest of those collectors around the stars." Duvar frantically worked his controls, reading the information as fast as it appeared in front of him. "Both battleships took heavy damage but are still functional. Six of the ten cruisers are out of commission and we lost all but twenty-five of the smaller fighters. I don't know if any of the reserve fighters can be launched. Communications are still out."

"What's our status?"

"Long range sensors are dead. Engines only have one-third power. Surge circuits tripped everywhere, but our hull is intact and we should be able to maneuver... if we don't push it too hard."

"Is our stealth cloak still working?"

Duvar punched a few more controls. "Yes, our shield only took a minor hit. We were close enough to the Tulop that it took the brunt of the hit for us."

Through the view screen, Maliche watched as the Skae vessels closed and opened fire on the virtually helpless Gorvins. Those ships still able to fight closed quickly with the enemy and laser fire erupted in a fierce battle.

"Can we contact Tufa?" Maliche scratched his crest feathers with his talons as he tried to think through the alternate strategies they had prepared. None of them considered anything like this.

Jontar returned to his station next to Maliche as the others brought their vessel back to life. "No, Father. We're on our own, at least for now."

"If we can get to that central collector, can you get inside and shut it down?" Maliche pointed to the focal point of the energy beams from all the smaller collectors.

Nalot and Jontar conferred and came to a quick conclusion. "No guarantees, but it appears to have at least two access points for maintenance personnel. If Yalmut and I can get inside, we should be able to connect with it and shut it down. The problem is getting there."

"I'll worry about getting us to the thing. You figure out how to turn it off permanently."

"They'll need protection in case the thing is protected by any Skae soldiers. Those Modiri probably know enough to protect such a vital key to their operation."

"In that case, I'm going with you." Seykel jumped down from her controls to stand in front of Nalot, hands on hips and daring him to disagree with her.

Nalot's mouth opened as if to object but shut immediately. His face contorted as at least four different arguments appeared to cross his mind, each one rejected before escaping his lips. He gave up and turned to Maliche, eyes begging for help.

"Don't ask me to try to stop her. I like all my parts right where they are." He held his hands palm up in resignation.

Nalot sagged in defeat and let out a mighty sigh. "The four of us, then. Let's make this quick."

Thyka ran up to her parents and enveloped them in a hug, or at least as far as her tiny arms could manage them both together. "Stay safe. I love you." Releasing them, she returned to her station, wiping tears from her eyes.

Fighting the urge to add his own cautions, Maliche gave the orders. "You four head to the airlock and get ready. Duvar, take the controls and get us to the nearest docking port on that satellite. Don't attract any attention if you can help it." He spared a long look over his shoulders, as Nalot was the last to leave. "Make sure everyone comes back alive. I'm counting on you."

Nalot simply grinned and waved a cavalier salute as he left the bridge. Maliche returned his attention to the main view screen as the small ship maneuvered through the wreckage of the ongoing struggle between the remaining Skae and Gorvin vessels.

"Those Skae ships are fast. The few nano-rail guns still functioning are having trouble getting a fix on them. Looks like this one will be decided by the fighters." Duvar kept a running commentary on the battle as they flew passed it. "There goes one of the Skae cruisers. The Gorvin are gaining the advantage."

"Not for long if that thing powers up and lets loose with another blast. How long before we can dock with it?"

"Another thirty seconds and we'll be there."

Back in the airlock, Jontar, Yalmut, Nalot, and Seykel donned breathing masks and armored pressure suits. Each picked up a laser pistol except for Seykel who attached her newly remade kital to a loop at her waist, stroking the blades with her fingers as she waited. A hard jolt and loud thunk announced their successful docking.

"Opening airlock door in three...two...one." Duvar's voice crackled in the speaker and the door slid up to allow them entry into the moon-sized collector.

"Keep your eyes on a swivel. Don't hesitate to fire at any Skae or Modiri you see. Don't give them a chance to shoot at you first." Nalot took the lead, stepping lightly on the metallic grid, which comprised the floor of this passageway. Dimly lit, the tunnel was lined with power cables and conduits, all labeled with warnings of high voltage, pressure, or temperature precautions, depending on their purpose. This facility displayed none of the artistic architecture typical of Skae designs. Pure functionality exuded every centimeter of the place.

"Take the next passage to the left. I'm sensing a small control room there. Not too far, probably some sort of remote auxiliary control center." Jontar removed his hand from one of the cable bundles and joined Nalot in the lead, his weapon at the ready.

"Everybody down!" Nalot shoved Jontar aside as an orange energy beam split the air where his head had been. "They must have vidcams watching the tunnels." Everyone dove for cover behind whatever protruding panels or bulkheads they could squeeze into.

"How many?" Jontar lifted his head only far enough to get a brief glimpse inside the control room.

"I counted three, but there may be more. You can be certain more are circling around to cut us off."

"Then we better act fast." Jontar raised his pistol and fired into the control room. Bursts of orange energy burned past him as the others joined in.

Shouts from both sides filled the air as the smell of ozone and burning circuits filled their nostrils. The return fire from the Skae diminished until only one soldier remained. Before anyone could react, Seykel's tiny figure flashed over them and into the room, her kital raised and flashing in the hazy light.

"Gentlemen, they're all dead. You can come in now." Seykel stood in the hatchway, smiling. Jontar stepped over the threshold, averting his eyes as Seykel yanked the kital from the last Skae soldier's forehead and wiped the blood off on his uniform.

"Make this fast, you two. We don't have much time." Nalot took up a position at the hatch they came through while Seykel guarded the hatch on the opposite side of the room.

"Yalmut, you take those controls while I work over here. You know what to do." Both Kolbri worked the controls as they sent their minds into the computers running the collector. Following the intricate pathways of circuitry, they gained control of the system, one system at a time, until their minds joined in the central processor.

"We need to burn out the controls allowing this thing to release the energy it collects. I found the files controlling that, but it will take both of us together to manage it." Yalmut's mind-voice showed Jontar the path to follow.

"Yes, I see it. Together then, but don't shut it down completely. We need it to overload slowly so we have time to get out of here with the others."

"Agreed. On my mark..."

Jontar and Yalmut leaned on the panels as they came back to their bodies. "It's done. We have ten minutes to get back to the ship and get away before it explodes."

"Follow me, then. Let's move." Nalot waved for the others to follow him, with Seykel bringing up the rear. As Jontar stepped through the hatch into the tunnel, he heard a thunk, like the sound of a heavy metal tool dropping into a metal bucket.

A flash of silver spun past Jontar's head and embedded itself in the neck of a Skae soldier a few yards down the passageway. "Get down! Fragger!" Seykel's scream, as she shoved Jontar to the ground, was drowned out by the ear-splitting explosion of a fragmentation bomb.

His head spun in dizzying whirls from the concussion. Jontar felt the trickle of something wet running down his face and slowly became aware of orange flashes of light above him. His lungs struggled to take in air as if a grendel were sitting on him. He distantly felt the pull on his arms as Yalmut dragged him down the passage and around a corner.

"Get him out of here. I'm going back to get Seykel." Nalot helped Yalmut lift Jontar to his feet, wrapping one arm around Jontar's waist and pulling one of his arms around his neck to support his barely-conscious friend.

"It's too late. She couldn't have survived that blast. You'll die if you go back." Yalmut adjusted Jontar's weight for better balance as he shouted at Nalot over the weapon fire.

"She's my wife. I'm not leaving without her. Get him out of here and get the ship to safety. I'll be right behind you." Nalot pulled Seykel's kital from the neck of the dead soldier and handed it to Yalmut. "You might need this. Now go!" With one last shove, Nalot let out a war cry and fired both pistols he carried while charging back into the control room.

Daring to look, Yalmut peered around the corner and nearly collapsed at seeing Nalot, holding Seykel's bloody and limp form in his lap, firing wildly, keeping the Skae soldiers at bay.

Tearing his eyes away, he pulled Jontar down the tunnel. "Come on, try to run. We don't have much time." He sent a desperate mind link to Jontar. *"Wake up! Run!"*

The effect was immediate, like a shot of adrenaline. Jontar, startled awake and needing only minor support, ran with Yalmut back to their vessel. Diving into the airlock, Yalmut took one last look down the passage before hitting the controls to shut the door. He yelled into the speaker. "Detach and get out of here as fast as you can." A lurch to the left and sudden acceleration sent the two crashing to the floor. Outside, shrinking into the distance, the collector satellite exploded in a massive burst of energy. The shock wave tossed the small Brin vessel like a cork in the ocean, but it held together and soon settled itself on a steady course back to the Gorvin fleet, or at least what remained of it.

A whoosh of air and the smell of fried circuits jarred Jontar's senses as the shock of Yalmut's mind link faded away. Strong arms, a pair on each side, escorted him to his cabin and helped him lay down on his padded cot. The room swam with his disorientation, but not as bad as a few minutes ago. Was it a few minutes? Or a few days? Hard to remember. He heard voices nearby, but they, too, faded as he drifted into a dreamless sleep.

He awoke to the touch of a cool, wet cloth on his face, and the sound of soft singing. A sad tune, but beautiful. He tried to move, but his muscles ached and decided it wasn't worth the trouble.

"So you've decided to rejoin the living. It's about time. Our friends weren't going to wait forever to celebrate their great victory. One less hero in the festivities wouldn't make too big a difference."

"Thyka? What are you..." The memory jumped back into him with both feet and landed hard. He reached out to take her hand.

"Thyka, I'm so sorry. I tried to... I mean, there was nothing I could..."

"It's alright, Jontar. Yalmut explained everything after we got you into bed. That was four days ago. There was nothing you could have done. The collector had to be destroyed." She sighed as her eyes drifted skyward. "At least they're still together. I don't think either one would have wanted to live without the other." She let out a tiny giggle. "And they died as two of the greatest heroes in the history of the galaxy. Mother would have enjoyed that one. She was always a little jealous of your father's stories of his ancestors." She wiped away more tears as they fell. "Oh, kupt. Here I go again. Not very Tolavarian of me."

Jontar grunted as he sat up and pulled Thyka into his arms. The two Kolbri clung together, each releasing their sorrow at the loss of their family and friends. Eventually sleep took them both as they lay together, comforted in their embrace and minds linked in silent, simple togetherness.

Chapter Twenty-Three

"Are you sure we have to do this again? I don't think I can handle another state dinner on another planet with another horde of adoring public figures showering us with titles and gifts." Duvar tugged at his neck, trying to loosen the tight collar of his ceremonial cloak. The past two months had been filled with an unending stream of parades and ceremonies celebrating the end of the war against the Skae. Untold numbers of interviewers on endless planets across Gorvin space and those from distant worlds once allied to the Skae, all wanted to honor the brave heroes from their own ranks. Tufa, greatest of the Gorvin heroes and much in demand, still limped from his injuries received during the final battle.

"You love every minute of it and you know it, Duvar." Jontar punched his friend on the shoulder and then put the last medal in place on his own cloak, grimacing at their reflections in the holographic mirror image. "This is the last of them, so we can go home in a day or two."

"How do you think a bunch of 'risen from the grave' galactic heroes will be received back home? They couldn't wait to send you and your father off to be incinerated in the sun."

Maliche stood in the doorway behind them, unannounced until his answer made them jump. "Ryma has been taking care of that little matter for us. She's made some significant changes to the Assembly since our departure. A few trusted allies were eventually let in on our ruse, and they helped gradually leak a few rumors about our survival. The traitor's trial helped expose the treachery they committed against our family and the people, swinging sympathy in our direction… and the broadcasts of all these celebrations touting us as the champions of this war haven't hurt, either."

"So you've been in touch with mother recently? How is she holding up?" Jontar tugged at his sleeves and collar, adjusting the fit of his ceremonial garb.

"Last night. She's well but is anxious for our return. The loss of our friends weighs heavily on her." Maliche shrugged and hung his head. A soft violet glow surrounded him.

Jontar approached his father in silence and laid a gentle hand on his shoulder. Yalmut and Duvar joined them, forming a mourning circle, heads bowed with arms outstretched on each other's backs. They held this circle for several minutes, each one lost in the memories of their departed companions, until Maliche broke the spell. "Time to go. We have a full day ahead of us."

Exiting their room, Jontar spied Thyka sitting alone on a small bench in the hallway. Her flaming red hair hung in long curls, intertwined with ribbons of gold and silver. She wore a long gown of deep green and displayed a heavy necklace of garnet, typical of the Tolavar. In her lap, she held a plain leather pouch containing her mother's kital. Her face was lowered with closed eyes. As Maliche and the others approached her, she gave a weak smile and rose to meet them. Jontar stepped forward and took her small hand in his. Together, they joined in their procession to the final celebration of their victory.

Chapter Twenty-Four

The farewell dinner, a private affair between friends, proved to be the perfect mix of somber reflection, and joyous celebration. The Grand Director of the Gorvin Congress had wished for a more formal reception, but discussions with Rutile, Tufa, and Dravite convinced him of the need for a smaller affair. He did, however, insist on holding the farewell celebration in his private quarters. No expense was spared. One of the finest symphonic orchestras on Kluton provided the music. Some of the finest artists and craftsmen donated pieces of their work as gifts to the departing heroes and all were on display. The table, finely carved stonework rising seamlessly from the floor and covered by a plain but beautifully woven cloth, held foods from all regions in the Gorvin territory.

"You do realize," said Calomel as she took another bite of something called blutak, a sort of red meat dripping in orange gravy, "That with the Skae out of commission, your young Kolbri are the only ones who have the ability to navigate the cosmic strings. Your world is about to become the new center of the galaxy. Are you ready to become the leaders of the new reality?"

Maliche preened his crest and swallowed a mouthful of a slightly sour brew called suth. "Yes, your honor, we have had some talks about this turn of events. Jontar and the others have already begun communicating with the other Kolbri, those who were being trained by the Skae and others back home, and they are developing a plan to take control over intergalactic transportation requiring strings." He hesitated before continuing, shoving a piece of something greenish-yellow around his plate. "I would hope we can count on your help in setting up a type of central governing body for all the planets, Gorvin controlled, independent, even former Skae allies. We are not comfortable setting up another aristocratic system and hoped to move toward a more parliamentary central body where all planets are represented equally and all have a role in keeping the peace. An Empyrean, if you will."

Calomel sat back, rubbing her broad chin as she examined Maliche with a piercing gaze in an unreadable stony face. "There will be opposition. Those who already rule over some of the systems may need to be convinced of the wisdom of such a move. You will have no trouble from us. We have always maintained a rather light touch on our systems and work closely with them to provide for everyone under our influence."

"Do you think there will be more wars?"

Calomel let out a rumbling, harmonic chuckle. "Nothing like with the Skae, to be sure. And, if you use your authority over cosmic string transportation wisely... as a prize rather than a punishment, you may be able to gain support without actual bloodshed."

Maliche tilted his head and raised a goblet toward Calomel. "You have much more experience with matters of this magnitude than I do. I would deem it a great favor if I could have your support and guidance as we move forward."

Returning the gesture with her own goblet raised, Calomel's harmonic voice took on a much deeper, richer quality. "I would be happy to be of assistance in anything you require. Our fees and compensation for such services can be discussed later." The corners of her mouth raised ever so slightly, a beaming smile for a Gorvin. "Nothing too extravagant, I assure you, but with politicians, nothing comes free of charge."

Maliche laughed in reply. "That I am familiar with. It seems to be a standard across the universe."

The party lasted well into the night with everyone sharing stories of battles, family histories, lost friends, and a good bit of politics and commerce filling the time. Long after the bioluminescent lamps had dimmed for the evening, Maliche and his companions said their farewells and returned to their ship to prepare for an early departure. Full stomachs and time spent in good company led to deep and, thankfully, dreamless sleep for all.

***

In the morning, cargo bay loaded to overflowing with gifts from dignitaries and average citizens across the galaxy, natural sunlight filtered through the skylights in the above-ground hangar holding the now-battered ship Maliche and his crew had commandeered so long ago. Jontar fought his way back to consciousness as a sliver of sunlight penetrated his cabin's portal and struck his eyes. A shifting of weight next to him and a small arm across his chest brought a smile to his face. Since his awakening after his injuries, Thyka had moved in to his cabin. At first, she claimed he needed round-the-clock care and this made her job easier. She simply never left after he healed and he did not object. She smelled good, and her touch stirred him in ways he never imagined. Though nothing was ever said to the others, at least not by him, they all smiled when the two of them appeared together.

He sent a gentle thought to Thyka as she slept. *"Time to get up. We're going home today."*

"I'm awake, just enjoying your warmth before we head off into the cold of space."

"The ship still maintains a constant temperature. It's not cold inside."

She dug a knuckle into his ribs before snuggling in closer. *"It's the principle of the thing. Just thinking about all that cold space makes me cold."*

Jontar broke the connection and patted her on the hip. "We still need to get up." He pulled the thin heat-reflective blanket off and lifted himself to his feet.

"Five more minutes." Thyka mumbled as she gathered the blanket around her and turned her face to the wall.

An hour later, Thyka waltzed into the ship's cafeteria, her face, hair, and outfit set to perfection. The leather pouch holding Seykel's kital hung from her belt. She leaned in, gave Jontar a peck on the cheek, and ruffled his meager crest. "Thank you. I feel much better today." She emptied one of the meal packets into a bowl, added water and sat at the table next to him as steam rose from the mixture and a fruit meal breakfast loaf prepared itself.

"I thought you said five minutes. It's been an hour. We lift off in twenty minutes." Halfway through this comment, Jontar regretted opening his mouth but could not stop once he began.

Thyka's narrow-eyed glare would have cut him in half if it were an actual blade. "Bring me some strong tea, my love. I can't deal properly with ill-mannered buffoons without my morning tea."

Without another word, Jontar filled a mug and backed out of the cafeteria. From halfway down the passage he called back to her, "Love you too!" and sped toward the bridge.

***

"Prepare for string separation in ten seconds." Yalmut called out from his post. "Kodut orbit in one hour at cruising speed."

A flash of light, followed by the black of space filled the main view screen as the ship pulled away from the cosmic string that had transported them home in record time.

Thyka sent out her mind link to the string in farewell. *"Thank you for everything. I promise we will be more considerate in the future. Those like me will be trained in proper etiquette before linking with you."*

A massive, nearly overpowering presence filled her mind as the string replied. *"The gesture is not required but appreciated. Be forewarned, however. Now that we have been awakened to the abuse of our inattention, we will be more aware of those who join with us in the future. We will not tolerate using us with harmful intent."*

"Rest assured we are of the same mind on this matter. We, too, will not tolerate a repeat of the Skae's abuses in so far as our abilities allow."

"And therein lies the difficulty we perceive. Our study of your kind has revealed a basic nature, which desires good but often results in succumbing to your baser instincts. The Skae fell to their pride and arrogance. How long before others fall as well? You mean well, but you have not the power to prevent the abuse of others. We will take steps to illustrate the wisdom of listening to your better nature."

A chill ran down Thyka's spine. *"What steps?"*

A burst of images filled her mind, and then the string simply vanished from her thoughts.

Seconds later, Duvar bolted upright in his chair. "I'm getting a frantic message from the Gorvin. Something about Seriph."

He listened with one hand holding his earpiece steady, his eyes growing wider by the second. "They say it's gone."

Maliche turned to face Duvar's station. "What's gone? What are you talking about?"

"The planet Seriph. The Gorvin say it just vanished."

"That's ridiculous. An entire planet can't…"

"Yes, it can." Thyka interrupted, her face pale and in shock. "The strings took it away."

All heads turned to watch her as she slowly took her seat. "I was thanking them for their help when they gave me a warning. They said they would give us all something to think about before ever misusing them again. Apparently they shipped Seriph, all the Skae, and Modiri, off to the most remote part of the galaxy, and left them there at some distant time in the past."

Maliche felt the pit of his stomach lurch. "But they'll all die if we can't reach them. Surely they maintained a route for us to supply them as they adjust to their new zero technology status."

"No. The strings deactivated the nanobots and the viruses, don't ask me how, and removed themselves from that region of space. No strings are within a hundred light-years of the planet now. We couldn't reach them even if we wanted to. They are far removed from us in time as well as space."

"How can they move an entire planet so far so fast? And into the past? I sensed they were powerful beyond belief, but this is beyond anything I could have imagined." Jontar fell back in his chair as he thought about the potentials the strings possessed.

Yalmut shook his head slowly. "They are completely isolated. Even with an ability to regain their technology, the Skae are no longer a threat to anyone."

Maliche preened his crest and resettled himself. "Inform the Gorvin of the situation and tell them to spread the word of the strings' warning. I pray to The Eternal it will be enough to keep everyone from doing anything stupid. For now, let's get home."

With the touch of a few controls, Yalmut brought the ship around until Kodut sat in the center of the view screen. It hung in space, blue, green, and brown like an oasis in a vast desert, growing rapidly as they approached.

Maliche touched the controls to open his microphone. "First Town space port, this is the Amaethon on approach vector delta four. Do you acknowledge?" A few anxious seconds of static filled the bridge as they waited for a reply.

"Amaethon, this is First Town space port. We read you and welcome you home. We've been anticipating your arrival. Synchronize ship computer settings to planet standard and set coordinates for landing pad one A. There's quite a reception waiting for you there."

Maliche watched as his crew collectively relaxed and began to smile. "Copy that, First Town. We're happy to be home."

Forty-five minutes later Yalmut glided the ship to a soft touchdown in the center of the landing pad. "All thrusters off, commencing shutdown. Releasing locks on outer hatches."

Nobody moved. Each member of the crew was lost in their own thoughts and feelings, coming to terms with everything they had been through.

"Come on, you bunch of stiffs. Let's go breathe some real home-grown air again." Duvar clapped his hands together and jumped to his feet, pulling at Yalmut's arm and grinning from ear to ear.

Roused from their thoughts, they hugged and slapped each other on the back. Duvar lifted Thyka above his head and spun in a circle. A look of fright on his face, realizing the risk he had just taken with the fiery young woman was quickly extinguished when he saw her lit up with laughter and aglow with joy. With a quick hug, he placed her on the ground before she could change her mind and rejoined Yalmut as he left the bridge.

At the hatch, they stood aside and allowed Maliche to lead them. Light from a bright blue sky blinded them briefly as it flooded the hatchway. Maliche led the way down the ramp, filling his lungs with the brisk, fresh air of home, followed by Duvar and Yalmut, arm in arm, and Jontar and Thyka, holding hands. Waves of shouts and applause mixed with a blaring horn band greeted them.

Maliche inhaled deeply all the familiar scents of home and reveled in the feel of the breezes against his face. He broke into a run when he saw Ryma waiting at the bottom of the ramp. He collided with her, gathering her into an embrace neither was willing to break. He took in the scent of her skin and hair and listened with near-rapture to the sound of her voice. It didn't matter that what she said was beyond his comprehension. He was home and with Ryma.

The throng continued to shout and cheer as the others stepped off the ramp. The crowd kept a respectful distance from the loving reunion until they could resist the urge to join the heroes no longer. Soon Ryma and Maliche found themselves the center of a crushing embrace.

Composing herself, Ryma addressed her family and friends. "We can continue this display in private later. For now, the public is eager to greet our returning heroes… the saviors of the galaxy." She gave Maliche a quick elbow to the ribs as she said the last part, and leaned in close to whisper in his auricle. "And that is the *last* time you will hear such nonsense from my lips. I knew you when you were a simple archaeologist, my husband. Don't think I will ever see you as more than you are."

She led them up a staircase to a temporary platform erected so the gathering throngs could witness the ceremony. Holo-vid cameras zoomed around them by the dozens. Their images, at least three stories tall, appeared on the walls of nearby buildings for the distant late arrivals to see. Dignitaries from all the guilds and cities around the globe sat on chairs attached to risers built into the platform. All of them were standing and cheering.

"Wave at the people. You're all great heroes now, so you need to play the part." Ryma, with Rilo and Neri close behind, signaled for the group to gather on the stage and greet the crowd, some of which had been gathering for days once their arrival date was announced. Stunned by the enormity and enthusiasm of the reception, none of them moved at first, until a gentle nudge by Ryma set Maliche in motion.

"Weren't these the same ones clamoring for your head the last time we were here?" Duvar said in Jontar's ear.

After everyone took their seats and a few brief introductions were made, each of the twelve guild masters took their turn at the podium to give their grand speeches, carefully edited and approved in advance by Ryma herself. Each one, while full of praise and admiration for Maliche and the others, included a well-crafted apology, of sorts, usually phrased in terms of being duped by the treasonous lies, and fabricated so-called evidence perpetrated by Nissend Honj and his family. Each one concluded with a declaration of fealty to the Rocker family and the Assembly.

The sun crossed well past its zenith before all were done. Then Ryma strode to the stand. Her long dark hair draped perfectly over one shoulder, the small tiara of her station as Princess to the Kolandi sat sparkling on her head. The simple but elegant white gown flowed regally around her. Interwoven threads of silver caught the sun and seemed to glow. She stood for a moment before raising one hand to bring the crowd to silence.

"My people, Brin and Kolandi alike, for we are all now one people, we are indeed here to celebrate the return of our loved ones and to celebrate not only the end of a long and cruel war," she gave the slightest of glances toward the guild masters, "but also to usher in a new prosperity. We have lost some of our dearest and most trusted friends." Holographic images of Seykel and Nalot appeared above and behind the stage. The two appeared to hold hands and gaze out over the gathering. "Their sacrifice is a symbol of the unity which should be in all of our hearts and minds. They died for each other and for all of us, Brin and Kolandi alike, so we could face the future together in their memory. Today, we celebrate. In ten days, we will mourn our loss. A new and bright future awaits us. Let us welcome it together and prove to all the inhabitants of this universe who fought and suffered on our behalf that we are worthy of their sacrifice."

Signaling for the others to join her, they rose and joined hands, held high. The crowd went mad with cheers and shouts. In the midst of the mayhem, those gathered on the stage witnessed Brin and Kolandi citizens embracing each other, and celebrating together as equals.

Maliche bent over to speak in Ryma's ear. "I hope this is not a passing fancy, soon to be forgotten in the resurgence of old prejudices."

"We will make sure it is not. The eyes of the galaxy are on us now. We have no choice."

Chapter Twenty-Five

As promised, ten days later, the funeral preparations were carried out. Of course the coffins were ceremonial; Seykel and Nalot's remains now rested among the stars. Representatives from not only the guilds but hundreds of planets attended. Calomel, Dravite, Rutile and Gnobis represented the Gorvin and offered Tufa's apologies. Despite his insistence of health, the doctors prevented his traveling in space due to his injuries and continued rehabilitation requirements.

The day reflected everyone's mood as thick grey clouds hung low in the sky, threatening to unleash the rains common in this season. A chill breeze blew, pushing fallen leaves across the ground. The kilometers-long procession wound its way through every sector of First Town. Throngs gathered on every sidewalk and hung from every window along the way. Banners, both manufactured and homemade, hung everywhere, displaying the image of Seykel and Nalot as they had appeared in holographic form above the crowd ten days earlier.

Leading the somber and nearly silent procession was the caisson carrying both empty coffins. Alongside them stood all those who, in life, had been closest to Seykel and Nalot. Brin, Kolandi, and Kolbri alike rode in the open air for all to witness. At the front, Thyka, only child of the two being escorted to their final resting place, stood gravely between them, one hand on each simple but elegantly-carved wooden sarcophagus. To her left and right stood Ryma and Maliche Rocker. Behind them stood Opet, and Tola Shatal, now The Elected One among the Tolavar, Danet, and Jontar, with Yalmut, Duvar, Rilo, and Neri at the rear. As they passed by, individuals in the crowds of mourners tossed brightly colored pieces of ribbon and white flower petals on the road before them in honor of both Brin and Kolandi rituals. The route took them to a prepared gravesite in Founder's Park, near the memorial built to honor Karm, Maripa, and the first Jontar Rocker. It was considered a fitting location so all who came to visit could be reminded of not only the struggle to survive on this world but the ongoing sacrifice required of all who want to thrive in a civilization built for them by those brave souls who came before them.

Tola Shatal and Haytk, high judge of the Assembly, acted as co-celebrants of the burial ceremony. The caskets sat on a catafalque standing in front of a marble mausoleum, carved with images of the two fallen heroes and scenes of significance from their past, including their final act of bravery. Each said a few words and performed funereal rituals of each race. At the end, Thyka rose, with Jontar at her side and her arm draped over his for support, and approached the coffins. She did not speak, but only said a silent final prayer of farewell, sending her thoughts into the empty boxes.

"Mother... Father, I don't know how I will ever go on without you and your guidance. I miss you more than you will ever know. Thank you for everything. Thank you for your strength and your love, even when I least deserved it. Your bravery has brought our two people together at last. I will use my abilities and my status as Tolavar to serve as a constant reminder so no one ever forgets." She paused, giving a brief glance toward Jontar under her lashes. *"I also ask for your blessings on Jontar and me. I pray we are as strong and as full of love as the two of you."*

She nodded silently to Jontar, turned, and walked arm-in-arm with him back to their seats. Maliche Rocker, newly reinstated as Head of the Assembly, rose and addressed the gathering.

"As we lay our brave and selfless friends to rest, here in this place of honor," he turned to look up at Karm's obelisk, "We remember hard times and good times. Today is a day for forgiveness and consolation. It is a day to celebrate a new beginning. We are about to embark on a journey unlike any other. The galaxy now looks to us. We must be prepared to answer. I will not mar this day with political speeches; our friends deserve better. I only wish to thank you for your heartfelt outpouring of sorrow, and to promise brighter days to come. I know we will embrace this brave new Empyrean we have been called upon to lead as one people, together and unbreakable, from within and without." He turned and stretched out a hand toward the two coffins. "May we prove ourselves to be their equals."

Chapter Twenty-Six

"Eight years and we've only begun to fill a fraction of the need for string pilots." Jontar paced his office, adding to the worn path already showing in the floor.

"It's a good thing we had so many Kolbri already in training with the Skae before we uncovered their secret. At least there are enough to cover most of the basic needs in every sector... for now." Duvar, surprisingly efficient and capable as an administrator, especially since his marriage to Thyka's Kolandi cousin, or third sister, or whatever she was — the intricacies of Kolandi family relationships still confounded him — sat with his tablet displaying holographic charts and tables of the recent training efforts. "We're still on track for meeting the growing needs, so long as all those Brin and Kolandi 'patriots' continue their enthusiasm for making new little Kolbri string pilots. Most of the little ones are showing plenty of ability for piloting. Your two are among the strongest, as expected for Rockers."

A sudden thought interrupted Duvar's chain of thought. "Speaking of which, how is Thyka doing? She must be ready to burst soon with your third, if my calculations are right. I heard she's still traveling to the Eastern Continent in her duties as Tolavar to her tribesmen. Shouldn't she consider settling down and stopping all her ocean hopping, at least until after the birth?"

Jontar halted in his tracks and raised his eye feathers. "You want to tell her that? Be my guest. I can always ask father if you can be buried next to Nalot and Seykel."

"She takes her work to keep us all united very seriously, doesn't she?"

"Yes, but she still finds the time and energy to be with us or bring us with her. Don't worry about us, Duvar. We're very happy and the children are young enough to still think of this as a grand adventure. We'll settle down someday, but there's too much still to be done."

"Tell me about it. Syla wants me to step down at some point and quit gallivanting around the sector inspecting the training camps. I can't do that until I've trained a decent replacement. That won't happen for a few years to come yet."

"Someday, my friend, some day."

***

Maliche, showing the grey crest and deep wrinkles of time, took his place at Ryma's side for the swearing-in ceremony. His knee creaked as he lowered himself into the comfortably-padded chair. The entire membership of the Assembly, now a fully-integrated compilation of Brin and Kolandi, with one or two of the oldest of the Kolbri, gathered for transfer of authority. Ryma, now chief judge after Haytk's retirement six years earlier and due to retire herself in a few months, rapped for attention. Still regal, even in the plain robes of the judiciary, her silver hair shone in the spotlight, setting off her brown face, now also showing signs of age.

"In the years since the end of the war and the return of peace to our world, we have proved ourselves worthy of the duty placed on us by those who have departed and now rest in honor. It has not been easy and there have been struggles, but we have overcome them as one and earned their legacy and the respect of uncounted worlds who have contributed to our prosperity." She waited as a wave of applause washed over the gathering. "But all things change. It is time to honor the past and look forward with eagerness to a new leadership. Will the honorees step forward?"

Maliche and Jontar rose from their places on opposite sides of the long bench of judges and stepped forward until they stood together in front of Ryma. The dignitaries all stood with a thunderous ovation for the father and son who had worked so tirelessly for so long and righted so many wrongs of their civilization.

After a few minutes, embarrassing minutes as Maliche would later recall, everyone took their seats.

"Hi, Daddy! That's Daddy!" A loud, high-pitched voice cried out from the first row. Jontar's youngest daughter, Eisoph, named after the Gorvin scientist who helped raise the first alarm to the Skae's nefarious scheme, sat squirming in Thyka's lap, trying to escape so she could run to her father. Laughter broke out among the crowd as they witnessed mother and daughter struggling. Jontar jogged the few steps to his daughter, swooping her up into his arms. Returning to his place beside Maliche, he jostled Eisoph on his side until he had a firm hold on her. The girl, all smiles, looked around the room until her eyes settled on Ryma. "Hi, Gramma! Can I have a cookie?"

After the dignitaries regained their composure once more and Thyka uncovered her scarlet face, Ryma called for attention and continued the ceremony. "It is with great honor and a full sense of personal pride that I now pronounce Jontar Rocker, having been duly elected and accepted by all those present, Head of the Assembly."

At her nod, Maliche passed the short carved stone staff, inlaid with copper and amethyst, symbol of leadership, to his son. Once more, the assembled body rose and cheered. Ryma stepped down to join her husband and son. Thyka, carrying one child and hanging on to the wrist of another, completed the reunion. Tugging on his shirt to pull him lower for a kiss, she held him level with her sparkling eyes. "Well, I hope this at least means you'll be staying on this planet now. There's a lot of work to be done

around the house and I've got your list waiting for you."
She winked and released him.

"I love you too." He laughed as he raised up,
returning her wink, and lifted Eisoph high above his head,
laughing louder than he had in years.

Epilogue

Deep in space, on a lonely world at the far end of the galaxy, a small group gathered to celebrate.

"One-hundred-twenty-three years and we are finally ready to complete our destiny." Tiphan, high priestess of the Modiri, raised a glass of torshill scent crystals and sniffed deeply.

"Our destiny!" The rest of the Assembly raised their glasses in return and also breathed in the nourishing vapors rising from the crystals. They were all gathered in Tiphan's reception hall. Lyrith and Zephyl, now raised to Tiphan's seconds, as well as Lek, former ambassador to the hated Brin, and Molk, commander of the former Skae battle fleet, now relegated to head of scientific development and coordination of efforts to rebuild their gravity well generator in this new region of space.

"Is everything ready for activation tomorrow?"

Molk seemed to stand at attention, even while seated. "Yes, high priestess. Everything is in place and ready for your command to make the facility operational."

Tiphan's smile would have reminded any Brin or Kolandi of one of the viperous lepti on Kodut. "Very well, then. With the power we will generate from our new generators we will take our fleet back across space, and with the invincible weapons powered by the devices, we will have our revenge on our enemies. To victory over those who oppress us!"

"To victory!"

***

As the new sun rose on Seriph, dimmed by the swarm of keugelblitz collectors surrounding it, Tiphan stood on her balcony naked to fully breathe in the morning air, reveling in the thought of the dawn of their revenge finally arriving. Her skin felt charged with the excitement.

"Would you care for first meal on the terrace, high priestess?" Zephyl strode through the diaphanous curtains hanging in the frame separating Tiphan's private quarters from the balcony, already dressed in her finest, a sheer light green wrap that left her midriff and long legs exposed and only barely providing cover for the rest of her slim form.

"No, the morning breeze has been nourishing enough. I will partake of the vapors when we celebrate the activation of the collectors. You may dress me now."

Three hours later, Tiphan strode into the main hall of the research facility responsible for completion and start-up of the collectors and gravity well generator. Lyrith and Zephyl followed close behind. The gathered Skae scientists bowed at the waist and lowered their eyes to the floor, except for Molk. She lowered herself into the travelling throne she used whenever visiting the planet and waited as her seconds adjusted her gown to perfection. With a clap of her hand, the scientists sprang into action, busying themselves at a wide array of panels, each providing updates and values of the collectors as everything was brought on line.

"We are ready for your word, High Priestess." Molk lowered his eyes, his version of a bow.

Tiphan surveyed the Skae around her and smiled her viperous smile. "You may activate the device."

A hum rose in volume as all displays indicated the collectors coming to life. On a large view screen, holographic images of their sun and the devices hung in space. Slowly one, then another, shot a beam of energy toward the moon-sized wave generators. As more collectors activated, a growing number of beams started the wave generators to show signs of building up their energy levels.

"Full capacity in three minutes." One of the scientists reported to Molk.

"Fire the generators when ready. Prepare for singularity formation."

With a flash of blue-white light, all seven gravity wave generators fired their streams of pure energy to a central point. Tiphan shielded her eyes from the brilliance. After a few seconds, the focal point of the rays seemed to collapse, replaced by a sphere of total blackness, surrounded by a film of swirling distortions.

"Singularity achieved and holding stable."

Tiphan nearly burst from her throne in excitement. "Prepare to energize fleet engines and weaponry. The fleet will depart before this day is over. General, are the directional reflectors in position? We will need —"

Alarms sounded at every station.

"What is happening, Molk?" Tiphan's excitement turned to terror.

**

In a distant region of space, a research vessel from Shyfar, once a Skae world but now assimilated into the new Empyrean, recorded data from distant stars in the hopes of finding new worlds to settle. In a region of space only sparsely populated by a few stars, so remote and not accessible by cosmic strings, that their light took a thousand years to cross the distance, a supernova burst into view.

"There goes a new one, sir. How do you want to catalog it?"

Peering at the view screen only half-heartedly, the captain shrugged and returned to his duty list. "Let the stellar astronomers deal with it. Make a note in the log and pass it along."

**

Thyka Rocker, revered Tolavar and mother, wife and reluctant heroine, sat in her cabin during one of her rare visits to space on a diplomatic mission to help celebrate the opening of a new Kolbri training facility. As was her habit on space voyages, she sent out her thoughts to the string, which transported them on their journey. With a start, and a catch in her breath, she sat up and looked out the hexagonal portal into space. There in the distance, in the midst of a vast black expanse, a single bright star, one which had not been there an hour ago, burst into view. A tear ran down her face.

"We gave them their chance. If only they had listened."

About Jim Cronin

I was born in Kansas City, Missouri and lived in Arlington, Virginia before moving to Denver where I attended High School and eventually college at Colorado State University, graduating with a degree in Zoology and a teacher certification. I currently live near Denver in the small town of Parker.

My career as a middle school science teacher lasted for thirty-five years, but I am now semi-retired, working part-time as an educator/performer at the Denver Museum of Nature and Science. I have been married for thirty-nine years to the love of my life. Together, we raised two incredible sons, and now have three incredible grandchildren to spoil rotten.

Social Media Links

Website: http://jimcroninscienceedutainer.weebly.com/

Twitter: https://twitter.com/authorjimcronin

Facebook:
https://www.facebook.com/JimCroninScienceEdutainer/

　　Goodreads:
https://www.goodreads.com/author/show/14203201.Jim_Cronin

Acknowledgements

This has been an incredible journey. Along the way, I have had the assistance and guidance of many wonderful individuals. I would like to take this time to thank all of you who helped me become the author I am today.

First of all, to my wife, Diane, thank you for your understanding and patience with me and all the times I spent hidden away in my office working on these stories. You are the love of my life and an incredible friend and partner.

To my brother Mike, who started me on this journey with his challenge to me to try writing a book, and all the brainstorming sessions we spent developing the characters and storylines. I may not have always agreed with, or used your thoughts, but you opened my eyes to a new world of exciting adventures and learning.

To all of my editors: Meredith, who bravely took on my very first attempt, as horrible as it was, thank you for treating my work with the same patience and understanding you give your students. Arsen, as much as it hurt to see the total dismantling and shredding of my first book, the time you spent teaching me why each change was necessary and opened my eyes to how a story is built from the ground up. Susan and Cat, your insights and suggestions proved to be invaluable improvements to my efforts and continued my education in the world of writing. Fred, your contributions added the final professional touches I needed to make the stories ready for the public. Each of you provided me with the skills and knowledge to produce these books and I appreciate all of your efforts. I hope my stories have proved to be a source of pride in your accomplishments and effort to teach me the English language and hoe to put words together appropriately.

To all of you at Solstice Publishing, thank you for your faith in me and all of your encouragement and assistance in teaching me the business of being an author. This has been, and continues to be a great adventure.

Finally, to all my readers, especially to those who have left such wonderful reviews, Thank you. I am always amazed when I read how much total strangers enjoy my novels. You continue to provide me with the fortitude to continue writing. I have more works in mind and in process, so even though I am leaving the universe of the Brin behind, I look forward to sharing more adventures with all of you.

Media and Purchase Links:

Amazon   (Hegira):
https://bookgoodies.com/a/B010E3EKC6/

Amazon   (Recusant):
https://bookgoodies.com/a/B01KTVTMNK

Amazon (Empyrean):
https://bookgoodies.com/a/B077ZBQWDT

Project 9 Vol. 2:
https://www.amazon.com/Project-9-2-Arthur-
Butt/dp/1625264372/ref=sr_1_2?s=books&ie=UTF8&qid=
1494881996&sr=1-2&keywords=project+9+vol+2

Project 9 Vol. 3:
https://www.amazon.com/Project-9-Vol-Debbie-
Louise/dp/1625266545/ref=sr_1_1?s=books&ie=UTF8&qi
d=1521392084&sr=1-1&keywords=Project+9+vol+3